The Alum M[...]

Stephen Chance

Wiskard Books

First published April 2013 by Wiskard Books
Copyright © 2013 Stephen Chance
All rights reserved.
ISBN: 1492995681
ISBN-13: 9781492995685

This is a work of fiction and certain liberties have been taken with events, dates, names and places.

Alum of every kind has
warming, astringent powers,
purifies the pupil
from darkening....

(Dioscorides)

Alum is made of a Stone
Digged out of a Mine, of a
Sea-weed, and Urine

(Daniel Colwall)

Contents

Prospect

1 Floating the egg

Snakestones - The piss boat - The assay house – Clearings - Floating the egg – Pallor - At swan and hoop - The red stain - Unearth

2 The charterhouse

Crossings - Weights and measures – Crows - The charterhouse – Reynard - Rogation day

3 Launde's journey

The making of the kelp – Rutways – Ossuary - Wild daffodils - Launde's dream - Launde's journey - One howe

4 Of honey laden bees

Crippled symmetry – Thickenings - Of honey laden bees.... - The cask - Fog and straw – Shards - Valerian

5 The parting keel

The alum cartel – Yield - Fish to fry - The parting keel

6 Meniscus

The jet bible - El azabache - At hilda's well - Sea fret

Postspect

Prospect

There was a fence post, some wire.
Rutted ground baked hard.
Wind harried the tough, bleached grasses.
Her hand rested momentarily on the post top, edges ragged from the mallet, as she straddled the fence and dropped into the gravelled trough of the dry beck.

On the post a twist of fleece, snagged: vermilion.
It clung in a splinter-crevice of the hammer-softened top, tugged by the wind.

She scrambled down the narrow gully, slipping and skidding. Scuffing up dust.

Under the dust on her face, under the scratches, heat flushed into the deeper brown of her skin. Expression set firmer than the required concentration of descent.

She bowled down the arid ditch between two spiky armies of marram, like rags flung by the wind.

1

Floating the egg

Snakestones....

Alcuin hesitated above Ness.

Below, flayed by human labour, the dust-grey landscape was a desolate, bare-scraped, treeless crater, like hardened ash from an extinct volcano.

Figures attacked the rocky slopes with pick axes, hacking out the shale. Lumps came free, and were loaded into barrows. Other figures moved the barrows among the spoil.

Sea fret dimmed the smudge where sea and sky met, and its blurred haze breathed in towards the ruined terrain. The first wisps drifted up towards Alcuin as he peered down towards the works. They mingled with the sulphurous fumes that coiled from the burning clamps. Those smoking heaps of stone were scattered like rough burial pyres across the crater. Fret unrolled its smothering gauze over the quarry floor.

Alcuin resumed his stride, marching down the track into the effluvium.

In the rain-scoured brightness of the morning, from the door of his hut, Fox peered up at the brow. Shielding his eyes against sky-glare.

He saw the works minister, Alcuin, descending the track that led down from the moor, past the great bowl of the quarry. Saw him skirt the works and come to the low headland of Ness. Going in hope, he thought ruefully, of salvaging a soul or two amid the stink of the seaweed burners. Watched as the morning mist softened and blurred movement, of the spindly figure in its cloak.

With a shiver Fox withdrew, shutting the door.

The tallyman's hut was a clutter of pens, scales, jars and ledgers. An inclined board had been set up, with a spar fixed at the bottom, to function as a desk or lectern. There were a couple of lanterns.

It was tiny and, for a primitive and badly patched edifice, surprisingly cosy. In dimness, Fox's form threw shadows into the recesses, competing with the dirty light from the little window. All round three sides Fox had hung wooden shelves and, while a number of these held papers and ledgers, many more had accumulated objects.

Most of these were rocks in a sombre range of hues. A great number of snakestones, shellstones, snailstones, splinters, tubes and plant forms gathered shale dust on these shelves. The snakestones outnumbered everything else. Fox might seem a high priest in the cult of Hilda, the former abbess, now a saint. She was said to have turned the snakes to stone, where they lie unseen until spilled by a pick thrust into the alum shale.

Fox was known to shrug off those that saw vestiges of superstition in his collection. The worship of saints as a throwback to the old church.

"Just some amusing shapes, that bring to mind plants, or maybe some creatures died and turned to stone."

Nevertheless Fox was known to observe the pickmen closely, not just to see work proceeded diligently. To see what turned up in the barrows. He was also to be seen pottering about among the spoil. The most 'amusing' shapes tended to find their way into the tallyman's hut. Fox locked it scrupulously – not only to protect the ledgers.

Fox's lectern didn't only support his ledgers. As the alum industry's accounts man he made workmanlike records of rock bared, shale mined, spoil heaped. He was also known as a prolific letter-writer. He drew the shapes of the stones and measured them, and he was engaged in lengthy calculations that were not about the price of alum.

Fox was largely left alone in his hut. The joke ran that the air was more poisonous within it than around the noxious clamps. For the tallyman, an amiable chap who liked a drink - often with Launde, the overseer of the steeping pits - was famously flatulent. In the hut there was an underfug of tobacco, overripe cheese or the under-exercised exudation of the tallyman himself.

The tallyman's small window condenses and frames the outside view. In winter he watches from his hut as Launde breaks the ice and walks into the freezing waters of the steeping pits, smashing as he goes. Watches as barrowmen reluctantly draw themselves away from the residual warmth of the clamps to bring burnt shale to the icy pits.

If he sees that Launde is there – a reliable fellow – he returns all his concentration to his task.

Content whenever possible to hibernate in his hut, Fox runs his hands through thinning gingery hair and wedges his gut under the edge of the inclined desk. Entering lines of figures, slow and meticulous, laboriously double-checking. Or starting new correspondence with a fellow enthusiast, a collector or classifier. Or moving his magnifying glass over a crenulated surface.

Weights and measures entered in long slanting script, his left hand arching over the pen, to avoid smudging. Or brushing the soil from a fragment to clarify the pattern of ridge or scroll or segment.

The roke suffocates the coastal wykes. Only a mile inland is clear. Here everything is veiled. Walls loom out suddenly. Blurred edges of branches only sharpen into thorns at the last second. Figures emerge and vanish, engaged in obscure acts.

*Hacking the shale. Thousands of tons, by pick and shovel.
Rockmen hacking the shale and barrowmen bringing it to the clamps.*

Smoke from the clamps, the heaps of burning shale, streams past Fox's window pane.

Seen from without, that pane - a flat square of grey. No hint of opacity. Except in darkness when occupied it lightens a shade, yellow-grey seeping through from presumed internal lamp-glimmer.

By day smoke streams across. Fifty yards away Launde sniffs and spits, supervising the construction of a new clamp.

To avoid double-handling, he aims for the shale to arrive at the clamp at a rate equal to its laying. It rises in alternating strata of brushwood and whins, substantial stacks of which are kept some distance away, to elude sparks. The gorse blazes intensely and rapidly, and the brushwood slows and smoulders as the heaped broken mine crushes down on it, cracking branches. Flames and smoke flare up between and around the rocks.

In a makeshift wood-lined pit nearby, labourers stir stiff clay that will be plastered around the clamp as it rises. Smoke-blackened faces streaked with sweat from the heat of the clamp and the toil of heaping stones. Worst, the noxious and feared fumesmoke that pours off the clamp, chasing after the men whichever side of the pyre they stand. These ill winds were said to cause all manner of sickness among the workers, who hacked up black phlegm, coughed over their pipes, and wheezed to early deaths. Various breath-strangling ailments of which works' owners, if they noticed at all, could make no connection with the black leakage off the clamps.

In summer, sulphurous smoke moves across the face of the sun. In winter, when leaden skies press down below the brow, the black fumes coil up into the dark clouds, twisting the earthen furnaces up to hellish heaven.

Smoke surrounds the little wooden hut at the edge of the quarry floor. Lays a film on its framed pane – a darkening picture on the tallyman's wall.

The piss boat

It was unusual to see Turner, the alum works owner, engaging directly with the foreign captain. A few heads turned. Several miles north of the Scarshead works the two stocky figures stood on the quayside of the main alum-trading port. A third man, Turner's aide, skulked in the background. A cluster of small sloops crowded against the harbour wall.

There was an unmistakable tang rising from the captain. Turner addressed him.

"Sir, alum and shipping, these are hand in glove. The alum is bagged in sailcloth. We keep a navy carrying chalders of coal from the Tyne. And an armada, if I can use that word, of piss.

Puncheons and hogsheads of our special flow heading everywhere."

"The Langbaurgh, they tell me, takes a hundred tons a time."

"And twice as much coal brought in, on the same boat."

"Some sorry boats I have seen too, taking the slam."

"Dangerous stuff, my friend, corrosive and poisonous. But like anything dangerous, toxic, these days there will be a purchaser and a vendor."

Turner paused, adopting a wry twist of his eyebrows.

"Not unlike, perhaps, your own trade."

The captain shook his head, lowered his gaze from the works owner's. Shifted his feet on the frozen ground.

"Not mine, this...."

The captain struggled for the right word in his weaker tongue.

"Only for a spell, sir, to trade thus. Before, it was the finest alum flour on my ship. This less refined cargo..."

A hard guffaw escaped from the mine owner.

"Piss? Don't turn your nose up at piss, Mr....?"

"Felipe."

A dismissive nod.

The captain was a little crestfallen. Turner lectured him.

"This is no paltry trade. In Yorkshire we need near four thousand gallons a day. That would be fifteen thousand men, making at least a usable quart. So for a reliable source, men not being reliable milkers at two pints a day, though often reliable drinkers, we might need a hundred thousand pissing persons to draw from. But that aside, count your barrels into sloops for that trade and tell me it's not a living! But float a few tubs of piss for me and we'll see if you might be trusted to run the alum back one day."

The captain shivered, waiting for the mine owner to go on. The owner spoke again, surprising Felipe in his own tongue.

"Nul hombre seguro in este mundo."

Thawed puddles, refreezing, lay around them. The captain, wrapped in a variety of coats, hats and scarves, stamped his feet and cocked his head to one side to consider this unexpected utterance.

Turner, impatient, repeated his phrase, anticipating recognition.

"Come on! It's one of your own!"

There was a bitter blast off the sea. The boats stirred continuously, restlessly. Twilight was approaching and the cold intensified minute by minute. The chapped skin of the captain leant a raw red-whiteness to the brownish, unshaven face, with its large dark eyes.

"Si Senor Turner. It is true".

Is this a threat? No one is safe in this world? The captain wondered to himself. He returned it in its more typical form.

"No hay cosa segura in esta vida."

"Well, what's that then?"

"Nothing is secure in this life, senor."

"Ah!"

Turner wrinkled his nose. The captain had come closer to translate softly. His fragrant trade.

"Yes, yes."

Turner turned to business.

"So for the chamber lye we are agreed."

"We return to London, we come back with the lye. Next time we take the alum."

"And please don't collect the *vasa urinae* just anywhere. Honest labouring men. Not too flush with ale money."

"Por favor?"

"Pure in urine, if you please. Not tavern slop."

"Of course! I would not even add my own rich stream – pure Spanish wine that it is."

And from somewhere within the folds of his over-layers the captain produced a stoneware flask and held it out firmly. Turner bowed mock-graciously.

The captain urged him to take it. Even a few seconds of holding the jar out was numbing his fingers. A few lights had come on in the inns on the other side of the quayside. The twilight deepened and the rough wind abraded his ears and cheekbones.

"Your *own*?"

"I *made* it myself."

He shrugged.

Turner took it, thanked him and, gesturing abruptly to his uncomfortable and shivering aide, handed it on.

The captain nodded, waited and spoke tentatively again.

"And my daughter?"

"Ah yes – what trade shall we find for the girl from the urine ship?"

The captain's outward expression remained unchanged.

"A daughter of the alum flow, *senor*."

Turner unfurled a large handkerchief and blew his nose noisily. He rubbed its numb tip for a spell, trying to get a bit of life back into it. He decided not to press his advantage - that the mariners of the small piss-boats were regarded with contempt – although mainly by those with no boats to their name.

A staple of the industry, stale urine was collected in London and Hull, and shipped up to Whitby. Or direct to the foot of the causeway, below the alum works. It was also carted across the moors in wooden pails, strapped to ponies in pack trains.

However, it was not just the imports of chamber lye that Turner wanted. Alum prices rose and fell. Its import was ineffectively banned from time to time, and pirates preyed on ships moving in both directions. Turner was keen to wager on exporting alum, but if he could profit from importing too then he might balance out the continual losses from the works. If the captain could help in any way to alleviate the debts that Turner lived off – the absurd loans from the adventurers – the owner would nurture him.

"The manager will look after her. She can help in the laboratory and the houses. That way you can be certain that she will be safe even if you return to Cartagena. You will only have the Pope's curse to worry about."

The captain's outward expression unchanged. The Pope's curse against anyone breaking the Vatican's self-declared monopoly of the alum trade. Within his wrappings two fingers crossed minimally.

Turner's head jerked back and fell emphatically forward again, an assertive nod.

"Bring her after Christmas."

The captain raised his cap slightly in brief assent.

At Scarshead, urine collected locally for the industry - girls with pails, traipsing from cottage to cottage - was merely a piss in the ocean.

In London Turner had seen whole streets, entire districts stuffed with ale and coffee houses. Packed sweaty crowds of red-faced men - and women - drinking, pissing, drinking. The casks overflowing. Regularly the ragged children, meekly or sneakily, pouring off the piss. Systematic collection and opportunistic theft. The urine finding its way back to collecting houses - great stinking yards. Barrels rolling in and out of gates. Carts coming and going.

Collecting from the informal communal latrines of the slums, and from the servants' doors of the wealthier houses, the urine and the night soil.

Turner thinks of the Empire, cresting the white-capped waves of the blue swell, cutting adventurous swathes across world oceans, white sails puffed out with quest and trade and exploration. Its eminence underpinned by this other – night shit, inn piss. Men digging out dirt, slate and coal from holes in the ground. Fuelling the processes, manufactures. Wool, leather, gunpowder, and alum.

Walking away across the frozen fish quay Turner remembers the urine carts, cutting a stinking swathe through the riotous streets. A vaporous cloud. Stale, dry and malodorous spillage on the sagging, softened boards of the carts. Pulled by animals and dragged by men. Rolling, rolling into the wharves, onto the docks. Rolling along the wooden staithes and jetties. Rolling onto sloops and barges. Borne on rolling waves, towards Scarshead.

* * *

Ana's father had come to the region via London, on the long journey from San Cerro de Cristobel, via Cartagena and Mazarron.

There had been a multiplicity of hazards for Felipe. The attempts to re-introduce and enforce the papal monopoly limited trading outlets in hostile countries that were trying to develop their own industry. Pirates, all the way up the west coast, across Biscay, and into English coastal waters.

In London, suspicion. A Spanish captain? Had we not long ago been at war? Now and then, manual work on the docks. His attempts to re-enter the alum trade thwarted. Hs knowledge as a sailor grudgingly accepted - a lowly hand on the piss boats.

An expensive and dangerous place - and every other person wracked with a contagion - he had sought to escape the city. Its piss stream flowing away from the capital. Its sour reek scenting his way to fresher air.

Too late. That city had taken his wife. On the journey he had prayed his daughter was merely seasick.

"I'm not a little girl."
Ana glared at her father. A little sensation flitted from within his chest to behind his eyes, which moistened slightly, as he recognised Ana's dead mother.

"Why should I be bartered like a Moor?"

"It's a job!"

Exasperated.

In the bare room of their temporary lodging a candle stub flickered shadows into the hollows of Ana's cheeks and eyes.

"I can fend for myself."

"How?"

"Even the girl from the piss-boat can gut fish."

"Ana that's not for you."

"The girl on the pedestal. The chamber lye maid, who will marry if not a Spanish merchant then an English gentlemen! After all I am the girl with a flower growing out of her arse!"

She scowled magnificently.

The captain marvelled – seeing her mother. Hearing his dead wife speak though his child.

No, not a child. Though apt to dress in tomboy garments, he noticed the filling out of her slender figure. And of her lips, her mother's lips, and his own large dark-set eyes. A young woman – he would have to dress her so for the works.

His eyes smarted, in the salt wind. He hardened.

"It's decided."

The assay house

January. In the cart, the journey was misery. She could see nothing for the fog. She simply squeezed herself tightly the whole time, chin down, trying to stave off the deep damp chill. Rarely looking up to glance out into the whiteness.

She'd mostly understood the cart driver but had not deigned to speak. In the cold she nurtured the one new word, repeating it like a charm to ward off whatever spectres the fog hid: nithering, nithering.

The cart swerved, and dipped, and rose with the track, but Ana had no visual sense of topography. As if the cart was stationary. Vindictive. Rattling her bones. Lurching and dipping, rising and jerking, a container of hurt. Like a rough blindfold game bullied into at the fair.

The whiteness thickened, and darkened, and in the drawing of night into the fog she felt only discomfort. With the leaching in of the darkness, the urge to lash out, stifled, and the urge to cry, bitten back.

Finally the cart shuddered to a halt before the gaunt form of a looming gable. At the front wall a yellowish glow smoked through a partly open door.

Ana was ushered into the cottage, like someone in convalescence pushed suddenly into the sun. A cave of candlelit warmth. The heat of the fire throbbed in her face. Damp steamed off her clothes.

A kind, careworn woman's face moved close to her and she was helped to remove some of the heavy wet garments.

"I'm Lizzie."

The woman moved aside to stow the clothes, revealing a lean middle-aged man, cast in firelit shadows, in a wooden chair.

"Robert Wynter....known commonly as Robbie."

He rose, came forward and shook her hand.

The girl took it timidly. This must be the works' manager. And his wife.

"Ana."

She glanced up briefly then returned her gaze to the floor.

"Welcome to our stately manor!"

He gestured flamboyantly, his expressive hands indicating the bare flags, and plain furnishing.

She ventured a response.

"Nithering!"

The three of them laughed to disperse the awkwardness, though it was quickly consumed. After that there was a silence in which Wynter became aware of the slight grating sound of adjustment in the fire embers. Of settling, and a little flame started up.

Launde broke the ice on the steeping pits. The hard frost dawn.

In the unsettling turbidity of the early morning gloom he grimaced as broken ice skittered away over the intact surface. The shabby crew of liquormen were trying to cling onto a few moments of sleep, until the ice had to be shattered with unavoidable violence.

It was bitterly cold at the quarry. Seepage from under the ice froze to the top shelves of the stacked shale. Ice dripped over the edge, arrested in fall. The wind was as sharp as any shovel, blade or pick. Under a sagging sky, heavy to unload a bulging weight of snow, men hacked the shale. Fingers feeling nothing, hands aching. Working to build warmth. Chilled sweat, frozen numb feet. Eyes watering from wind laced with acid vapour streaming from the clamps. The calciners, hot faces, cold backs, freezing feet. Labouring to keep the temperature up in the clamps.

Grey-blue light, inadequately distilled from night's suspension. A few flakes drifted down, whether ash or snow. The sour scum that drifted into the leafless thorns, or the damp touch of settling crystals. It thickened. The rockmen paused, looking up into the grey swirl. A dark swarm, thickening the cloudy cistern of heaven.

Launde launched into the freezing waters of the steeping pits, smashing as he waded. Barrowmen reluctantly drew themselves away from the remedial warmth of the clamps to bring the burnt shale to the icy pits.

As head liquorman Launde waved them back. He had to appraise samples of the burnt shale before immersion – had it mellowed sufficiently? In the pit Launde picked some of the shale out of the freezing water and examined it. The chill seeped into his limbs. In a few moments his hands began to ache, his teeth chattered. He dropped the stone back in.

Beside the tank two apprentices had started up a fire to dry Launde after he emerged from his inspection of the pits. They were spinning it out to maximise their own warmth.

"Hobbs, get that fucking fire going."

The two lads nodded, and went about their task with the requisite amount of youthful nudging and irreverent snorting. One wafting with a battered tin plate, the other looking vaguely about, as if wood would collect itself.

"Now!"

He lifted the gate to a culvert which ran the liquor off into a nearby cistern. Often he would send one of the boys in to release the opening to the outgo drain, but today he needs to get in and make a close inspection. The water level dropped around Launde, revealing the ruinous state of the sides of the old wooden settling tank.

The boys cracked logs onto the fire and sparks flew up into dregs of the sullen night sky. Winter morning brought its cold light to bear on the tight constrained world of the quarries.

Released along the wooden culvert the liquor splashed into the second pit, over the dry mine. Launde waded out to the fireside and quickly swapped clothes with the new pile Hobbs held out. Stamping and prancing and gasping, slapping and smacking his arms around himself he forced heat back into his arms and legs. His feet and fingers would soon be an agony of chilblains. Hobbs held out a bowl of ground alum powder which he rubbed on his knuckles and the knobbly parts of his feet. Finally, socked, booted and caped he belted around the quarry in a fierce canter that brought some life back to his extremities.

Beyond the quarry floor, the spoil heaps and the cliff edge, the day brightened perceptibly over the dark gleam of the sea.

Stopping as he completed these faintly ridiculous circuits he spotted two figures in the lifting gauze of light. The works' manager Robert Wynter, with his wife Elizabeth, walking up through the spoil heaps to attend to the water weight of the pits.

Damp grey cold day. Alcuin wakes early to the stench of burning kelp and steps outside. Smoke drifts across his view of a grey sea. Too early for teaching his class, to escape the stink he hauls himself up the steep path above Ness, to the headland. He sets out briskly for the alum houses. Strides down scutty, sheep-sheared turf, dew-soaked sedge, towards the works.

There is activity everywhere. He sees Robert and Elizabeth walking up the frosty meadow towards the quarries. Sees men trudging towards the alum houses. He is aware of the sinister drift of fumes from the clamps.

Alcuin crosses himself whenever he merely thinks about the alum trade. Men toiling at the cliff face, others carting the rock to and fro in their primitive barrows.

The stripping of the land, the razing of the whins.

The burning of the rocks.

Others trailing along the shore at low tide, scraping the green slime off the rocks.

Piss gathered in the crowded wickedness of the cities. Everything stirred into a malign soup, to coarse imprecations.

Not least the sorcery with the egg.

Alcuin mumbles a few lines of prayer, but the wind seems to grab them, mingle them into its own mutterings and hurl them away.

Wynter made some calculations on the ground beside the pit, with his stick, in the powder-shale. The liquormen watched from a distance. He shielded the action from them by turning his back, his jacket draped to one side. He let Elizabeth see.

Rising, he moved away from her towards Launde. She watched him indicating towards the pit, and then the recently calcined shale. His hands fluttering and swooping , defining a trajectory of process.

Liz felt a familiar feeling stirring inside her.

Liz loved the way Robbie moved his hands, when he handled the egg.

The hands seemed older than Robbie. The veins and knuckles stood out, the sporadic tufts of hair on the finger backs. She held these hands at night, and traced routes across their landscape by candlelight. She moved them down to her thighs.

She thought of her husband in his laboratory, his assay house. Robbie with the egg – sleeves rolled up. His array of assay dishes. His notched bottles, and scratched flasks.

The bottle filled with spring water and weighed. The balancing weights ascertained. The dry bottle weighed, with the lead shot in it. Then the bottle filled with its liquor.

Robbie laying shot on the counterweight.

Robbie setting the egg on the surface of the liquid.

As manager and liquorman conversed, a little distance away, Liz watched light gleam on the wind-worried surface of the steeping pit. Watched the level fall as the pit drained.

Liquid flowed down stone troughs. She followed their line all the way downhill to the distant alum houses. Where the furnaces steamed, the vats boiled. The casks brimmed over. The vats cooled. The egg floated. The alum crystals grew in the barrels in the Tun House.

* * *

In the assay house Ana looks around her, wondering where to start.

Mr Wynter, elsewhere, has told her about cleaning the vessels, the glassware and pots, the utensils and the preparation surfaces. Clean, the manager has told her, so there are no 'contaminants'.

Que?

Nothing unclean, to spoil the work.

The laboratory a simple shed, whitewashed within. High windows. The child that is usually here, the apprentice they call him, has gone to collect wood.

Ana and the boy can barely understand each other – her accent, his dialect. She looks at the jars and flasks. Everything seems clean already, but she sets out to wash it all again, boiling water on the fire for the task.

She will do this, heat water, sweep the floor. It's warm in here at least. He says he will tell her later how to weigh and measure. How to collect materials. She is content. Alone, thin limbs, thin clothes, she allows herself a graceful movement across the floor, expressive of music unheard.

Clearings....

Ana watches Wynter in the lab, around him trays of dry seaweed. Thin vegetable strands, brown dry bubbles, fresher slime. In trays on scales, grey powders, sifted and graded. Scummy jars of brackish yellow-brown. These, she has learned already, with the lid off will clear the room in seconds. She will be outside, one hand on the weathered doorframe, retching into the grass.

Winter notices her looking at the jars, and then back to him.

"Ana."

"Si."

She grins, reddens.

"I mean *yes*."

"It's time you started to learn why the glasses must be so spotless. What we do here. How we do it."

She smiles. Straining to understand. She thinks she grasps it.

"Go to Elizabeth. Say you will help Milly with the round."

"Round?'

Her elegant brown finger traces an arc, rotating at her thin wrist.

"Ah! No."

A quiet stutter in his nose, she thinks, of amusement. She slides from the bench and swivels, stepping towards the door.

A movement in a dance he thinks, turning back to his flasks and crucibles.

She catches his words as she lifts the latch.

"Liz will explain."

Wynter sighs.

Becomes self-conscious in the fresh silence. Scans his calculations doubtfully. Generations of established practice for adding the urine, none for the kelp. The small thrill of experiment, balancing the new additive, and the low fear of lost output, if put into full-scale operation.

He stretches, yawns, and sits. Elbows on the desk, hands run back through thinning hair. Rests his eyes. Thoughts drift. Drift to Ana.

Ana exults in the salt tang of the wind, while she shudders at its chill. Not quite sure which way to go she scuttles between the sheds and storehouses, the scattered buildings of the works, and across the muddy yards. Smoke or steam seeps from the cracked pantiles of one building. Sensing warmth, the wind gusting to blow her off balance, she heads towards it.

At the calcining place, Launde looked anxiously at the largest of the clamps. He felt the wind freshening. Years of experience and worry scored into permanent furrows of his forehead, as he peered at the flames and gases escaping from the heap.

It's too hot, he thought.

In the cracks between the stones on the leeward side the dull red of optimum heat had brightened alarmingly.

Launde supervised the difficult task of removing the burnt shale and adding new. The windward side of the clamps was covered with a shale render, which needed constant patching and filling. He called men to pulverise small shale residue, to start plugging the cracks on that side. The dangerous work of plastering the sides of a living furnace in malicious winds.

Wiry, hollow-cheeked men crushed the stone to near powder and, adding some water, stuffed the gaps. The shale powder itself, being alum bearing, was waste. But he must keep the temperature down.

The men cursed and spat through dust-filled mouths. Eyes tightly squeezed and caps pressed down low. Faces cut and stung by flying wind-borne shale fragments. Blood tracking a staggering path through stubble was dusted dry by the styptic shale powder.

The plasterers scrambled around the base or, higher, on rough planks of wooden scaffolding. The clamp had been burning for some eight months now. Towering above them it shifted unexpectedly as it burned and settled, grinding and creaking, opening new cracks. Always threatening to roll red-hot rocks down onto them.

They laid futile siege to its ramparts like starving peasants to a castle keep.

Launde considered this clamp almost ready to be left to cool.

The wind roared through the rock furnace.

He wondered how much of the elusive extract was rushing into the late afternoon twilight with those coloured gases.

Perhaps a third, Wynter had told him, of the theoretically obtainable alum, might be lost at calcining stage. It could account for an extra twenty-five tons of shale needed per ton of alum.

"Dear God!"

He had been present when the minister Alcuin, hearing this from the works' manager, had exclaimed.

"One quarter of the cliffs torn up and thrown into the sea for nothing!"

Wynter had replied matter-of-factly.

"That is just the burning stage".

Launde knew this was one of the most difficult stages in which to make any improvements. In a hundred years there had only been two new ideas.

In the old days the clamps had simply been piled up and left to smoulder. The effervescence would appear. After some time the shale, if closely packed, and particularly if mixed with jet shale, would smoulder, and in extreme cases, ignite.

At some point German alum workers had been brought over to advise. Ever since then, clamps had been started with a base of furze and small faggot wood and fired. Even now, how long the shale should lie exposed to moulder, before being fired, was a matter of dispute.

Wynter believed it should lie ten or twelve months to mature. At other times it was simply a matter of pragmatism. If too much shale was bared it would get fired up. If the markets were slow, or the supply glutted, it would be left anyway.

Launde peered grimly at the upper reach of the clamp. It was a hundred feet high and had been built up continuously while burning. The tricky business of extracting the burnt shale, while adding fresh. Two years before, a youth of twenty years, plastering a badly built clamp, had been buried under a fall of red-hot stones, and roasted like pork before he could be dug out.

Launde tried to estimate the amount of cold shale to add. He instructed fissures to be opened, to get the wind inside like a chimney, as the shale was piled on.

As he worked Launde mirrored the manager's worries as to how much was lost in the calcining process. Wynter relied on his long experience of gauging the significance of the colour of the shale. Of the different hues of smoke and gases.

Anxious, Launde had spotted flowers of white sublimation on the surface of the heap. The fire penetrated right through the body of the clamp to the top so it was always likely this effervescence would break out somewhere.

As frost would settle on the moortop standing stones, even in June.

Below the quarries the discarded shale was simply thrown downhill where it constituted a great tip of loose debris, grey leached-out rock. A barren heap of waste, gradually starting to acquire a mould of gorse, bramble and nettles.

A cart laden with Scots Pine boards stood in the quarry by the steeping pits. The fragrant, resinous wood withstood the attack of the acidic waters produced in the lixiviation.

Launde scrutinised it, inspecting the quality, smelling it, and lining his eye along the planks for straightness. Meanwhile, Fox checked off the quantities for his records.

With a sideways nod the carter indicated his load.

"This is virtually the last you will have."

Pine had been in good supply until the recent clearing of local woodland. Cleared for agriculture, sold to industry.

The carter tried to engage Fox while he tallied up the load.

"Sea is the way for that."

Launde frowned.

"So the prime lumber gone, these boards are leftovers?"

"No. This is the main crop."

"Which is why it's twisted, and stunted?"

The carter considered his options, replying nonchalantly.

"Your pits will last a bit longer then?"

Fox interjected.

"At that price."

The carter looked doubtful.

"A tallyman would know the meaning of terms that I hear much of, nowadays..."

He spat.

"Well?"

"... of supply and demand."

Fox raised his eyes heavenwards. He glanced across to Launde, who scoffed.

"You'd make that glue sack on spindles walk all the way back up the track with a full load?"

The carter looked at his pony, patient, blinkered. No blade of grass in the desolate bowl of the quarry, among the dust and rubble.

Steam from its nostrils exhaled into the cold morning air.

"No hurry. Easy stages, then all the way downhill to Stoupe Brow."

Fox and Launde could see they had little leverage. They gave the carter some beer. They digressed. They toyed at bargaining a bit longer. They paid up. The carter would accept no impests or promises or postponements. Turner's as good as his word, he had said, meaning that the owner's word was a good as his cast-off corn.

He turned to depart, offering them final philosophy.

"It's free trade that made the Empire what it is."

Alcuin had finished attempting to teach for the day. Wrapped in his cloak he went among the alum houses. The blustery wind flung handfuls of hail, stinging Alcuin on cheek and forehead. Even without its load of shot the wind had a keen abrasive quality and Alcuin's face quickly felt a surface numbness.

For its shelter and warmth therefore, Alcuin headed for the Boiling House. He wrestled briefly with the wind for possession of the door and, passing through, pressed it shut by leaning back on it. There he stopped, just inside. The Boiling House was full of steam, and figures were partially visible in its intermittent thinnings. Conjured momentarily and then occluded. This was partly a trick of the light, what little there was, brightened, dimmed, by the vagaries of the clouds. They boiled across the roof outside, troubled by the wind.

It was warm in the House, and dense with conflicting smells. The steam poured off a row of giant lead coffins, which boiled furiously. The coffins tilted from head to foot, deepened at the toe end to help drain. Iron pleats supported these boiling pans over the brick-lined hearths.

A sulphurous tang of the smoky fog.

Alcuin coughed.

The boiling went on continuously night and day. The shrouded workers around the pans checking as the levels fell, stirring into the thickening broth the residues from urine or kelp. There was an ammoniac sharpness to the air.

Stirring, stirring with the wooden paddles, the stirring poles.

A yellowish scum hardened around the edges of the tanks and the boilermen scooped out or poured in milky liquids.

Alcuin had heard that the stone for the furnace house had come from the Abbey remains. A crime redoubled, seeing these cauldrons brewing up their poisonous fumes. Farms built with stones pilfered from the sacked religious houses would be cursed, it was said. In which case this business would be twice cursed, doubling the Pope's.

They boil every day, even on a Sunday.

But the alum will help the dye take into the altar cloth, and size my manuscript.

I could illustrate this scene, he thought, and tried to imagine how the steam could be captured in line and wash. Not too much. A few marks to hint at what obscured. The greater part of the page blank, with steam.

He was aware of six or seven shapes of the housemen tending the tanks.

Dark enough to render in charcoal? Certain lines stand out in the fog, other parts are mere shade, or texture. Perhaps try this out with some burnt wood on a stone.

There was a slight lull in the background sound, which for the first time made him aware of it. The foul residues were being chipped and scraped off the bottom of those tanks which had been drained.

The housemen, he knew, carried burns from the slopped liquor, or from the fires, smooth patches on faces or hands, hairless skin on scalps or forearms.

The steam rose up into the rafters where it leaked out between the pantiles, the same places the light leaked in.

Chilled behind, where cracks between boards in the door leaked probing draughts, as under it, where damp boots chilled. Warm at front, where the steam filled his sleeves and leggings.

Feverish.

This pestilential air. Breathing in the piss from London and Hull.

He was in the shade under the lintel, in warm fog, when for a second it drifted clear across the room and then something punched him from inside his chest as he saw the girl. Squatting down by the far wall, looking across at him with piercing intensity. Like the owl's gaze, he thinks, which pierces the night forest and pins to the stump of a tree. A furnace-drawn bright hot wire of moonlight, fixing its prey.

The pounding in his chest was accompanied by the sudden seeping of red dye into his flushed face

Floating the egg....

"Lift the lid!"

Ana grimaces in disgust.

"See if it's full!"

She lifts the stone lid of the jar tentatively but the lid flips unexpectedly and in drawing back sharply she jostles it. A thick rank tepid brackish shock of smell slops out. Ana is immediately nauseous; she spins and gags, coughing. Milly puts her hands on hips and her fishwife mother cackles through the child.

Subsiding, she beckons.

"Come on we have to empty it into the pail."

Ana shakes her head with vehemence.

"We have to!"

Just the thought of it and Ana retches again.

Even on the urine ships she had clung to the windward deck, enduring the cold spray, as the residual stink would instantly trigger a recurrence of seasickness.

Milly looks little concerned. She grasps the heavy jar but she cannot easily manage it herself.

With a shiver of horror that is also of determination Ana, drawing a deep breath behind her and spinning back to advance on the jar, removes the lid. Tilting, the heavy base of the jar grates on the flag like a mill wheel. Spillage runs over her hand, tracks back along her forearm to the elbow and drips onto her skirt. Together they manage to lift it and the cloudy ochreous soup pours out into the churn. Jar set back, lid on, but the invisible pestilential cloud still fogs the fresh morning air. Ana retches again, just short of vomiting. She mutters under her breath, imprecations in her own tongue.

Later, the morning mist evaporates and the day unfolds into sunshine. The breeze stirs the leafless branches and a little warmth thaws through when it stills. The raw wire of the churn cuts into her hand as it gets heavy. It knocks against the sore sides of her knees at each step. The retching lessens with successive pourings as Ana gets used to the reek which, it disgusts her to realise, is becoming her own from accretive spillings.

The child, Milly, carries this smell always about her, like a neglected baby or an incontinent elder, or a vagrant.

Lizzie is laughing.

Ana is folded into the big wash tub that her clothes will afterwards be stirred into with the soft, furred, bleached wood of the paddle. Naked, she is mortified with embarrassment. At the same time in physical bliss from immersion in the enveloping heat of the steaming tub water. Liz is pouring hot water into the gaps between Ana's slight frame and the tub sides, and between her knees, taking care not to scald her. The sickening reek of the piss-collecting has steamed off her like a fog lifting to the kitchen ceiling. Ana covers the stark brown berries of her tiny breasts and grins widely, the heat rises around her, and she accepts the modest shadow that nestles between her thighs as concealment and succumbs, eyes closed, to the blissful luxury of hot wallowing.

In another room Robbie is a ferment of imaginings as he hears the slap of the water pouring, the mingled laughter.

* * *

"A sorry tale of scarcely believable fortune put scandalously to waste long before Mr. Turner became the owner of this extensive shithouse, with its profligacy of shithouses."

"How so?"

"Well...."

The tallyman paused, sieving something up to the mind's surface.

"....when Chaloner came back from Italy, his curiosity piqued by the particular location of certain wildflowers, he had the good fortune to make a connection with those of his home. Those growing on his own land, above rocks he would, consequentially, later excavate. Rocks found to teem with a certain spiral stone. A snaking stone. Rocks of a certain shale we now know so well."

Fox was watching the shale sliding from a tilted barrow into the shallow depths of the nearest pit. A primitive brazier burned against the cold in the fast-failing late afternoon February light. Launde, rangy and lean, a foot taller than the stocky tallyman. Strong, but undernourished. Ember light shadowed hollows under his eyes. Sharpened the stubbled bones of his cheeks.

"But, knowing the right shale apart, what clues did the Italians have for the rest of the whole ludicrous performance? That play we daily enact? The torments we inflict on those snake-stuffed stones?"

Launde shook his head.

"Maybe that after Prometheus, delighted with his new toy, they simply burned everything. If a raw pig could be so much sweeter singed, then why not a stone?"

Launde smiled.

"And it takes no imagination to see why a red-hot stone might find itself in a cooling bath."

Launde nodded.

Fox rubbed his hands over the brazier. Neat buttons down his circumference, twice Launde's, reflected the glow. Customarily tidy, like his ledgers, tokens of being the owner's trusted money man decorated his neckgear and cuffs. In contrast to the worn leather of his practical friend the liquorman.

"But then to imagine that exactly that stone, abandoned in its own puddle, would evaporate out a little crust around the edges."

"Now this is becoming far-fetched."

"Perhaps thinking that, to the burnt pig a little salt added so much, it was natural to try this ochreous crystal scum."

"In a spirit of experimentation... "

Fox shrugged.

"....or in desperate times?"

"Both. And finding it only detracted from the porky charcoal they would have ranged around for other value."

"Thinking perhaps..."

"Of chilblains, oven-bun milkmaids and the pox!"

Launde lifted his sweat-salted cap and reseated it.

"Perhaps the pot was not so clean before the same was used to boil up wool with madder or onion skins. Some bright lad would have noticed the lasting effect that unfading shawl created on a village girl..."

Fox held his arms out before him, palms up, eyebrows raised shrewdly.

"Self evident."

"After that of course its only a matter of time before someone – out of malice perhaps, or just laziness – decides to piss in the pot."

"Some say it was contaminated, by the leaking of latrines."

Launde acknowledged this with an inclination of the head.

" Its possible. Or there could have been more forethought – after all, its many a process that piss perfects. Think of degreasing the wool, of the tannery."

"The fuller's trade just once removed from the dyer's?"

"Something to consider while the fuller spends an hour or two trampling in a barrel of best."

"Which would be the local stuff of course. Not the piss-poor product shipped here from the Tyne or the Thames!"

"So in this we see a keen application of observation and experimentation. A little more urine, or a little less."

"But the dogshit man. Where is he? Surely they must have floated the turd alongside the egg? The kennel collectors and street scrapers – the 'pure' gatherers? Missing it seems..."

Fox frowned, considering the head liquorman's question.

"Hmm.."

"They must have dished the dirt?"

Fox had to agree. Reflecting on tanning, and on tawing.

Reflecting on 'pure' – as the shit was known. Launde seemed to read his mind.

"But this is a process of purification, not of 'pure'. So this would be tried and dispensed with."

"And so on, and so on, until naturally we arrive at the refinement of the kelp, the delicacy of the piss. Sure enough it leads to that whole ludicrous performance, as I call it, of evil-smelling quackery that is our so-pleasant business here."

"We're not talking about a few weeks?"

"Ha!"

Fox laughed.

"No this is from Rome to Yorkshire – via Wade's Causeway."

"No, never as direct as all that!"

"So, as a matter of purification, we would have to look to the brewery."

"Yes!"

"Boiling and stilling."

"The best water!"

"No doubt!"

Fox gripped his chin in his hand, covering his mouth, frowning, and looking down. He looked up at Launde, holding his gaze for a few seconds. Launde brightened suddenly.

"Yes! – this line of enquiry can be pursued further with a glass of the best water."

"Might was well idle there as here."

It was darkling anyway, and the two men set off at a brisk pace up the track.

Meanwhile, in the gathered dark by the alum houses, against February's viciousness, Launde's wife Marion pilfered a few lumps of coal from the heap. This was tolerated so long as it had negligible impact on the overall pile. It was a scuttlefull of unpaid wages. Marion wrapped a few in her apron. Her husband was a highly regarded liquorman but pay was often months in arrears.

Brushwood was forever feeding the clamps, and deforesting the district. As fuel for the hovels in dwindling supply. But coal was a commodity the works imported and, expensive though it was, while they operated, the pile would keep being replenished.

In The Flask, Fox rounds up his history of the alum trade with a joke.

"You know that alum is used in the leather trade, in tanning? In 'tawing', to be precise."

Launde sips his drink.

"Well its purpose can be to tighten the leather."

Fox makes his hand a claw and closes it, as if around an imaginary ball or fruit.

"Tighten it, you see?"

Launde shrugs.

"Well for that reason it was sometimes used, when a young woman was to wed, let's say as a guarantee, that the wedding night would be the first time."

The liquorman glances up quizzically.

"Well, in a village not far from here there was a girl. A beauty. It was said she had entertained several of the young swains of the district. When she finally came to accept a proposal of marriage she first went to the wise woman of the village, for a concoction of alum you see? To apply, as it were, to certain parts!"

Launde grunts a low dirty laugh.

"So, on the night of the wedding itself the young man makes a good account of himself in the bedchamber, and after many hours of lovemaking the bride, is both surprised at what has taken place and more than satisfied. She has only one question:

My dear, she says, how can you perform so well, for so long, and yet fail to say the words 'I love you'?

And the groom replies....Mmmmmmnnnn.....mmmmnnn!!!"

Here Fox emits a stifled murmuring – his mouth apparently stuck tight.

Mordant fog fixes moisture to the ash dusting every sprig and branch. Fixes water, fixes frost. Grains of ice freezing to the hazel twigs are tiny crystals of fog.

Here and there, in sudden thinnings, in partial clearings, rumours of findings. Taints of possibility in smoke-mist. Hints pungent of wet coal, bitter-sour ash and woodsmoke. Inert stone, mute shale to reveal secrets.

Sent to find the manager, something made Ana pause at the door of the evaporating house. It was slightly ajar. Into the interior murk and steam she peered. A dim cloud-whorled shaft of grey light penetrated from a slipped pantile. She recognised the hunched back of the figure that squatted down by the pan. The head was bowed forward of the shoulders, the thinning crown. The manager's stillness conveyed concentration on some unseen activity, screened by his torso. She hesitated to enter. Steam shifted, and slightly to Robbie's left she saw the shallow pan mirror skylight gleam. Ever so gently his hand moved over the liquid, holding something tenderly. Furtive this lonely activity. She felt she should not watch. Nothing moved in those seconds save only the vapour drifting. In that moment she realised what Robbie did. He lifted his hand to reveal, the egg. It floated on the still vat of liquor. Grey light washed its surface. She thought perhaps now would be a time to go in. She sensed other movement. Out of sight. Robbie was trembling with some further act, of which a grunt of concentration emerged.

Stealthily, she backed away, troubled, and went.

Pallor

"She is almost pale with it!"

Wynter pictured the usual dun lustre of Ana's skin.

"Robbie, you idiot, this keeps recurring doesn't it? Like a fever that burns and abates? But it's not a fever. Lets get this straight. She feels very weak. Faint. She is pale. No appetite. A loss of blood is it not?"

Wynter seemed clueless. He stared at Liz, his expression blank.

She flipped her hand at him, dismissive.

"Oh god. You nincompoop. Go away. I'll see to it."

The women laughed and joked, discussing Ana's anaemia. The girl sat among them, bashful. They made ribald remarks.

"No good fainting on the job, when it's the only safe time."

"No pickling beef or salting bacon."

"One glance will tarnish a mirror. No man will want you at that time."

Another disagreed, observing Ana.

"I wouldn't barter on it!"

The tenor of the conversation was clear enough to Ana. Though she understood little of the chattering, many of the cruder gestures of the women left little doubt.

"They will refuse communion either way. So if you can't be holy after doing it, and you can't be during your time, then the time itself could be blessed!"

They laughed again, with much tutting and expressions of mock scandal.

"Come on Ana."

Marion brought her over to the table.

" Someone might see in the dark with this, or stop the shits. But for you it will help the cramps, and stop up the blood."

She looked into the bowl, recoiling at the livid purple emulsion. There seemed to be some bits of leaf, even dirt and twigs, and a spiral of cream colour was being spooned into the thick paste. It looked inedible.

"For dyeing?"

Perhaps it was a joke. Or were they trying to poison her. They thought it very funny.

"Not for dying, pet! For living."

Ana shook her head vigorously.

"No, no, for dyeing colour."

More laughter.

Marion brought the bowl close to Ana's face and she breathed a rich fruity aroma.

"Ah."

Marion gave her a bemused look.

"Bilberries pet, of course. Unmistakeable."

Ana looked bemused – a new flavour, though familiar? It was some kind of preserve, the fruit in a jelly, but watery.

'With buttermilk and nutmeg, and a little... secret ingredient."

They laughed.

She looked doubtful. Still, though strange, it seemed edible. She spooned it up. She felt a bit sick.

The entertainment over, the women started to go back to their chores.

"Bilberries – the cure for everything round these parts."

As the women, outside the cottage, peeled off singly or in pairs to head back to the kitchen garden, or the works, there were muttered remarks.

"Good job she is having her time I'd say."

"Yes. I'll wager it's not overwork that's tiring her out."

Ana felt a little better. She made her way delicately down towards the lab. But she was not happy. For several days she had felt lightheaded.

The previous day she had just about fainted outside the door of the lab. Wynter had found her, pale and listless. He worried that she was sickening. Ana could not explain. She said it just happened sometimes.   In fact it often happened at her time. She lost a lot of blood; her appetite went at the same time. The stomach cramps came. She felt weak and faint. During the day drowsy, at night awake with the pains. She stuffed the rinsed rag in. It was very uncomfortable.

The bilberries had made palatable a bitter undertow taste. Some distilled spirit was mixed in, perhaps something to reduce the pain? Before the lab door she sat down on sun-warmed sandstone. A gentle breeze fanned the feathery wisps of the grasses, waving above the yellow flowers that they called the cups of butter, the feet of birds or the ears of cats. She closed her eyes. The sun warmed her, and soothed the pangs.

At swan and hoop....

Tyrian purple.

In London, the banker leans back in his chair. Closes his eyes to alleviate ache from the previous night's inebriation. Shifts his backside on soft leather, stretches against the polished oak back, and daydreams Tyrian purple.

His mind a whirl of colours and scents, a mercantile babble of Low Country docksides, and a thick fog of masts in Venice's Lagoon.

On his desk the report he has just read, interpreting the researcher's scrawl. Discontinuous, full of conjecture. Almost certainly misleading, erroneous and based on other fabrications. Nevertheless, nevertheless, he muses, a revelation!

This alum flour, a dirty dust, without which it seems the colours of kings and emperors would simply run to the peasants' drab.

Opening his eyes, he flicks through it, alighting here and there as words leap out to brighten his imagination.

The fact stark enough: alum, a mordant. A fixer of dyes. With it – wool, cotton, silk, linen – colours are brighter and more fast. Craftsmen it seems, have passed on this knowledge for thousands of years. This quality has always had dramatic commercial significance. Fact two – money follows alum.

He takes his pen and underlines some words: Imperial purple. The porphyry, the account states, of Byzantium, and later Greece – a dye made of whelks! Highly valuable – and the wearing of it proscribed, except for royalty. The banker has a hazy image of ruined columns, sunken baths, thinking of sketches from Grand Tours he has seen worked up into etchings and prints.

Cloth brought in galleys from around the azure Mediterranean. The alum brought, it seems, from the island of Milos, from Libya, from Vulcano, from Naples, Persia, Spain....

He leafs through the papers, muttering names: dark ages, monopolies, alchemy....

He glances over tables and figures – sackfuls, boatloads, unquestionably a vast trade - and alights nearer to time. Venice, Florence, Flanders, Bruges....

This period he can picture. If he saunters down to the Thames after his mid-day meal he will see this scene: merchants' houses, wharves, the unloading of ships. But...the scale, the insatiable demand. The report states bluntly: the golden age at Venice, the Florence of the Medicis. English wool! Flemish cloth! London, Ghent, Lille....the market squares and tiered and jetted merchants' houses. Dripping wealth, he thinks, and alum shipped as ballast! Under the lighter, more precious goods, alum. Alum – essential to the Venetian dyers, the Florentine tailors.

English wool – from the monasteries apparently – and now, now he thinks, reflecting on last night's tale at Cornhill, in the Swan and Hoop – English alum.

His eyes drift down the blotchy ink. Cordovan, Castilian – the Moorish al-kemiya, and here's the rub: the dammed mystery of it! How to make it, how to guarantee that purity needed, how to use it?

Ludicrous recipes the report quotes: blackberry, honey and alum – for a sore throat. Excrement of hound, a pigeon and a hen – with gallons of fermented urine – to dye a hide! Gum, water and alum, with egg white - for distemper. Verdigris, quicksilver, saffron and vinegar – plus alum of course – to make gold! The banker pushes himself back from his table. Chair legs scrape on the flags. He feels tired, but there is more.

England. The efforts so far in England to benefit financially. Pitiful. A brief history of rogues and scoundrels. Monopolies broken (the curse, it seems, of some Pope – cheerfully ignored) and fortunes hanging in the balance. Cases of corruption dragging through the courts for years.

Now this Yorkshire nonsense. Oh yes – alum indispensable, alum priceless, alum the history of empires before our own. All this glorious history of purple, of galley slaves, of smoking volcanoes, of Venetian barges laden with colour, of togas, of turbans... and all come to this! A stinking, remote, freezing north sea cliff-land, and an upstart landowner with a beady eye on fitting out a jumped-up farmhouse with the latest Italian gardens, looking to borrow a fortune to demolish headlands and burn rocks.

The red stain....

On Ana's first visit to the Tun House Robbie Wynter had brought along the priest, Alcuin, and one of the men, telling him to bring the drill and saw.

In the quiet gloom of the Tun House, a compact narrow shed running crossways to the other houses, the bulky shapes of the casks lined each side of the room. They sat on large flagstones, with stone culverts running along the foot of the walls on each side. The casks were lined up like choristers, it seemed to Alcuin, in the stalls of a cathedral choir. Ana they reminded of chessmen, particularly since on one side the tuns were intact, portly barrels of dark curved planks wrapped around with iron hoops, while on the other stood the crystallised alum, set hard in the form of the tuns it had recently occupied.

These large chessmen, the light and the dark pieces, faced each other like the back row of nobles and bishops. Ana thought of themselves in the middle, on the flags, as the released pawns, venturing forth in loose arrangement.

"The naked and the clad."

Robbie's comment brought a blush from Ana, and tutting from the priest. The workman laughed, raising the saw.

"The naked and the dead!"

Robbie shook his head.

"Not yet."

Lightly, Robbie held back the hand with the saw.

"First, lets show them how we strip the willow."

Ana was thrilled by this lightness from Robert. The contrast with the reverential stillness of the assay house.

Wynter explained that the wooden tuns had been there eight days, and likewise the stand-alone blocks. On one side, barrels of concentrated alum liquor, setting. Opposite, the set blocks hardening, before breaking down for grinding. It was therefore time to strike the timber barrels, the clad, and to cut up and remove the blocks of set alum for grinding. In this way Ana's white pieces would swap with her black, Alcuin's *cantoris* with his *decani*, and the naked would replace the dead.

The workman went out and returned immediately with another man. Between them they set to dismantling a wooden tun.

"Here the alum must stand firm, once the boards are removed. If it collapses the batch is wrong. It will be re-dissolved and added back."

Ana wandered over to the nearest cask, taller than her, and reached her arms around it, reaching perhaps a third of the circumference. Turning her head back towards Robbie she grinned cheekily.

"Port wine!"

The workmen levered off the iron bands and lifted one of the planks free. They then removed the lid. The casks tapered in one direction only, sitting on their wider bases, heavily truncated cones. The whitish granular surface of the block within was revealed. Carefully the two men detached each plank.

With an auger, one man drilled into the pillar of crystal above the base. From the interior a reservoir of thick whitish liquid was drawn off. A nod from the manager and the men took a big two-handled saw and commenced to cut down into the hard sugary cylinder. The blades scoured and snagged. The men strained and grunted. Wynter watched Ana. Her large eyes, slightly bulging, whites all around the deep brown gleam. Rapt? Engrossed in the sweating labour of the wiry men, brothers perhaps, not young, ribs at unbuttoned collars, prominent stubble-strewn jaw lines. Finally, they cut in with the big-toothed saw at a level base and a big heavy slab was lifted carefully aside, leaning on a swept flag to avoid contamination. Alcuin and the girl drawn as one to peer into the jagged aperture. Wynter stood back, noticing Ana's eyes widen a little further. Just the tip of her tongue over the full lower lip.

The men prepared to saw up the removed piece and grind it to alum flour.

Early morning, Ana senses a particular stillness and gleam behind the window rag. Rising she brushes it to one side. Between the curtain and the windowpanes stands an invisible slab of cold. Ana shivers and waves her hands, thinking to disperse it. What she sees beyond stills her, her lips part involuntarily. It is the most radiant and astonishing scene. Her first thought is that the world has been sprinkled with alum crystals.

She rubs away moisture her breath has laid on the panes, and feels at her eyes icy draughts that leak in at the cracks. Peering out through the glass to the foot of the house's boundary wall, the dark spines of the reed grasses poke up through white candescence. Swirling flakes in the brightness above, catch light. She imagines the boards torn off dozens of roaching casks and the wind spinning in the tun house, twisting around the unravelling casks, spiralling up out of the unroofed building. Like smoke boiling off a moorland fire and drifting over the fields. It deposits like ash over the fields up to the rounded brow above the quarries. It sprinkles and settles over the headland. The heavy grey drapes of clouds wind-whip aside and a clear turquoise blasts through. Sun pours across and the dirty crystals, individually lit, and dusted over the fields, form a sparkling bright blanket of dazzle.

Later, Ana would come to hate snow like the rest of them.

This morning it unifies the ravaged landscape. Drifting against spoil heaps, clarifying out the horizontal strata of the quarry and distinguishing only by textures the differences between bracken, heather, grass, gorse, and spoil. Thin dustings, coarse coatings and wind-heaped bankings in the purified air.

Only at the clamps, she notices, is business as usual. Smoke spins up off the clamps, twisted by the wind.

Ana piles on all the clothes she can find and scampers through the chilled house. It is empty, she realises. She grabs a couple of oatcakes and some cheese, and goes out.

She is surprised by the granular texture of the snow. There is a heavy wet-cold cloth of wind that slaps her cheeks and eyeballs. Gusts shiver the melt-water of track puddles. She follows the sandstone liquor trough down to the works. The stringy white grasses and the odd small yellow flower straggle over the tooled stone of the trough. The grainy hail lies in the drain as though the liquor straight from the pits has simply settled out into alum.

By the time she covers the short distance to the laboratory she cannot feel her toes except as a deep ache within the bone. The wind seizes the door and flings it into the laboratory with her still holding the handle. Amid the sudden gull-wings of airborne paperwork, and the shattering of glassware, she is aware of her wrist gripped and the door heaved shut.

It is instantly calm. The lab is warm. Acrid fumes of stale urine immediately make her retch. Robbie ignores it. He is matter-of-factly reassembling papers. He takes the broom and starts sweeping up fragments of a flask. She goes to the fire and sits down.

In the order of the neatly crowded glassware, the rack of surgeons' implements, the light from the large window, she feels even more than usual like a badly stitched together rag doll. But the lab is often the most peaceful place, where even in her customary impulsive disorder some of the manager's calmness rubs off on her.

"Drink?"

There is a pot hanging over the fire and from it Robbie pours into two mugs. She nods, a little timidly.

"Feet are numb."

She inclines her head in the direction of the high window, where the snow on the sill is backed up flat against the glass.

"So beautiful – *pero mucho frio.*"

"Here."

He hands the mug. She wraps both hands around it and sniffs. A herbal concoction. She sips, slurping the hot liquid noisily to cool it.   Spicy.

"Mmm."

He draws up the stool opposite and without a word he removes her shoes and the wet woollen socks. These he places in the hearth. Throws a couple of logs on and the sparks fly up. He takes Ana's foot into his lap and massages the wrinkled rubbery toes gently, clasping his fingers around for a few moments at a time to impart warmth.

Ana is quiet.

The logs crackle and settle. The embers pulsate. Light from the high window swirls through the external fluttering of flakes and glints on the glassware.

Years later Robbie will reflect. This was the moment. Not the later glances. Not the accidental physicality when he helped Ana lift the heavier pans. Not the gradual playfulness of their exchanges. It simply formed. Everything else was an elaboration, a refinement. That time.

Ana looks up at him through the steam, wary and inquisitive, over the rim of the held mug, just the two eyes holding his.

Years later she will remember. That time. The reigned-in, expectant curiosity as he gently, an unfolding surprise, brought feeling back into her toes. Later, she will think, the most unexpected and complete moment of exquisite tenderness in my entire life.

She observes him over the fragrant punch, through the steam, body warming almost to the point of drowsiness, mind alert. He looks down mostly, at his handiwork. Glances at her only briefly. Finally, reluctantly even, he stops, with a final ever-so slightly extended squeezing of the toes of each foot. Her socks have finished steaming. He hands them back dry. She puts on her shoes. He goes back to a pot and, lifting the lid on a disgusting vapour, stirs its brackish contents thoughtfully.

She gets up slowly and, seeing a collection of soiled glassware, takes some water from the pot, and the bucket, and starts rinsing.

To protect the slight, skinny foreign girl from the famishing wind Launde's wife had knitted a woollen jersey. Now, with the material Ana had been given by her father, they prepared to dye the wool.

Marion observed the little roll of cloth Ana had brought.
"You're lucky to get hold of this Ana."
Ana smiled. Embarrassed about something, or just hesitant with language?
"My father."
"A present?"
"*Si.* Yes."
She didn't add anything.
"I reckon it's expensive."
Ana shrugged.
"He had some... I think...."
Marion felt that she would get little more. She unwrapped the red-stained cloth, spreading it open on the wooden table to display the pigment. She was entranced by the intensity of the bright red crystalline powder, tinged with an orange glow. She rolled the back of the wooden spoon over it, crushing out any lumps.
"I don't know how much to use."
Ana shrugged again, looking at Marion brightly. She shook her head slightly.
"All?"

Marion was a little shocked.

"If you think so."

Marion weighed the woollen garment she had made, and measured out a quarter of its weight in alum. This she did by guesswork, using, after rinsing it, the wooden spoon.

She took a big pot, filled nearly to the top with water warmed over the fire. She stirred the liquid, adding the alum flour gradually until the grainy mordant was fully dissolved. She added the woollen gently, kneading it carefully to fully and evenly saturate it in the solution. Two tiny mittens knitted for her own daughter Ellen, she added to the liquid with Ana's permission. Stirring as it warmed, she heated the pot, back on the fire, until it bubbled gently.

There was a calm, homely atmosphere. Ana relaxed into it like the woollen opening out into the warm mordant liquid.

Marion turned to the substance Ana had brought along – the powdered cinnabar.

Ana's big brown eyes widened. She yawned and stretched like a cat in front of the fire.

"Well, we have to leave the alum to cool overnight. Then it will fix properly."

"How does it work?"

"Ah Ana, it doesn't pour through the gaps, with the liquid. It sticks to every hair."

She stirred the woollens round again in the mordant, and then lifted the pot from the fire into the hearth. Lid on, to keep out any ash or cinders, and weighted with a stone on top.

She indicated the pigment on the table.

" I think you should wrap this up again. We'll dissolve it in the morning."

Ana was a little disappointed. She looked at it, and turned to Marion, yawning again.

"Cansada."

Distractedly.

Marion looked at her affectionately.

"Tired."

"Stammel over your homespun, Ana. That'll make them stare!"

She sighed, then smiled, flashing her eyebrows up a second. Ana simply looked embarrassed. Not understanding?

Marion stretched upright, holding her back, suddenly tired herself.

Next morning. Bright sunshine. A clutch of meadow flowers in a jar in the deep, lime-washed recess of the little window. A shaft of sunlight fell across interior gloom, onto the dirt floor, animating the motes. The rest in shadow.

Ana's eyes accustomed.

Marion stirred the mordant liquid.

"Right. Lets have it."

Indicating the wrapped cloth.

Ana handed it to her, grinning.

"Vermell"

"What's that?"

"Vermell? Vermeillon?"

Ana looked doubtful. She explained.

"My father says it."

"Vermilion?"

"Si." Yes. Could be."

Careful not to waste any, Marion opened the wrapped cloth over a small pot of water, letting the powder fall into it. The water clouded into deep red. This she set to heating on the new fire.

After a second she dampened the rest of the set-aside wrapping and squeezed it gently to seep the remaining dye into the wrapping cloth.

"This I can make into a small bag for you. It will start bright. But of course, without the alum, it will gradually fade."

She set the cloth to dry.

She boiled the small pot of dissolved vermilion powder for about half an hour. Filling the time with domestic activities in the hovel. Ana was disinclined to help, she noticed. Content to stare into the flames.

"With the stammel you'll maybe find a man with a maid!"

Ana smiled. But she didn't get the hint.

Marion didn't mind. The quietness was companionable.

Ana came to life when they drained the mordant from the big pot and stirred in the liquid dye. Heating it and stirring all the while as the intense red swirled around the woollens, which they lifted clear occasionally, checking the effects.

This went on hypnotically for some time.

They had used all the cinnabar and the woollens, even after the rinsing, came out with startling intensity. Finally, she took them outside and draped them over a couple of logs to dry in the breeze. Marion worked the garments, stretching and laying in anticipation of the final shape. Laid in the sun, they glowed radiantly, as if lit from within.

Liz and Robbie in the Cooling House. Robbie measuring the kelp, the burnt seaweed ash. Strewing it into the tanks, sowing the tanks. Stirring the tanks. Robbie measuring the stale urine from the stews of Hull. And in the casks the liquor cooled, cooled. In the Tun House, within the wood and straps, within the outer crust, liquor cooled in the casks. And the alum crystals grew in the dark. Hard and clear of purpose, sharp and precise.

The stench in the cooling house was obscene. Its undertow was the smell inside beach shells, of the molluscs, the smell and taste of it.

Robbie pulled out his cock and pissed in the tank. Liz saw the hands that held the egg delicately to float it, holding the cock. She went to him and squeezed the last drops for him, and she held it. The cock came hard and hot. She milked him. The liquor jumped into the cooling tank.

Robbie floats the egg. Liz stirs the soup. Alum grows in the dark. Robbie pisses in the tank. Liz drinks from his cock. The crystals grow, like Robbie, sharp and clear of purpose.

In their bed, Liz lies in the dark, next to Robbie. Nothing grows in her.

Unearth....

To feed the clamps.

Hack the shale, by pick and shovel. Scalp the overburden, peel the green layer. Level the cliffs. Scour the quarry scoops. Raise the planking and scaffolding.

Thousands of tons by pick and shovel.
Pick and shovel. Dig. Or starve.

A workman hacked into the shale at knee height in the quarry wall and suddenly a heavy undercut seam sheared off. Collapsed down, like a breaker banging onto the sea. Rocks above toppled down, glancing him as he leapt backwards.

A long malevolent shadow was baked into the rock.

The worker turned and ran.

2

The charterhouse

Crossings....

Rumour of the monster in the rock was crackling through the crowd like a bracken fire in October wind. It had to be the manifestation of the Pope's curse.

Some wanted to down tools.

The monster was extraordinary – black, with a long snout, with stunted legs, a powerful fishtail. Its empty eye-socket an admonishing glare.

The tallyman came out to inspect the monster.

On second thoughts however, he gave it only a cursory glance. Scrutinising instead its circumstances. Half concealed by loose debris, above a considerable heap of spoil and dust.

The quarry was deserted. There had been no need to order the digging to stop. Still, he set about erecting wooden posts and roping off that part of the rock face. For good measure he cordoned off a wider area too and knocked up a board on which he painted a symbol. For the literate minority adding a single word - danger. Returning to the alum houses he put about that the cliff was unsafe and likely to collapse. Soon after, he sent a messenger via the pannier routes that fish traders took, to York.

Meanwhile, Fox ordered the men to return to the older quarry. Reluctantly they started clearing the recent brambles and gorse, and shoring up the collapsed terracing.

Alcuin drifted back from somewhere, summoned by a noise in the church upstairs. A mouse, perhaps. He became aware of his knees and chose to suffer them for a spell.

The crypt of Kenelm's parish, the church beneath the church. Which Alcuin is encouraged to use as a well of faith. He draws on its ancient spring. For ministering to the alum hamlets empties Alcuin's resources. Teaching the children, disheartening. Ministering to the apathetic workmen, a drain.

He took in the play of dim light on stone in the ancient crypt. The round arches. The dragon's head carving from the old abbey – "in the haunts where dragons once dwelt shall be pasture" – words from Isaiah. The pigs-back tomb the Vikings fashioned. The Saxon crossheads.

He considered the rams' horn capitals that held up the stone vaulting. A simple, pastoral people he thought. Whose pasture grew too small, a strip around their rocky islands, for their multiplying generations. The roughest disinherited sons, the outcasts, criminals and adventurers. Those unlucky in love. Those in fear of rivals. The listless and the trapped.

They all climbed in their boats and came here and smashed everything. But the rams' horns came after they left – carved by Christians, or pagans or simply peasants? People unafraid of the devil perhaps? Afraid only of people wearing horns.

It had grown shadowy in the crypt and, unusually, he felt no nearer to god, no compact with the ancient monks, and something distasteful and unsettling – fear?

Eventually he rose and stood stiffly, trying out his limbs like they were newly fitted. Wearily he mounted the stone steps into the nave. He took his bag, cloak and hat and left the church at once, closing the heavy wooden door behind.

He tramped up the track out of the village but strangely, he felt lighter. Not because he was heading home – there was nothing there. It was a chill, gathering dusk and a few weightless petals of snow fluttered. The moor opened expansively to receive him. The sky lifted, light crept round the edges and into the exhilarating dome above him huge clouds trundled like mill wheels.

It was muddy. His boots slipped back on the track. He kept to the edges, skirting standing water, frequently hopping onto the heathery tussocks to keep his feet dry. Quite quickly he was in a vast space bounded by distant low hills, with brown heather ranging away in all directions. In places the earth was scorched black where there had been moorland fires. Here the white bones of the dead heather were scoured by the wind and sleet, which now intensified with each step. The burnt heather would resurrect, reclaiming lost ground.

The monks, they said, had created the moors. Had felled the trees and drained the land. For pasture, or crops. Later it was lost to heather and bracken, where the hag-worms - the adders - were comfortable. But to Alcuin this would always feel like the oldest landscape. The one he knew God had made, but felt, at a deeper instinctive level, to be older than Genesis.

Momentarily, before the land dipped, he glimpsed Ainhowe Cross - stark silhouette on the horizon. A myriad of the old monks' paths crossed the moors here and he kept his mind focussed on that summit.

The sky was bubbling up a boiling storm cloud. He could see it must be snowing already in the valley to the east. To the west a chink of light prised open the black coffin-lid of cloud propped over the tombstone hills. Pinkish blues and crimsons, silver edged, leaked out.

The cross appeared again, now closer. It was a comfort. Although the thick oils above were light, the ground was nearly dark. He could see the track only by the gleam of water in the ruts. It was clearer looking back at the path behind – a silvery snake slithering back to Lastingham.

Head down into the gale, eyes to the ground, glancing occasionally to the cross, until suddenly he was out there, fully exposed, the wind lashing him around its shaft.

The flaying onslaught of the wind howled about him, but the sky above opened its full splendour of light. Marvellous cloud masses – the denser grey imbued with the deep salmon-pink of the western sky. To the south a woollen edge like ripped felt. It was a spectacle of hues and pigments, fiendish to replicate, and the colours mixed and stirred. He launched himself from the cross mound and hurried on. Out of the blast a thickening swirl of snow gradually hardened into a field of needles. Hail was a thicket of thorns and he hunched into it with his hands shielding his eyes. His cheeks stung painfully. At last he located the firmer track that wound down into the shelter of Rosedale.

On the return coach to York, Turner ruminated on his expensive evening in London's Swan and Hoop.

The report he had prepared for that meeting, its covers lavishly bound in an approximation of the imagined Tyrian purple, had lain on the inn table unread while his ground surveyor held the company in rapt attention.

Prospecting was a diviner's science, the surveyor had told them.

"It sweateth out a saltish aluminous hoariness, and little by little scaleth away into earth."

At Cornhill, in the Swan and Hoop, the group of London bankers listened sceptically to the prospector's account of how exactly he had established the occurrence of alum-bearing shale in a new location. They had the unrolled, sketchy charcoal-smudged map pegged down at the corners with brandy glasses and decanters. Turner was nervous, starting to wish he had not brought the prospector along for veracity.

The bankers were a secret society of speculators, and they had resources to burn. But they were not yet persuaded.

"Please go on. I have yet to ascertain the precise nature of this 'mouldering' and quite why I should consider heaping money on it."

Turner nodded, and the prospector carried on.

His description carried much truth, if not about cause and effect, at least about prospecting itself.

Turner's thoughts wandered from the prospector's rambling account to what he recalled of the history.

It went back to Chaloner. The family had purchased the monastic estates at Guisborough priory – so much dissolution accumulation. Yet the Chaloners had not been cursed, rather blessed. Although the various Chaloners – Thomas the second, John of Lambay and Thomas the son – had claimed the discovery in north Yorkshire, it was also said that John Atherton had a claim.

However Chaloner claimed to have recognised the Yorkshire alum – and claim it he had – it was most likely due to that 'aluminous hoariness' the prospector alluded to. The crystalline effervescence of 'hairsalt' had sometimes been detected during coal and iron mining. In this respect it was recognisable by a diagnosis of the murky ground water close to the rock, notably below iron mining. Also, some said, by taste.

Some of these early rights owners *must* have made money, thought Turner. Lambay, for one, as claimed discoverer, was said to have received an annuity of some forty marks, lasting till his death.

The shale more frequently came to light through coastal landslips. Turner thought of the dangerous instability of the cliffs at Scarshead.

In the early days the exposed shale would 'smould to pieces' – and leaving it to smoulder would indeed be the crudest and most accurate test of whether alum was present.

Copperas had been extracted in this way, and likewise used in dyeing. Now alum was used, with more predictable results.

This had not stopped experimentation of every kind. It was the same goal of transformation undertaken to try and conjure gold from almost anything. Or attempting to turn iron into copper coinage. John Medley had tried to make copper from copperas and had died in a debtors' prison. Not that it held anyone else back.

"...detected a smell like that of the vapours procured in *aqua fortis* preparation...."

As Turner heard the prospector saying this, his attention snapped back to the exposition. He thought to interject, but saw the bankers enjoying the saga.

"....and detect the copperas by tasting."

The prospector mimed an exaggerated grimace of distaste.

"Nearby runs a styptic fountain."

This enthralled the bankers further.

"Vitriol, mixed with saltpetre, would be distilled by the alchemists, and used to dissolve silver."

Neither the vitriol nor the nitre would dissolve gold, thought Turner grimly, but the bankers had a more reliable formula for manufacturing and dissolving *that* substance.

The bankers digressed to wonder about saltpetre and gunpowder, and whether there might be a lucrative spin-off in trading explosives. Turner steered them back. He indicated for the prospector to resume.

"Nearer to hand, who has not had regular need to staunch the shaving wound?"

"Ah, I often crave the haemostasis!"

Laughter.

"Well this fountain would both wash and staunch."

The prospector and the entrepreneur, a hilarious double-act from wild northern regions, gave much mirth to the moneylenders.

"Its waters, like to the alum powder itself, can be added to the handbitten nails..."

"Like ours! It's a nervy business lending to phantasmagorists such as yourselves!"

More laughter.

"...yes sirs, and bound in a waxy stick will salve the razor's revenge."

"And is there much of this amazing material?"

Turner was relieved to come back to this. It was proving an extended and expensive evening.

"The mine itself would stretch all along that hill and be exposed in such sort to the breath of the sea and of the sun and the wind which are the only ripeners of the stone."

The prospector was pleased with this.

He paused for effect before a final flourish.

"And of course last but not least, or should I say first but not least, the top layer of sandstone which is a valuable material itself, the main stone of the region, which has seen many a majestic minister or austere abbey constructed from it."

"How can I tell it's not a North Sea Bubble?"

The bankers laughed at that. The prospector looked pleased. Turner winced inwardly. Very droll. He laughed along.

"I've heard of the East India Company, and wagered speculatively there to great profit. Perhaps this 'North Yorkshire Company' is worth a bet."

More laughter.

The decanter was refilled. As the prospector went once more over the details of the proposed new shale beds, Turner drifted off into thinking about his last few days here in London. Eating anchovies, going to the waxworks and the opera.

Turner had been transfixed when the curtains were drawn back on the theatre stage. Extravagantly dressed and masked figures moved onto the stage, dancing curiously. Some kind of elfish tableau followed by songs and music relating to Arthurian stories.

The bankers had been less spellbound, pointing out women and nudging each other. Noisily unwrapping their hams and chunks of cheese. Eating, spitting bones and heckling the performers. The rest of the otherwise genteel audience behaved in similar rowdy fashion.

Much of the performance, with the exception of one or two of the dialogues, had eluded Turner. Nevertheless he was much impressed by the spectacle. He was also amused by the account of the entertainment's devisor, the composer Mr Purcell, and his untimely death. As one of the bankers told it, he had been locked out by his wife and, on returning home late from the theatre, perhaps from the company of a theatre lady, had picked up a chill in the sooty frost of the capital, and died soon after.

His attention returned once more to the private room in the tavern. Its dark wood-panelled walls gleamed with reflected firelight. Pewter and copperware along the top edge of the panelling, each item with its small consignment of fire glitter. The candles had burned low and light twinkled in the heavy lead glassware of the decanter and glasses. The logs were allowed to die down to glowing embers.

Turner sensed that the evening was coming to an end. Conversation had mellowed to a few low remarks. He realised no deal would be concluded this night. The bankers yawned, their entertainment over.

"Well, let's all sleep on it Mr Turner."

Rattled by the rutted road, rattled by the remembered conversation, in the coach Turner reflected on the hardened tone of the next morning's brief re-assembly.

"Please explain to me how opening a new works will help to repay debt when you are not yet even producing the annual quantity we agreed was the basis of our investment. Furthermore, what you do produce sells below the target price, and finally that price is not as low as the imports from abroad!"

"Sirs, this is not a business of quick returns..."

"You're telling me!"

"... but of substantial and steadily increasing reward over time."

"More specifically?"

"The current price per ton is low. There is an overburden of dead stock, in the short term. The country is not always quick enough to protect the sloops..."

"And your fisherman are smuggling it into the country as fast as your sloops are shipping it out!"

"Sir!"

Turner feigned shock. The banker waved his hand dismissively.

"Oh, go on."

"Sir, there is.... an idea..."

"Yes...?"

'...to concentrate production in a few places, by a gentleman's agreement."

The banker waited.

"It would pay us to stop production."

"How much?"

Turner paused.

"Perhaps £400 a year."

"Good God! We produce the precious material at £10 a ton and it makes a loss. We do nothing and we rake it in?"

"If we were to start a new works - at the place the prospector described last night – and start investing in pans and cisterns then by the time the agreement takes hold we will have to be paid to stop. In due course the price will rise as flow is controlled – then we will be in a good position to produce plenty at £20 or £25 a ton."

The banker sighed deeply. He toyed with the pen. He scribbled figures. He set the pen down. He coughed, stretched, leaned back. He rubbed his face vigorously with his hands. He lifted his hat, scratched, and lowered it. He grimaced. He shook his head.

"No."

The first hopeful day to hint winter's departure. Cold, weak sunlight and a hint of mist.

Word had reached Alcuin to return swiftly to Peak. A disturbing message – garbling together an accident of some kind, the supposed curse and a physical emanation?

Alcuin left the open land of fields and tracks and entered the fringes of the forest. Immediately the slight chill under the canopy. The sense of small sounds, closed in, made him more circumspect, and alert. There was a watchful peace in the shaded wood and although sunlight filtered down, and birds moved among the branches, he felt uneasy. A commoner in the city might feel this way, entering a cathedral. The trunks of trees, in shade, formed a grisaille and he thought of charcoal lines over rough parchment. He imagined shading between these verticals.

It was relatively clear of undergrowth and he moved stealthily, instinctively trying to reduce the noise of his movement, as he followed a narrow wandering trail. He knew that the forest was far from empty. Indeed, he thought, the shrinking forest must be getting more crowded.

The forest was under attack from all sides. The constant demand for feeding the clamps, which burned round the clock, months on end, as more and more alum hamlets sprung up both along the coast and inland. Other industries, shipbuilding, mining, razed acres for manufacture, propping structures and fuel. The forest dwellers themselves felled the trees. They would make clearings for planting their little communities of woodworkers, smiths and nailers.

Alcuin discerned a fragrance of woodsmoke mingled with the dusty bark smells. Squatters lived in the woods, he knew, and not just the odd solitary fugitive, deserter or political exile, but bands of tradesmen or merchants – the so called masterless men – and the casual labourers for the mines, kilns or weaving houses. Also, the dispossessed, which for that state alone were considered criminals.

Alcuin knew them to be self-possessed types, banded together or single, benign or otherwise. Both defensive and potential aggressors. Alcuin's heavy stick was no real deterrent he knew, nevertheless took comfort in its weight. Useful for briars at least, or the odd wild pig or dog.

He had heard that these self-determined groups would just as quickly seed and water their sects. The self-sufficiency of the artisan led the individual to dispense with the need for the church as an intermediary between man and maker. By a logic that Alcuin both feared and admired, this sectarian spirit nurtured both a dissenting bent and a disdain for authority. Kenelm had told him about the implicitly treasonable statements the 'diggers' had made at St George's Hill: "We have chosen the Lord God Almighty to be our king and protector."

A keener whiff of woodsmoke made him twitch his nostrils. Glancing ahead he detected a haze among the higher slanting sun lines that threw raking shadows across the twisted verticals of the trees. He peered into the confused spaces between them. He caught the crack of wood striking wood, a shout.

Alcuin skirted left, veering away from the direction of woodsmoke, clipped axe-echoes and voices.

He had been named after the great wanderer, that other Alcuin, who in the eighth century had travelled as far as the court of Charlemagne. His antecedent, who had been put in charge of the great illuminated 'golden gospels'. Who had been there when news came of the sack of Lindisfarne. Had implied the sinful monks brought the Vikings on themselves. And taken a strict line against harpists and versifiers.

Like his earlier namesake, Alcuin became a teacher. In less exalted circumstances. Asked to perform a double role at the alum works, minister and teacher.

His older brother was the first-born. He would inherit the lands. Alcuin's father had mapped out the familiar path of the second child – which historically had been into the safety of the monastery – laying the first stone slab on that trod by the name he gave his son.

As a boy Alcuin had developed, and been encouraged to embrace, solitary ways. Reading came easily to him. He also drew, as a way of telling stories back to himself, through which he learned about the world. His father's friendship with the village priest,

Kenelm, brought him into contact, through his stories, with the idyllic world of the Carthusian houses. Each monk with his own little stone house nestling against the protective wall of the monastery boundary. Each house with its door onto the great cloister, itself an inner sanctum given over to contemplation and prayer. The monks in solitary meditation, or in artistic endeavours. Their food delivered to the little stone alcove by the door. Taken through an L-shaped recess so as not to afford a glimpse of the provider. No window to the cloister. Only the individual cell garden.

The outer sanctum still a protective enclave – the one the lay brothers occupied. Coming and going between the priory and the surrounding villages and fields with their horses, their worldly trades.

Two things particularly appealed to him in Kenelm's evocation, and to these imaginings he returned continually over the years.

One was that each monk's little stone house was also a workshop – for weaving, for making pictures. For books to be written and illuminated. In Alcuin's vision a shaft of dusty light fell from a high window across the quiet interior with its lime-washed walls. The shaft fell over the hand loom where the woven strands of the gospels came together into a tapestry litany. The honeyed light fell across parchment, cloth for the books. Lighting pens and brushes, inks, charcoals and pocketknives. Linen, glue and leather.

The second was that each stone house had a walled kitchen garden. Here herbs and vegetables could be cultivated. In Alcuin's mind smoke rose from all the little chimneys of the cosy cell-houses around the cloister and drifted into the canopy of trees in the surrounding woods.

The daily routine, as Ken had described it to him, evoked in Alcuin a picture of a perfect world. The people of the surrounding villages and manors – nobles and serfs alike - contributing to the upkeep of the monastery. Supplying meat and grain, fish from the coast. Trading salt and spices. The wealth donated to the monastery's upkeep. The monastery taking on the intensification of the region's contribution, translated into prayer. In addition, fostering and protecting learning. Cultivating artistry and philosophy. Protecting libraries and paintings. Bestowing grace.

Long after the original Alcuin had mourned the sack of Lindisfarne, long after the destruction of Egbert's great library at York, long, long after the Romans had come and gone. Through the darkest period in England and far abroad, with lands overrun by invaders from the east, for centuries this second flowering of these remote monasteries – connected by stone trods and daffodil-strewn trails – had kept a light of learning burning through plagues and wars.

Alcuin circled over the geometry of this ideal, looking down like a raptor onto the pantiles and thatch, the green square of the cloister. The textured rows of the little herb gardens. Smoke gliding into the trees that clustered round the neat boundary wall of the monastery in its clearing. He drew this hawks-eye dream continually over the years, roughing out perspective over the monastery. And he portrayed himself within as he imagined it, in his comfortably austere cell, filling in the outlines of elaborated letters.

Kenelm had also told him, that dream had been smashed long ago. The outer gates broken, the stained glass shattered, the thatch burnt, the pantiles dragged off and cracked. Or intact brought to roof cowsheds. The stones pushed over. They found their way into grand houses, into pigsties, into limekilns, barns, mines and alum sheds. The horses bolted, the stores ransacked. The libraries pilfered or burnt. The cloth spirited away. The monks cast out, humiliated, beaten. Imprisoned or hanged. The raptor circled above the smouldering ruins looking for carrion.

The Dissolution. The icon smashing. The flagrant grabbing of the monastery fields and fisheries. All this and more he heard from his father's friend.

That priest had also given him his most treasured possession – the little book, mainly blank pages, that had been started long ago and abandoned, lost. A few pages filled out with colour and form. In the book the unknown artist – a monk, he likes to assume – had been able to finish only two things. Both were versions of Caedmon's hymn. One in the common tongue, in reference to the author's tongue perhaps, or for preaching to the lay people. The other in Latin. In the first he saw an echo of his own calling – pre-arranged for him as it was. The common version was elegant enough, with its modestly embellished first letter and its marginal sketch, he thought, of Hilda's Abbey. The Latin was set out in exquisite calligraphy and the title word turned into a small exegesis, by staff and snakestones, of Hilda's acts. The illustration providing the contextual story within which the hymn was to be heard. The two complementary versions creating, he feels, a small parable of aspiration for himself – to teach the workers' children, with stories set in *their* world.

So with his raptor's view of the pre-dissolution religious houses, the Carthusian priories, and with his unfulfilled book that brought the monk and lay brother together with the same song, he willed his way into service.

Alcuin's mother had died in childbirth with her daughter stillborn. His father's loss was turned towards a redoubled nurturing of his two sons. Gradually Alcuin had come to understand the care with which his father had prevented any risk of rivalry between the two brothers. It was a piece of craft to let his friend Kenelm kindle the fire of vocation in the younger son (for god had never spoken to him except, by implication, through his works). It was a piece of craft to procure a deputy more able than the hesitant, and somewhat fragile, older brother to help him seem to run the lands with such success.

So Alcuin respected his father for his fairness, and understood that he was loved, indirectly, through actions, and he in turn loved him. With this understanding he channelled the more abstract notion of the gospels into familiar and familial examples.

By the time Alcuin came into his position in the church however, it was not only transformed from the pre-dissolution vision in which he had been inculcated, it was fragmenting into so many splinters that the centre might not hold.

The liturgical monastery of his calling was now not much more than a straggle of mismatched outbuildings. The raptor swooped over them in turn. In one shed the Anabaptists, in another the free thinkers. In a smouldering field a near naked woman danced into euphoria. In a tumbled down lean-to someone argued that He was in each of us, argued with those that saw Him everywhere and those no-where.

The physical monastery of his calling was the same. The ramshackle collection of the alum houses. The work not of light and artifice but the crudest work of smashing the stones, and burning them. And the human wreckage.

Why try, some argued, against so much blasphemy, superstition and sin – so much dung and piss and filth stirred into the mix. Still he was drawn to it, to sniff and taste, and wonder if something might crystallise out.

Alcuin came up out of Stape and crossed the Roman Road. His mind turned to stories of the Romans in England. They had worked here with such purpose, despite their own chaotic cacophony of gods and prophets. Set to it with the application of the puritans. He considered the ruin of the Roman Road. Its rubble overgrown, stretching each side of him to the distance. Abandoned after they had gone. Later, Patrick in Ireland and his own namesake in Northumbria had re-established the Lord. Their fellow monks came afterwards to criss-cross this landscape with their trails and trods.

Walking was a form of meditation for Alcuin, if not quite of prayer. His task to bring the Word into the hard frontier places where the alum was made, all along the coast, was a challenge to his faith. Perhaps my only purpose, thought Alcuin.

He was moving through areas where the forest had been cleared, and small fields enclosed and ploughed out among the trees. From the path he could see the heather up on Howl Moor, and the open skylines. The bright afternoon that he had set off in was gone. Quietly, gloom was gathering under the wayside bushes and trees, and an unwelcome chill materialised as he ploughed down into the increasingly dismal vale. Locating the river, he followed it trudging northwards for a long time to the fording place. It was darker by the stream but its reflection lit the route and its gurgling reassured him.

Evening dimmed and in the deepening murk, struggling up from the river, everything was in conspiracy. Unable to see the overgrown trail he blundered uphill against callous hindrances, deliberate snaggings and trippings. The various shades of darkness were a confusion of thorns and brambles. Some vicious rose briars or gorse thickets drew dashed lines of scratch, spotting blackly with blood. Why didn't I leave earlier? He slid, feeling a strain in his groin, his ankle nearly went over. He suddenly felt like a child again – mad and tearful. On the steeper sections he slid back with nearly every step. His cloak tore and fleshy parts of his hands snagged as bushes tried to hold him. He was really quite scared. Feeling frantic and desperate. Now late and the light almost completely gone.

Suddenly he scrambled onto the track and straight ahead the dark looming silhouette of the inn reared up against the dregs of light left in the sky beyond.

Unoccupied?

The door swings open too easily with his hand on the knob and he half stumbles into the back of a high pew, just behind the door. The simple reddish glow of the ceiling beyond is enough to raise his spirits immeasurably. The transformation offers itself up as a parable that he is too tired to explore.

The front room of the Saltersgate is just enough for a fireplace and two high-backed wooden benches. They shield the draught from both window and door, enclosing enough dirt floor for a small table of rough planks.

Alcuin notes the diminishing glow of the embers, the bare, rubble-stone wall which recedes past the fireplace. Beside, a curtain concealing, presumably, a passage.

He notes too the still life of food remains on a wooden plate. Snapped-off pipe stubs, an empty tankard, crumbs, some darker spillage. He looks for a log to toss on the ashes. Finds none. Sits heavily down opposite the hearth, notes the slight throb of the shadows, some dark ochres and maroons.

One sudden involuntary shiver is enough to warm him. His eyes close and he sleeps. Sometime later he wakes, throws off a tiny panic of confusion, remembers, lies lengthways on the pew, head on his boots and sleeps again.

It was several days after his arduous trip back from Cornhill. Having failed in the Swan and Hoop, Turner had managed to obtain other finance from three London salters and dyers, to expand the number of boiling pans. This he would not do, given the supply problem, but some investment in the works might bear fruit, if the mooted gentleman's agreement did come to hold, against the costs of closing down, and then of re-opening. More urgently, there were repairs to his home at Stormy Hall that would be essential before another winter.

In fact the money had been eroded by the need for a paid security escort between London and York, and for the exchanging of currency between silver and gold. The stopover in York had been required to cash in bills of exchange.

Turner felt tightness in his chest – this new investment could not easily be paid back. It would subsidise previous debts of interest, delaying the day when all might be called in. No wind of it must reach the workmen. Already men were grumbling against the lack of flow in wages, against the hated system of impests.

News came of a man returning goods in lieu, who was making all kinds of accusations against quality and measure.

He despatched a lackey.

"Tell him I have returned from a wearisome journey to London, raising finance just for him, that I have wisely invested on his behalf, in a new whip."

He ate dry bread the dour innkeeper grudged him. Unhappy to find a sleeping priest in his stale parlour. Alcuin, stiff as the bench he has creaked into life from. As he soaked crusts in mouthfuls of weak beer he mused on the moorland crosses that waymark his wanderings.

Alcuin thought of the tree that became the cross. How the wooden cross came to be remembered in stone. How, after the felling of all the moorland trees, the paths and boundaries were marked with isolated trunks, stone ones, in the form of a cross. Those he encountered time and again on his solitary journeys across the desolate tracts. Setting out for one or other of his ministries within the alum trade. Or returning home alone. His roving ministry attached with Kenelm's blessing to his friend's parish. Heading back to his submerged ark, the stone boat below the stone boat, the church beneath the church.

Mauley Cross, that he passed the day before. From its high vantage point he can look back over open land to the top of Two Howes rigg, west towards his home.

He thinks of his path today - a dreary traipse east to the ancient cross on Lilla Howe – with Scarshead a lonely windswept prospect on from there. At Lilla the Saxon nobleman fell, taking the blade intended to end the life of his king, taking his own. That nobleman would have trod the Old Salt Road, the hollow way that passes the door of this inn. Or some other trail that preceded it by many centuries. Here blocks of salt, or more commonly fish, wound up the pannier-way. Walking this road Alcuin would often stand to one side as the passive Galloways, stout ponies of the traders, and the impassive men, straggled by.

Before Lilla, Alcuin will wind out of the thin companionship of the bare Saltersgate, and weave the nab-side to Malo Cross. A reminder to keep clear of the dangerous bog at May Moss. Heading north he might pass Old Wife's Neck, not a cross, but a standing stone, and find the reassuring weathered stones of the long trod as it falls to the foss.

Departed, without a grunt of acknowledgment, from the Saltersgate Alcuin took the old hollow way beyond Lilla, crossed the boggy dale to Bleak Hill, where the land ranged away in all directions bare and featureless. Alcuin stood on the tussocky howe and considered the possibility of the burial place below. Where beads of jet might be found. Pins of bronze.

Imagining the hummock for a stone base he stood erect, holding his arms out on either side in emulation of a stone cross. His cloak flapped in the breeze. Eyes narrowed against the wind he peered north east in the direction of the sea, invisible from here.

Here I could petrify, he thought. Like a stone in the collection of the Scarshead tallyman. Here would I serve a useful purpose, guiding travellers, panniermen and solitary ministers across harsh terrain. Looming out of the fog, sticking up blackly above deep path-obscuring snow. Indicating higher ground from the avaricious bogs. Dryer ground, to rest a while.

Named among my brothers of the cross. John Cross, Ralph, Percy...

Alcuin felt his feet sinking slightly into the soft turf of the barrow. He felt his roots reach down into the earth like a tree. Tensing his calves, his feet pressing to adjust his balance as he swayed to stay upright in the bluster and fall-away of the rough wind. Arms out, he kept as still as he could, but swaying slightly like a moorland alder.

Crossing these moors Alcuin often felt he traversed the oldest landscape. The bleakest tracts, open heather, wind-scoured tracks. Riggs peppered by cairns and howes, pits and dykes. The broken bases of lost crosses, standing stones. Old kilns, peat cuttings, beacons.

Olden land, its people of wood huts and mud walls, of peat smoke spiralling up, long-lost. Like ourselves, and those to come after. Leaving only the stones.

Alcuin held his arms out until they ached. He imagined the surprise of an approaching traveller, making his way from distance to this cross, suddenly amazed to see its silhouette flex and stir, its shaft divide, and step off its base and walk.

Which, growing cold, it now did.

A Lazarus rising. Or a Perseus mirroring Medusa – turned back from stone.

Soon he came to John Cross itself. Tracks led in several directions from the battered shaft and base of the cross. Its left limb sheared off in some brutality, of frost perhaps. Its right remaining like a sign post pointing him over towards Thorn Key, where the banked earth and ring of stones told of old graves.

Thinking suddenly of his summons to Scarshead. What of this unearthed body? This so called monster, of which he has been given only the barest outline? This emanation. This...revelation? Black corpse in a shale coffin. To erect a cross?

"They also marked the site of a murder or sudden death."

Sometimes Alcuin feels he treads a graveyard. The whole landscape scattered with remains. The gaunt marker stones of the vanquished being the moorland cairns, standing stones, and crosses. He imagines the countless little piles of bones, under the heather roots, under the turf. Like the splayed ribs of birds, the bleached structure of rabbits and shrews, he encounters on his travels. Picked clean, spread to the sky for the rains to anoint and the stars to sorrow over.

But the stark crosses are uplifting to Alcuin. In summer he places his hands against the warm glow of the rough sandstone. Alone he embraces the column, pressing his cheek against the warmth of its grainy surface.

He also loves the handstones and the guidestones. Those that spell the destinations of the pannier roads. The lane head stones, and their cryptic markings.

TO STOXLA. THIS KIRBY ROAD. S-TH

And the hand stones.

The flat splayed hand, fingers slightly apart, palms up, shallow-carved into the shaft of a square upright stone. There was one, a little to the north and west of his church below the church.

He can lay his own hand, right hand palm down, thumb pointing down, while he reads:

Roadto Pic krin:o r: Mal ton

And on the west side, another hand, which his left fits. Above it:

Road: to:Kirb y: mor :side:

Alcuin inspects his own palm, and he remembers the old hand stone on Urra Moor. The hand in relief, rounded fingers, palm up, with a hint of cuff, or bracelet, and words below.

THIS:IS THE WA Y. TO. KIRB IE:AND

A hundred yards or so beyond that hand stone stands a much more mysterious marker. A puzzle to Alcuin, a friend he can never fathom.

The face stone.

A round face, with the simplest markings to denote the eyes. Two horizontal slits. The nose a vertical line, the mouth a horizontal one. Inscrutable. It neither smiles nor frowns. It peers. Intently. A human face certainly. Like the one man sees in the moon. As if the moon man has finally woken up to give earth proper scrutiny. An owl-face, as the moon's owl, seeing its prey for the first time, the earth, narrows its eyes with intent. Like the girl's in the Boiling House.

Pressing on from the ring cairn Alcuin passes the standing stones. Here he feels the wilder places behind him. In less than an hour, if taken, the old salt road will deliver him to its source, winding down among the tightly packed houses of the fishermen, direct to the swell, surging up the slipway into the village.

Instead, having ventured north to avoid the barren high moor and the boggiest trails, he cuts down the sheltered wyke to where the becks converge. At the ford heads onto the sudden ravaged industrial waste of the plateau. Leaves the old grave-strewn world of the moors, leaves the period of the monks, their scattered remains of walls and ditches, like so many skeletons of small moorfowl.

Catches the sharp stink of the modern day. The sulphur from Scarshead. A festoon of timber along the desses, clinging to the bare hewn face of exposed scarp. He starts to see grey scum clinging to whins and hedges. Close by, and ahead, steam pouring off the shed roofs. Smoke streaming into steam and all of it merging with the lifting cloud of fret hovering above the cliff edge. Invisible, somewhere above the fume-filled fields an ineffectual sun, masked. The tug of sea breeze absent as men appear, singly at first, then in groups and then tens, scores as they pick their way, in grey ragged clothes and caps pulled down. Picks carried, sacks, barrows, carts. Reaches land criss-crossed by muddy pitted tracks with black standing water. Reaches land not of tiny dents and hummocks, of marker stones and bones, but today's land - stripped off, lifted, peeled, rubbished, laid waste. Man everywhere. And his works.

The eruptions of the clamps. Misshapen volcanoes seething dull red. Smoking with resentment. They are just the tip of the sore. Cone of the boil. Hell bubbling up, wreathing its poxy outbreaks in sulphur. Cloth-rotting and skin-rotting vapour.

Alcuin droned one of his prayer-charms mechanically and, suddenly aware of himself, found that it consisted only of 'God help us', repeated obsessively, like a phrase muttered by an exhausted mother in a sick household.

He cast his glance over the grey landscape in the failing light. Dirty grey and white scum clung and coated all the hedges and trees in the vicinity. Many dead or ailing. What survived hung mindlessly on.

Weights and measures

A few days after Fox's pannier road message, a tidy looking man appeared at the quarry. Slight, short and neat, he was soon deep in conversation with the tallyman. Accompanying him, a rangy youth in ill-assorted garments, which lent a flamboyant air. The youth set to without hesitation, drawing an outline of the monster. Having got it roughly, measuring it piece by piece, he added notes to the drawings.

In wooden boxes Fox had collected various pieces that had been damaged by the picks, or fallen loose in the spoil. The visitor and the tallyman sifted several of these out, turning them over. The visitor peered at them with a magnifying glass.

To one side of the steeping pits Carey put down a bundle of dry gorse and lit it. The gorse blazed fiercely. Carey was gazing not into the flames but somewhere far beyond. In a moment or two the gorse started to die down and, with an exaggerated blink, Carey was back in this world. He added kindling and quite soon had a decent fire going with a good few embers. He produced a little pot and, requesting some water from a butt by the tallyman's hut, boiled up a small quantity. A few of the workmen glanced over, half interested, half bored.

Carey prised the lid off a small battered tin and scooped out a handful of coarse brown grainy material, which he allowed to sift down into the pot from his folded hand. A precise methodology, thought the tallyman, matching the sober style and neat raiment of the visitor. Carey lifted the pot onto the earth beside the fire. A small pewter cup materialised with which he scooped liquid from the top, having allowed the grittier contents to settle.

Finally he sniffed it, swirled it around in the cup, sipped it and grimaced, and then held it out to Fox.

"Coffee?"

With a sceptical look the tallyman stepped forward, took the cup, and gulped.

"Urgh"

Screwing up his eyes. He had also burnt his tongue.

"Horrible."

Carey produced a third receptacle, and spooned honey from it into the cup, stirring it. He offered it to Fox again who, in the interests of experimental science, took a more cautious taste. After a moment of absorbed analysis, cooling it, swilling it, he swallowed. Fox shuddered lightly, refraining from comment. At last Carey made a second pewter cup appear and poured a further measure for himself. He stoked up the fire, which flamed wanly in competition with a patch of weak sunlight. The two men squatted beside it.

When Carey eventually broke the silence it was not to pronounce on the coffee, still less the black fragments he and his assistant had been summoned by the tallyman to observe.

"Xenophanes believed the stones found in the mountains were shells that must have come from the sea. They weren't a loose collection, but were embedded in the rock strata."

Fox nodded. He was reasonably well read for an industry accounts man, but the Greeks were not his strong point. Carey continued.

"Hooke mentions it. He has often compared petrified objects with organic specimens. Broadly, he agrees with the Greek, and no doubt with the Greek's assertion that there is a single deity, rather than a multitude."

Fox rubbed his lower lip, and scratched his chin as he interjected.

"Hooke must be sane, I suppose, designing as he is the Bethlem madhouse."

Carey hesitated, to consider whatever measure of dark humour the tallyman intended with this remark. Unsure, he pressed on.

"His colleague Ray begs to differ."

Fox took another sip of coffee before replying.

"Yes John Ray was nosing around these parts more than once."

"Really?"

That interested Carey.

"Did you know him?"

"Met him a couple of times. He was getting on a bit, and his inspection of findings from the shale seemed to pain him as much as enthuse. But with the shits and the leg ulcers perhaps that was unsurprising. He would lug around his 'Catalogus Plantarum' and make comparisons with the markings in the rocks. Apparently, he rarely strayed this far north."

"No, his patrons were Midlands gentlemen, and Ray was frequently impecunious. However, he did get as far afield as France, even Italy. His little group liked nothing better than pressing the flora, and pegs on noses, cutting up dead animals."

Fox sniffed.

"He had little time for the likes of us. Keen to get away he was, but some of our findings were irresistible to him. Hobbling up to the quarry from an urgent shit in the gorse, or inspecting his weeping shin wrappings."

"He was puritanical of course, and no doubt saw his lack of temporal funds as promise of plenty in the next sphere. Ray could not quite dare to conclude that, for all his comparisons, the formed stones came from plants and fish."

"That would put a weapon into the atheists' hands!"

Carey was irritated that Fox had jumped ahead of his discourse.

"Yes, Ray was a Cambridge man, and Hooke, like me, Oxford."

He hoped to re-assert scholarly superiority.

"A humble blacksmith, apparently."

"What?"

Carey had spoken more sharply than he intended.

"Ray?"

"It was his father, in fact."

Carey, regained his thread.

"In his Wisdom of God sermons Ray worries about the formation of the stones and considers the Flood. But for him it is too risky to assert His wisdom in these particularly puzzling works of creation."

Fox shrugged.

"Even Hooke runs up against the church, and prefers to peer down his microscope, so they say."

Carey smiled. He shook his head ruefully.

Quietly they sipped their coffee, which Carey had topped up from the dregs.

Fox peered sourly into his cup.

"The last taste fulfils not the promise of the first sniff."

"Ah. Like so much in life, like so much."

"Lot's wife was turned into a pillar of salt."

Fox ventured this wisdom as the inn discussion returned once again to the monster. An evening after Carey's initial inspections, that gentleman not being present. The tallyman had given a guarded account. Speculation in the inn however, had grown excitedly, with many contentious opinions, despite the presence of both the minister and the manager.

"From this it's a small step to petrifaction."

Alcuin knew Fox for a sceptic, one with considerable bible scholarship, of which the tallyman was usually circumspect.

"So the creature could be a miracle, or as the workers will have it, a curse?"

Fox held his hand out towards Alcuin.

"Perhaps the clergy will explain this fellow's place in the order of things under heaven."

Alcuin shifted, gathering his thoughts. A shout interrupted.

"Maybe there were two of them in the dark?"

Wynter, after a few drinks, was getting a little provocative.

Alcuin addressed the tallyman cautiously.

"Are you suggesting, that this is some creature interred? There are any number of oddly shaped rocks, that hint at forms to the imaginative or overly suggestible."

"Well, we will see when Mr. Carey has him fully unearthed."

Robbie brushed his hand, palm down across some spilt ale on the wooden tabletop.

"Unearthly is the word. My workers argue fervently whether the monster should be smashed to pieces or given a Christian burial."

Others stood just outside the firelight where the manager, tallyman and works minister sat.

"But those rocks must have fallen on the fellow at the time these hills were created. Or before."

The inn was a known gathering place of dissenters.

Another voice commented gruffly.

"Any papist curse is worth about two pots of piss."

"And yet this fellow must have sinned mortally to get this treatment."

The tallyman was briskly confident.

"When Mr Carey has the fellow extracted – and reassembled - then we will see how he shapes up."

Alcuin was amused.

"You will need a large shelf for that one Mr Fox."

"Who knows, perhaps Mr Carey might have a shelf for this one."

Wynter cocked an ear at that.

"Might he? Turner will be intrigued to hear that!"

An uncomfortable shuffling ensued. Fox bridled a little, coming back brusquely.

"Robbie, since when did Turner take an interest in mine spoil? Except for tonnage shifted."

Alcuin was not so sure.

"I'm sure word of it has reached Stormy Hall, if its reached my unworldly abode."

The men snorted. As itinerant preacher to the alum works Alcuin's route could be a conduit for news, particularly since the printing presses were so productive nowadays.

Wynter was more certain.

"Turner will sniff out value, wondering who pays for Carey's draughtsman to take such care to capture the fish."

Several voices at once.

"Fish!"

Though Wynter had said it, Fox was flustered.

"Well Mr. Carey ventured an idea.....just one of many."

The drinkers swiftly elaborated that one.

"The monster swam up the cliffs! A thirty-foot fish jumped up the beck like a salmon! It crawled across the meadows like a seal. And it bored into the rocks like a mole!"

It was hilarious. But when the coughing and spluttering stopped more than one shivered, and the less sceptical crossed themselves.

The tallyman however, recovered his poise.

"Stranger things have happened than a seal or a conger died on the mud and sank."

There was laughter.

"The conger curled up like a snakestone."

But that had them frowning too.

Wynter drained his glass, holding the empty to the lantern light.

"Well it's surely a sign to use more kelp and less urine!"

Alcuin thought that the manager might not be altogether joking. Nevertheless, the tone lightened and the subject shifted to the vexed question of which additive would best aid the alum crystallisation.

Alcuin was grateful for the change. The company of the sceptics was the most stimulating he knew. Carey's assistant had fired his imagination with his drawings, but he was still floundering to fit the monster into his picture of the world.

He thought back to earlier that morning. Alcuin and Robbie had walked up to the quarry from the manager's house.

The previous night they had stayed up talking late. The manager had touched upon many worrying things. These were anxious times at the works and for some the monster was a clear manifestation of this underlying unease.

Nevertheless they had risen early, as night's turbidity clarified into day. As grey settled out of the early morning light and the sky brightened behind the clouds out at sea. The idea of seeing the monster had kindled Alcuin's nervous excitement.

They strode up through the wet dew, slipping on the tufted grass and reeds. They scrambled over the gorse-edged rim of the plateau, where the clamps brooded, and scuffed across the scabbled floor of the quarry.

They encountered a ritual of pipe-lighting and spitting. A straggle of men kept close to a meagre fire. A flagon or two of small beer was being distributed. Carey was already there. On the fire, he prepared a soot-blackened pot of something noxious, which to general admiration he then drank.

Thus fortified he indicated the various portions of the monster, explained how it should be extricated, and demonstrated the itemisation of the pieces. Some of these he referred to, disconcertingly, as 'like to fingernails.' Beside him the assistant drew, stopping occasionally to peer and frown.

Robbie and Alcuin could make little of the black shape, which appeared fused to the rock face like something burned, baked to an unrecognisable residue.

Alcuin noticed Wynter's close attention to Carey's methodical approach. Certain procedures, Alcuin imagined, might be overhauled in the manager's laboratory. Alcuin turned his attention to Carey's assistant, admiring the youth's drawings. He thought he detected significant embellishment tending towards animalistic, or plant-like forms.

They brought to mind the illuminated gospels, in which fanciful creatures, scaled birds or winged worms took the form of the letters introducing John, or Mark. These books had long held a fascination for him.

Seeing the assistant's notebooks he imagined a kindred spirit. He would consider showing him his own book. He watched the assistant outline a roughly circular hollow, visible in the revealed surface of the stone, and with one or two more strokes conjure up a fanciful eyeball.

Alcuin kept quiet, frowning over the drawing of the loosely ordered fragments. He was shocked to see how clearly certain rows of stones seemed to suggest the spine. He wondered what Kenelm would have made of it. He looked back to the rock figure. At three or four times the size of a horse's skeleton, this looked disconcertingly like something the workmen would have called the devil's work. But fear was ripe to suggestion he knew, as tree boles beside the trail on a moonless night, given the vaguest outline by a frost of dim starlight, conjured figures.

Afterwards, Alcuin had sketched the eyeball into his own book but, shocked at its verisimilitude, quickly converted it into the central disc of a stone cross – adding a shaft and etching in a tuft of heather at the base to ground it.

A sudden uproar returned Alcuin's attention to the inn, where the monster was under discussion again. The tallyman was stoking the argument by asserting that St. Hilda could petrify a conger eel and that his collection might be all elvers and hag-worms.

There was another shout from the back.

'We die like beasts and after we are gone, there is no more remembrance of us – just as Raleigh said."

Robbie was quick to shout back.

"Not here! Just dive in the mud like this fellow. You'll live forever."

Carey had a piece of ground cleared, close to the original rockfall. It was first rid of loose rocks and pebbles, and afterwards swept with a besom. A low canvas tar was erected over it, and the dust watered and smoothed, and allowed to dry.

After that, for long periods Carey and his assistant disappeared under the cloth. Occasionally they ventured to and from the shale face, carrying lumps from the baked black scar, or from the spoil around.

Slowly, over several weeks, the workmen would see the gradual erasion of the monster in its shale bed, and assume its reappearance under the tar. Which activity the workmen observed with set faces. Under its shade Carey cursed the dust that blew in, and the snap of flapping canvas in gusting wind. He juggled pieces endlessly in speculation – arranging and rearranging, to try, conjecture and guess.

A black mass of rubble began to aggregate into a flat undulating island, in its dust sea. A craggy outline, like coastline on a portolan. With a long foreshore promontory at one end and a reef of intermittent islets twisting from the other.

It was an island of as many inlets, and inshore tarns, as dry land, for the greater part of Carey's jigsaw lay, tentatively labelled, in the wooden box. The same quantity again simply in piles of frustratingly similar pieces. Mixed in, a proliferation of the fallen alum shale, temporarily kept from the pits.

Once, Carey and the assistant lugged over a heavy unwieldy shale-embedded fragment. A long dark tapering stone, bigger than a horse's thighbone. The island grew, like a volcanic tract emerging from falling sea level.

At the centre of this expanding lava-stain island a spiralling reef of thin curved splinters radiated in a mazy proliferation. Aligned along the necklace of knuckle-shaped bones, at right angles to them, almost like a spine and ribs. Carey pieced in tiny shards, lifting and rotating them, reversing them, and lifted them out, and tried them elsewhere, as the stubborn pattern emerged.

It was frequently crowded under the cloth as the tallyman, Carey and the assistant all pressed in around the jigsaw. Thin pipe smoke curled around the edges of the canvas. Periodically all three emerged and the tallyman was encouraged to indulge his growing acceptance of Carey's brew.

Whisper of these activities unsettled many among the alum workers and grew to muttered speculation.

In his book Alcuin draws a looping line of charcoal. He crosses it roughly with another, hacking the mark sharply from a cutting angle. A piece splits off, leaving a hard dark gouge. Quickly he cuts more lines with the broken edge of the charcoal, slicing and slashing with its broken blade. Curves and arcs mesh densely. He stabs with the charcoal – bits splinter off leaving dark star holes. He smudges with his thumb. He drags the back of his hand across. He shades closely, rapidly, in dense patches. The page fills quickly. Thickly, blackly. He smears again. He dots the page with sharp taps of the stick's end. It snaps. He takes another. He jabs it in quick hard movements. Finally he slams his fist down on the page and clasps the book closed with his open palms, feeling the gust off it on his brow. A whiff of charcoal dust. He slaps the book on the table, the charcoal fragments within emboss, like darker stars in a black firmament. Slams his fist down on the leather binding. The night thorns prick viciously into the black tangle of undergrowth.

"Launde is rich?"

Robbie laughed.

"Why do you say that?"

"He has many pennies...."

"Ah."

He smiled. Ana went on, her eyes wide.

"....and an even greater quantity of half pennies and then again a fortune in farthings."

"Indeed so."

"Yet he says he will go to the owner, saying he is starving?"

Robbie's eyes narrowed a fraction. He had not heard whisper of this. He measured his response.

"Not in such a way rich, or in such a way poor."

"Gah! So roundabout the bush Robert. Like always. In one word. *Por favor. Si or no?*"

Robbie grinned.

"I'll show you."

He lifted some of his assay bottles down from the shelves, handing one to Anna.

"Ana take this and weigh it."

Ana put the bottle on the scales and added the tiny weights until it balanced. Robbie then filled the jar with water.

"It's fresh. From the spring."

With a gesture to the girl he made her take it and, full to the brim, watched her weight it carefully. He noted the weight, subtracted that of the empty bottle, and then divided it by eighty.

"We're rich!"

She beamed. Then frowned.

"How?"

"80 pence!"

"Que?"

He raised a forefinger.

Robbie felt his forearm brush against the soft, matting felt of Ana's sleeve. Her thin brown wrist, the vermilion cuff. Ana leaned in close. He could smell her hair. A few seconds passed.

Robbie took the bottle from her, emptied it, shook it and blew in it until satisfied it was dry.

"Now."

He took a stoneware jar of liquor fresh from the leaching pits which, he explained, Mr. Launde had brought down that morning.

He filled the bottle with the liquor and passed it carefully to Ana. She weighed it and, moving the tiny weights on and off, at last satisfied herself it was balanced, looking to Robbie for approval. Finally she showed him the new weight.

"Ah. Ninety. Ten pence more."

"What! How?"

He shook his head.

"Now this is from the coolers. After the evaporation."

Once again he emptied, dried and refilled the bottle. She weighed it and he jotted down the result."

"Profit!"

She clapped her hands. Then frowned.

"But how?"

"40 pence more!"

Ana scowled fetchingly.

"So not real pennies?"

"No. Not real. The water weight divides by 80. That is a unit they call a 'penny'. The steeping will make the water heavier. It contains what we need – the alum. The evaporation will remove water we don't need. When heavy enough it's ready to start the first crystallisation."

"So Launde remains a poor man."

"Sadly, yes, we all do. Yet in a sense this enrichment does take place, for the heavy water is what we need. Its why we do what we do."

Ana looked at the heaviest liquor.

"So this will make the crystals."

He nodded.

"Yes. You saw them finished in the Tun House. But something has to happen before that."

Light in her eyes, glancing up, under dark lashes.

"Do you want to go and look?"

Launde circumnavigated the wide disc of the timber lid that kept diluting rainwater out of the raw liquor while it settled.

Unhappy with its condition, he looked around for someone to repair it. At the same time he saw Wynter and the girl going in to the Evaporating House. The manager nodded to Launde, who wandered over to the cisterns to fetch a carpenter.

"The first solid alum is made here. By precipitation."
Ana was perplexed.
"We add the salts, and let the liquid cool."
"Salt?"
"Here we piss in the tanks."
Her eyes widened.
"No. You are joking Mr Wynter."
She grinned widely.
"*Si*".
Mimicking her cadence. She pulled a face.
"Yes. But not entirely. Fresh is no good. We collect the old stuff – as you know - and let it stand. Yours will do though. After a time."

She wrinkled her nose.
"Or, more and more these days, the kelp."
Puzzled.
"The burnt seaweed ash."
She nodded, happier.
"And then the urine!"
"Pah!"

This was also true. Robbie led her through into the hot stink over the cisterns. The foreman was stirring stale urine into the broth. She felt her gorge rise. She half coughed, half retched. She tried to breathe in as shallowly as possible. Turning back to watch, to be brave.

The foreman moved the liquid round continuously with a wooden paddle. Around him were little notched glasses and assay dishes. Winter noticed, to his satisfaction. Good.

"Once this has stood for a few days we drain the 'mothers'."

He noticed her perplexity return.

"The residual liquid - the 'mothers' we call it - don't ask me why. We run it off and collect it. It goes back to the quarries to add to the pits of calcined shale."

He paused, moving to a drained cistern close by. He scooped up a sludge of brown sediment. She saw that it was made up of small rough crystals.

"This is the alum flour."

"Easy!"

She grinned.

"First salt, then flour – then you bake it – bread!"

He laughed.

"Very good! You learn fast."

She gave him a darting flash of her momentarily widened eyes. Dark spark, a quick fan of glow over tiny cinders.

"Brown bread. This has iron in it. These crystals will be purified. Our aim is white flour. So this is washed, and washed. The roaching as we call it. Water and mothers, as the foreman decides. Reheated till the bad stuff drops out. Finally, we crystallise again."

She nodded obediently, with a hint of mockery.

Robbie pronounced, mock-solemn.

"Where the baking is not of bread, but the baker's wife is turned to salt."

Here she was completely lost again.

"As you have seen."

She frowned a little parody of infuriation.

"Lot's wife. You remember? With the priest? Giant chess pieces you said."

"Yes. But the baker's wife?"

"The roaching casks. Inside them when broken – you remember? We call each one Lot's wife. His wife you see, should never have looked back."

She was exasperated. He smiled.

"You have neglected your bible studies. Ask the minister."

She guessed he was joking. The bright spark of mischief in his eyes, when he teased her, easily dismantled the mockery.

Having instructed repairs to the raw liquor cistern, Launde had come into the Cooling House and was engaged with the foreman by the settlers. Seeing him, Wynter beckoned him over.

"We need to step up the evaporation of the purge stream. The West Yorkshire pharmacists and cloth makers are demanding more Epsom Salt. Launde, get someone to set up a separate evaporator for the purge stream, to cool and crystallise the purge. The residue from that to go back to the alum evaporators."

Launde laughed.

"A lot of constipation in the Pennines is there?"

"Oh yes. Stiff with shit they are over on the west side!"

"I wouldn't drink that stuff, however dilute."

Wynter grimaced theatrically, and then nodded.

"Though it does soothe a bruise."

"For the fields too, of course. It feeds the soil."

Launde departed. Robbie turned to Ana.

"Here, in the coolers, or settlers, the liquor stands for four days."

She looked. Crystals were starting to form around the edges of the lead-lined cisterns.

"At the base too."

He drew in next to her, aware of her body warmth as their arms rested gently side by side. He pointed, and she peered into the cloudy depths, seeing the sediment at the bottom. Leaning forward she grabbed the pointing arm for stability, crooking her elbow around it, oblivious it seemed, though not to Robert, as it nestled against her breast. In that position they remained slightly longer than necessary. When they broke off he gestured to the wider room.

Beside the settlers there were wooden draining trays, where any surplus trickled back into the tank. Here the crystals harvested from the cisterns were placed.

"These will be stored in the alum byng. Then we sweeten it."

Close by were some tubs into which the crystals were placed, once drained. Fresh water was added for the edulcoration, to wash away soluble impurities.

"And this?"

A barrowman pressed past Ana, as she indicated the yellow sludge within.

"Ah, the 'slam'. Most is removed in the Clearing House. It's the waste. This residue we throw."

The toxic waste of the slam would be tipped into the sea, or for convenience over the side into the wooded wyke.

"Sometimes we ship the slam. Unpleasant stuff but there's always someone will find a use for it. The bottle glass men will take it."

Ana smiled at him, without comment.

Amid the stink and steam, the coming and going of men, the bubbling and coughing, the scraping and swearing, Ana and Robbie stood stock still – watching each other.

In March the weather improved, but for the men things got worse.

William Fenn, a barrowman, unpaid for three months, had subsisted through the last winter on the residue of bad corn, reluctantly accepted in lieu. The corn was Turner's. The owner had a monopoly on corn produced in the region and sought to install a captive market amongst his alum workers.

At first Fenn had demurred, going instead to local merchants to seek credit. It transpired that they had succumbed to pressure from Turner not to give any.

Having no alternative, Fenn returned to Turner and, being once more refused payment in cash, negotiated a quantity of corn, some to use, some to sell. Not only was the quality poor, but the weight dubious and the price high. Later he sold the surplus at a loss.

Fenn was twenty-eight, without wife or child, of sturdy frame and modest habits. In late March he collapsed at the shale face and, falling heavily against his barrow, cracked two ribs. Afterwards breathing became restricted.

Wynter moved him to the settlers, for reduced pay, although the effect of buying expensive corn and selling at a loss had already implemented that. He replaced an older man who, over the cold season, had fallen to a fever thin soup had failed to assuage.

In the works Fenn grew disengaged and troubled the others with suggestions that they all withdraw labour.

In March also, Turner made one of his rare appearances at the works. Oliver Clarke, a barrelman in the tun house, had confronted him. Corn that had rotted, bought above the market rates, and some cheese, which in trading down he had found to be worth only half the price. These in lieu of wages had brought him to a desperate edge of anger and despair.

On impulse, seeing him riding past, Clarke had stopped Turner on the track a little way from the works. A few men watched from a distance. Turner, on horseback, appeared to strike out with his whip. The altercation continued, with Clarke keeping his distance, and Turner's horse shifting agitatedly on the spot. Suddenly it seemed to rush at Clarke, knocking him to the ground.

That day Clarke left the works and took temporary employment in the fields. They heard he had threatened to sue Turner for unpaid wages and that he had been dismissed on the spot.

Later still Oliver Clarke returned anyway, compliant, having found little else in the region to be paid to do.

Another, pickman John Cuthbeck, had taken rye and oats for his ticket of unpaid wages. This after a long period of badgering Wynter for money. In November his wife had grown listless, withered and died, leaving two bewildered infants.

Cuthbeck left the works, and later returned to lower pay. One of the children died. The other was left with a relative in Whitby. Cuthbeck sold his few remaining goods of any value, mainly pewterware from his deceased wife's family. He moved into another household where his contribution of impests, meagre goods of doubtful value, would be a further drain on that family.

Despite these deprivations, all over the region but particularly along the coast, the landscape was being transformed by the feverish hacking of desperate starving labour. Each man could barely get enough food to lift the pick. Yet the cumulative effect, over decades, had made enormous despoliation. The razing of woods, the ploughing up of the furze and the plundering of the sandstone crown.

Wynter heard strike rumours from Launde, who had the ears of both the manager and the men. He persuaded Launde that demand was so low anyway that Turner would close the works if there was a strike. Wynter knew he might pay with his own position. In which case none of Turner's other three alum ventures would be available to him.

Alcuin and Robbie had walked down to the laboratory together. Inside, he noted the usual neatness in the manager's preparations for the daily alum rites.

And its contrast with the disassembly he had witnessed on the way over. They had met the girl. Alcuin had ceased to exist for a few moments – might well have been turned to stone. Robbie had opened a faucet of charm and cajoling, but he was translucent as a rock pool. Alcuin had seen right down to the bottom. The manager was sending the girl on some begrudged errand. The girl said a little, but Alcuin felt some bargain was being negotiated. Felt the manager, for all his status, being manipulated. The atmosphere became suddenly tense, closeness as before a storm. It was like the clouds raced over feverishly, flashing brightness and hail, lightning and heat, all in a few moments.

Then the girl had left. Skulked off along the track.

"Hot blooded that one."

Alcuin frowned over the ambiguity of this comment.

After that they had walked briskly down to the lab in uncomfortable silence. Sulphur smoke and gull cries followed them.

Once in the laboratory Robbie had regained composure. The sure ritual of his processes stabilised him. Heat was turned off and the turbulence stilled.

Alcuin watched thoughtfully as Robbie arranged the jars and glassware. A box of ash. A flagon of kelp leys.

"What do you feel when you go through this?"

"It's a job."

"But it's a search. You are constantly experimenting with ingredients, temperatures..."

Winter was dismissive.

"Seek and you will find."

Alcuin persisted.

"That's what I mean."

Robbie shrugged.

"You keep note of everything, you make adjustments."

"It's guesswork, Alcuin."

"Robert, you have faith."

"It's the blind leading the blind. That's why the industry has made paupers of everyone."

"Like Turner?"

"In time."

Alcuin looked around the room at the workbench, the shelves, glassware, instruments.

"It's very well ordered, your universe."

"It's the girl."

Alcuin frowned.

"It's what she does. It's her vocation."

Hint of a sneer. It was a challenge.

Alcuin said nothing.

The atmosphere of calm in the laboratory was pervasive, despite the underlying volatility of their subject. It brought to Alcuin's mind the little Carthusian house: the loom, the parchment, the cloth, the shaft of sunlight.

Alcuin resumed thoughtfully.

"I could work like this. It's a work of transformation."

"From rock to rock."

He paused.

"Alcuin, its just one step following the last."

"Yes. Each one takes you into the vicinity. To know the goal nears, I envy that."

"The steps could be in the wrong direction."

"Then you reverse, resume. You have a procedure you can believe in."

"Its guesswork and common sense, but whether it takes us where we need to be?"

"If I had those reassuring steps.

"If you lose faith we all do."

Alcuin shook his head.

"I can't be faithful for everyone."

Wynter was wandering on Scars Head, inland from the crumbling cliff edge above Ness, by the old tower. Roaming uneven ground of rubble and earthworks, where they said the Romans lit beacons. Where they still do. To guide or lure the ships. A dark glint caught his eye. He stooped, and seeing something, squatted down. He turned over the object with his nail. It was small and black, lustrous. Instinctively he swept his gaze swiftly around him. No one. He quickly pocketed.

Crows

It lay in her open palm.

"What is it?"

Ana studied it intensely.

"It's whatever you make of it"

It was a small flat pendant, little bigger than a bead, with a hole made through towards one end. He took it back, rubbed it briskly on his tunic and held it over her forearm, raising the hairs.

"Ah!"

She shut one eye, with the other glaring wide, and grimaced comically.

"El azabache - to keep the evil eye"

"To keep away the evil eye? You have this?"

"Yes, we have this. For the evil look!"

She squinted through the hole. Puzzled, she squinted through at Robbie.

"Who made it?"

"It's Roman"

"*Que?*"

"Roman. They made the old road on the moor. They left this."

She looked serious. Impressed?

"One thing. If you keep this you must tell no one. If anyone sees it, a labourer made it. From something found on the beach"

She peered into it closely, as into a small dark mirror.
"Why?"
"It might be valuable."
"Give it to Elizabeth"
He was silent for a moment.
"She'll sell it."
"Only if she has to."
Silent again.
"If you don't want it...."
She grabbed it away.
"Mine!"
Her eyes flashed like jet.

Later, in her room, she puts the brown stone pensively to her lips.

Shouts carry across the blanketed fields. Muffled. Suddenly sharp. Sounds of tools scraping, rocks splitting. Far hiss, as of a quiet kettle, approaching boil or, in its murmur, the sea.

Voices carry from buildings that quickly materialise, close to, their high windows streaming.

"I know where I am from. But how can I tell you?"
"Try".

"It has always some sun, *mucho calor*. Here it's...*frio*. It's always f..."

"Freezing?"

"Always fucking freezing."

"Tch."

"Well this word is not so bad in my language."

The lips push forward. A petulant rebuke, which he mimics. She grins false, sudden, and returns to stirring the dirt with her stick. The pout a reproach? Or a kiss?

He tries her words.

"Un beso."

"Fuck you."

Throws down the stick.

Fox's network of beachcombers brought back rumour and gossip. This is how he heard about some rough music due to be meted out to the manager. Some nonsense planned for the upcoming Rogation festivities, he guessed. Mischief. Which knowledge he kept to himself.

His informal band of informers patrolled the foreshore below the unstable cliffs. Their main purpose was to search for jet. Striking an actual seam was rare but, as the cliffs were prone to regular falls of shale, certain ragged men, human crows, thought Fox, would be found at the ebb tide, scavenging for washed jet.

Jet had its skin. Dug from a seam its outer layer would need to be chiselled off. But on the shore a lucky find would see the stones worn smooth and the skin near melted off by the scouring of the rocks – like scales rubbed off a herring by a blunt serrated blade.

Fox's crows were largely desperate and unreliable, straggling solitary or in pairs, picking over the beach rubbish. But they knew he valued more than them the snakestones, which shared their beds with the jet shales below the dogger. Destitute crows might barter their pickings and peckings of jet to a local craftsman. And for a pittance, evocative specimens of petrified marine semblance could be traded with Fox. A lucky crow might celebrate a decent find of raw jet shale with a gift to the tallyman of Hilda's unwanted cast-offs. At other times Fox would wander down below the cliffs with the ragged men, trading their preferences with his, like a skulking gull amongst the crows.

The jet collectors were a superstitious colony, and they were glad to be rid of devil's toenails and snakestones alike.

In Fox's palm he held a little collection of recently traded 'thunderbolts' – the sharp little fragile pointed cones that Carey called the belemones, the 'little darts'. The scavengers were uncomfortable with all the shapes, from the shells to the worms, and would keep about themselves little witch-post charms of jet - crosses and hearts stuck with pins - only to be sold in abject destitution.

So, wandering, turning over stones, exchanging a few words here and there, Fox had picked up rumour of the planned mischief. This sort of thing was not just restricted to the night before Gunpowder Treason, but could build under the pressure of malicious speculation, like something boiled up under a battened-down lid. The coming Rogation Day was often an occasion to prise up the lid a little. Thus, by implication it seemed the general drift of whiff and whisper concerning the foreign girl and the manager was building to a release.

> "I know Turner."
> "You do?"
> Quick to a rush of jealousy.
> "I met him."
> "How?"
> "In Whitby."
> Wynter, exasperated.

"That's where"
"With my father."
"That's who with."
Ana put her tongue out.

Alcuin squatted on the beach beside the assistant, who had sketched the merest outline of a common snakestone.

The assistant sat on a large rock with a few pieces of charcoal and a piece of dry bark he had stripped off some driftwood. He drew on the inner face of the bark.

Alcuin observed how he shaded along the sides of the coils, but only half their girth. He then shaded off the form around the roughly circular relief, where it lay still half-embedded in the split shale. In this way the light of his primitive page was captured, and used to throw light on the other half. In a similar way the raised cross-bumps of the snakestone – that might imply segments of joints – were swiftly brought into relief. The assistant cross-hatched a hint of shadow under one edge. Here a little sand-flea might have scuttled underneath the sleeping snake, before Hilda's judgement.

Alcuin looked up and around at the curve of revealed foreshore around the bay. The rippling sea lay like a shimmering cloth pulled back from goods laid out for inspection. He saw Carey and Fox looking over the wares, picking them up and replacing them. Trinkets laid out on a market stall, rearranged to renew interest, juxtaposed to entice, in new combinations, by the furling and unfurling of the sea.

A grey drifting saturation enveloped the deserted quarry. The tallyman's hut alternately loomed out and was obscured. The atmosphere was three parts drizzle, four parts fog, and three parts smoke. It could cure you, or kill you. Desolate, the rubble-strewn floor. Occasionally the rim of the quarries' brow would appear against the lighter gloom of the gauzy luminous sky, ragged with edge-growth. Hawthorns and other bitterly twisted briars fruited with heavy water droplets.

The smoky grey fog sucked in spirals around the hut. The updraught wind moaned as it explored the sodden boards for weakness and twisted up, wreathing the little chimney pot, where it ritually conjoined with the woodsmoke emerging from it. It melted into the larger volume of luminous turbidity. Falling ash from the clamps precipitated through it like flakes of dirty snow. Mingled with the steamy vaporous murk came the muffled sound of voices.

Inside, the hearth was a little furnace of cheer, where the consuming love of the flames burned among the pulsating radiance of the logs. The tiny fireplace constructed of flat layers of steeped and discarded shales, built up with soft corners and rounded edges, a small hive of warmth that, blackened, narrowed towards the timber roof. The hut had been built around this chimney, of quartered logs and various boards, patched with salvage and driftwood. Some boards bore the characteristic curve of ship's timber. All said, the hut was a sturdy edifice, and although the wind groaned through the cracks and prised at the edges with creaking fingernails, today, inside, was a little shrine to the god of creature comfort.

The assistant had adjusted to the background redolence of Fox's flatulence and was conversing animatedly with him over strong coffee, which the tallyman had developed an affinity for. Sweetened with sugar and laced with brandy. The subject was a fiery exchange the assistant had witnessed the previous day, between his master and the itinerant clergyman. Its kindling had been Mr Carey's quoting, or paraphrasing at least, the words of Francis Bacon.

"God wishes man to rediscover his mastery over nature, which Adam squandered at the Fall, and therefore a clergyman's obligation must be, *must be* - I tell you - scientific enquiry."

Carey had gone on.

"Yes we have quack medicine. Yes we have mad doctors and lunatic prophets roaming the country, competing to flog their myriad special elixirs of salvation. We also have the geomancers and the alchemists, whom these upstarts seek to make history of. But we also have the god-fearing scientists. Stephen Hales you might know of? No? A scientist who fixes prayers to his apparatus!"

Alcuin shook his head.

"No. And yes, I acknowledge the many clergymen scientists. But their science is subservient, not a primary activity. They look to find an expression of the spiritual life in the life of things."

Carey was scathing.

"But this is to find an answer and look for the question. Its *phlogiston* in all things – assumed not proven."

In the hut, the assistant gave the fire a poke, and explained to Fox the meaning of Carey's remark.

"Here at the clamps, why do the alum rocks burn?"

"I am not sure. They have some tarry substance, like jet or coal, although it's not black."

"You could theorise, and many do, that the mysterious substance that is in all things that burn is the material that combusts. This name they give *phlogiston*. This word contains its only substance, *phlox*, the Greek word for flame."

"But all stones do not burn."

"No. But those that do must contain the substance, and so must other materials that burn, thus wood, paper, cloth, even animals and man."

Fox looked sceptical.

"Why not say only that these things burn, and others do not? Sandstone say, or clay. Many things will only harden or glow. Try burning a snowball!"

'Yet it will be consumed.'

Fox sipped his coffee. His shins roasted. His back shivered, as draughts wheedled under the door.

"The priest...."

The assistant searched for a name.

"Alcuin."

"... yes...Alcuin...I heard him tell Mr. Carey that the Holy Spirit burns in man. But Carey was sharp with him, saying: *Frankly, what I have seen of men in these parts, it dwells no deeper than their lips.* To which the priest bites back: *These men have enough to do keeping body together!*"

Fox nods sagely.

The assistant shrugs.

"That maybe. But Father Alcuin says he is at least trying to keep that holy flame alive. The one he says the monks sheltered and fed in the dim dark ages, as he put it - *stitched into their robes, stained into their windows and painted into their manuscripts.*"

The assistant expanded further. This *phlox* theory was a reasonable one. It took one in the direction of a solution, and in itself it was good enough for some. But Carey was a scientist who would worry away at the how and the why of it. He would bring reason to bear upon the matter. And this reason, the assistant hypothesised, was Carey's *phlox*. It would take him wherever it led. Reason was a divine gift, Carey argued, which, employed rationally and objectively, applied scientifically, would lead back to God. The assistant mimicked his master's reedy whine: *"So good Christians should not be afraid of it, whether of the orthodox or dissenting view."*

But the assistant ventured further, telling Fox that, for Carey, following where reason led was his faith, and where it led did not reveal itself in advance.

The tallyman fidgeted with his empty cup.
"May I?"
The assistant took the liberty of putting the pot on for fresh coffee. He flung a couple of logs on. Sparks flew up and the fire creaked and settled. The shadows of the two men fell on the walls. The multifarious shapes of Fox's collection, half modelled and half in shade from the shelves they sat on, cast their own shadows on the painted boards, glowing roseate, elongated.

The two men tinkered with their pipes, whose fog filled the hut and was drawn up the chimney with the woodsmoke, to flavour further the saturated exterior gloom.

In the acceptable silence the tallyman remembered another occasion, when the works' preacher had visited him here in his hut. That was a bright hard clear morning of fulgent sun after early frost.

Alcuin had scrutinised all four walls, inspecting the collection on the shelves. He had taken his time. Moving around the room in the cluttered space surrounding the desk. Inspecting ledgers, piles of shale (those with interesting excrescences or indentations), papers, chairs, a toolbox, a pick, some staves. Fox made small talk about the weather, the activity at the works, and enquired about the other alum houses that were on Alcuin's preaching circuit – Loft Houses, Wath.

"All bad bordering on dire then?"
This said very cheerfully.
Alcuin ignored the comment.

"What do you call these?"

Fox looked past him, through the bright rectangle of the little window, and saw a man pushing a barrow along ramping boards, past raking desses of the quarry walls. He spoke to the view.

"Any one in particular?"

"No. All. The general term."

"Ah. I call them my stones. Others refer to them more sceptically. Fox's collection, some say. Or the tallyman's enthusiasm. The passion, sir, the preoccupation, the fixation."

Alcuin smiled. Fox continued.

"A pastime I tell them. A little relief from the excitement of figures in ledgers, of poundage, of barrowloads, of debts."

"A singular enthusiasm."

"Perhaps."

"And the term? For the accumulation, for the array?"

Fox shrugged.

"I have heard the term *fossils* used."

"Fossils?"

'Things dug up."

Alcuin nodded.

"Ah yes. Scholars no doubt, falling back on the Latin."

"A ditch for the nose to run."

Alcuin stroked his upper lip thoughtfully.

"Hmm. This little depression?"

Fox shrugged.

'While a *foss* in these parts is a waterfall too.'

Alcuin nodded sagely to acknowledge this, and gestured vaguely to the room.

"Individually?"

"Various. These curling on themselves like a fern, say, we call snakestones. Hilda made them. St Hilda."

"So clearly, Mr Fox - you remember the lively debate in the inn? - they were made later than the flood."

"Seems so. They must have been lurking here in the rocks, but there was no escaping that miracle. Her reach must have run deeper than the surface worms."

Alcuin frowned. He pointed again.

"Those?"

"The devil's toenails."

Alcuin's smile returned, though he made the sign of the cross. Rather ambiguous of sincerity, it seemed to the tallyman.

"Dig the foss deep, like any pit, and a sulphurous tang will arise.'

He was testing. Getting no purchase, Fox continued.

"Shell-stones will do. Beakstones."

Fox took over the pointing.

"Bullets, father. Darts say some. The Bethelemities I've heard, dissenters, but on the right side of Old Nick."

Alcuin saw he was being spun a yarn. He returned to the largest snakestone.

"Like a coiled rope on the quayside. With its own keel. And this?"

Indicating a large piece of flattish shale on the wooden floor of the hut, with a shallow undulating indent.

"Something very big stood in this I think, father, when it was soft."

Finally Alcuin picked up a split pebble that nestled comfortably in his large palm. Its exterior was unremarkable, a smooth drab grey. It's interior was a dense field of crystals.

Alcuin's lifted eyebrows framed the question.

"Fruit-stone is one I like. Though the juice is all dried."

The minister moved it around to catch the light in the crystals, of pale gentian. Fox took it from him.

"These same scholars you referred to earlier have called this a *geode*."

Alcuin nodded. There is geometry to it, he thought. The facets sparkle, opaque and reflective. The colour elusive - of lightly bloodstained water. Or after washing from berry picking.

"I call it the Tun House."

Alcuin looked up, interested.

"Or more accurately perhaps, the Roaching Cask."

Alcuin remembered.

"Yes, I saw the opening of the alum tun and the sawing of the block to reveal the crystals, with Wynter and the girl.

The tallyman remembered his final remark to Alcuin that day.

"This is a secret the manager could learn. It would surely strip down the process. This egg floats itself. It gestates in its mud womb. No seaweed or piddle brew needed. One day it falls out of the rock, splits in two and hatches. Man has no meddling in it."

A fierce squall rocked the hut, bringing the tallyman back to the present. It was gloaming so he rose and lit the lamp. Outside the little window the mist had turned to drifting sheets of filmy mizzle.

The geode was not from this region. Fox had swapped it for a good size snakestone. His eyes naturally strayed to its space in the corner, where it displayed to the room its impassive outer shell.

The assistance was roused too, from a reverie, by the squall.

"I must be making tracks Mr Fox."

"Oh."

"The gnomon above the manager's door is dripping six o'clock."

"Hmm!"

He nodded, smiling appreciatively.

They smoked out their pipes, making further small talk about the manager, and washed the bitter pipe-juice down with a blast of the cold, laced coffee. Earlier, the assistant had sketched some stones from Fox's collection, and he gathered up his papers before departing.

The charterhouse

Bright, blustery day. Its breezes had dispersed the early fret and frost. High clouds hurried across the blue, while flashing sunshine glanced across waving meadow grasses.

In the lab doorway Robbie's eye caught a fleck of piercing red. Slanting down the sloping wedge of green it moved, just over the field's brow. Ana, as if wading waist high, saw him and raised an arm in a wave. Bright red garment, wide teeth in a grin, and black hair roughly tied up, she neared.

Eyes screwed up against the sun, head to one side, smiling up at him. The vermilion, rough, felted, pushed back over her brown forearms. Goose pimples. He reached out and took her arm, running his hand over the cool skin, despite the sun, and smoothed and warmed it to disperse the tiny surface stippling. Then he tugged the red sleeve down to the wrist. He took the other arm and solemnly, meticulously, repeated. His eyes strayed briefly into hers, glancing back to his work. He tugged the other sleeve down.

Ana hugged herself in a little symbolic gesture of chilliness and, smiling, to disperse the awkwardness, went inside.

Robbie felt everything in his body was flying around within its skin.

Alcuin entered the lab. On his way over he had watched a man nearly blown off his feet crossing open space between two of the houses and, reaching the lee of the wall of the second, scuttling along in its meagre shelter, keeping tight to the wall, like a rat scurrying beside a skirting board.

They make their way to work like shivering vermin, thought Alcuin.

In the lab, Robbie had expostulated bitterly.

"This is a god-forsaken place, Father."

"Don't say that Robert."

"What else can one say! It's a blessed paradise!"

"Have you thought about erecting a sheltered way?"

"To what purpose?"

"How can the men approach their work in the right spirit if they have to struggle through these brutal weathers just to get from place to place? Up at the quarries of course it would not be possible, but they have their fires. Here all the houses could be connected up by passages. Let's say the wind usually comes this way. Not always I know, but often, so its side would be a wall – of timber or stone, and on the other side, open with posts."

"These men approach work in a spirit of necessity, at best"

"A little comfort..."

"They'd go soft!"

"Like a cloister."

Robbie screwed up his face – a mixture of scepticism and distaste.

"It's better than working in the fields, Father. That's why we are never short of labour."

There was some truth in this.

"Better than worst is not equal to good enough, Robbie. It's hardly Utopia."

Robbie looked up, awaiting further exposition.

"Have you heard of More's Utopia? It is an account of how things could be in an ideal world."

"I thought that was after we've gone?"

"A better one now, Robbie, that's not to be ignored."

Robbie shrugged.

"What you have here is a little world Robert, it's one where your workers live and die, they bring up their children, they work and play. All within these few acres. It's a village that works to produce something useful. Your mysterious alum flour, that helps to brighten our world."

"You idealise it."

"It's to imagine how it could be."

"Even so. With your mystery and your faith. This is a practical matter. It's a fact. At a certain temperature it forms.'

"And what about your secret, Robert?"

Wynter started.

"Sorry?"

"The egg, Robert. Your mystery, when you float the egg."

Robert breathed out.

"Father, its just something that works. Yes, it has to be learnt, exercised with care. But it just works, that's all.'

"Years of trial and error – with an ideal of purity,"

"Subsistence. The men come. The stones burn. The liquor flows. The crystals form. The men go. Another turn of the wheel."

"As for all men Robbie, even the ministers and the monks. The daily ritual."

He paused.

"You've heard of the charterhouse at Mount Grace perhaps?"

Robbie shrugged.

"Its over the western edge of the moors. Was."

"Was?"

"Destroyed Robbie. Like all the others. Another of your 'turns of the wheel', in a long trundling of wheels and axles. Many of the stones remain. They have to be built up again."

He paused.

"Like the brothers had, in the charterhouse, Robbie, you have your community here."

Robbie smirked, seeing how earnest Alcuin had become.

"Its business."

"Even so. You are like the abbot. You are the linchpin between this world, the community of the alum houses, and the outside world, where the traders come and go, where the owner works."

"Works?"

"...works to raise money.."

"Pah!"

"...and where you find men to come to the works..."

Wynter sighed heavily, as if resigned.

"So I build a sheltered way..."

"Between all the sheds.."

"...and the men stroll..."

"..warm, willing..."

"...they saunter along the cloistered wall, thinking holy thoughts.."

"warm at least..."

"...of the innkeeper's daughter."

"Robert!"

"All right Father, sorry, I mock, but really, if I had the wherewithal for your cloister I would first use it to mend the crumbling houses themselves, then patch lead pans... this would be long before the men file along your covered ways, dreaming of a proper breakfast!"

"Well fed men would willing workers make."

Robbie was exasperated.

"More would be utopia to us, father. More would be merrier. Just a little more."

Alcuin was startled by the bitterness of it.

"No doubt you'll mention your idea of 'Utopia' to Mr Turner, that well-respected forward-thinker and champion of the common worker."

Alcuin was stung.

"I *will* talk to him."

"Failing that perhaps someone will come and mercifully burn this lot down ..."

Carey looked at the exposed crater side of the Scarshead quarry. He observed the striation of the face. The different coloured bands, below the furze topping. He considered what he had learnt visiting other alum works in the region, courtesy of Mulgrave, the local landowner.

At Loft Houses he had noted mixed shale and sandstone on the tops, beneath which they dug through the band they called 'dogger' – those rusty orange stones glowed above the darker shades. The sandstone he knew, in some of the local districts, would yield ironstones, and much mining of these occurred in the region. At Saltwick the rocks above the dogger would yield up what he saw as remnants of primeval trees. The bark astonishingly lifelike, though petrified. Under the dogger the rocks would sometimes split open with an oily reek.

As he peered at the layered rock wall of the Scarshead quarries, he turned over in his pocket various small stones. Bringing out a handful he picked one, returning the rest to his jacket. A pale brown stone with a rubbed patch polished to black. Though he had not tried it he knew the rock would burn.

Handling the jet took Carey's mind back to his recent discussion with Mulgrave at his hall. Mulgrave, a powerful landowner with several alum ventures operating on his property.

Visiting his works at Sands End, a blackened universe where barely a blade of grass remained. Here the cliffs themselves were the quarry, reduced to grey stumps and lumpen outcrops. Dust heaps above the sea. Directly below them the alum houses, the sheds and warehouses, right on the foreshore itself. He had been impressed by the scale and effectiveness of the industry. A ruthlessness and a single-mindedness he had expected to find reflected in the owner. But Mulgave had proved different.

During Carey's markedly cool reception there, Mulgrave had been reluctant to reveal to him anything about the inkstand. The small black, Negro's head, mute on Mulgrave's desk. Having asked to take a closer look, Carey had held it to the light, studied the unpolished base.

"Like the barky relics that turn up in the dogger, it seems to bear the semblance of annular rings."

Mulgrave had chosen to ignore this, ventured nothing about the curio's origin, its obvious link to slavery. But was happy to ruminate on English jet.

"What did Bede say? *We have much and excellent jet, which is black and sparkling, glittering at the fire.*"

Disturbed by workmen swearing, Carey glanced around the quarry. He looked at the ropes, dangling from the scrawny overhanging foliage of the top, down the cliff face of the excavation. This rigging was sometimes used by men to shin down the face, to the narrow exposed seams that contained the jet. Even small pieces would be rescued for making charms.

"They use it hereabouts to ward off witches."

Carey had raised an eyebrow towards Mugrave at that. In the rush to the new dissenting cults there was little evidence of the old superstitions continuing. He thought to himself that the polished bare head of a captive Negress would make a potent charm against a witch, or for one.

As if he had read Carey's mind, Mulgrave continued with the lesson.

"The Vikings were the first slave-owners here. It was our ancestors they shipped back. Until they took a fancy to these sheltered inland valleys. In thrall to our daughters. Then they stayed. They found jet here – in the Mulgrave cliffs – but that was much later than the Romans had. Who liked to offset the garishness of their chalcedonies."

He was grudgingly impressed by the broad inclusive sweep of this scholarship. But Mulgrave was skating over the surface.

Again Carey raked his scabbling gaze over the Scarshead quarry's rocky surface. An observer would have marked his peering intensity of investigation, but found the object of its search wanting.

Below the dogger was the large expanse of the alum shale. Here Carey saw, as always, a mysterious translucency of material. As if the rock was a giant block of amber, in which many creatures were trapped.

He had asked the landowner about amber.

"As Pliny the Elder noted."

Mulgrave had proved well versed in amber lore too.

"In Northumberland, as he recorded it, with its insect life trapped remarkably intact."

Carey surveyed the quarry – conjecturing flying lizards and sea creatures, land animals and insects, birds and leaves, even flowers – laid out in a block of amber like nuts in treacle.

"Not to be confused with the precious material the whalers return with."

Mulgrave astonished Carey as he alighted here and there.

"The oily perfume of the whale."

Amber would burn too, knew Carey, like jet. Carey had the whole infested amber block of the shale cliff behind the quarry, in a block, in his pocket. The joy of classification. Ambergris, amber, jet. He thought of life solidifying its processes out into material – light and dark, clear and opaque, mirroring and obscure.

Carey studied the dark polished patch of his pocketed jet. Occluded, a dark obsidian mirror, where no image swam to the surface to reveal.

Looking up, there was little activity to witness, since the newly imposed go-slow in alum mining. Carey cursed. Why would the still young century not drive its brute energy forward to level the cliff? All its monsters and reptiles would crawl clear, its birds lift clear and its fish once again seek the blue depths.

'The Vikings also brought this."

Carey had taken the small round pebble from Mulgrave's hand. Dark green with red spots.

'The heathens didn't know it was made with a drop from Christ's side. They only brought it this far from Scotland. You are a learned man – it's the bloodstone to us, but you might know its name for following the sun – like the sunflowers and the marigolds – as the heliotrope."

Carey had smiled.

"As the earth turns after the sun, according to ....."

Mulgrave had given him a hard look, and taken the stone back.

"This is inert.'

The rock sat in his palm.

'Unless someone turns it.'

In the quarry at Scarshead, Carey looked around, taking in the whole landscape. The towering shaleface before him echoed the sea cliffs behind him. Its scooped-out material was the debris of the ebb tide. The spoil-scattered slopes below it were its foreshore and beach, where all manner of interesting specimens could turn up. Buried in the land, just as in the deep. As in the *Cartus Marina* of Bishop Magnus, *there lie monsters*.

Tinkers had arrived at the works and were gathered by the cottages, bartering with the women and the workers. Technically it was illegal, and the tinkers were chased from parish to parish. Their wares were cheap, no one needed to ask why. So they were tolerated, so long as none of the owner's agents was around.

From a distance Wynter watched the tinkers. The men in sombre clothes, the women decorated with bright strips of coloured rags. He noted the dark, gaunt faces. The sharp cheekbones. Wide mouths, big gappy teeth, high bared gums, as they gesticulated and haggled.

Ana was there. He perceived her rapt attention. The glare of scarlet wove among the darker strands. Ana moved to the edges of different conversations. Wynter imagined that as the group gathered up the pots and utensils, wrapped up their cloth bundles, sticks and trinkets, leading their threadbare donkey away, Ana would simply move off with them. One of their people, to wherever tinkers go. The tiny pinprick of red being last to grow invisible as they merged into the distance.

After a while Ana saw him, detached herself from the animated gathering, and came over to him.

"Extraña!"

He looked at her wryly.

"You're a tinker."

She grinned.

"Fine people!"

"Really?"

"*Sí*. Where from?"

He shrugged.

"Everywhere and nowhere."

"Like me!"

He nodded seriously, thawing into a smile.

"Thieves, troublemakers..."

She looked over at them admiringly.

"Illiterate, spreading diseases...."

She frowned. He regretted saying it. Spoiling her enjoyment. Feeling old. Ungenerous.

"Good musicians."

She brightened immediately.

Every few seconds, he thought, new weather.

Noticing a piece of twine around her neck he glanced quickly around and then, grabbing a handful of red wool at her belly, drew her towards him. With the other hand he raised the string and the jet pendant lifted clear of the neckline. Her eyes blazed up into his. He felt his face hot, blood pound, cock thicken within rough cloth.

He released his grip, letting the pendant fall. Looking around again. He nodded past her to the tinkers.

"Go on."

She looked over her shoulder.

"Go on. While they're still here. I'll have to make them go soon."

Ana looked at him impassively.

He flicked his head again.

"Go, I'll catch up with you later."

She stood there.

He turned. Moved off, in the direction of the alum houses.

Alcuin entered the tap room. The men in the inn were gathered in a raucous scrum around a table. Jugs of ale stood on its wooden boards. Alongside, various sheets of some printed illustrations were being studied, brought within range of the candles, or held close to scrutinise.

Alcuin drew up a chair on the other side of the table and the landlord brought over a tankard. He took a long draught, relishing the cellar-chill and the sour tang.

A flicker of intent between the landlord, moving to throw a log on the fire, and the group, registered with Alcuin. Complicit. He wondered if he had interrupted some political meeting. Or a sect gathering. He knew several of the men. Among them a likeable liquorman from the works, and a couple of roguish panniermen. Mumbles of 'evening, Father'. He nodded, raised his mug, and took another long draught.

"Artistic."

One of the men, to snorting and laughter.

"Finely engraved."

"A most pious nun."

Spluttering laughter.

Alcuin glanced across the broad table. He felt relaxed, the ale working, but something about them unsettled him.

One or two men glanced up at him, furtively.

Finally the innkeeper spoke.

'Forgive these sinners Father, they cannot read. They mock to cover for their ignorance"

A pannierman pushed one of the sheets of paper over towards Alcuin. He straightened the sheet and looked at it. A coarsely printed engraving, figures praying. In the foreground a kneeling girl, wimple lowered over her eyes. An infant in a manger.

It was very hot in the inn, he realised. Red faces, waiting eyes, bulging in expectation.

"The virgin kneels..."

Explosion of cackling and guffawing. He heard the dour innkeeper grunt.

"...in ecstasy."

Alcuin's bemused expression provoked further hilarity. The panniermen slid another page over. More ale was sloshed from the jugs. Men gulped beer down. There was a bright-eyed fervour sparking among the drinkers. They topped up Alcuin's mug.

He surveyed the next sheet – equally crudely drawn, printed with smudged lines, rough paper, much handled. Ale-stained. Hardly reverential, he thought. Two friars, bald headed, both apparently sporting monstrous red carbuncles on their fleshy parts, but none-the-less smugly pious-looking for it. They sat back-to-back with their flowing friar's sack-cloth, holding symmetrically foaming tankards before a small fire with dark flames. It was a curious design – a bit like two faces in profile, that together make a candlestick. There was a title beneath, that he read aloud:

"The Holy Friar's Dream of Heavenly Bliss.'

Another blast of laughter. A couple of helpless men, barely recovered from the last utterance, collapsed again. Arms sprawled over the tables, heads back against the wall, or down. Eyes squeezed and spluttering. One heaved himself to his feet and staggered outside.

Alcuin half rose, in exasperation, with his tankard, but the pannierman put his hand on his cloak.

"You see father....the men see it differently. They see it this way."

He quickly flipped the sheet round, top to tail. For an instant Alcuin was blank and then, in a sudden, like a lantern held up sharply to his eyes, a spread-eagled, viciously crude, naked woman's form flashed in his face. Mouth distorted by a sneer or a scream. Eyes looking to heaven. Armpits sprouting, legs flailing apart. He jumped, to his feet.

"Oh grow up!"

He flicked his hand dismissively.

"Another drink Ben...."

He gestured behind him.

"....for these children. And one for me."

He flushed hard.

The laughter subsided.

Outwardly he struggled to remain above it. Inwardly, the image was struck like a brand. He felt its heat. Despised the crude line. Shrank from its potency. The smeared mouth, gasping its urgent cry to the dark smudge of the straining legs. He tried to slam shut on this image, which might invade his prayers.

He was aware of some of the men making their apologies. He shook them off. They could suffer. The panniermen smirked. The innkeeper mocked him he thought, but Ben tried to explain.

"Printed in London, and gawped at in every tavern in the kingdom."

Alcuin shrugged. But it was a convulsion kept to a shiver.

"Madam Creswell's famous brothels."

No response from Alcuin.

"Well, you might as well know."

He shouldn't have called in here. He had no friends in this inn. He looked at the ground. To stay he risked further compromise. His cloak encircled him. On the floor his shadow shifted. He felt a brutal anger rising in him. Christ would have felt this, when he turned the tables over, he thought. But I will be laughed out of the inn tonight. Mustering sardonic, as best he could, he spun to the room.

"Goodnight gentlemen. Sleep well."

There was a brief lull, as the door swung shut. Then jugs were refilled, and the heavily thumbed sheets fought over again, turned and re-turned. Eventually interest palled. A pannierman gathered them up, together with his takings, and packed them away ready for the next inn on the trod to York.

Where was he?

She was hit by the wall of heat, opening the door to the forge. The red hot hoops, gripped by tongs, hammered over the anvil. The apprentice boy, pale in the furnace glow, weakly wielding the leather bellows. Straps to bind Lot's wife in her wood-walled cell.

From the smith, a hot sneer of malice and disdain, seeing her trespassing in his demesne. She didn't bother asking. Returned an insolent face. Slammed the door.

At his desk, Alcuin was trying to put together a more coherent version of his charterhouse ideal, as applied to the alum works. The analogy he had drawn for Wynter had just sprung to mind, but now he was struck by the power of the parallel.

In his book he drew two rough rounded squares side by side, a line with an arrowhead at each end connected them. Two further arrows, one entering, one leaving, penetrated the first of the interconnected squares. The second, or inner square as he considered it, was itself dotted around with small circles, and from these further faint grains of charcoal radiated.

The diagram represented the vanished ideal of the charterhouse. In the inner world the monks worked in their little houses, apart from society. The community looked after their welfare. The work of the monks, of art and craft, glorified God and reflected well on the wider community. The landowners and nobles demonstrated their virtuousness with splendid artefacts. With their patronage the parish churches were endowed. Each monk honed his skill, and the cloth, the books, grew finer and more rich. To feed and clothe the monks, the grain, meat and fish, wool and flax, were brought into the outer square, the world of the lay brothers. The world that panniermen, farmers, tinkers, and occasionally landowners, entered. The abbot moved between the two worlds, filtering and purifying from the outer one, perfecting and improving the inner. The charterhouse chapel, at the intersection of the inner and outer courts.

Kenelm would have laughed at him. And also despaired. Kenelm would tease him, seriously. *Always trying to improve the lot of your precious alum makers! Instead of preparing them for their own transformation. Sometimes I think you would prefer to roll up your sleeves and open a seam in the blessed shale, rather than open the Book!*

Thus it was that he mulled over this diagram, and tried to apply it to the alum works. All this to try and clarify his arguments about the works. Why not a perfectible world? Like the charterhouse? Perhaps Kenelm was right. He kept looking to serve God in this world. And if Alcuin couldn't hear God, then his works were still a way of presenting acts for approval. Even if undervalued, they might still be of use in practical ways.

He drew a rough square for the works. Above it an arc, representing the quarries, and an arrow from the arc to the square. Below the square some wavy lines – the sea – and another arrow, from the works to the sea.

Then he imagined the different houses of the alum works, the roaching house, the settlers, the tun house and so on, ranged all round – like monks' cells around a cloister. Finally, he drew a rough oval. Here, in this protected world was perfected the mystery of the floating egg.

It was neat, but in reality the alum houses were all in the corruptible outer world, pierced by others' arrows. Where the owner strode in, the traders rode in, the filth the printing presses churned out blew in, blew about. Smuggled goods came, even, he thought, women came, the girl came in.

So, he considered, with some anticipation of pleasure at the task, this needs improving. He imagined the quarries and the workers all within one square. He reflected on the idea of the laboratory as an inner sanctum, containing the mystery of the egg, like the church within the charterhouse, but penetrated by both worlds. Although, the memory of the girl there troubled him. The obscene image from the inn troubled him.

And the point of the diagram? The workers in each trade, more free from hunger, cruelty and disease, to perfect the craft of each.

He pondered God's place in this perfectible world. Saw himself, the ragged itinerant preacher struggling in, into the one square. Another pollutant, tolerated at best, otherwise ignored. He drew over the outline of the lab, marking it more strongly, and then he drew a cross on it. As, he thought, a wooden cross, lifted onto the ridge of a barn. Idly he drew round and round the perimeter of this laboratory-chapel, wondering which it was. Or if it was both

Finally, he thought of Lastingham. The chapel under the laboratory: learning founded on faith? Or the lab under the church: faith founded on fact? One undimmed by the other, he thought, as he closed the book, or, perhaps, one undermined by the other.

Suddenly tired, he thought to pray a short while and sleep.

Reynard

Wynter was furious with the tallyman.

"What the hell is going on here?"

Laid out on a flat cleared patch of ground beside Fox's hut, within a rectangular space defined by twine and pegs, were some loosely assembled parts of the so-called monster.

Wynter demanded angrily of the tallyman.

"Who is actually working here today?"

Fox blinked rapidly, saying nothing.

"I have got a works rife with rumour, people refusing to dig. I have people saying a waist-coated quack, waving dubious scientific papers, is in charge of the quarries. I have heard that the tallyman is playing jigsaws with a quantity of burnt charcoal."

"Mr Wynter, sir..."

"I have men picking gingerly at the old overgrown face, fearful of opening a seam to the underworld!"

As he spoke, Wynter became aware at some distance of Carey and his assistant. They were examining the shale face near the rock fall. Hearing Wynter's raised voice they had stopped and turned and now, looking towards him, appeared to converse.

"And some fawning foppish dandy with the luxurious role of making pictures. Illustrating old landlubber's tales with fanciful creatures of the far-flung deeps. The same nonsense I gather, as the old scrimshaw men can embellish on a bit of bleached whalebone."

Fox was biting his lip. He felt it was too soon for interruption.

"So what is this black sorcery? This devilish parlour game?"

The manager addressed Fox. His hand flicked dismissively towards the fragments within the twine enclosure.

Fox spoke gently.

"I had to move the men until we inspected the face. It could fall again."

'Nonsense! Its no more unpredictable than usual! Get some support planking rigged up. This fall has done several men's work for a week. They can move direct to sorting and breaking it down for calcining."

"But recent rains...."

"Mr Fox. The science of 'recent rain' is simply that the rocks will fall one day. The men know this. You know how the cliffs retreat from the sea. Have you been along the top of the causeway recently? Cracks back from the edge – they could shear tomorrow, or a year from now. I worry about that, but what would you have me do?"

The tallyman shrugged, and spat.

"I could be forever tending the path, shoring it up. Great projects of levelling, propping, buttressing. Of unproductive tasks. Sending the cost of extraction soaring, while the price of alum ever drops."

Fox moved his head, as if to speak, but the manager continued.

"Yes, and I go up above the causeway with the galloways, and I stand under the cliff inspecting the unloading. I watch the cracks and the little becks and slacks and gills, how they alter with the seasons. I watch it rain, think about the science of absorption and saturation. And down below, the scouring and undermining. Wondering where, when....."

"You feel a responsibility, I know."

"...wondering when, exactly when it will all fall. Then some poor bastard will be lying down there on the foreshore, pressed flat like your fucking monster."

"Mr Wynter, I know. That's why I have to take some stock of the quarry face up here. To see if another fall is likely...."

"And until then?"

The manager was running out of steam. Fox had heard this all before. Wynter would share his burden, getting another opinion, as it were, but the decisions would still be his. The tallyman thought about the barrowing of the fall for calcining. How it would not allow for fine sifting of the rubble for further fragments. He abruptly changed tack, gesturing slightly in the direction of Carey and his assistant.

'He'll pay."

Wynter's eyes flickered across, and back to Fox.

"For this.... wreckage?"

Fox watched the other two men, keeping his voice low.

"You know the big snakestone?"

Wynter shrugged impatient, frowned.

"I kept it on the shelf above the door."

The manager waited.

"It'll keep me in drink for a night or two."

Wynter looked sceptical.

"A rock fall is a harvest, like windfall apples."

The manager was irritated by the direction this was taking. He spoke angrily again.

"We know rocks can be harvested man! That's our business. Perhaps Mr Carey knows what your prize exhibit can be reduced to?"

"Even so...."

"Black flour?"

Fox was put out. He ranged around for something to add.

"Even so, it's not worth anything around here."

Wynter cut in.

'So now you're saying they're not worth anything? These rocks you just happen to spend half your life looking for, picking them and pocketing them, cleaning them and ordering them and..."

"So if he has a market for it?"

"Alright!"

Wynter relented.

"So how much for the corpse?"

Fox puffed out his cheeks and exhaled.

"I don't know."

"Leaving aside whose it is to sell, and who the eventual buyer might be."

"Turner will not be interested. He doesn't need to know."

"I said leaving out who might be the vendor."

"Carey says there is a specialist. At the University."

"And leaving out, for now, who might want it later."

The tallyman stopped short again. He didn't want to tell Wynter what Carey had said. That they must spend much more time arranging the pieces. That they must sift through the rest of the rock fall for every minute fragment. That they must try different arrangements, sketch each one, try new permutations, imagine the missing parts. And that they must find a way to explore delicately around the site of its coming to light, in case there were others. That this should be a matter of weeks not days. No price he could think of could justify this. He didn't mention something else Carey had said.

"In my notes Mr Fox, I will of course mention your role in this, and how your amateur collection led you to identify when something special was found. Your name will be in the footnotes, Mr Fox, and until we have some category to place him we will, just between ourselves, call him Reynard."

Fox came back to the present conversation.

"Mr Wynter, sir, I will tomorrow start inspecting the area above the fall. I will also be instructing the picking through of calcining rocks and setting aside the worthless spoil. Then we will start shoring and constructing desses accordingly. In the meantime there will be extraction enough from this surplus and the old quarry."

The manager waited.

"And this area will be made less conspicuous."

He waited.

"And I will talk to Carey about price."

He waited.

"Until then no-one will know much about it. Mr Carey will be asked, told, to be discreet, and the men will work elsewhere."

Wynter nodded towards the two onlookers, who again appeared deep in conversation.

"You can start now Mr Fox."

Then he set off down the slopes.

After the decorum of some minutes' wait, Carey and the assistant came over and by certain gestures it would have been apparent they discussed something laid out on the ground before them.

The manager and his wife listened to the priest with affectionate tolerance. Alcuin was struggling to convey the diagram he had roughed out – alum works as inner cloister.

Wynter interrupted him.

"Father, where the men live is not really a village, even a hamlet."

Robert was shaking his head gently, glancing from the minister to his wife. The priest replied excitedly.

"It's the inner cloister!"

Robert flung his arms out suddenly, as if to embrace the place under discussion.

"Alcuin! For goodness' sake. They're here because it suits the owner. All the alum houses of the coast have their little rows of hovels. Grazing rights, places to grow a few potatoes. Yes, to grow what they cannot afford to buy!"

Wynter considered it dismissively, but Liz was more serious.

"This is the new way. The new cotton mills, I have heard, have everyone kept close, like the chattels of the owner."

They looked at her.

"Far from the church..."

She shrugged.

"...or the inn."

She smiled.

"Unlike here."

Wynter was dismissive,

"That's not how it is here. Not yet. Though Father Alcuin would have us clean up the place until it glitters like a cathedral. Some hope – soap strong enough to scour this filthy racket which is our livelihood!"

She eyed them both, mysteriously, singing softly.

"Oh burn the birch
Pot the ash, bye and bye
Lime and tallow
Pot the ash, lye and lye.."

Alcuin was bemused, but Robbie chuckled, rubbing his hands around themselves.

"I'm washing my hands of this."

Liz and Robbie laughed.

Liz closed her eyes, allowing a sleepy warmth to circulate. Allowing soft rippling sensations to subside.

Women in her family had links back to Lilburne, and her namesake his wife. In that successive congregation among women she had learned how to enjoy lovemaking, and felt it was no sin. Therefore Robbie had learned what Liz liked, and in their private world she was happy to feel she did not sin. They both felt this private matter a strength in their marriage.

Beside her, no longer agitated by the morning's tensions and frustrations, the vexing argument with the tallyman, her husband snored loudly.

Rogation Day

Everyone knew the Rogation Day rituals had descended into farce. The only aspect of the litany that retained any tradition was the movement from the mock-solemn ritual of the outset, to the anarchy of the conclusion. They also knew these arcane ceremonies could not easily be dispensed with.

A straggle of traditionalists and early revellers scattered and regrouped like mobbing crows around a few brown-clad burghers. Tramping the boundaries of the so called 'parish'. Children hung around the fringes, chasing each other with sticks, or pausing to decapitate hedgerow flowers.

The local landowners customarily coughed up for the Rogation Day rituals. A rare surfeit of meat and fish for the under-fed alum workers, washed down with plenty of Turner's ale. Which once dry would be followed by the output of various potent bothy-brews and poison from illicit stills, with predictably catastrophic effects.

At this early hour the marking of the bounds involved reminiscing about the debaucheries of previous years, and frequent nipping from pewter hip flasks. Starlings kept up a commentary on the perambulations. A man with coloured ribbons tied around his knees and elbows knocked on a baronne with a pestle. He chanted rhymes from the 'old religion' whilst the burghers' priest for this occasion was required to commit some mumbling and crossing. This was repeated at field corners, certain trees and one or two other places. For reasons no one remembered or cared about.

Earlier still, Alcuin had absented himself from the local beating of the bounds to attend the more solemnly marked Horngarth, the 'Penny Hedge'.

There had been ominous tides.

The heavy metallic swell, muscling towards the shore through the bright sharp spring morning. There was a chill wind. It explored the cloaks and rags of the assembled onlookers.

Alcuin, hat pulled low, cloak tight, merged into the meagre crowd. He watched the planting of the stakes below the high-tide mark, dark sand still wet from the receding waves, and the weaving of the horizontal branches. These sticks had been cut in Eskdale-side woods the previous night - the stakes, the 'strout-stowers' and the yedders. These varying sizes of boughs, branches and pliable twigs had been bundled and carried on the backs of the three men and brought to the shore ready for the service.

This ritual, established several centuries ago and restaged every year since, marked the murder of a hermit by three boar-hunting nobles.

The hermitage had been occupied by a reclusive monk of the abbey, for solitary prayer and contemplation.

A day came when a badly wounded wild boar, chased by hounds, was given refuge by the hermit, Accepted within, it lay dying from its wounds. The dogs bayed outside, and hurled themselves at the door.

Finally, the hunters arrived, Outraged at the thwarting of the kill, they attacked the hermit with their sharpened staves. Seeing the man was dying, the hunters then sought sanctuary at the abbey. But they were refused, and therefore facing penalty of death.

The dying monk however, forgave them, on two conditions. One, that they offer their souls to God. Second, that they serve penance by the horngarth, the planting of the hedge.

Those men, and their successors over all time, were required to cut the wood in Eskdale on Ascension Eve, and bring the wood to the shore at Whitby. Here to build a hedge that would resist three full tides.

Does this express resistance or futility, Alcuin, thinking of Canute, asked himself. No answer came. Rogation, he thought, from the Latin to ask. John's gospel: ask and you shall receive.

Alcuin felt a shiver that was anticipation, not just the chill. This service reached some part of him that was instinctive to the needs of continuity and ritual. The cutting and weaving of the hedges in spring, the linking of them into field boundaries. The control of their sprawl. This he guessed was as old as the claiming of ground for cultivation. Other gods might have presided, long before the hermit's demise.

The men hammered the stakes in, through the soft pebble-strewn sand, through thin gravelly layers, trying to anchor a strong upright. They buttressed the stake line in both directions with raking posts, tethered to the uprights with wrapped briars of springy fresh cut growth. Gradually the hedge took shape as an undulating lattice of limbs. Not too close a grid, so the tide would strain through its net rather than batter it down. Its waving line added strength in both directions.

Green leaves were woven in too, decorating the hedge, Giving it the semblance of a living thing. Finally the horn was blown three times. Alcuin's goose flesh shivered. The bailiff shouted.

"Out on thee!"

So, over a black huddle of ragged people, as the tide turned from retreat to attack, under a cold sun, black clouds with silver-edged rags massed like armies.

Some would wait for the first of the three tides to engulf the hedge, but Alcuin, the building of the horngarth witnessed, turned into the wind. He headed towards the foot of the cliff path, and trudged up through sodden wind-dragged marram.

In the house the manager, having avoided any official early duties, was lowering eggs into a pot of boiling water one by one. Liz was stoking up the fire with branches. Ana was sifting flour into an earthenware bowl. She kneaded in some lard.

Liz observed the exaggerated formality with which Robbie lifted the eggs in and out.

"The science of pancakes."

Ana looked perplexed, glancing between the two of them.

Robbie demonstrated.

"Six eggs. These two are fresh, this one is fine. This one is borderline, but edible. These two are off."

He handed the four to Ana, nodding towards the bowl. She cracked them individually against the rim and dropped them onto the flour. Liz crushed a pinch of salt in. Ana stirred it all into a thick slurry.

"How can you tell?"

Robbie had a seventh egg and he lowered it into the bottom of the pan where it stayed. He scooped a handful of the salt crystals and with a serious expression allowed some to fall gradually into the boiling water.

"The bad ones float."

Ana shrugged.

Liz watched wryly.

"Please Professor Know-all, do tell us why." said Liz.

"Several hundred scholars, graduates of the land's finest universities, together with eminent tutors, clerics, nobles of the king, bishops, lawyers and merchant-adventurers all tucked into a feast of boiled eggs. Each egg was first duly lowered into boiling water, noted for its position – horizontal, angled, vertical or floating...."

Robbie indicated the different positions with his forefinger. Ana and Liz shrieked.

"..and having interpreted – recorded for size, colour and origin. Then fully boiled, served with or without salt, butter or sauces, and eaten. The learned gentry ate a dozen each. Finally, the results. Which turned green – the gentry I mean – which men grimaced, which smiled. Those that bent double, those that felt queasy, those that slept, replete, and those that vomited colourfully, violently or continually. Afterwards the conclave concluded. Smoke signals were issued and interpreted, learned papers were written and at great expense printed and circulated. Reputations made and ruined. At least two died. Many reported flatulence, several constipation, several more unstoppable lust. Some broom-handles lasted for days despite the compassionate attention of other nobles' wives, courtesans and innkeepers' daughters..."

"Robbie!"

Ana understood little of Robbie's lecture, but marvelled anyway.

"...until at last it was decreed. Bad eggs float!"

The two women applauded, and then as Robbie added more salt to the pan the remaining good egg lifted from the base and floated up to the surface.

"Venga!"

Pronounced, like a magical word, to Ana's delight. Robbie scooped it out.

"This one is for me....for the liquor."

Liz explained.

"He needs to use a good egg to test the alum liquor. No good if it's floating already. It seems that older eggs, or damaged ones, must take in air through the tiny cracks, and that is why they go off, and also why they float."

Ana nodded seriously.

"Entiendo!"

Robbie raised both arms flamboyantly and, taking the bowl from Ana, and simultaneously dancing a jig on the wooden floor, he beat the pancake mixture in triplet time with a spoon.

Liz took the mixture and, melting more lard in the flat pan, fried the pancakes over the fire. The three of them consumed them in relative silence, at the table, with hunks of bread. They drank small beer that Robbie topped up with the stronger stuff brewed for the party later.

After the washing-up some of the anticipatory zest dissipated, but nevertheless, they left the house in good spirits. Ana and Liz had their best garments and ribbons on for the celebrations, and Robbie was jacketed, with a red neckerchief. The trio strolled down to the works, the manager feigning nonchalance, with a fine woman on each elbow.

They arrived at about the same time as the Rogation patrol, which was necking back porter at one of the long trestles. A roped-off enclosure had been staked out between the works and the cottages.

Ana nudged Robbie.

"You knew it would float?"

Ana asked in admiration. Robbie was nonchalant.

"An egg laid on Ascension Day will never go off."

"*Sì?*"

She elbowed him.

"That is true. And we put the egg in the attic - for luck."

Ana frowned.

"And....?"

Robbie shrugged.

"Months later we find a chicken skeleton."

Ready this time for the elbow. He grabbed it and pulled her to him to stifle. In the hot boisterousness of it both flushed.

A small distance away a cloud passed fleetingly over Liz's brow.

Robbie spun her free from him. Ana stuck her tongue out. He was aware of his cock stiffening slightly against his breeches.

A sizeable crowd was also gathering, as individuals and groups made their way from nearby hovels or from further away, over the surrounding fields. There were a few of the owner's lackeys' horses, and a number of chapmans and donkeys. Dogs skulked around their masters' heels, barked at children or chased each other among the crowd. Scrubbed-up children were already flushed and dusty. Scrawny lads pushed and shoved each other. Sallow girls of thirteen, fourteen with over-large eyes in emaciated faces, with nails cracked from kelp gathering, or garlanded with meadow flowers to drown out any lingering whiff of urine collecting, kept close to their mothers. Those same eyes searched out the faces of boys in fear and anticipation of ill-formed inklings of Rogation Day misdemeanours.

Their mothers delivered hard eyes to those same lads, hoping to hang onto their valuable child workers without having to feed another. These girls, even if of age, might not be too malnourished to conceive.

The same youths eyed with fascination the girls of the travelling fair. Scared of the pox, and without money, they nonetheless hoped for some fumbling after dark. Those same women ignored them and hung around the fops and lackeys, admiring their horses, or chatting to the musicians.

Ana was trying to comprehend the game at the far end of the fair. A rough-looking group of men were jeering and swearing. They didn't notice her hanging back, as all were fixed on the turmoil of the activity. Drink was supplying its own thirst and flowing after it. Money was being flung around, and in the centre of a ragbag scrum a bull was chained to a post.

Vicious dogs were by turns whimpering back to their owners, snarling at each other, and menacing the tethered bull. This looked like it had been going on for some time, as all the animals, and one or two of the onlookers, were bloodied. The bull was chained to three heavy stakes, hammered into the ground in a tripod arrangement and tied together with ropes. Even so, the alternate lunging charges and rearing retreats of the bull looked like they were starting to loosen the tether. Rarely, the man with the sledgehammer got near enough to deliver a hasty and ill-aimed blow before the bull, or one of the wilder dogs, went for him. An urchin boy, armed with sticks and stones, circled him like his own ragged dog. The boy used his ammunition to try and protect the hammerman from the bull-baiting dogs. Bystanders were much entertained by this enjoyable sideshow. They also enjoyed the anger of the dog owners, lest any of their hounds should take a hit. Indeed the urchin had been clattered hard about the head once for a stone that had knocked a tooth out. In any case the dogs were just as likely to get jabbed back into the ring by the pointed sticks of their owners.

So, frantic and enraged by their wounding, the dogs attacked the bull more recklessly, goaded by pain and fear. They flung themselves at the bull with frothing red mouths and teeth.

Ana was exhilarated by the near anarchy. At any moment the bull or the dogs or the watchers might all be loose among the fair, tearing each other apart.

Crammed next to Ana on the bench, men from the works on either side vied for her attention, yelling in her ears. From somewhere she had acquired a tiny kitten, which she stroked.

Fish head, greasy with blood. Eye staring. Off-white breeches, string tied around the knee, smeared with grass stains and cowshit. A split sack, spilt grain, spilling seed. Gulls and crows, necks jerking, plunging to plunder pulps. Stamped into the mud, churned with ale-slop. Blur of an infant, running squawking past, its hand around the neck of a live chicken. Mad-eyed mongrel leaping up at it barking. Yanked above head. Piggyback fighting. Riving each other by the scruff. By red ears, scratched cheeks. Sticks shoved between knees. Sprawling. Crashes against a trestle, staggering. Cracked on the head by a brutal fist. Teeth moving on fishmeal and bone, scales stuck to lips. Spine and fins spat out. Tail sported as stick-on moustache, swilled off by laughter-slopped drink. Vermilion fleece, sleeves rolled up over brown arms. Head down on shoulder, face in the fleece. Pressed close on the bench by bodies leaning in on both sides. Dusk twinkled. Some lanterns and the shadows danced. Hems lifted for feet to move. Squeezed sack fed the drone for nimble fingers. Pockets picked through petticoats. Faces leaned in over the trestle. Jugs crashed down noisily. Neck frills pulled lower over loose bodices. Stars pricked up, and the world shrank. Liz whirled breathlessly, a child's mask tied on her face. Chancers whirled her dizzy. Spun her back as she buffeted the shrinking arena of bodies pressed around the dancers. Fingers furiously milked the pipes spurting the elbow-pressed air into the night. The dancers reeled. Hands pressed onto ulcers. Inflamed skin, flaked and raw, caressed. The healer went from table to table. Tolerated, abused, paid, kicked. Scornful sufferers sought him later. He blessed them too, for good measure. Alcuin watched the healer, watched the wise women. Herbs and heather flowers. He listened for old spells. He drank too fast. Mud-wig, splattered on a bald pate. Teeth picked with splinters. All God's work. Alcuin felt his feet walking away from him under the table. The music called them. Basting, basting – the spit turned. Grease dripped. Turner's man guarded it. A woman's hands worked upon him slyly behind her back. Men staggered almost to the edge of the lantern light and forgot to piss in the collecting pots. Seeping bandaged stump, rocked past on creaking crutches. Drum beat, slipping out of time with the piper. Voices. Crying. The pig squealed in its headlock. The vicious teeth clamped the log. The knife. Dogs kicked back from it. Its hooves tied together. Launde's wife pulled out the clotted linen crammed between her legs, beyond the firelight. Launde pushed her against the tun house door, under the shadow of the lintel. Red slurries dropped from the slit pig. Hands shoved into the hot jellies grabbed the oiled tubes and firelight glistenings. Launde bucked numbly, for a drunken age. His wife gasped. The old carcase, thrown off the spit was set upon by dogs. A bear raged at its cage on a cart. In the dark. Boys jabbed at it with their sticks. Cream cloth tacked on the hem of worsted dragged in the dust. Robbie. Danced with Liz. Their bodies collided. The spiked rod skewered down the pig's throat and through to the rump. The unaccustomed bellies heaved. Liz reeled from the dancing. The stars spun. Spewed against the wall of the cottage. Two moons slid apart and converged. The brow above the quarries dipped sickeningly. Her upper body swooned over. She felt a thick grainy flood into her mouth a second before her throat convulsed it forward. Drained it with a concluding retch. More surged up into her mouth and splattered the moonlit grass. Sweating. Hand aware of the rough sandstone. She swirled round and stumbled. Knees in the damp grass. Hair forward stomach convulsing she spat. The earthenware flagons banged on the table as Turner's men relished the vicious slander of the long-departed owner. Perfunctory appearance. Ana, dragged into the dance fell near him. Close as he lifted her to her feet. The bandaged stump whirled past. Robbie lurched off-balance his bristled sweat glanced onto her neck. She deftly avoided the wreckage. Fox retrieved her and made her look like the dancer she was. Robbie grabbed someone's flagon and barged through the crowd to the edge. A breeze off the sea chilled his shirt damp on his back unbuttoning fast and drinking pissed. One leg damp. Liz breathed. Her forehead chilled. She crashed against the cottage door, thinking to go in and sleep. Instead she rolled, upright, along the cottage wall. Spewed again. She set off back towards the flickering figures and the music. Robbie watched Ana dance. Felt the weight of her body, the balance of her against him, registered deep inside. Intoxicating him. His body felt torn off from its completion. He drank to steady himself. Over Fox's shoulder, for a flickering eternity, her eyes fastened on his. The world reduced to its dark carbon essence. Light sparked across the gap. Cloaks of rough woollen, gathered around shoulders. Hoods. Two pannier chapmans brayed. The wheel of a cart turned. Sacks hauled off the back. Surreptitious, flagons of bothy-stilled spirit passed under the trestle. Numbing lips. Off-glow from the feast area uplit steam folding in billows from the Boiling House. Lights sparkled in lancets or stone cracks from parts of the works still active. A skeleton crew guarded all the doors not double-bolted and the watchman did his rounds. Off limits. No mischief night in the houses, Turner's orders. A bonfire started to crackle up between the tables and the cliff top. Low fret settled over the headland – visible from the chilling external dark. Straw figures dragged to the fire shadows. Set aside while drink sought. Closed in tight the firelight, the lantern light, the dancers trapped in the hot skin of the pipe and drum. Heavy leather, a spit-guard's apron wrestled aside. Her hot mouth pushed him to a corner of sandstone. Numb-rough against the under-hide of the leather she swung his uncurled ammonite. Discomfort fought through the drink dullness with the sudden surfacing of quick pleasure as she squeezed his sack. Dripped from the hem of the apron. The knife cleaved a scallop of pork from the spit-rump her reward. A big rat, from the stores. Sleeping, a pannier man spread-eagled beside his cart. The patient pony's nostrils steamed. Rough wood – the dice rolled into the cracks between the planks. Tilted between faces on the table to cries of cheating. The wood lice raced, randomly, craving the peace under the stones. The tabletop an obstacle course of breadcrumbs and liquor drops. A hand-carved die, made of crystal alum, its dots superimposing if viewed before a candle flame. Shares of rotten impests gambled away a child's meal.

Forfeits of a lesser sort made evens with garters. Payments for drinking contests. Under the table children fought off the dogs for scavenged morsels or spewed stolen flagons forgotten by the dancers. You're not like the other girls here, Ana. It's a provocation to the men. You tease without knowing. Maybe. The way you dress and speak. I never know what's on your mind. He could check the doors of the houses. Tugs her sleeve. Ensure all locked. Carey saw them flicker out to places where the light drained into the ground. He turned over a devil's toenail in his pocket. Turned it over and over. Vermillion linked through the tweedy elbow of the manager. Their chaste round checked by several observers, they knew, as they dipped in and out of light. Fox, warming to his task of showing the women how to dance led Liz and Carey into a jig. He gathered up a maid from Turner's hall. The tin whistle trilled, the ale flagon crashed rough time. Should I change? In the diagonal shadow from the house corner her eye and nose in light. She looked up at him. Do you want me to? No. Her face slid up into the pale golden light. Loud cracks from the fire logs. Stars and sparks. Lips vermilion parted on the verge of an utterance. His head lowered. The soft collision of lips. She stepped back he moved with her into the shade. Breath moaned sharply from their nostrils. Mouths sucked tongue pressed and withdrew juice slobbered teeth bumped noses dampened hair sweated arm and hands explored in a sudden anarchy of belly, cotton, armpit, mouths closed on collar bones, ears, flowed, sweat, grumbles and breath gasped in too short spaces a wild fragmentary moment of fumbling cut abruptly short. A voice horribly near, shouted. To them? Seen? Unseen. In a flash Ana appeared in the light and moved to the fire, perhaps returned from a piss. Robbie went round the other way, stopped dumbstruck by the constellation of Orion as this sudden new knowledge flickered around his consciousness. He could gallop the rogation circuit, energy flowed into him. He squatted down just to steady. Strands of thin music reached him. He bounded up, crunching the gravely mud behind the shed, a terrific thirst woken in him. Thin wisps of roak drifted through the invisible hawthorns. He shivered one violent chill tremor through his whole body. He bounded towards the fire, grabbing and draining a flagon. Pushed into the thickest throng of the men around the dancing and swayed among them to the music.

3

Launde's journey

The making of the kelp

He became aware he was awake. There was a composition of purposeful sounds, which came to him muffled. Liz was up and attending to the domestic routine.

Half opened one eye – subdued light. He brought into focus with the one squint the wall, close to. He was facing it. He rolled from his side onto his back and his head jerked with it. His eyes squeezed tight against the sudden crack of nauseous pain as it seemed an internal storm breaker slammed in his brain. It drained out, like an icy tide, leaving clarity. He steadied himself and the choppy swell in his gut subsided a bit. He emitted a low groan.

He opened his eyes again in the soft grey light and allowed his gaze to rest on the grubby whitewashed ceiling. Kitchen noises drifted up the stairs, like pack-horse bells jingling in a far valley. He registered the familiarity of each sound – chopping of vegetables, the pot lifting onto the hook over the fireplace.

As if the world was unchanged.

As if the bees were back in the hive, the escaped cattle grazing peacefully, back in the field. The mutineers surly, back on deck duties. Rioters quelled, beaten, back in their cells. Spirits, back in the forms of their familiars – hares in the hedgerow, cats on the barn roofs. As if nothing had changed.

Robbie was sweating, hot and feverish under the blanket, which he hugged to himself nevertheless. He felt such nauseous sweetness as he re-imagined soft tumbled moments of brief revelatory elation. Heart jumped, head throbbed. He turned back into the position of a sleeping infant, hands clamped between his thighs.

That kiss.

Had rooted him to the earth the way a lightning bolt wriggles down through an oak tree - scorching it, burning it into the ground.

A ticklish nervous feeling prickled in his chest, its emotional welling was close to tearfulness. It overrode his customary hangover concupiscence – a curdling mix of fear and desire. He considered muscling up a physical desire, with a few hard shuttle-shuffles of the hand loom, to weave the warm wave over the tight tense headache and subside back into drowsing...

"Robbie?"

He heard footsteps ascending the stairs. He rolled back gingerly onto his back once again.

"Ah, you're awake!"

Liz, coming through the door with a bright tangle of meadow flowers in a small mug.

Facing the ceiling, rolling his eyes down to see them gave him a jolt of pain. This caused her a wry smile.

"Ana picked them. For the invalid."

A hot confusion swept him, the way a sudden gust washes across a cornfield.

It seemed necessary to muster a response.

"You're looking bright and breezy".

"Oh I know what will sort you out".

She smiled, her hand darting under the blanket towards his loins.

"I know you the morning after."

But he closed up against her. He felt sick again.

"Suit yourself."

Hesitating at the door she spoke brightly.

"Shall I pop back with a drink?"

His one mangled utterance revealed to him his dust-baked mouth, hoarse voice and worn throat.

"Not ale".

He braced himself as she came back in to open the shutter but there was little difference.

"Foggy. It's sat here all morning."

He grunted.

"But it'll burn off later. It's going to be hot."

He closed his eyes, flinched inwardly at that thought. But then he consoled himself with reliving the kiss until, with a guilty start he re-awoke from a drowse to find Liz back, holding out a jug of yarrow and camomile infusion, the handle towards him.

Later, Robbie came into the empty kitchen. On his own in the house. Mid-morning. Bare, his feet registered the gritty unswept texture of the flags. The wind probably blew it in. The broom was in the corner. He reached the wooden chair by the hearth and his hands smoothed absently over the dirt-polished curve of the top rail. He stooped in the hearth, picked up the poker and broke the crust of coal. The scuttle was empty, a few logs beside it. He picked one up, weighing it in his hand for lightness, judging how dry, and lobbed it on.

He sat in the chair and looked around the tidy, dusty room. Grey mid-morning brightness revealed nothing. Not listless, but with a velleity, his thoughts skated over things he could do. Tidy the workshop. Walk up the lane. Nothing alighted with any weight.

"Ana."

The word out loud, quietly. The word failed to evoke. He leaned forward in the chair. Looked in the flame for something.

"Ana."

The door flew open and, in a turbulence of breeze and cloth, branches and bundles, Liz bustled into the room, like a flapping pigeon.

"There you are."

His cheeks were cooling and the word must have died before Liz entered because she beamed, and even as his pulse steadied she was around him, radiating enthusiasm and vivacity.

Wrestled into her embrace he instinctively ducked the smell of her mouth, which he could only really manage when wine and smoke overlaid. He dropped to her fleshy shoulders where the musky scent of fresh sweat smell, as it always did with Liz, brought him sluggishly to life. He pulled the cloth from her left shoulder and dropped easily from the armpit to the breast, sucking in most of the milky surround along with the coarser nipple. Breathing in the smell of her. The smell that after bathing in the bay and running the length of the beach, rose from her when she gasped on the hot sand.

She grabbed his stiffening crotch playfully, but then she was up – rearranged – and on with other things. Emptying the bundles with their pebbles, flowers.

With the word still echoing soundlessly in the room, and her busying herself at the fire to start baking, he fell back into torpor again.

Ana pinched her nose tight. Watching Robbie stir.
"How do you know which is good....*pis?*"

In the assay house Wynter toys with the three ingredients: liquor, piss and kelp. The urine, by tradition, they have always used. It works. But the kelp, the ash, might work better. Unpredictable, it destabilises his whole operation. So much hard won liquor could be spoiled.

Light fluctuates in the assay house. Buffeting at the high windows.

Wynter orders the separating out of the different kinds of seaweed. Egg wrack. Felicitously named for floating?

Bladderwrack, dabberlocks, wireweed. Sugar kelp, and the red and green weeds.

The liquor in small batches, separate pans on the boiling fire. His plan, to start with crude quantities. His controls: one of alum just with urine added – several samples, of varying quantities. The second of kelp – here his problem already starts to increase – of ash, par-burned, of which variety?

Turbulence in the lab, a sudden cooling draught as Ana struggles with the heavy lab door in the wind.

"Help her – quick!"

The apprentice boy dashes over and together they heave it shut. The roar drops. It remains as a taut whine around the building corners, exploring crevices for a hold to tear at.

Ana bends, agile, cat-like, to pick up a few sheaves of paper that have blown to the floor. Robbie raises his eyebrows in good-natured approbation. The boy returns to picking through the mixed piles of seaweed, roughly sorted, lifting out any varieties in the wrong place. He prepares to burn selected batches in the heavy cast iron pot by the fire.

Wynter collects ash that the blast from the doorway has scattered. Checking for contamination, and replenishing any diminished batches.

'Dry the saucers and glassware thoroughly, Ana.'

Her movement to the bowl, like sunlight through a candle flame.

Wynter tries to concentrate on the structure of his experiment. The number of possibilities multiplies alarmingly – each type of seaweed par-burnt or reduced to ash. Each added pure in at least three measures: single, double, doubled again. Then the possibilities of mixing the kelps – a profusion of multiples. And the possibilities of varying the proportions of admixtures – part urine, part particular kelp, part mixed kelp. Quickly he can see the combinations increasing from dozens to hundreds.

Wynter thinks of his father, passing on his knowledge. Everything defined, established, evolving only as modified by the smallest changes based on observation over generations. He steels himself to measure up to his father's persistence, but in a much broader field of enquiry. That might lead to ruin. He thinks suddenly of how his father's sight failed him.

Warm in the lab. Smells of stale piss and burning. Slime-tang of seaweed piles, still wet. Wind hurls rain at the window glass.

He watches Ana rinsing flasks at the basin. Thick fleece of vermilion pushed back with wet hands to the elbow, over the slight, smooth brown forearms. Small hands, long fingers, rotate the suds, rinse and upturn to dry.

Ana brings the glasses over. He folds back the loose sleeves that have slid down, rolling them up. She stands arms raised, hands drooping, dripping.

Aware of the apprentice's presence neither speaks. This simple act is now taut with potential.

An inner kick. Come on! He forces himself to the endless repetitions of his examination, knowing that this is the only way to information, to knowledge. Like the miller returning continually to the stone.

Has he sufficient liquor from this one batch to ensure consistent tests across all the permutations? What if this batch is itself deficient, substandard?

He realises he needs to double every test, with a second batch at the very least. His eyes close in frustration. Behind the eyelids a vermilion glow.

And in the air, which is chilled, stilled, the sharp undertow of sulphur. Caustic, at the nose; bitter-sour on the back of the tongue. Not just smell and taste, something breathed in with the mist – dust, or ash, tiny flakes of grey.

Wynter gave instructions for the burning. The making of the kelp, the seaweed ash. The seaweed came in by boat from far afield, Ireland and Orkney, since the local harvest was no longer enough.

He remembered hanging out seaweed to dry. His mother bringing out the washing. The clothes and the seaweed interspersed on the line. The clothes to tempt a sprinkling. The seaweed to foretell the shower.

Some of the locals rented scars, rocky outcrops, exposed at low tide, where seaweed attached. What they collected barely paid that rent, since kelp from the islands was so cheap.

Peter Hogg, kelp-collector, steeping burnt seaweed ashes, put one finger to his nostril and blew. A stream of soot-blackened snot shot out.

Squatting by the tub, wiping his nose on the back of his hand, he turned back to the kelp.

For kelp collected he had earned not wages but some bushels of red wheat, and some of white. These he had tried to sell on, being offered only a paltry sum.

Bitter, breathing sour smoke, and disillusioned, in frets and roaks, he stayed on in slender hope of some pay. There was no way he could afford to transport his collected kelp elsewhere, and the cheap imports dragged the price down. With little choice he bent again to the burnt weed. Hogg took the powdery ash and steeped it, with the help of a shivering ragged child. He slapped the child occasionally, to encourage and warm him. He was under instructions from Wynter to supervise the soaking of his own kelp and that of others. Also, under strict method of the manager, to oversee the burning. Raw stink of seaweed bonfires smoked across Ness. Which strict methodology he followed as suited his mood. With the bushels of bad corn to live off, and renting the corner of an earth floor in an undercliff hovel, his attitude of procedural accuracy was not euphoric. Of the leys a sample was to be taken to the lab. The rest to be stored by the evaporating house.

Below the headland the old worked-out quarries – that bare tract actually the former headland. Hacked down by quarrying to a rough plateau perhaps half the height of the former cliff. A desolate plain of burnt out shale, spoil and bare rock. Some tough grass and gorse reclaiming.

Here the kelp was burnt. A straggle of mean cottages close to the undercliff on the landward end of this terrain, known as Ness. Ness had been the main quarry some fifty or more years previously. Beyond the ossified shoulder of the shale edge the sea.

Above Ness the underhung edge of the higher cliff threatened with soft slippage. Behind the cottages, between them and the face, a stone rampart of loosely piled debris to catch the odd fallen boulder of rain-loosened overburden.

The most inhospitable place, particularly when the wind swung to north. The poorest workers wasted there: the kelp collectors and burners.

Alcuin moved among them. Children carrying out the task of burning, and leaching. If he can wean them away for an hour – under the reluctant glare of the women – he will try and interest them in learning to read. Orders from the manager's wife, not from the owner.

Acrid smoke, the burning weed, the astringent sapidity of leeching kelp, the pot-ash lees. Ash and smoke blowing into the hovels. Their begrimed clothes lines flying rags. The shit-pile behind, the urine buckets out front for collection. Here the underclass of the undercliff. The illiterate, deformed and backward. Spurned and to some degree pitied by the alum workers and quarriers above. Even so, though an essential part of the making of the alum, when imported kelp was too cheap, they starved.

Survived infancy, unlike one in three. Long hours from young, tending livestock, curing fish, hoeing and weeding. Or tasks around the works. If not mangled from childbirth then limping from accidents met in these tasks. Too tired to recover properly. Kept from doctors for fear of surgery, quack cures and fees. Malnourished.

His class.

Alcuin watched them tenderly.

By the sea, the raw material of shale; of whins, of seaweed. The raw material of men, of children. He thinks of Kenelm's words.

"Don't you see, Alcuin?"

Kenelm exasperated, as so often, with his friend.

"You see, God put everything they need in one place!"

Their tired faces. Some of pallor flushed with eagerness to learn. Others dulled already. Boys ready to hack the shale, push barrows. Girls discouraged by their parents from attending his reading class, insisted on by Liz.

He tries to retain the attention of fidgeting children. Layers of thick clothes in the winter, hard to dry, rarely washed. Soiled from squatting by the becks, in the corners of fields, behind trees. Itching with lice, fleas. Bedbugs, worms.

Jobs for children. Mixing human and animal shit with the sand rich in broken shells. Spreading on the crops. Collecting urine. Threading needles for poor-sighted elders. Collecting wood from the forests. Bleaching.

Why should the girls read? He considers the fears of the mothers. Leading to ideas. To transgression and breakdown.

Pamphlets of carnal excess circulating. Promiscuity, breakdown of marriage, vagrancy, prostitution, disease: toothless from mercury treatments.

If lucky, girls would be among the further one in three, unmarried. Provided they could spin or weave. That way never a deserted wife or widow, thrown upon the roads.

Boys? To become men. To work sixteen hours a day in a Yorkshire alum house. Hard work, and often dangerous. The fears of the fathers. Where would books lead but to ideas: of fairness, liberty? Of sedition or revolt?

Liz would have none of this.

"Lilburne flogged in the streets so we can read without the vetting of you priests!"

So Alcuin put in his hours, up and down the coast, teaching the children between their labour and domestic chores. Steering a course between the owners and the managers, with hostility or indifference in the alum hamlets.

Rutways

The fret's energy runs out as the land climbs inland towards low hills, towards the sun. Sudden clearings reveal the season. Insects, bracken, gorse. Something blue above.

At times Ana was inevitably drawn to the cliff edge. It was captivating, exhilarating.

She had been nowhere like it. Sheer to the surge and suck of the ocean.

Where Ana now perched plummeted several hundred feet sheer. Down to the wrack-strewn rocks. If the tide was in, sheer to the sea

Skeins of white slid towards the foot of the cliff. They slid over the foreshore scars.

Knees drawn up, wearing boys working trousers, rolled up at the ankles. Her arms around her knees, wrapped in the dirty, felted and knotted vermilion. A flat cap pulled low shadowed her dark eyes. Peering keenly out from under the peak of the cap. Glints. Relishing the sheer blue immensity of the sea beyond the meagre waves of the foreshore.

Scandalising Robbie, to the amusement of Marion and the ambiguous humour of Elizabeth she had given up all woollen underlayers, petticoats and aprons for their infrequent laundering. She had taken to her temporary garb and resisted changing back. Wynter was unsettled and drawn to it. The rest of the workplace seemed quickly to have got used to it. Another eccentricity of the foreign girl, provoking comment then easily ignored.

Small fishing cobles cut across the bay, moving diagonally through the scars towards the village which crammed into the wyke below the far headland.

Ana watched from the clifftop. Her lips moved to the soundless practice of terms she had been taught for all the craft to identify, and her method of memorising. Barks, like dogs, ketch, if you can, sloop, bread in the soup, coble, making shoes badly, flute, whistles, dogger, not bark, hoy, there!

There were always cobles. Fishermen used them, but the boats also plied between the bigger boats and the foreshore, acting as tugs or service vessels.

Gulls glided below her, disappearing below the edge to find ledges.

Down on the shore, below the waves that explored the foot of the cliff, looking for weaknesses, were stone remains of a breakwater and sheds. Foreshore store houses, long abandoned.

The initial convenience of quarrying the cliff and making the alum in such proximity must have been overridden at some time. Maybe a storm overpowered the breakwater, wrecking the sheds. Maybe the cliff sheered off an ominous landslip, its warning heeded.

A gull flashed by her, elevating into view suddenly from below the cliff edge. It swerved past, tilting one beady eye towards her, reflecting red.

She stretched back, legs extended nearly to the edge, feet rolling apart, the boots touching at the heels. She leant back on her arms, stretched out straight behind. The cap's peak shaded her dark eyes, closed to the high blue lid.

Each hand bunched a bundle of cliff top grasses and flowers. Yellow petals over the ripening seed pod, and small spikelets dangling on slender stems. She would take them back to hear Liz recite the names: mouse-ear, hayrattle and quaking grass.

Ana was sent down to the rocks to find shellfish. Not quite sure what to look for she grappled first with the limpets, sliding them along the rocks if unaware. Otherwise they gripped tight. Soon bored with this she peered into the pools, watching the feathery tops of barnacles.

She was confused by the hasty instruction she had received and aswirl with unfamiliar terms: dogwhelk and bladderwrack. She looked for these without expectation of success. Tugging off the stringy threads of tightly-bundled black shells or poking at red beadlets.

Quickly tiring of any practical search she gazed into the watery underskin of the pools. A little sunlight penetrated the drifting ferns and glossy side-slime with its miniature crags and shaded dells. It was soothing. The vague twin anxieties of hunger and the futility of her given task receded. A balmy peacefulness held sway in the pools, where little translucent insects drifted across the grasp of wriggling tentacles. Weeds ebbed and flowed in the invisible currents. Fish darted suddenly and more unfamiliar words surfaced – the gunnel and the blenny.

She crouched cramped. Face shadowing its reflection as she inspected the interior world of the rock pool. She was entranced by the sway and drift and at the same time aware of a growing temptation to press her face to the flashing skin of water. She leant forward until just the tip of her nose touched its sombre twin. In a flick of an instant all the gliding life of the pool darted to the edges. Each beadlet closed, each shell snapped shut. She pressed her whole face into the pool and lifted it quickly, the disturbed surface rocking to realign as drops splashed into its fractured light patterns from her wet face. She rubbed her eyes, nose, sniffed and spat.

Suddenly bored she started scouring the sides with a flat rock that was lying nearly, and in haphazard fashion harvested a few winkles. She started to feel cold, and also to notice the filling of the pools and the steady lowering of the exposed scars under the in-rolling waves. This was enough. She had been told countless times to beware being trapped by the treacherous incoming tide. She gathered up her meagre haul and traipsed back towards the foot of the cliff path.

Rock surface dried in hot sun. Still, the parallel tracks water-filled from the receded tide. Rutways. Their hard lines cut across the scars. Hard bright ribbons of mirror holding skylines. Glinting with reflected sunlight. Troughs of mercury diverging, somewhere beyond their vanishing point, at the waterline, where their cargo spills out, still as mercury, into the brimming rimless vessel of the sea.

Cutting rutways. Men with chisels, chipping away at the hard rock of the foreshore. Scars on scars. Work fit for felons, punishing enough for the toughest labourers. Raising not a palace, but sinking a drain. Mere channels for the humble cartwheels. For the donkeys, the galloways, to plod through the shallows, trundling the wheels in the lines of least resistance. The guideline gouges, the hand-hacked scars. An axle-width apart. Chiselling as light practice for the serious work of cutting the dock that the rutways serve.

A murmur of disgruntlement, anger laced with fear, spread among the kelp collectors out on the rocks. The tide had long reached its extremity and was starting to surge in again. Beyond the dark bobbing heads of the seals the sloop stirred at anchor. The gatherers swiped at flies that darted around the sweat at their eyes, and rose in clouds above the rapidly drying seaweed – stretched thin and translucent over the rocks, in tight straps. A sharp reek rose off the weed, equal parts piss, rot and seawater. The sun beat down.

At the jetty, Robbie shielded his eyes and peered out to sea. One or two carts were waiting beside their patient donkeys, ready to be moved along the rutways to the quay. Waiting for the imported kelp.

"Makes a good *sopa.*"

Everything she says a provocation today. He looked across, lips pursed. Ana was seated on a nearby rock, in a tomboyish outfit – trousers rolled up from bare feet, flat cap – and poked around in the nearest rock pools with a stick.

"Like jelly. It sets and you cut it into little squares."

He sniffed.

"You're very knowledgeable."

"It's better than yours and cheaper."

"Ana!"

There were a few workmen around, but probably out of earshot.

"Be careful what you say Ana.'"

Always so brutally frank.

"To speak your mind so, even in this county, that's not always wise. People are bitter. Envious."

"But you are the kelp-master, Mr. Robert."

"Oh yes, its an ancient mystery passed to me by the wise ones, and I practise the dark arts."

It was light on the surface, but it had a sardonic undertow.

She wrinkled her nose.

"Yes, I mix it in with the liquor, it sets in the tanks, and I toss the egg in. It sits on top like a goose egg on fresh peat. And everything is miraculous. The waters clarify, the crystals perfect themselves, the casks know when to lay their planks down, the workmen sleep in the fields and the ground shoots forth fresh loaves of bread."

Ana didn't understand it all, but felt the anger and bitterness rising through it. She kept quiet, knowing that this would be equally galling.

Robbie screwed up his eyes. The local kelp collectors were moving in towards the beach, gathering their skirts, and balancing the baskets of kelp, picking their way delicately over the slippery sharp rocks, like sea birds.

Ana squinted up into his weathered face, admiring the crow's feet. She glanced past him, back to the cliff below the works. A steep diagonal causeway had been hacked out of the cliff and it could be seen as a shadow against the shale. Here and there the causeway was buttressed with stone and arched in places over the steep rills. She saw a desultory straggle of pack horses making its way down to the beach, panniered, to help bring in the Irish kelp that would undercut the local market.

The steady progress of the tide swallowed the outlying scars and rolled over the flatter foreshore of rock. Small boats and ropes to the shore helped guide the sloop into the shallow dock that had been hacked out of the lower strata that ran diagonally out into the bay. Alongside the crude dock a rough staithe of timbers spanned between piles sunk into postholes chiselled from the rock.

"Gah!"

Ana's nose wrinkled fetchingly, and Robbie grimaced as the unmistakable deep stench of the rotting cargo flooded into the rapidly filling dock on the rising tide.

Robbie laughed, teasing with her words.

"*Buena sopa!*"

Ana flung her stick down and stormed off. She felt both queasy and hungry. She wasn't particularly annoyed, it was just time to swap one location for boredom with another.

Robbie watched after her. Good. She can wait.

The ship drifted into the dock with its ropes to the land crew and its cargo of discontent.

Everyone unhappy or fearful these days, thought Wynter. Half the people cursing the monster. All turned worse since that black lighting streak through the seam. Not long after Ana arrived. Perhaps some made that connection too?

Two more pack horses arrived next to Robbie with their drivers. A little cloud of fly-proof pipe smoke enveloped the packmen, and he felt a pang of want, patting his tobacco pocket, as they stood by. The two men were involved in an argument of self-justification.

"He told me we should refuse to bring it up."

"Just slaughter a pony and eat that I suppose."

"Said we could bring up the local stuff. But they can't pay for that."

Sure enough the flock from the beach were making their way round the headland, away from the causeway. Baskets on hips they would scramble up the path below the old tower and back round to the works the long way.

"Said we couldn't trust the locals to pay."

"Well it's the devil or the deep blue. No cash no ash."

"Besides, they think nothing can fall from a pannier on a slippery path or a rut-baked one."

Wynter listened in. The panniermen were not young. Sweat stood out on the white chest-hair of one. The other had whippet cheekbones under his cloth hat. Neither looked particularly ill fed. Panniermen had a reputation for taking a toll of their own from the baskets, which supplemented the sporadic wages for the pack trains. They were not tied to Turner like most of the alum workers and could turn seasonally from alum or kelp to lime or cereal, as gluts and shortages dictated.

"But we mustn't burn our bridges. What if the imports stop?"

The pannierman peered down the shore at the diminishing figures, skirting the promontories to avoid being cut off.

"Once they're above high tide, they can rest. We can pick up the local weed once this sloop is emptied and moved aloft. I'll go and talk to them."

One pannierman started going down the foreshore, trailing the local collectors.

The local seaweed would be taken up to Ness for burning. It would produce a quantity of ash for steeping. Precious little, considering the constant demand now that Wynter was steadily increasing the kelp component, and experimenting in small batches without urine at all. The kelp on the boat already reduced to ash would be a much greater quantity.

As the boat was made fast a couple of carts, each with a pair of galloways, trundled onto the first rutway leading to the dock. The rutways guided the wheels of the carts once the tide had covered the tracks and it was still shallow enough to wheel across, and also at night.

She darts over the brow and scampers down, scurrying onto the steep side of the shale sea cliff. Dashes zigzag down the loose sliding surface of the shale that falls perhaps six feet with each footfall. Little gasps of exhilaration as speed gathers and the slide of the shale running with her every leaping step threatens to skitter out of control.

She hears a sound. Like a grouse startled out of the heather he shoots over the edge behind her, arms and legs wheeling with huge primeval strides, he flaps across the shale after her. Larger footsteps crashing onto hers as the distance narrows.

Across the steep face of the cliff, the whole of its surface alive and sliding, sliding. Striding, on the edge of overbalancing, they rake across, race across the steep diagonal shale scree towards the beach.

She hits the beach first, registers a jarring shock at the solidity of it, of the hard sand. She staggers at speed across into the pebbles, ankles registering sprains and knocks, and propelled by her own momentum splashs into the shallows. An instant later he gallops into her, picking her up under the armpits as top half toppling, he carries them both into the waves where they collapse into spluttering and laughter.

The cold of the sea makes them gasp, the rough physicality of the spray and salt. Water-borne sand among their rived clothing and the collision of lips and teeth and spit.

Ossuary

Alcuin knelt in the church beneath the church. He rehearsed the words that he would one day, when his wandering ministry ended, illuminate.

Oh lord, I feel the heavy stones of this floor holding down the pagan earth of this place, that even now moves to make them lie uneven, that moves the little blades and thorns up between the cracks. I sense this crypt, hulled around, with its warped boards straining to keep out the heavy swell of the damp earth, as it lies too low in the unquiet deep, as it lists. I see these old stones, these carvings which, although hewn for you, draw for their artistry upon the old patterns of the land, and its plants and animals. Oh lord, I feel the heavy burden of this work, of baling out these drowning souls, of maintaining this ark.

I feel the ponderous, overwrought and leaden imagery of these words oh lord....

Alcuin drifted back, disgruntled, failing to find conviction.

His work in progress, his self-satisfying manuscript that would one day be written was no substitute for prayer and he felt a brief blaze of shame. But today in the crypt, he felt strangely protected from the full glare of God's scrutiny.

And then, just then, he sensed movement and then, he was eye to eye. The little high level window that outside in the graveyard was at ground level. A glass-framed icon. Sun flashing the grasses, points sparkling with sharp little spherical worlds of dew. The stopped squirrel, its alert sidelong gaze. Like a page quietly turned, the creature gone – just the little jar of grasses, stirring slightly like weeds in a rock pool.

Alcuin felt the acute tug of the warm sunlit world above, and he stiffly rose and left the place where, usually, he could be closer to certainty than anywhere. Here he tried to shore up the strength to pound over the moorland, the strength that would dissipate among the reeking smoke of the clamps, dissipate among the freezing slake of the pits, among the hard stares of the alum men, and their sullenness, their unspoken aggressive challenge. Come on then, save us.

Alcuin, with his provisions, his trappings of the trade, and his wide-brimmed hat, rose from the chill of the crypt and mounted the stone stairs to the nave of the church above the church. The newer church above the ancient crypt. He passed through the insect-drowsy, already warm churchyard and set off briskly through the village.

Climbing on Rudland Rigg, Alcuin stops at one of his favourite hand stones, and takes out his book. By the track he spreads his cloak over woody heather and, sitting on the springy half-comfortable clump, he sketches the stone.

This hand he likes. Outstretched as in greeting. For a handshake. Welcome, open palm. Thumb up. He carefully delineates the shallow relief around the thumb growing out of the stone.

The words he likes too. The simple usefulness of the text. This way to Kirby. Also the pattern, arranged in a square, the letters and hollow stops between them. Like the opening text of an illuminated manuscript.

He scores in the words, with the charcoal, lightly.

Around the base, the clustering straggle of spiky grasses tight around the shaft. He sees suddenly the shaft rising from its pubic tangle. The outstretched palm and fingers a mockery of hand and shaft. He thinks of the girl in the Boiling House, thinks of the images in the taproom. The friar's dream, the virgin kneels.

Blushing, probably alone for miles. Shaking himself, he concentrates on surface, making himself look into the grain of the stone, of the lichens.

Soon he is lost again to the detail. Each surface hollow and mark given depth. The play of shadow across the undulating and pitted surface. The dry lichens clinging to the north side. The hard shadow cast over the baked earth by the stone.

Finally he rests a while. Unwraps dry bread and crumbled cheese, chewing absently.

After the food he suddenly gets up briskly and approaching the stone first lays his left land over the stone's right. This way he shakes hands with the stone. Then he moves behind, and laying his hand onto the stone hand, fits his fingers to their shadow. The two hands meet palm to palm. This way the hands meet in prayer. In this way he cancels out the crude image in the stone, and eyes closed, feeling the residual warmth in the stone, becomes aware only of the wind with its earthy scents.

Before long he is on his way again.

Turner was eating anchovies. Heavily salted. Washing them down with wine. Discomfort in his guts, as so often. Some slices of cold fried kidneys. The heavy Portuguese liquor, chilled from the stone-flagged cellar, sitting heavy in his stomach.

"There was a time when every gentleman in the north would keep a fool in his household – but that position is extinct now. And yet I have a surfeit of fools applying. You are merely one of them, and though well-qualified, not outstanding from the rest in any way except that I have to ask myself why am I not put in good humour?"

Listening in silence as he ate. As Alcuin explained about the Carthusians, about the perfectible world. About the alum works. Turner poured an amber wine into two short sparkling tumblers. He waved his glass towards the minister. Alcuin sipped it. Sweet but with a dryish back taste. Smells a little of straw. He let the mouthful accumulate under his tongue. Sourish. He swallowed.

"Agreeable."

With an appreciative nod.

"From the Spanish captain."

Alcuin waited.

"A good man the father of your friend's mistress."

Alcuin frowned, but otherwise kept Turner's eye. It was always like this. Turner trying to unnerve him. Usually succeeding. But he was getting used to it now.

"Do you take his confession?"

Alcuin shook his head.

"Mr Wynter's I mean."

"No."

Turner let that subject lie for a few moments.

"So what are you preaching now Father? Sedition?"

"Perhaps hope."

He hoped.

"You give hope to those rogues and vagabonds? That thieves and blasphemers and beggars will be welcome in the next paradise?"

Alcuin looked past Turner's feet, the shine of the polished boards, over the bright threads of the lavish rug, up to the window alcove and through, past the foreground of lush lawn, over the early summer green of the beeches, to the low pastures and beyond to the blue haze of the heather topped moors. Light filtered through silver edged clouds like the ones in paintings in Turner's hall.

"Some of the men try to tread their own trail, sir.'

"And you round them up, barking, and bring them back into the fold?"

"Some of them don't want me on the works."

"Yes. They prefer the back rooms of inns and they plot heresy and revolt."

"Men with insufficient to eat will look where they can for succour."

"These are austere times, Father. What does your bible say about an honest day's work?"

"The lord does not preach starvation."

It was too late to withdraw it. Turner gave him a sharp look. It's harder for a rich man but Alcuin quelled that. He softened his line.

"What I mean is that his example is of brotherhood, of charity"

"And faith."

Alcuin let his breath out quietly and slowly.

"Yes."

"That's why I gave you my blessing – to go into the works. To preach to the men, teach to the children. So be it. Mr Wynter will bring the men out to hear you. You can preach about adultery. You can preach about pilfering from those that feed you. You can condemn the squalid cults of the taverns."

Turner paused to sip his the sherry.

"Good stuff this papish mead."

Alcuin emptied his glass, but he didn't raise it in return.

"And you find alum to be the devil's trade too I gather. Disfiguring the green sward."

"Mr Turner, sir. You are an educated man. Since Bede wandered these parts the cultivating of the land, the fishing of the seas, has fed people here and the landscape grows back, the tide rolls in."

"Droughts come. Storms. Pests. The plague."

"The water comes again. Winds calm. New crops. New generations."

"Superstition. Folklore. Witchcraft."

"Flasks bubbling in laboratories, alchemy, spells – what's the difference?"

"Oh, come on – it's a mining business, with a little science. The science you preachers fear most. Even your Gnostics."

"But the works are something new – baring the whole earth. The flesh off, the bones burned! A few inedible weeds return!"

"Prometheus – stealing fire. Only to bake bread, brew beer?"

"At least the old tasks were in the family home. Not the children in the works – the coarsest world."

"Well this is the age, father, this is how it will be from now on. As the mines deepen, the ships get bigger, the foreign traders crowd in. To buy and to sell. As the demand grows from your bishops for purple that doesn't fade"

In recompense for that little triumph Turner refilled Alcuin's glass.

"So out of this, those of us who are intelligent will increase the comfort and shelter, the finery, of this world and rightly share in it. Those of us in hock to the king, to London merchants, to lawyers in York and Leeds, we who take enormous risks, will increase and partake of the bounty of this earth, here endeth the lesson!"

And Alcuin thinks, this region was once a bright blanket of green, embroidered with the violets, lilacs and golds of meadow flowers. A profusion of colours, woven to the far hills with rippling folds. Here we moved in happy drab. Must we make this world drained of colour and life – just to give a few richer people the privilege of hue? Is this the dyer's art? Making alum to fix colour for garments? My God! We turn this world grey! He only mutters.

"And our coast will be left as cliffs of dust."

Turner stood awkwardly, stiffness in his knees, and tottered around the room a little impatiently. Alcuin's soles sweated in his sandals. He could see Turner's shoes – new looking – pained him.

"Father, collect a side or two of meat as you go. Take some other provisions too."

It was the signal for Alcuin to leave. He realised he had been on stony ground, sowing his seed about the ordered community of the works. The owner had simply ignored it.

"Just preach a little common sense down there."

Alcuin rose to his feet.

"And when the archbishop's robes are bright long after his august personage has melted in his lead cloak, let's praise alum."

He lifted the dregs and finished them. Alcuin did likewise, crossing himself discreetly.

A lackey showed Alcuin the door and as he passed down the path a few brownish leaves scuttled over and, in a freshening breeze, spots of rain fell.

The smell among the heather when they kiss is heady, like something fermenting. The heather's springiness is almost funny.

Warm air, bees swoon over.

Robbie leads her from the narrow path the sheep make. Dust-spores in the bracken make her cough. They fall into the hillside, waist high bracken, and disappear. She laughs her harsh cackle. Her smell, earthy. The bracken breaks their fall, they topple slowly. The stems fold under them and form a mat. After they depart the bracken creaks back a little, hollow with the memory of their bodies.

Carey gazed at the headland. His eyes bored into it. To Carey the cliffs were an ossuary. A solid black specimen case with no laboratory lantern trained on it. Or a chest of drawers, every one crammed full, so they would barely open. Or a heavy book on a dusty shelf in a locked room, in a forgotten corridor.

Carey imagined a heavy leather-bound book, each page filled with flattened specimens – fronds, meadow flowers, compressed lizards, insects, dried fish, small rodents, spindle-boned birds, emptied egg-shells, mummified skin, desiccated hands – all clamped tight in the pages of the book. The whole book squeezed down hard under the heavy plate of the printers press. For an eon. Until the book formed solid stone, a fossil book. The book was a cliff, battered for centuries by the purposeless quest of the sea. The island book of Albion. Gradually the sea would gain ground. England would be eroded from all sides and shrink. Gradually all the specimens – perfect stones, of every size, from the sea horse to the white whale, would be released, from the stone aquarium. The sea would wash over the whole land and the field creatures – spiders, cats, sheep, boar, the freshwater fish – crayfish, salmon, oyster, any bird that cannot land on the waters, and the children, grandmothers, the beggars and priests and scholars and parliamentarians and court hangers-on, would be laid down for their future preservation as mute stone.

Mute? He thought. Not at all. And he brushed the dust off his breeches, scrambled to his feet, and slinging his jacket over his shoulder started loping down through the hillside bracken, his boots snapping the brittle stems and sending up spores.

That evening Carey writes a footnote among his papers.

Cleaning and classifying the specimen (they call it the monster!) will take time. Meanwhile I intend to learn the alum process – so much seems quackery and mysticism. There is even a roving priest here, claiming to teach the ragged urchins. However, this alum business has some method to it, which I hope to understand (there is much room for improvement – perhaps a patent or two?) – also this method is distinguished by much ineptitude – deliberate or otherwise – and a public show of ill-remembered facts and gropings in the dark. This Mr. Wynter, however, is smarter than he seems.

"It was the colour, I suppose, that led the chemists to seek to distil gold. The trail seemed to be signposted with evocative clues. The appalling reek of the fermented piss, for a start. Boiled down to thick brackish slurry. Lifting the lid a second or two would stink the room out with its acrid ammoniac fumes. Brand, the alchemist, distilled the bitterly pungent lant, catching its milky vapours in a glass retort. The white deposits finally sifted out and stored under water. A grain or two, dropped over a flame, in a large glass, suddenly filling with a blazing white light. Flaring out into the dark corners of the dim laboratory. Where Hennig Brand failed, failed absolutely, to find gold. To turn piss into power, lant into lucre."

Everything on earth was alive, they thought. Grew in the earth, and would live and die, rust. Could be purified into gold.

The light grey cloud swirled in the jar.

"Later Boyle used the white phosphorous, sizing paper, like the monks did with alum, and scraping into flame a sulphur-tipped twig."

Carey seemed to be ruminating to himself. He turned towards the manager at his bench.

"But this whole ritual of yours is alchemy!"

Wynter shook his head.

"A simple procedure."

"The very words you use here conjure alchemy!"

"Do they?"

"Calcining, for example."

"Heating in the air?"

"Yes, in your 'clamps'. The purifying fire. What is the residue from your calcining?"

Wynter waited.

"*Calx*. Literally, lime. Latin for lime. Chalk."

Wynter shrugged.

"If you say so."

"So this residue, the calx, was of essential substance to the alchemist. Transformation through consumption by fire. Most magically the red calx, for that must surely lead to gold."

"As ours does of course, in a manner of speaking."

Carey frowned, puzzled. Then smiled.

"Ah yes."

He went on.

"So here we have the base matter, calcined. The phlogiston - as my assistant is so fond of relating - the combustible essence, departed, consumed, burnt."

"Leaving the calx."

"Exactly so!"

Carey waited to see if Wynter would add anything, then resumed.

"So the mercury calx leads to gold, the iron calx is merely rust. And you, I believe, practice the dark arts here in your laboratory."

With your muse, he thought, your little witch.

"In your sorcerer's workshop or laboratory, or 'assay house' as you prefer to call it."

Carey was smiling, teasing Wynter.

"Making your alum calx. With the alchemists you amalgamate, you calcinate, calculate and crystallise. The language is pure alchemy!"

Wynter smiled.

"As if these were words I would use."

Blast!

Carey curses his clumsiness with the charcoal. He vows to get the assistant to provide a more serviceable version of the diagram he is attempting, once he has had a chance to verify it. His best guess at the picture of everything alum, from the soil to the sail.

Under the plan he adds a few lines.

I have stood some time beside a fellow of few words, gazing with him at smoke signals and fire spirits. Whether he divines by sight or smell I have yet to work out, but he watches the clamps for a sign as the various colours of flame play around the burning shales. Some elusive transformation (as at every stage in this slippery and reckless venture, it seems) is sought by dint of temperatures of the calcining, the tones of the flame tongues, and all this constantly modified by the substitution of shales, the clumsy plastering of the windward side, the opening up of 'chimneys' and all manner of teasing and poking and general not leaving well alone. I am absolutely none-the-wiser but it seems that if this is wrong then 99 tons of waste from a 100 of shale (deemed a success!) will be one ton more waste or 100 in percentage terms. My God, if the funders got wind of this....

Carey rubs his tired eyes and extinguishes the candle.

Turner shakes his head in exaggerated disbelief.
"They literally make their own soil!"
Wynter sucked on his glass of beer.
"So do I."
"Very funny. But seriously, Mr. Wynter, the western islands are so rocky, every field is simply a field of stones. Rocks plucked from that field are piled up to bound it. Lichens attach to the rocks. They drag the stones out of the ground and smash them. There is no soil! The Irish gather the kelp and they mix it with the crushed rocks."

Wynter clamped his glass to his chest with his right hand. His left cupped his right elbow. Why? He thought of his father. The same posture.

"So they mix the kelp and the dust from the smashed rocks. They piss on it, shit on it. They make their own soil! And this before they can even start to think about planting a single seed."

"And still they can sell their precious wrack and urine to us? And undercut our starvelings?"

Turner's slight movement of the head a rebuke to the manager.

"With the industry the way it is, we must cut costs where we can."

"Well, we have kelp on our doorstep, or at least the weed to burn it from, and we only have to pay to collect. But others use it too - even in this the market squeezes us - as the soap boilers, stirring kelp with quicklime, and the glass blowers, both need it."

Turner topped up Wynter's glass and then his own, emptying the jug. When the innkeeper came to refill it Wynter pushed some coins over to him. The mine owner raised his drink towards him.

"To seaweed. Once your experiments are concluded I am sure the yield will pay once more for the local crop, which muck the Lord at least spreads on our doorstep."

Wynter's thoughts drifted to Ana, lying back on the rock after the swim, in the sun. The green streamers of the seaweed gleaming on the rock. Legs apart, trailing into the water. The suck of the tide under the outcrops of the little rock pools. Wet dress up, the water lapping up between, the narrow trail of hair leading down from the navel. Hot skin smell. His own shoulders red and burning .

Turner broke into Wynter's reverie.

"Your wretches, their own seaweed too expensive. Their own piss no good when they're broke, because they mix it with sea water, and no good when they're not, when they drink so much."

"Well yours wouldn't be much good!"

Turner mock outraged. Drained his glass.

"Well I'm out for one now. Get them in!"

Turner walked heavily towards the outside door. Wynter noticed the sheen on the shoulders of the owner's well-made suit. He looked at his own clothes. Threadbare in places. He could ill afford to drink with Turner, ill afford not to. Alum had not brightened his own rough linen and woollens but it had surely seen Turner's silks.

Wild daffodils

Marton, by way of Broughton, to Spout House. Here Kenelm will stay two days before heading south.

The more he hears about Alcuin, his novice as he thinks of him, the more he worries about the wavering of faith. For this reason he has embarked on a mission to find him, at Lastingham, the church under the church - if he cannot draw sustenance there, then where? – or failing that at one of the dreaded alum works. Last he has heard is he is often at Scarshead where some say, village nonsense, a devil has been unbottled, some rock spirit.

Near Cuthbert's church in Marton he had looked in on Cook, a Scottish farm labourer, and his wife. He had known Miss Pace before her marriage, a local girl. At a year and a half the second child was doing well. Grace was clearly expecting a third.

A day later, under the low thatch of the Spout, Kenelm was drinking. The farmer was known to keep a room or two available and brewed a respectable ale from the spring water.

Kenelm's ministry to the widely-strewn farmsteads of the dale would afford him a few more friendly pourings from the jug, on the meandering trail south. Fertile land between here and the ruined abbey, and again the other side to the market town. No trace of hell fires, ash and ritual burning this far from the alum-poisoned coast.

Out of dense woodland, Kenelm's trail wound down into a small hamlet. Merely two or three stone hovels. There was not a soul about. The light was only just intensifying, leaving a few dregs of twilight lingering in the dale. The cottages were blank and mute. There was no sign of occupation, and the hamlet had a gloomy atmosphere. Impoverished and forlorn.

No one witnessed Kenelm as he passed the small, mean shut-up houses. A glimmer, glanced through the blurred foliage to his right, revealed the direction of the Rye stream. Now seen, he simultaneously caught its murmur. He swung south, away from the hidden beck, and dimly felt, rather than clearly saw, the broken masses of craggy stone assembled in the brooding murk.

There was nothing distinct about the crags, for everything was draped with heavy swags of ivy. Deep shade of wooded slopes behind.

Kenelm peered grimly at the daunting, austere edifice, gradually making out a row of arches and, higher, the triple opening of the nave's window. Not far short of two hundred years had elapsed since the abbey's dissolution and nature had claimed its carcase with teeth and claws of briars and ivy. Kenelm imagined the *trental*, the thirty requiem masses for the souls of the lord that John Storey had paid for his son William. Chanting drifting from tenebrous chasms. Voices massing between the ivy-raddled ramparts. Claustral remnants.

Kenelm shivered. He coveted the warming room, where the scribes prepared ink for the parchment, and a great fire would have burned. The chants would have been faint and weak, Kenelm imagined, as the warming house was used for the ritual bloodletting. An equivocal ministration, which promoted musicality, but diminished the strength to sing.

The chanting dissipated, the way the last few monks had done as the royal commissioners neared.

A little more light had drained into the valley. Under the alleviation of murk the floor of the clearing revealed a waste of bramble and gorse. These would have been the market gardens and oatfields, Kenelm thought, and the occupants of those cold cottages, at that time, would once have laboured here. Or perhaps the *conversi*, after breakfast in the lay-brothers refectory.

Inevitably, reflecting on monastery life, he thought of Alcuin. In a day or two they would meet. He looked forward, but anxiously, to their sparring conversations, so enjoyable when Alcuin was a boy. Still stimulating, as he took on his present role, but lately more tense. He sensed a distance widening between them that he was hoping, literally with these strides, to close.

A mist clung around the stones, like a vapour the ivy exhaled. It dissolved in the brightening light, as if strained through layers of dark unbleached cloth. The sandstone warmed into honey. Visible now, ranges of ruined masonry and suddenly Kenelm was hiding in a deep stony trench of the outlying walls. He was a small boy again, playing hide and seek, and his brother was somewhere overhead, running among the rubble in pursuit. It was peaceful down here. He crouched down, legs astride a stone runnel. It was damp and mossy at the base. Sunshine bathed the flank of stone above, while he squatted in the chill shade. They often hid and sought, taking turns, among the ruins here. In the hiding was the exploration, the sense of self and solitude, and the excitement of concealment. In the seeking was the heady rush of running among the stones in the hot sun. Pelting down corridors of stone, the rapture of cloistered openings flying by, the sudden clearings into roofless outdoor rooms. The deep diagonal incision of shadows. The expectation of a sudden leaping out, mutual shock of discovery.

"Found you!"

Kenelm was back in the Rye valley, and realised that his reminiscence had been triggered by a child's voice. The sounds, from someone nearby but out of view, had both transported to his childhood and recalled him. His shoulders lifted with a quick involuntary tremor. It was cold and solitary in that runnel, and always would be.

Kenelm resumed the path. Perhaps the one Sylvan had taken when, after coming from Scotland to succeed Aelrad as abbot, he later covered the few miles to Byland, to die. Kenelm followed this path only a short way. Then turning southeast, downstream, he skirted the riverside thickets and headed over the fields towards the market town. Above him the picked-dry bones of the former village called Grief, also dissolved when the 'white monks' left.

By the stream were a few small wild daffodils.

"Nhn!"

Wynter exhaled sharply through his nose, followed by a wave of pain across his forehead. It was early, grainy pre-dawn light. Drinking with Turner. He felt sick – so much money. Had he spoken out of turn?

Launde's dream

Ana was bilberrying above the quarries. Launde stood nearby, at the reservoir. He was doing something at the outlet duct. Making adjustments or repairs. The wind blustered, flapping up strongly for a few moments, and dying away. The sun burned down hot in the still periods. Ana's brown nape, above the delicate ridges of the spine, burned pleasurably. She stumbled and tripped, snagged on the tough-rooted ground cover, as she came over to Launde with a purple hand outstretched. Mouth widened to a grin with the teeth together. Purple–stained, seedy. A gust swept her roughly clipped hair over her face. She wrinkled her nose. Fumes blew over from the clamps with the gusts, and in the lulls left a trace of soft ash. Launde was unaware of sulphur smells, born in the stink. His expression of humour and puzzlement. Wrinkles deepened as he narrowed his eyes against the bright sky behind Ana's silhouette.

"Acqui tiene."

She laughed.

He gathered the proffered bilberries from her outstretched palm, holding her hand aloft gently. The soft skin mobile over the knucklebone. He thought of Ellen. His daughter's hands.

"You were telling me about home. "

Launde spoke as if their conversation, actually of some days ago, had momentarily lapsed.

Ana shrugged.

"Was that all of it?"

Shrugged again.

"Maybe."

"So tell me a bit more about the black pigs."

Whistling a jig, Launde sat down on purple heather, back against a wooden post. His bootsoles clapping together at the edges to beat time for the tune. She peered at him, hand shading her eyes.

"What?"

"Anything! You feed them, you eat them, you ride them, you talk to them!"

Ana tugged up a few leaves and tossed them at Launde.

"How do you hold them?"

"What?"

"When you ride them. You hold them like this?"

He indicated wrapped arms.

"No!"

She tilted her head coquettishly.

"They have fleas."

"So like this?"

His wrists mimed holding a pair of ears, and then he tugged his own.

"No. Like this."

She mimed a similar posture, but she slapped herself on the back of the neck.

"Loose skin on the back of the neck?"

She was kneading the air like pastry.

He imagined grasping the loose fleshy folds of the pig's neck, alive with bristles. Have to be wary of the teeth. Of the head swivelling.

"Just one hand."

Holding the other hand high above, with an imaginary cap.

"Then they charge like the bull!"

Eyes widened to express incredulity.

"It must be easy to fall off."

Launde laughed aloud.

Near them, a little distance away, another liquorman was attending to the bank of the reservoir. Out of earshot, but a mutual awareness made them quieter. She indicated, clamping her right arm between her thighs.

"They grip here."

They both glanced round at the other liquorman, who nodded imperceptibly. Launde took some more bilberries and for a second or two imagined Ana gripping the bristled rough abrasive muscular flanks of the black pig with her stocky thighs.

"People race them."

Launde loved it.

"On those little legs?"

He might mean Ana or the pigs.

"They have pig-back wrestling. They dress the pigs in bright clothes and choose the best. Everyone drinks hot red wine with herbs in."

Launde grabbed a handful of bilberries.

"The most beautiful ladies..."

She paused for effect.

"...dance with the pigs. They wear veils. The pigs stand on their back legs."

Ana tried to reach back beyond the memory of the fetid claustrophobia of the urine ship. She could remember nothing of Spain. The black pigs were a fairy tale from her childhood – heard in a crowded rooming house near the water stairs, by the pool of London, where her father looked for a ship, and her mother shivered in July, in a smoky fog, in a threadbare shawl, telling her about the dancers.

Ana leaned forward and flicked a fly off Launde's perspiring brow. Under the bilberries there was a rank smell on her breath. It brought Launde back from his reverie. He sat up a bit straighter, and crossed his legs. He would need to be back working soon.

Launde loved to hear the stories of Ana's homeland. He didn't care to sort fact from fiction. Launde's father had been a seaman. He had his own stories. Tales of narwhals, giant tortoises that swim and fish that fly. Launde's world rarely stretched beyond the works and the few surrounding villages. After his father and brother drowned at sea Launde grew up to take land work, in the alum trade. That was fine. But a hidden part of him wanted to be more than one who sat in thrall to the tales in the inns. Someone with his own stories.

Launde imagined himself driving the herds of black pigs over the scorched landscape of Ana's homeland, stopping by the alum works there to trade techniques for saturating the liquor. Asking the locals for the loan of a hen's egg.

The wind buffeted around and brought a tang of the sea. He stretched stiffly to his feet and resumed tinkering with the outlets to the culverts. Ana wandered off.

In Launde's dream he is cramming his mouth with bilberries. The juice and soft crush of them as he bites. He crams more in, it's like wine. The juice and berries overflow. Ana laughs soundlessly. Mouth also crammed. Tongue churning. She smears a purple liquid stain across her cheeks. Her teeth rise and fall and berries fall out. He sees her mouth very close. The stained teeth and tongue. Their mouths crash violently in a fever of cramming and kissing. His hands go all over her, moving the loose skin over the bones of her body under the mobile skin of her light tunic. Their bodies sluice with hot moisture like sweat or juice. His rough bristled thighs wrap around her. His face burrows into the coarse hair of her nape. She slides round till she is on top. He feels his neck hot, loose folds grabbed by her. She grabs his hair. Her sex is hot wet juice oiling his back. She slides round him on the oiled spit of his spine. He pushes his face into the liquid neck under her ear streaming with hot crushed berries flowing. She squirms round his cock hard against her flank.

He awakes pressed face against his wife's damp breast, his cock crushed against her thigh. He needs to piss. Sliding from the blanket he goes to the back door and in the sudden sharp cooling of the night air his cock relaxes and he starts to urinate. The air cools his belly and thighs. A few stars, and the piss hisses soothingly onto the earth. Inside he regains the cool damp patch of the bed and, in a few moments regains a fragment of his dream, clutching his stiffening cock, and seconds later is back asleep.

Launde's journey

Launde had breakfasted on the hinder-ends of peas. He had taken some bread with him to the works. During the morning lugged sacks of impure crystals to the Alum Byng. Dragged other sacks to the roaching pans. A sullen overcast day. The heat seemed to be contained in the air. Steam rose from the boiling vats. He sweated. Had little energy. His legs were weak, but he hoarded the bread uneaten.

At midday he returned to his cottage. Ellen, his daughter, scratched in the dry soil of the vegetable patch, murmuring some rhyme over and over. Just as he was about to call he saw her dig up the root and chew it.

He felt momentarily dizzy as something tensed rigid in his throat, a violent unfocussed anger, jaw clenched. Suddenly he decided.

"Ellen."

She glanced up fearfully.

"Come inside!"

Marion was stirring something by the fire. She looked round. For the first time he saw that hunger had not just made her thin, and pale, but had aged her. She smiled, but a frown hovered.

"Give me some of that."

He scooped some of the strained stock and put the bread from his pocket into it, stirred, and gave it to Ellen. She wolfed it.

He spoke to his wife.

"I'll go to Turner."

She stopped stirring.

"Richard...."

"I have to."

"Go to Wynter. Turner will give nothing."

"Wynter has not been paid either. The works manager, and his own clothes won't hold their dye. The wind goes through. He's no stronger than us...."

"He's scared."

"He's ...."

"And he's feeding three."

Launde checked. Wynter was childless.

"Marion..."

Launde was exasperated.

"And you too find time for her stories."

"Oh for god's sake! I'm talking about us – trying to feed our family!"

He sensed it was a diversion. She was troubled, but not about this, it was a red herring. Or a manifestation of a different anxiety. He went over to her, and gathered her up into his arms. It was like twigs, gathered into a bunch of kindling.

She wriggled free.

"Ask Robbie to go instead."

"No."

"Tell him we can't live on air."

"He's never wronged me, unless his hand was forced. His problems are his. I'll go tomorrow."

He made a show of poking the coals. But he felt weak. Frightened. She poured out some stock, and he dropped a few of the peas in, watched the light bloom of mould dissolve. Afterwards he could not keep awake. But after a few minutes his wife woke him and sent him urgently back to work.

He stopped by the manager's assay house.

"Mr. Wynter."

"Richard."

Then he saw the girl was there. She was looking resolutely away – but he could tell she was smouldering like a coal. He had interrupted some kind of row. The manager was distracted and kept glancing back.

Launde forced his attention.

"Sir, I'll see Turner tomorrow, as the production's slack, and he owes me."

"Don't be stupid, man. Turner will whip you."

He was angry – but Launde sensed it was towards the girl. Launde was tentative.

"Sir, I know you've asked."

Wynter glared at him.

Launde sensed the girl was enjoying it. She had looked across. There was a hint of amusement. He took it as mockery. Black pigs. The dream. Ellen. Now the anger from the cottage garden surged through him. He could strike her. Steadying himself he looked down.

"Mr Wynter...."

He stopped. He would not say out loud his family was starving.

"Unless I'm needed tomorrow...."

"Mr Launde... Richard....you'll decide. But Turner...."

"What choice do I have?"

He left.

In the old storehouse, Ana lay on her back. Hot, breathing hard, slowing. It was shady and warm in the shack. Smell of dust, woodsmoke. Cobwebs on the inside of the small window opening spun together gaps in the dense ivy that grew over the outside. A green shade. Brindled sunlight flickered over Ana's bare damp body, which was mostly in shadow. Robbie produced the egg and laid it gently in Ana's navel. It was dry and cool. He looked at it thoughtfully. Ana peered down between small flattened breasts, chin tucked in. Her belly muscles quivered slightly. Robbie noted the faint mud streaks on the egg, its grey colour. He thought of it solid, like a beach pebble. He thought of it light and hollow, as when blown. Ana looked sideways at him, apprehensive. She spoke in her smoky voice.

"Never knew it like that before."

He looked at her.

"Honest!"

Robbie smiled gently. His eyes passed from the egg to the bush of moist hair in the shady valley between Ana's legs. The bushes which hug the becks in the steep gills which tumble down to the cliff edge. Playfully he spiralled his fingers in the cooling moisture of the hair, noting its sticky resistance. On his damp thigh Robbie's cock stirred sluggishly.

Ana watched the egg, and beyond it the knuckles of the caressing hand. He parted her and slid a slow smear of her liquor. She let her head fall back. He rolled over, pressing her apart with his thumbs, letting his fingers slide in and out. Heaved onto his palms either side of her waist he watched the egg wobbling in her navel hollow as he pushed his cock in slowly. Gently, firmly, in and out. Her little exhalations. He pushed in and in. The egg trembled, and then he fell forward his mouth crushed over hers, their tongues squirmed like eels and her gasps escaped around them. His stomach smashed the egg onto hers the liquids leaked out, they felt the little shell pricks and he pushed in and out harder and faster and he pushed in and in until at the last second with a huge effort of will he lifted himself out and slid forward over the yolk-slime of her belly, pumping albumen. He pressed his face into the wet hair behind her ear. After a while he slid down her body, his mouth slick with fresh yolk and jellies, licked her gently, slavered his tongue lavishly in her, till she cried out in her own language.

Later. Midnight. Alone in her room.

She looked out of the window.

Snow? In midsummer?

She stared at the bright, white field of grass.

The moon was somewhere. Full. Behind the house.

The angled shadow of the house cut across the grass. Like the shadow of a ship, raking across harbour surface gleam.

Not snow, she saw.

Just a field of white dew. In the bonelight.

She shivered, and went back to bed.

In the first inklings of the morning Launde moved over the rough flags. Leaching darkness in the hovel. The smell of ashes in the grate. The moist damp warmth of the folded-in cosiness, chilled on him immediately. He raked the clinker. Dry leaves around the edge of the hearth trembled slightly in the draught under the door. Launde wrapped up in layers, determined to use the pre-hunger balance of the body from sleep to walk as far he could before the thought of food nagged him.

He pushed open the door. A couple of stars were still visible. The moon was down, the sun not up. In the half-light a couple of figures were visible moving towards the works. Fumes drifted down from the clamps.

Launde pressed up the steep rise at the hinterland of the bay, with the village away to his right, a cluster of dark cottages crowded in the wyke. His boots and trouser legs were quickly soaked in the heavy dew condensed in the grasses and low bushes. They would dry later. The sky lightened from deep blues to pale greys. He was aware of one or two rabbits, and thought to remember that. Sudden movement, a hag-worm probably, flickered away from near his foot.

Behind Launde the whole wide bowl of his universe was laid out like an offering.

This world was gripped tight at each end by the headlands. They were two arms that held a shallow settling pan between them, the sea. On its surface of cloudy grey the odd spark of silver. The splinter-light of the rising sun, crystals forming in the liquor. At the far meniscus the invisible outer rim was blurred in a slight light haze. At the near edge, some scum drifted towards the closer lip, of the land. Foreshore breakers.

Features of the landscape grew sharper. The left arm sheltered a few rooftops of the fishing village, where wood smoke drifted up. Beyond, a coble picked out a path through the scars to open sea. In the ravine, trees and scrub huddled down in the shelter of the valley. At the right arm a knuckle jutted up above the knobbled hand of a cliff edge – the old tower's silhouette. In the crook of the arm, in the elbow and the armpit, was the steam and smoke, the continuous hum and throb of Launde's world – the one formed by scraping away the rock, and making the place to burn stones.

Smoke drifted up here and there, up into the enormous dome. The stilled vat of the sea gleamed with reflected light. The bowl was lifted up, brimming with light. The air filled with cries of birds. Warmth flooded into the gorse and the hawthorn blossom, into the sandstone, and the light fell onto the grass with long early shadows. One or two sheep materialised, a mistle-thrush darted. Insects lifted off dung. Adders slid onto stones to warm. Purple flushed into the first clumps of heather. Bracken exuded its smell. The arms cradled the pan of the bay; a skin of silver cooled on its surface.

All this Launde would have seen if he had not pressed on, oblivious, over the shoulder of the ridge and on, towards the moor.

The sun was well up. There was a buzz in the air and a warm fermenting smell of dung and peat. Blossom on the moorland shrubs, a heady honey-ish aroma – perfumed, thought Wynter, and cunty.

He moved towards the brow of the hill overlooking the works and the bay. Remembering his words to Liz earlier.

"I feel like a bit of fresh air before spending all day in the sheds".

Liz had smiled, embracing him warmly.

"I love you Robert".

He had hugged her tight. She had light in her eyes, a spark of mischief. He kissed her.

Nevertheless, he now bounded up to the brow like an escaping hare, sprang up the hillside. He took the long curve to come out above the clamps, but away from the drift of the smoke. High summer. Where the paths converged at the top he saw Ana arriving. After an anxious glance around they embraced. Her smell of fresh perspiration, and they kissed carelessly and his hands sought out the moist places. Soon they were gasping and sticky.

Almost as soon the ache of imminent departure. Fear of being missed at the works.

He sighed.
'You go first.'
'Robbie....'
'I can find an excuse to be late.'
She went.

Squatting, peering over the rounded summit, Robert could see the sharp arc cut from the hillside by quarrying. The concave hollow of the quarry echoed the scallop of the bay. Immediately below the floor of the quarry, spilling down the lower slopes in the direction of the works, were heaps of spoil. The long bumpy tumulus of spoil was ablaze with its colonising gorse, a livid rash of yellow.

He scanned the quarry floor, thick black smoke was pouring off the clamps. Around these great piles of burning rocks, twice the height of trees and double again in length, figures came and went. The great hills of stone smouldered on their bases of coal and brushwood.

Bees hummed around Robert, and the sun imbued deep warmth to his face, neck and forearms. For a few seconds, he felt deliciously drowsy. Reluctantly he got to his feet and started to scramble down to the quarry floor.

Approaching the clamps, two burning piles towered over Wynter, and a third was being built.

He could see an impressive co-ordination of labour. Barrows were being propelled at speed down the shallow incline of the quarry floor by half-running barrowmen, their carts tipped up steeply to load the weight just above the equilibrium point of the trundle. Those with empty barrows scampered back up to the foot of the rock face, slipping frequently on the spilt shale. A third group loaded the barrows with the alum shale, dragged back from the face by the pickmen, who hacked recklessly at the rock.

Normally this would be a cause for satisfaction for Robert. This was an impressive performance by underfed men labouring in the steadily rising heat of the morning, in the reflected glare of the bare rock face, on little more than the promise of impests. He understood it well. It was driven by a desperate hope, borne of need, that their targets of so many half-barrows or quarter-barrows would translate into a few shillings. But today he remembered what Turner had told him about overproduction.

Robert spotted the tallyman preparing a pipe over by the steeping pits and, skirting the heaps of brushwood, made his way over.

The tallyman nodded.

"Morning Mr Wynter."

"And a fine one."

Robert took out his own pipe, and snapped the end off the stem before filling the bowl.

"There seems an unusual zest this morning, Foxy. One would almost think they were getting paid."

Fox flickered a sardonic grimace. Robert registered that he was under the same delusion.

Fox started tentatively.

"There's a rumour...."

"As always."

Pause.

".... that Launde has gone to see Turner. The men say you sanctioned it sir."

Wynter sucked on his pipe stem.

"I refused to refuse."

"I heard his wife has spoken of his determination to succeed. She is not a foolish type."

"No, Foxy? But still she sticks by him?"

Fox appeared to inspect a pebble by his feet, frowning all the while, and then he kicked it away.

Wynter looked down at his house, and beyond to the works, and the workers' cottages. Finally to the lime kiln on the cliff edge and out to sea. A number of small vessels moved to and fro. The horizon was not sharp, blurred with a haze. Winter felt a slight cooling breeze on his brow and, noting that the wind had swung round to easterly, considered the possibility of a sea fret.

"Mr Fox, I let Launde go, since we have more than enough in full casks. Frankly, short of sacking him I had little choice. Turner is looking to cut back production. There is foreign alum flooding in cheap and all up the coast here we are producing too much. You know all this."

"Well, Launde has the guts to go, and that gives the men hope."

"Foxy...."

He knew that was a goad aimed at him. He saw Fox's pursed lips. Almost petulant, he thought, almost like Ana's.

"Foxy, Launde is going at the wrong time. If the price is low Turner will not see this as a time to pay more."

"So what else is there?"

Wynter spat. He put his pipe away. It was bitter. He took little pleasure in it, but it put him among the men. Ana, however, occasionally in the lab, took to it with evident relish, sucking, coughing and widening her eyes. It appalled, scandalised and attracted him.

A cloud stole over the sun. He felt the harsh edge creep in. A flicker in his mind almost recognised it as jealousy. Ana flirting with the workmen by the tun house. Fox's petulance. The sour reek off the liquor pits of the steeping burnt shale.

"Mr Fox. You're the mathematician. Work it out. Either these men work fewer barrows, or they get less per barrow or some of them go to Stoupe Brow."

Fox coloured. Like he had been slapped. Both men knew labour was being offloaded already at Stoupe Brow.

"Tell me when you've decided."

Wynter headed down the track beside the wooden trough which ran towards the works.

After leaving Robbie at the brow Ana had cut across at the spoil heaps below the quarry and picked up a line of channels bringing liquor down from the steeping pits. The sandstone troughs were half sunk in the thick meadow grass and in places dipped below tussocks as culverts. In other places makeshift timber sections carried the liquor over hollows, chocked up on wooden crutches.

Sunlight caught the cloudy thick liquor which surged down the trough like spunk. The slow squeeze as Robbie came nearer to coming and then liquor jumped. It flowed into the troughs, down towards the sea, as from a primal spring. The sea - everything smelt of sex down there – the seepage from the shells, the reek off the kelp, the sun on the skin of the workers, the rank hot flanks of the pack donkeys toiling back up the causeway from the beach. She felt her own liquor fall through her and felt with her hand, smelt and tasted. For half a second considered kneeling on the grass just there but instead ran down the trough line, dashed past the manager's house with eyes ahead only, and scuttled into the yard by the roasting casks.

Turton, a houseman leaning in the shade by the Tun House wall, registered immediately the spark of mischief in her eye. He caught a hot whiff off her as she came to a halt embracing the warm timber of one of the casks. Turton was waiting for the order to open the casks, and until it came, idle. Arms hanging down, his sinewy brown hands tapped idly at the wall at his back. That would soon be prizing apart the hoops that held together the loose planks of the casks. She suppressed a shudder. A driver led a small team of packhorses past the open end of the yard. The driver stopped off to speak to Turton.

"Not ready yet?"

His panniers were empty.

Turton shrugged, non-committal.

"What's happened?"

"What?"

"Everything's shutting down – no flow, not enough 'mothers', one of the clamps out? The causeway so untended the pack could slip over the side at any time?"

The driver ignored the girl.

"Launde's gone to Turner."

"He'll be back."

Turton's inactivity mimed unconcern. Disguised saving his energy. He was hungry. The packhorses nibbled the grass at the edge of the narrow trail. The driver nibbled a square of seaweed.

"The manager's distracted?"

Turton didn't react.

Ana slipped into the shade of the Tun House, through the open doorway. It was cooler inside and the few inert barrels stood in a row, cooling. Ana cooling. Quite soon she went into the room where the cooling tanks were and, after lingering there, to the laboratory where the assay dishes and other paraphernalia for floating the egg were kept. Here she commenced her daily task of cleaning the equipment, tidying and putting it away.

Initially Launde crashed across the moorland with a sense of purpose and some buoyancy. The sun had no real heat, but it warmed a little optimism. He stopped and peeled off a layer, tying it round his waist. He drank some stream water and it awoke a pang. The hunger suppressed by the deeper twinge of fear that underpinned, despite his steely purpose, his nagging concern.

Turner would have to see his point. Alum was a precarious business, but the owners were selling the goods and the wages not filtering back to the works. The wicked system of impests had been imposed on those too desperate to say no. Launde told himself: Turner would see that a loyal, hardworking man with acute knowledge of the trade was a valuable asset and should be paid a living wage.

The rill ran between soft, spongy banks pricked with bunches of spiky reeds. The type Ellen wove into plaits, in a pattern that resembled flattened ears of corn, which Marion tied in their hair. The sound of the stream – gentle. He scooped up a handful of water and popped a couple of dried mushrooms from his knotted cloth into his mouth, chewing them together. Launde saw it all again. Ellen, squatting down, picking the root from the dust, her eyes flicking across to see her father, seeing her. She registers wrong. The root between her teeth long ways. The tip of the tongue playing slightly with the gritty surface. Biting it tentatively and then throwing it away. Spitting. Running into the house. The bright intent of desperation. She picks up the root. Before she sees him and runs.

At length Launde reached the inn.

Masson was outside, doing something among the hens. He was moving a couple of clay slabs, propping them against the wall. The inn was a simple pantile-roofed, stone building. Ivy grew over one end.

"Richard!"

"It's been a while."

"An unexpected pleasure."

Launde's mouth twisted ruefully.

"I'm going to Turner."

Masson spat.

Launde looked around. Suddenly feeling desperate.

Masson must have registered a trace of it.

"Come in. Some bread?"

In the woody, smoky, sombre interior there was an impression of a sheen, from polish or from wear, and a pewterish gleam. Launde sat at the heavy table.

"Here."

Masson brought a jug of small beer, some bread and cheese. He watched Launde's hands tremble as he tried to eat without wolfing it down.

"Marion?"

"Well. There are three of us now."

"Of course. Little Ellen. Age three?"

"Five."

Masson pursed. Registered a half sideways nod.

"Something stronger?"

Launde felt the urge to settle in. There were a few logs on the fire. The chill was off the air. It would be easy to succumb. A few drinks. Masson would get lively. He was excellent company when he shook off his natural lugubriousness.

Masson went out back. Launde closed his eyes, remembering.

Here as a youth, Launde had bowled off the meadows, in a group of others after the shearing. They wrestled each other to the ground, and then rolled down the sheep-shorn hillsides. Raw on faces, forearms and necks, from the sun. They tore along the dry rugged cart track past the farm. The sun low. Golden on the sandstone of the outbuildings. The wool heaped for degreasing, then for the spinners, the dyers. The alum for the dyers. Past the hedges with the unripe brambles. Grabbing a handful, careless of the thorns, spitting sour juice. At the yard the lads burst into a run for the inn door and pressed into the opening – seven or eight of them, wedged tight, squeezing in gasping and giggling. He had cricked his neck as, part forcing, part resisting, he pushed under the low lintel and the group sprang into the inn like horses bolting through a left-open gate.

The fire was stacked. Their shadows looped up the walls and encroached on the ceiling. Beer and smoke. The room stuffed with the shearers, the farmers and the villagers.

They packed in the furnace heat of the inn. The throng heaved with boisterous, raucous activity and noise. With drink the earlier fluidity of the youthful coil and slide becoming the wrestling stagger and topple, and torpor.

Marion had been there, delivering something from the farm and she stayed, glancing over at Richard. They knew each other. But this was away from both their homes. She went back into the storeroom. Richard resumed his distracted interest in the group. But he glanced back frequently, seeing nothing.

Later, he had been sick once, but was getting a second wind. He went out the back into the balmy night for a piss. One hand on the wall, leaning he fumbled to re-button. Suddenly Marion was between him and the wall. She kissed him. Once quick, and then full and wide and soft. She pressed her soft warmth against him. The energy surged through him, a shiver and a burst of excitement. He grabbed her using his arms and knees. As boldly, she reached into his partially re-assembled pants and yanked him out, milked him with a few long full fist pulls and he shot out with a gasp. For a second he leaned against her. She squeezed his cock tight a couple of times and then, just as neatly she slipped to one side, brushed off the wet, re-layered her skirts and slipped back inside the inn.

Two other lads came out to piss. The stars were bright. Quickly he made as if to finish and go inside.

"Such a waste of piss," said one youth.

"We could sell it to the works."

"It's worth nothing with all that drink. They prefer the nuns'!"

"So do I. I'd sup it myself from the spigot. They can sell mine back inside here."

Launde reopened his eyes. A bright dust-column of sunlight struck the deep window reveals, and folded over the sill and down the whitewashed stone. Masson had come back into the room, bringing a jug of buttermilk, seeing that Launde needed something more.

"Now, what's your business with Turner?"

"Thomas... we have not been paid for months. The impests fetch half what we've swapped in wages for them in the markets. The measuring is light."

'This is old news."

"The alum gets made. The backers lend more to Turner. The alum sells."

"Only at the rate the smugglers charge!"

"Yes but it sells. Turner is getting it both ways. And giving nothing."

"And the manager?"

"He does his best."

'So I've heard."

Masson's brows lifted imperceptibly.

'Oh God! The whole coast is feeding off that story, and waiting to eat!"

Masson shrugged.

"So he's too busy to go?"

"He's shit scared!"

Masson sniffed.

'Like you."

Launde's anger rose. He was half out of his seat, but Masson laid a hand on his shoulder.

"Fine. So you'll go."

Launde left with some more crusts in his pocket. Masson watched him go. He turned back to the yard and started lifting the slabs.

There were bilberries to eat on the dry slopes. The little blue pills popped like the pockets in the bladder wrack, but these yielded sweetness. Launde crammed his mouth. He kept some for later, and bruised berries among his sweat-dark clothing leaked ink.

He toiled up and over the heathery top from Black Moor to White Moor and stopped at a large upright rock - the Blue Man.

So you are the god of bilberries. The dry unyielding god of this place.

He stared at the mute standing stone, baking in the sun on the treeless moor. Well, drink this. Squashed a few of the bilberries on the stained stone.

I've a few more stones to collect before I get there and Turner will be last.

Launde pictured the setting of the stones from the Blue Man to Fat Betty, the White Cross – the tumuli, the workings, howes, riggs and cairns. Shortly after the Blue Man he drank at a little spring, and slapped water over the left side of his face, the reddening neck and forehead.

For several miles Launde simply shielded the glare of the sun, and tried to keep his feet on the unpredictable sprung roots of the heather. His walk became a labour of footsore, joint-wrenching stumbling, powered only by a low stream of curses.

At Wheeldale Launde was wracked with doubts. Faint and tearful, he lingered listless, feeling far from help or encouragement. He stopped at the stream and drank. He tracked the beck upstream a little way from the ford as far as a clump of rowans. Here, remembering rowan's supposed power, he cut a pliable branch, twisted it around itself to form a stable loop. He slipped this hoop over his hand and up to lodge at his elbow. Thus augmented he scrambled back down to the wath and crossed by the rough boulders placed there.

Launde laboured up to the Roman road. It was hard going, up the steep side into the hot sun. The gravel soil slid under his feet. At last he toiled over the rounded brow and onto the rubble road – which stretched off in both directions. To the south, straight to Rome. To the north, to the Wall. So they said.

The great straight wide spread of the rubble-strewn road marched to horizons. Its significant camber buttressed by the heavy wide slabs of the kerbstones. In a few places neat slab metalling was in place, but generally it was uncomfortably rough walking, with many unstable rocks. Much of the stony underlay was covered in tough heather clumps, or invaded by grasses, and in the boggy hollows, reeds.

A plump dark brown bird stood on a rock ahead of Launde, with its tail towards him. It seemed oblivious as Launde hobbled painfully forward, delicately as possible, on his aching feet. Nearing, he saw its head turned to one side and noticed its startling eyebrows, the colour of rowanberries. He was within a few feet when its sudden single note of alarm triggered a quick fire cackle complaint, its monotonous clatter-rattle, as it flapped clear and landed again some distance away. This happened repeatedly as numbers of dark brown moor birds broke cover ahead of Launde's erratic footfalls.

Mr Carey's theory, Launde remembered - and he seemed exceptionally well informed about most things in the region, for an outsider - had been that the Romans drove through here to clear the wild tribes of that period. A task, Mr Carey had said, indicating a motley collection of alum workers hanging around nearby, they had singularly failed to do.

After the bird flew off Launde rested. He lay back on a large slab of the Roman road, shielding his eyes with his arm. The road had been built, they said, on the line of an older path, that the giant Wade had made for his wife to roam with her enormous cow. Wade lay in his grave near Lythe, that stood now above the alum works there. His footstone stands, a hundred feet from his headstone. That Wade was a horseman, of impressive size, seemed common to all the tales. He was master of the seas over which he came to find his new home, and his boat moved magically beneath the waves.

Launde was drowsing when he awoke sharply to the faint sound of a bell. A train of packhorses was making its way over one of the old hollow ways – silhouetted against the rigg – higher up the bank.

Galloways, thought Launde. About fifteen of the short stocky horses, with wicker panniers, trundled along the track. Launde slid down out of view. He couldn't see the driver, but he wouldn't be too far behind. Moor coal, or lime, thought Launde. Or returning with salt.

The little row of bells on the collar of the lead gal jangled, tongues of solidified shot. Launde had nothing to fear from the drivers but they could be Turner's men.

The gals stumbled over the peppering of hard-baked hoof holes in the track.

Launde kept his head down.

One howe

The captain wrinkled his nose. A fly meandered off. There was an intense smell of smoking fish that mingled with the keen aroma of seaweed drying on the rocks. Warming in the sun after the receding tide. Flies lifted off, regrouped and landed again continually. He leaned on a stanchion of staithe that cut across the narrow fringe of revealed shingle around Whitby harbour. Eyes closed. The warmth intensified. Nameless mental and physical tensions eased out of him and dispersed. All his limbs relaxed.

Eyes closed, a rough dwelling of irregular stones and adobe materialised. In the cleft of the branch and trunk he felt the rough bark through his damp shirt. Against an ochre and green backdrop of baked hillside and chestnut trees he saw his father stride out of the doorway and set off across the land with his shadow at his heels. The stocky figure of his father moved with its barely perceptible limp, across the screen of olive trees, and the cork oaks, that straggled up the hillside behind. Behind his father, from the dark shadow under the hut's lintel his mother emerged and headed into the yard. The hens scattered and regrouped. His mother entered the deep shade under a rack of climbing vines.

From his vantage point high in the chestnut tree the boy looked in the other direction once more. His father had reached the black pigs and, as every day, braced himself to approach them, remembering the bite that had wrecked the muscle and sinew of his left knee. The boy sensed rather than saw his hesitation and self-girding. His father began some task at the fence post. The lower fields shimmered. High above, a black kite circled on the air currents, spying prey. He looked beyond his father, beyond the black pigs, where the escarpment dropped a shoulder to reveal the sea. The boy peered intently into the uncertain blue distance, searching for ships.

"Don't you fucking talk to me."
Pause.
"What?"
"I said ......"
With deliberation.
"What!"
"Just wait a while."
"Fuck...."
"He won't see you."
Pause.
"If you don't calm down, he won't see you."
"I am calm! I can wait. I can grow roots. I can turn to stone here."
The gatekeeper sighed.
"Just wait. I'll tell him."
"What?"
"I'll tell him there's a gentleman to see him. A quiet fellow. Respectful. Hoping to see Mr Turner at a convenient moment. Who has a matter of business to discuss. A tradesman. With a proposition."

Launde had been kept from entering Turner's gates. Hunger made him irritable. His head felt like it had shrunk. He couldn't sit for fear of simply dissipating into the ground, like a meagre watering on a parched plot. He had been waiting over an hour. The sun was low. The shadows slanted over the impossibly green pasture of Turner's grounds, each side of the track from the gate. The long shadows of the horse chesnuts, the deep shade beneath the spread branches.

"Fuck you."

A kind of compassion hovered around the eyebrows of the gatekeeper.

"Fuck you."

Said without malice or fervour.

Several minutes passed.

Launde's anger subsided a little. He could see the man was threadbare. But he could see that the sprinkling of compassion would dry out. He wanted to smash the man to pieces against the gatepost. But Launde never fought anyone. His wife bit him. Threw things. She slapped him violently. The child hammered her tiny fists on him. He turned his anger inwards. A muscle tensed in his throat. His teeth set. His stomach gnawed.

He breathed out slowly trying to calm.

The man smiled.

Launde propped his back against a tree to wait. Allowed his wobbling legs to fold. Sat under the canopy in the gleam of the low sun. Suddenly desperately tired. Eventually he dozed.

He awoke to a violent kick. Scrambling to his feet only to be pushed hard in the chest. He fell back on stones that jabbed into his shoulder blades.

He was unsure who his assailant was. A couple of layabouts smirked. The gatekeeper was absent. Turner was standing back, the last sun was behind him, his face in shadow.

"Sleeping on the job?"

"What?"

"Sleeping on the job. One of my workers sleeping on the job. Miles from the cooling house. Sleepwalking no doubt. Across half the country. A sacking offence, no question."

"What".

"Thank you Mr Launde, by your actions you give me little choice. There are men walking the length and breadth of the land looking for work and you are dreaming Mr Launde."

"No"

"No?"

"No, sir."

Launde dragged himself to his feet. Something was draining out of him. Leaking from his blisters through his cracked soles and into the unsteady earth.

"No sir. Mr Wynter has granted me a day sir. To see you, sir."

"Wynter encouraged you to see me?"

"No, sir."

"So...."

"He couldn't stop me."

Turner just swivelled round and started to walk back to the Hall. The two men yawned. Launde gawped. His arms flapped up raggedly on either side like startled crows. He shouted.

"Listen to me! Listen sir."

Turner never slowed.

"Sir you do us wrong!"

Turner walked.

"You wrong us. Sir, you owe me."

Possibly Turner's walk checked, slightly.

One of the lackeys shoved Launde in the chest, and over. From the ground he raised his head and yelled.

"Turner, you have not the balls to face me. While my child eats mud from your boots. You owe me and a gentleman would hear me out."

Turner had stopped.

They had stopped short of whipping him. But Launde was left in no doubt that violence was just a breath away. They had worn him down with their brutal interrogation and the unfair bargaining that had emerged from it.

He had been forced to accept the triumph of his mission. To secure, but only in lieu of wages, some bags of rye and beets. The corn was weevilled and close to useless. Even this he was unable to take with him and had agreed to return another day. Launde would be in no position to question the measure.

In despair Launde walked south, away from the Hall. He had been offered nothing to eat or drink. Rather than track onto the barren moor top again, he trudged unsteadily down into the head of the dale.

Around the valley a long looping track followed the level shoulder. Rutted with wheel marks, peppered with hoof prints of sheep and pannier horses.

To the west, below the rigg, mine workings dotted the hillside. Above was the inn, he knew. Penniless he turned to face the other way. The eastern slopes were bathed in pale roselight of the set sun, the other side in shadow.

He set out along the dusty trail, painfully slow. In a daze, in the fading light. He felt hollowed out. Outside he was a mere shell, a bruised and dented one, but pain made it a reality at least. Inside he was scoured out by injustice and hurt, but his rage had gone, replaced by emptiness. He was light-headed and free of either purpose or resolve. His feet moved forward, in their turn, of their own accord. Flies buzzed, birds flitted among the heather, never settling.

The long valley stretched ahead. Fields of vegetables and woodland clumps straggled up the lower slopes. Bracken and heather roamed down into it. A few sheep were visible as white forms, on distant patches of pasture, like maggots on mould. Dogs barked, scenting him early and Launde looked for a stick to wield as he skirted solitary farmhouses. Finding none he chose to take a wider path, where the heather slowed and tripped him.

For a spell his bitterness returned and all the things he might have said and done raged in his head repeatedly till he cursed to try and rid them. The jeers and humiliation. If he came across Turner or any of them now he would kill them. Yet a dog barked and his guts turned to water.

After an age he came into an impoverished hamlet – a row of stark cottages, lacking glass in many windows. Beyond them were some crumbling limekilns. At the first, he begged bread. After initial refusal he was given some to be rid. At several the door remained closed. At the last he received water. He ate half the stale crust with the water, gulping it down uncomfortably past his dry throat.

Resuming the track at some point he simply sat. The legs decided, crumpling under him. Later still he awoke with the day gone, swifts wheeling, and a display of cloud which, had he noticed it, evoked the panoply of heaven.

By old priory ruins he cut down the steep bank and moved through the outskirts of Rosedale village, avoiding farm workers that he occasionally spied.

On the other side he trudged up the steep incline and veered south as the trail levelled out on the top towards Hutton.

Blisters and cuts brutalised him from the track, as the light drained quickly from the emptying sky. The clouds soaked back into the marine depth. A cool breeze disturbed the heather tops. The pain displaced the inner hurt, the feet trudged. The body ached but it no longer craved the dry crust. The head was dizzy, the stomach queasy. He refused to stop or rest. A deeply instilled instinct told him that even in desperation this was no place to spend a night.

He passed One Howe Cross, barely noticing, and finally, accompanied by a couple of stars, with little light left, he came down the long path into the village. He moved towards the church above the church.

Through the dark graveyard he flitted, like one of its occupants. Into the porch where he leant heavily against the door whilst lifting the latch, expecting it to be shut firm. Instead it gave, and off balance he tumbled into the chirch, falling heavily on the flags. It was black, but before long his eyes grew accustomed to the first moonlight and by patches of lighter and darker black assumed pews, or space. He kept clear of the crypt – fearing some black stain from the wrong side of history would seep out of it and engulf him. Instead he crept back towards the door where, groping amongst objects on the table beside it, to his surprise found coins on a pewter plate.

These he took, leaving, after a pause, the smallest.

Robbie jabbed the fire. He exhaled sharply, realised his jaw was clenched. He dropped his shoulders, breathing in deep to release the tension, exhaled more slowly.

It clenched.

Come on!

He couldn't risk going out until Liz came back. She might see him and follow. The little opening he had prised, its draught of fresher air carrying a whiff of danger, was swinging shut. He sat with his coat over his knees. It kept the heat off him, except his face. The coals glowed a little brighter under his intense gaze.

Noises outside.

As a premonition of the night air reached him, he heard the door, and rising, turned towards it. A small child entered the room.

It swung shut.

The child looked fearful. Uncertain eyes in the pale emaciated face. Launde's child, Ellen.

"Were you going out?"

Liz came in behind Ellen and, leaning over her, crossed her arms over the child's chest, kissing the top of her head. Liz looked up brightly, the child hesitantly.

Momentarily thrown, Robbie took a step towards them and stopped. Then nodded vaguely in the direction of the works.

"I thought I'd do the round."

"It's hardly necessary."

He sniffed.

"I said you'd tell Ellie a story!"

Shut. Locked.

Liz gestured towards the child.

"Richard has gone missing. His wife is searching."

"Has she tried the Flask?"

"Robbie!"

She smiled at the girl, and moved her towards the seat by the fire. She gave Ellen an oat cake. He noticed how she set to it, and then by force of will slowed down, keeping mouthfuls unswallowed.

She lowered her voice.

"Richard is missing, he didn't come back today."

He watched the girl vacantly chewing the mouthful of mush.

"His wife is out? On her own?"

"Some of the faceworkers are with her. With picks."

Robbie shook a brusque shrug into a gesture of impatience.

"I need to do the round."

He turned to go.

"Where's Ana?"

"What?"

She didn't repeat it.

"How should I know?"

"Maybe upstairs."

"Maybe gone fishing with Mr. Launde."

He spoke sharply – regretting it instantly.

"Robert!"

The girl had twisted round in the chair and leaned over its back, at the sound of her father's name.

"What's wrong with you, Robbie? You don't need to do the rounds, and you should know where Ana is, for the captain. Besides, you usually do know. And Launde is not just your responsibility, I thought he was your friend!"

Robbie hesitated. Exasperated. To do the round? To enquire into Launde? To stay?

He dithered at the threshold.

The threadbare woollen was wrapped tight but the wind unpicked any residual warmth. Ana was very cold. Unfamiliar noises carried in the near pitch darkness.

He's not coming.

In a second she decided to go. Rounded the shed and hurried carelessly across a penumbral yard, with the tun house in silhouette against a scarcely brighter sky.

She hacked up the muddy track, buffeted by squalls. Nearing the manager's house light leaking out cast onto a form of familiar movement. She heard Liz's voice.

"He'll tell you a story when he gets back."

Liz calling back into the house. At the same time lifting Robbie's coat over his shoulders. He stepped out into the enclosure before the house.

Liz on the step. Ana came through the gate.

Robbie thought of some buffoonery at the local fair, or a mocking show, like someone had shoved him onto a stage.

He spoke the leaden script he had been given.

"Where have you been?"

She shrugged.

A lamp flashed in Ana's eyes. Liz's voice came out of the glare.

"Robbie has to do his round."

She walked up the to the step, passed Liz and went in, muttering.

"Mas tarde."

Liz shrugged her incomprehension at Robbie.

He shook his head. He headed in the general direction of the works. Kicking a stone violently into the dark grasses beyond the fence. He stomped off on the now pointless circuit.

Kenelm is alarmed to hear the mingled sounds of crying and retching coming from the direction of the graveyard. He makes haste along the road, as it scoops down to where the wall dips. Sight of the rising bank, thick with upright overlapping slabs, silhouettes in gloom, and their weathered inscriptions. Popping his head over, he can see nothing. He races round to the gateway and from there, passing through, he is startled to see the twisted face. A hunched gargoyle of anguish, eyes squeezed tight, body spasming. The man kneels on a fallen gravestone, his hands gripping its edges as he strains forward towards the rough grass, retching long and hard, ending in a dry cough, producing nothing. Wracked sobs jerk him, and he moans an inner diatribe of woe or grief.

Stopped in his tracks and then instinctively moving towards the shelter of the porch, unseen Kenelm is dumbstruck. Not a little afraid, he watches in consternation and repugnance.

Perhaps the man has a contagion. Seeing someone sick is not unusual but the wretched desolation of the man's inner pain unnerves him. Is he deranged? Has he been beaten? All these likely possibilities flash through Kenelm's thoughts. Finally, summoning his vocation unwillingly, he leaves the lee of the porch column and starts across the open churchyard in the half-light. Still at some distance, hesitantly, he calls out.

"Hello? Can I help? Are you alright there?"

Launde starts like a frightened animal, and then, like one in a trap, seems rooted. He still grips the edge of the fallen slab, but his head turns and his eyes fill with stupefied fear, as if expecting a blow. He flinches, and retches again.

"It's alright."

Hand raised in greeting or supplication.

"I can help."

Launde stricken, swaying and shivering like a wounded dog. Kenelm is almost as afraid. Evening birds twitter. The hot day has subsided into a chill twilight. Kenelm slips his cloak off and holds it out.

Absurdly, the man holds out his hand with coins, offering them. Kenelm, gently, closes the man's fingers over them and pushes his hand back, shaking his head mildly. He lays the cloak over him.

With difficultly, Kenelm supports him and helps him to stand. Gradually, with much stumbling, he leads him out of the churchyard and, having no provisions with him, over the road to the primitive inn, where he pays for bread, soup and small beer.

The man is beyond explaining, almost beyond speaking, but he thanks Kenelm between sipping tentatively at the soup. After recovering sufficiently to tackle the bread, he seems withdrawn and unwilling to converse. He indicates that he will sup and go. The landlord and Kenelm discuss discreetly whether the man is a vagabond, in which case he should be whipped and driven out of the village. However, having some money on him, it is decided not. Kenelm leaves and soon Launde requests strong ale. The landlord decides that with those coins he can stay, and serves a glass.

The gloom has deepened in the inn. Candles are lit and the fire stoked up. It is a tiny tap house and, after a couple of other men enter, it becomes quite jovial. Launde is left to his own for a long time, where he sways and mumbles, but at length others draw him into conversation. Eventually, in the course of a long evening, they extract Launde's story.

He can never return, Launde tells them, over the final round. Even as they depart his eyelids fall, like heavy sacks.

* * *

4

Of honey laden bees...

Crippled symmetry

The dog had its legs bound together and it was strapped to the table. Several assistants held the quivering animal, which emitted high-pitched whimpers that keened into screeches ending in high yelps. Its jaws were partially muzzled in a cane basket with leather straps. The assistants struggled to control the muscular convulsions of the animal as the bellows were forced into the lungs through the removed section of ribs. After emitting metal-edged shrieks, and wriggling in spasm the dog appeared to lose consciousness – its eyes open and glassy. The bellows filled and drained the lungs. The surgeon's hands rummaged among the organs, the lungs and beating heart.

Carey excavated a few layers of his notes and brought to light certain scraps and jottings. Ah yes. Steno had found fossil teeth on a mountainside in Italy. This he felt had given weight to Xenophanes' surmise that fossils were the remains of living creatures. Studying the Tuscan teeth at Florence – they closely resembled shark's teeth - Steno himself proposed that they were evidence of marine life in regions that were, in his time, both inland and raised above the surrounding countryside.

Carey glanced over a different sheet, faint and dog-eared. I must get these written up into a proper journal. Leonardo too – seeing fronds of ferns, comparing fossils with shells on a beach. But what did da Vinci conclude? That the Flood could not have carried the shells to the mountains? How long could this process of petrifaction take? The fossils must be older than the Flood? Antithetical to the church's teaching. Alternative explanations? Placed in the world by Him – as with all things- with deliberation and exactitude. Fully formed and there from the start – waiting to be found. To a purpose yet to be discovered? To be analysed and discussed by scholars and priests.

His discussions with Fox had thrown up some interesting notions, but crudely expressed. In Carey's journals these would be integrated into his own more sophisticated argument.

Carey had cleared a tiny space in the crowded jumble of the tallyman's hut. From the small window he watched the dirty steam curling round itself as it lifted from the alum buildings, expanded and drifted off in the direction of the headland. In obedience to some combination of scientific laws and principles, he thought. Perhaps this is His plan – that over time we will discover His more integrated purpose and come to regard the earlier explanations as the nursery rhymes we learnt as children. Carey felt the familiar thrill of approaching heresy – the combination of guilt and excitement – with which he outraged his colleagues at the Royal Society. Which he also manipulated to increase his reputation, or notoriety.

Shaking off the claustrophobia of the hut, Carey clambered above the quarries and looked down over the long shallow-sloping fields. They flowed from the base of the spoil heaps down to the cliff edge. He observed the straggle of outbuildings that constituted the stubborn boundary of advanced science and manufacturing. The alum industry – its barns and sheds scuttling down the cleft of the wooded gorge, to the brink of the cliff. Its ropes, pack-horses and men going over.

They hang on there, he thought, like the cliff-edge hawthorns. Those ancient deformities, teetering over the verge, their agonised roots clawing into the splintering shale. Their branches leaning back in to land. Old crone's fingers bent imploringly back, callused with berries, stiff with thorns. Limbs dense and huddled, with a folk-memory of survival.

Carey lifted his gaze out to sea. Here the longships came. Their crews learned and adopted cultivation and put down roots in place names, fair-hair, blue eyes. Swapped their teeming pantheon for the one master of work and stoicism. Their grandchildren helped rebuild the little stone minsters, seven hundred years ago, that their grandfathers had toppled.

Beneath them, great reptiles swam. The powerful thrust of their huge tails – they swept under the longships and moved towards the shore like an advance navy.

Long before them, Carey speculated, the monsters had spawned small, like elvers, and fought their way tenaciously up the spurting waterfalls of the cliff wykes. Once on the fertile plateau above the cliffs they grew, fattened on the animals that roamed there, rabbits and voles. Growing larger on wolves and deer. Some grew great three-toed feet whose claw prints, according to Fox, occasionally turned up in the shale. The workmen smashed the infernal prints to powder, with the assent of the local wise-women, and the clergy.

In a second theory Carey had them spawning in the high moorland pools, flushed down to the sea in autumn spate, gaining in size as they go, like salmon. Out of the becks and ditches into the crashing tides that claim them from the rocky foreshore. Once at sea the monsters grow on the teeming underlife of herring and conger.

Once old, and grown unwieldy, Carey imagined, they feed deeper and deeper until they come to some dark oblivion, far below the sun's trickle through watery translucency.

Those that spawned on land, or those that returned there, he thinks, grew heavy and slow. They fell into the hidden tarns and bogs which can still swallow up a careless man easily. They sank into the mud for centuries.

Carey wonders not why God deemed the monsters and their ilk disposable, as the church might have it, but how. Did they grew short of food, like men, as the sceptics might hold? Were they hunted perhaps? He hopes to unearth material for better theories, or to prove these.

Accused of embracing scepticism, even atheism, Carey was fond of quoting Winstanley: "To know the secrets of nature is to know the works of God."

Crippled symmetry.

Carey's assistant was redrawing the monster, re-inspecting it minutely.

From a distance it had the look of a flattened canoe, with a couple of paddles fore and aft. The front slightly larger. Its prow would slide between the steel breakers of the North Sea, its stern tailing behind, to balance and steer.

A second impression was that of some kind of squashed lizard, only on a frightening scale. Blackened and dried in the sun, as if rutted by many cartwheels. Its texture was like old skin, and its backbone, as Carey clearly identified it, was like a vein standing out on the crinkled back-of-hand skin of a blackened corpse. That spine was perhaps the first disturbing thing – it seemed to wriggle with snake life, like a charge of black lightning.

Each paddle was flat, like an oar's, but the surface was covered in dips and ridges, like adzed wood. It was only a step to see the oar's invention, modelled on a flipper, and that flipper stuck awkwardly on the streamlined body of an antediluvian seal.

That skin. He imagined a small child playing with the loose skin over the knuckles of a grandparent's hand, sliding it over the hidden bones, veins and sinews. Its fine etching of lines suggested movement, something fluid, through water. He hatched a semblance with his charcoal. Movement as a forward lunge from the swish of that spine as it resolved elegantly, beyond the hind paddles, into a long powerful tail.

The second monstrous detail that gave the casual observer pause was the hard straight thrust of the prow – that nose or beak, that narwhal-horn pike, that swordfish-strike spearing of its clenched jaw bones.

It seemed to the assistant that the specimen appeared simultaneously in top and side view, slit open and flattened out, spatchcocked and kippered. It gave a semblance of three dimensionality, which he rendered tangible with a little shading. In a few strokes it rose from its slumber and could shuffle forward like a stranded seal, but with menace. He deepened the shading. It stood out in the harsh sun-bleached desert of the page, the dark shadow of itself.

Then the eye socket. The final troubling detail that no sceptic could avoid. A pebble-pit perhaps, that could explain its unsettling stare to the imagination. A rock crater, pressed in by the weight of the rocks. Just accidentally, coincidentally there – between the paddle-shouldered spine top and the serrated blade of the incisive prow. There, where the head would have to be, the predatory brain searching the hostile world with its grotesque fish eye casting pale lamplight in the cloudy depths.

Part by part, patch by patch, he picked over the scorched black form of the monster's surface, shading up its relief, drawing its coastal outline, etching its rutted terrain, its stony outcrop, until a deep feeling of unease crept over him and, with a shiver, he packed up his draughtsman's tools for the day.

"This...monster...?"
She broke off.

"They say it's the Pope's Curse."

A tremor rippled her bare skin. She hugged her nakedness. Shivered.

"Why?"

She crossed herself.

"I shouldn't worry. If the curse is as effective as the one to stop Queen Catherine's annulment."

"What?"

"Fat Henry, after he ditched his Spanish queen, was cursed, he thought, to be without a son. And he chopped the head off the next one. Then later he got a son anyway."

Ana shook her head in good-natured bafflement.

"Y el monstruo....?"

"The Pope's curse on anyone working alum against his own monopoly. Designed to scare off competition. It's a black monster like one of your *moriscos*."

She crossed again.

"One I wouldn't be surprised to hear your grandmother had met."

She scowled at him while she made time to work that one out.

He dodged a slap.

"Well, they mixed in plenty of alum when they tanned your hide!"

He was pleased with that.

Her little fists came for him and he grabbed the thin wrists to check the renewed assault, quickly turned her over and slapped the naked backside. Red rose. A muffled gasp. He slid his hand down past the buttocks and rubbed forward between the legs with the back of his hand, pausing to raise its scent – peaty – to his nose. He returned the hand, to resume with purpose.

She buried her face in discarded vermilion and smothered the sound as her tremors subsided.

Roughly he raised her to her knees and pulled tight into her. A surge of energy and he succumbed to the force of it – arms clasped around both her thighs – yanking back and forth. He grunted as release flooded through them both.

A draught from somewhere fluttered across their sweat and liquids and they both shivered, whether from the baleful stare of the monster, from the Curse, or other fears.

On her own, his light-heartedness evaporated off the stubborn anxiety of the curse.

It's a stillborn curse. So he had said. It was born petrified.

But we should be cursed! She had said.

That had annoyed him but he had quickly softened.

God and his holy wars brought you to me. You don't seem too afraid of *my* monster.

But in the stifling heat of her room she kept seeing the single eye, the all-seeing socket. Sleep either eluded her or troubled her. The monster shifted shapes in her fitful dreams – scavenging dogs worried her, shapes of men in the shadows threatened her, the black shape suffocated her like a heavy cloak, its muscular tail slid up her thighs as if slimy from the rock pools. The heat as if close to the alum pyre. Finally, in the gritty dawn she dragged out to piss painfully, to think about raking the cinders together to start the new day.

Yet again, Carey picked over the corpse carefully. He examined every inch of the skeletal anatomy, taking care to consider the gaps quite as much as the extant fragments. Deliberating how one piece tapered, or flared, towards the next. Or towards the void, towards each space in his conjectured sequence.

He checked back frequently between the actual pieces and the corresponding record made by the assistant. He added scrawled notes, or question marks. Everything must be tested and verified, with theory and exposition. As Hooke had put it: to discover, argue, defend and further explain, everything that is material and circumstantial in the entertainment of the Society.

I have discovered that wily Reynard is not simply collecting the snakestones and toenails but that he uses them to identify a certain shale! The more rounded toenails, like solidified eggs, indicate a rock freer of the 'cementstones' which for some reason are unattractive in the burning process. Octagonal geometries of the 'fools gold' also show up, for some reason more welcome (alchemy!). Goodness knows why the only place in the country where alum shales turn up is this god-forsaken county of bumpkins! Still, more is known than these idiots let on.

Carey knew all the different kinds of adherents to the small, obscure cult of specimen-collecting. He nurtured them all, gathering all their different emphases into his one comprehensive knowledge.

There were those who were the historians of the cult. They would relate how Athanasius Kircher recognised the bones of giant humans, which he claimed in Mundus Subterraneous, were a people that had died out before our own. They would talk about Paolo Boccone, walking in the Sicilian hills with Agostino Scilla, turning over the tongue-stones that the locals used to ward off evil. How he had argued for a scientific explanation.

Boccone identifying plants and flowers. Scilla painting and drawing them. How the tongue-stones were sharks' teeth, which in their lifetime Fabio Colonna, the Neopolitan, epileptic botanist, taking extract of valerian, had also claimed.

Organic matter absorbing earthly particles from solution, to later solidify? Inevitably, they would link their work, hinting as it did to species extinct, to the work of Steno. But they would not overlook that before Scilla, Federico Cesi, colleague of Galileo's, collected Umbrian specimens, stone wood. Which his friend Stelluti assembled as evidence of stone growing from stone, with his drawings and notes. All this the cult historians would present, with self-satisfaction, to the Society.

Besides the historians were the classifiers. They logged the objects formed within the rocks, as made distinct by Steno, separately to those formed outside of the rocks. For this type of cult follower the proliferation of specimens was most important. The more objects grouped the more clearly each group was made distinct.

The diluvianists, turning to Scheuchzer, and his ossified, child flood-victim, floating to the surface in a Swiss quarry, looked to promote evidence of the Deluge. They argued against the Aristotelians – who held that seeds of the living grew in the ground and not only gave forth new living versions of themselves, but the petrified simulacra. These priest-scientists, sermonising to the Society gentlemen.

Carey's colleagues within the cult at the Royal Society, whose predecessors had translated Steno and nurtured Hooke, and published the counter attack by Lister, also cast light on these 'theologians'. The earth had 'shivered' during the Great Deluge, and the world had collapsed into particles and reformed. None of these more recent followers would stomach Kircher's theory, of a few decades previous, that something could become extinct. Not even a convoluted shell, let alone a giant human.

Lister had drawn attention once again to the poor headless snakestones, ammunition to refute Steno.

Most recently Reamur had fought back over the flood, arguing that many yards deep of broken shell, trapped in a rock layer, could never have been laid down during the biblical year of the deluge.

Another cell that Carey nurtured contained no academicians of any flavour. They were simply the collectors. These for whom possession represented the objective. Their motives were various, but ownership was king, with value, one-upmanship, and other self-aggrandisements being natural bedfellows.

Amongst them, once he had bolstered his reputation at the Society with his presentations and publications, would be one to relieve him of keeping the monster pet, for a tidy sum.

Rags to riches – the cloud tatters torn to gold.

Thickenings

Evening. Winter absent from the lab. The assistant, with the manager's permission, borrowing the assay house lamps. Glassware moved to one side. Catching the light. The minister absorbed, watching him.

"How did you learn to draw like that?"

The assistant put down his brush, with which he was highlighting the outer ridges of a snakestone, with white lead.

"Imitation. Of course."

Alcuin shook his head.

"It takes more than that."

"A little perhaps. Hours in the libraries. It was an advantage that my parents' friends tended to have collections of books and manuscripts."

He smiled. He leafed among his papers for a while, and then he produced a sheet, carefully rendered in charcoal on a pale blue ground. Several snakestones and a devil's toenail. Together with some outlines of leaves, or parts of plants. Little squiggles as of foliage between.

"I copied this."

"Beautiful."

"It's Hooke. A sketch really. Hooke was not a patient person. But he captures it. He taught himself to draw well enough with chalk and ruddle. Also, with Hooke it was informed by knowledge. He studied them under his microscope. Looking into the grain and the texture."

The assistant paused, scrutinising the drawing. He handed it to Alcuin.

"Your fellows are a lot to blame."

Alcuin's brows rose.

"Mine?"

"Yes. Of course. Latin scholars. Translating from Greek. *De Materia Medica*. In their monks'cells, reflecting the natural world in the style of your manuscripts. For centuries, waiting for someone to come along and draw things more the way they are. This is all apparent in the libraries. The flat, ornamental style, to augment the words. To tell the story in the pictures too. Then the later styles – closer to the real thing. Now the words can be in English. The pictures only need to show – as it really is.

"Drawing for the block perhaps?"

"Yes. Woodcuts too, copied from the drawings. Engravings, commissioned by royal patrons. After that the adventurers, returning from conquering the far-flung places, bringing back a world of new things. Objects, animals, plants. New species."

"So you copied them too? Who were they?"

"Foreigners, some of them. Still with us today. Recently I met Van Huysum, who was illustrating rare plants for a man called

Martyn. He colours beautifully, in a very natural way. In the libraries however, wonderful works! Besler's sunflower, marvellous engraving! Richly coloured – staring out of the page like Cyclops!"

The assistant looked at Alcuin.

"Sorry – you have to see it really."

Alcuin shrugged.

A change came over the assistant. He lapsed into a ruminative silence, frowning slightly. Alcuin studied his elongated profile, the youthful skin, curling hair.

"I need to be out there, Father."

Alcuin was puzzled.

"Outside? It's dark."

"No. Out there!"

He swept his arm extravagantly, opening his hand at the finish with a theatrical flip.

"Carey is most at home at the Society. He takes enough back to bolster his reputation. Oh yes, I know, he seems very interested here. In fact he is. But his is an accumulating spirit. Everything to be dug up, catalogued, in the cabinet. More importantly, in the paper, in the lecture, in the journal."

"As a mere minister, I don't see the sin in it."

The assistant smiled now.

"You know perhaps that on the Golden Hind were many plants and insects? No matter. Drake brought back all sorts of spoils. Winter's Bark for example - no relation to your surly manager - which is used for scurvy. A certain Frenchman, the grandly titled Charles de L'Ecluse, drew it. It's among his aromatic plants. In his book I mean."

Alcuin listened attentively, wondering where the increasingly animated assistant was leading.

"So you certainly won't have heard of Lionel Wafer, little more than a Welsh pirate, a floating butcher or self-styled ship's surgeon, who nevertheless got himself round Australia with the Englishman William Dampier. Both dead now. Both left books with delightful hand-coloured maps. He brought back a fortune, stolen from the Spanish in various parts of the watery world. Also writings on the plants and animals, as well as varieties of unusual humans! All illustrated by the ship's clerk.

"You know so much."

"Yes, and so little travelled. Only venturing in the libraries. But it's remarkable how one book leads to another. One man's botanical drawings leading to another. One explorer to another."

He paused.

"However, to change, that is my aim. One day to be setting forth on a ship of investigation, artists and naturalists, heading for .... well, for wherever."

"Artists, naturalists, scientists and Quakers no doubt."

"All comers, Father, prepared to look, listen and to record."

Carey joined them in the lab. The assistant settled to drawing quietly.

Carey produced a large crystal and held it up. Its facets caught the light, flashing.

"Father – what about this?"

"It's alum."

"Yes, alum. Beautiful isn't it? An octahedron. Eight sided. Wonderfully compact. Like a great cloud of steam condensed to its dense icy core."

"Eight sided."

Carey interrupted.

"Yes. Eight. Mystical significance?"

Alcuin frowned.

"Exactly. None."

He rotated the crystal in the light, where it sparkled.

"All of equal, equilateral triangles by the way."

Alcuin shifted his feet. Smoothed his cloak over his knees. Carey handed it to him

"Eight sets of three edges. Three in one."

He peered intently at Alcuin.

"Well!"

Alcuin smiled, relaxing. He placed it triumphantly on the table.

"You wouldn't expect something as perfect as that to be an accident!"

"Yes, very neat this. Reminds me of a diagram. A square within a diamond."

He licked his finger and drew on the table.

"At the corners fire, earth, water, air. As the ancients had it."

He refreshed the drying diagram with new spittle.

"Four triangles, and a square. Four equal, equilateral triangles. A flat alum crystal or half an alum crystal or....a diagram of the elements and humours. Between fire and earth – dry. Between earth and water – cold. Between water and air – wet. Between air and fire – hot. Science of the world, Father. In a crystal nutshell."

"This is a backward step, Mr Carey, this juggling of elements and humours. From the perfection of creation back to the Ancients' struggle to understand. Before our Lord."

"Well, perhaps. Then maybe this is a further step backwards?"

Carey opened his palm to reveal a small, tightly coiled, flat snakestone. Both men studied the stone quietly.

The centre was not quite a point. More an absence. A recess. A tube spiralled from it, thickening and therefore raising its girth above the previous encircled. Springing from the tube curved arcs, ridges, like the chevrons on dressed building stone.

"Aptly named...."

Carey raised his eyebrows, breaking the silence.

".... for a coiled serpent."

Alcuin nodded. Carey continued.

"It's a shell isn't it? Made from stone?"

The minister looked sceptical.

"It.... has.... that semblance."

"Very much so, father, very much so!"

He looked brightly.

"But how did this form I wonder? We know how the crystal formed...."

"We do?"

"Ah.... well, at least we know it did so, saw it form in the alum broth, when that liquid was thick enough, heavy enough."

He paused.

"But this.... other. This formed in the rock. Out of the shale. Out, perhaps, of the heavy rock. Perhaps, perhaps.... when the rock formed."

Alcuin shook his head vigorously.

"No, no. When the rocks were made."

"What! This snake? This shell? At the same time as the rocks?"

"Don't put words into my mouth, Mr Carey. Your questions. Your answers. Not mine."

"How then?"

"Made of stone, as you yourself suggest. Admittedly a semblance. Quite why remains a mystery. A curiosity."

"Certainly a curiosity. Certainly I, for one in the scientific world, am curious. Maybe this is not the mystery, but the clue."

Carey had taken his curiosity up to the quarries, in a brisk breeze with spots of rain. Under ominous clouds he tested Wynter with subtle interrogation.

"This 'laying in' of the shale, Mr Wynter, seems a tedious business."

Carey was picking over the pile of recently excavated mine, as suggested by Fox, to see if any other monsters, large or small, whole or in parts, were lying there. The shale would shortly be barrowed clear to a further heap, to be left to mature before steeping. The 'laying in,' Wynter explained, allowed the weathering to start to break down the shale. Regarded as important to allow it time. A source of frustration to Carey.

"There is no urgency to process this stone. And nature is the labourer here, which is a very economical workman."

Carey nodded.

"Agreed. But surely a certain through-put, a minimum level of production must be required to keep above the break-even point?"

"There is supply and demand."

"But there are many fixed costs, and no doubt substantial investment to repay. So a certain output of alum would be needed to ensure profitability."

Wynter kicked over a few slates, flipping them with his toe. Carey glanced at them for patterns or shapes. Wynter scrutinised them for alum potential.

"Whose profit would that be then?"

Carey raised his eyebrows.

"Point taken, Mr Wynter. Nevertheless, this mouldering and soaking business intrigues me. Is it not the mark of our era to have improved on nature? I am no philosopher, but if I was I would be looking to transmute my stone more sharply than this, this...laying about."

Wynter shrugged.

"Vitriol, for example."

The manager waited. Carey sensed some interest.

"Vitriol. The medieval philosophers considered it the secret salt of purification. The glassy salts that burn by liquefaction."

"With what success Mr Carey?"

"Ah no, in gold, probably none. In making copper from iron, little more. But in making a reaction much success. In solving, quite spectacular. In your steeping pits I'll wager it would save much time."

"Hopefully no-one will fall in."

Carey chuckled.

"Yes. That would surely change the recipe. *Modify* the results."

Wynter smiled too, and they were silent awhile. The sound of crunching on the shale piles, from their boots. Carey struck up his theme again.

"As a laboratory man you will no doubt know that nitre will burn too."

"Yes. To what purpose?"

"Well, one of your local men was in with Fawkes was he not?"

"They say."

"Chaloner himself wasn't it? The local champion and founder of the alum trade hereabouts?"

"There is a confusion with his son, but no. No. It was Percy. After the discovery, a musket stopped him. Stopped Catesby too."

"I see. Well anyway, in the plot, a fuse of nitre would have been to the purpose. Of course this was always made with that most useful by-product – urine. And whether decomposed over straw and compost or dung and wood ash, would at some point be crystallised for gunpowder. A quick way perhaps to quarry the shale."

Wynter shook his head.

"Yes, it would be, but here the land slips frequently. It often catches us unawares. Think how your monster freed itself. Twisting in its bed it wrestled free of the rock which fell away. Fortunately no workmen were buried that day. Your monster came back from the dead, not too completely decomposed, and certainly not blasted to smithereens."

Carey acknowledged this with a curt nod.

"Coming back to vitriol then. The alchemists' elixir was *aqua fortis*. Their 'strong water' made as you will know, from mixing alum and vitriol. Adding the nitre, the *sal petrae*, and increasing the gravity, much as you do with the alum liquor."

"Go on."

"So here we have a whole family of assailants for your stone that would be more effective than water. Vitriol, saltpetre, aqua fortis."

He paused again. Stooped to pick out a fern impression, delicately incised on a shale fragment. Shale settling under his feet as he stretched up again, simultaneously pocketing it. Addressing the manager again.

"Faster dissolution, smaller quantities of liquid, quicker production, less labour, more profit. Those you alluded to, who profit, need not know. Lay off a few souls. They will hardly be worse for it from what I see. Give yourself more time in that cosy little lab of yours."

"It sounds neat, Mr Carey, very neat."

Carey nodded to acknowledge.

"And we can make vitriol from the process, although not in much quantity – and being the corrosive stuff it is, not easy to store. It would soon burn a hole in our pockets."

Wynter realised that this was unconvincing. He tried another tack.

"But this is an industry where innovation is avoided."

Carey raised an eyebrow.

"Surely not! Why would that be?"

"First – it always needs subsidy, and money is not flowing in this business. I can only buy what Turner will permit."

"He will not sanction the production of vitriol? Even though the sulphurous gas off the heaps already rots the worker's rags?"

"He will not invest in any improvements, because – so it is rumoured – the new London investors' money is simply being siphoned off in small increments to pay back something to the old investors."

"My God, is that true?"

"Who knows."

"But surely, that is building on sand? It's another Bubble, waiting to burst."

"No one will question the laying out of the cards, while the pack stands."

"And you?"

"Where else can I go?"

Carey frowned. This was not just troubling, it was bordering on scandalous. He had a thought. If the work stopped, then the free excavation of monster-bearing cliffs would also cease.

Oh this conjuring with the egg! Showmanship? Some 'red herring' – they eat them round here – or deliberate obfuscation. It sinks in the mess of stinking ordure, bubbling in the vats like witches' brew – where the place? upon the heath! – and then after a certain amount of boiling and tipping in of the weed and the urine, my God! the head scratching, frowning and general tossing in some for luck – lo and behold up comes the egg, cooked no doubt – no man would taste it – though a fresh one is essential to start – and this is the signal for the dirty crystals to start appearing out of nowhere!

(Later note – I have gleaned that there is some tinkering with weights and measures going on behind the scenes, while the egg is served centre stage, but to what to end I have yet to fathom).

Carey addressed the owner.

"I have been doing some research into this alum business with Society friends of mine and it reveals a remarkable history."

"Does it?"

Turner's impatience palpable.

"Yes – from ancient Egypt to Greece, and Rome. Fortunes have been made...."

"And squandered."

"Naples, Milos, Venice, Tolfa...."

Turner puffed his cheeks out.

"And nearer to our time the fortunes made in the mercantile houses of the Low Countries. Of Antwerp, Ghent, and Bruges. Thousands of tons of alum brought to here. The same of English wool, Flanders cloth, exported – to Florence, to Venice. Tyrian Purple, kermes, cinnabar...."

"Yes, yes.... all controlled by the Papal monopoly until thankfully Henry had to find someone who would give him a male heir."

Carey was exultant.

"And now it's here! Great cliffs stuffed with alum. Of all places – in this godforsaken, backward..."

"Oh yes?"

"Well – I mean to say – this glorious history come down to a few ragged Yorkshiremen scrabbling away in as remote a part of the kingdom as you would find from sailing the globe...."

Turner folded his arms.

"Mr Carey!"

Carey stopped sharply, mid flow.

"It's my leniency that you are on this site. The enterprise can be fragile as it is in this market, without you dabbling. As you rightly say, a few thousand years of refinement has gone into perfecting this procedure and we don't need your reckless experiments – diverting the men from time-honoured methods, and promoting expensive and dangerous materials!"

Carey speechless with exasperation, but Turner wagged a forefinger in front of his nose.

"You are in danger of overstepping your bounds here. Now you kindly stick to your old bones! Or I will find a glue maker for them in a trice, mark my words!"

Carey crafts the letter carefully to his Society colleague:

My dear friend, please keep these contents and this letter to yourself entire. But I must tell you something of my activities in this inhospitable, wild and god-forsaken place! This much I can tell you now, a hunch perhaps, but a strong one. As I wrote to you before, I have been piecing together their so-called monster (though monstrous it is indeed!) This unparalleled organic specimen of so extraordinary an 'animal' measures 15 feet in length, and 8 feet 5 inches" across the paddles. The neck is 6 feet 6 inches long, inclusive of the head. Along the multiplicity of 'fossil petrifactions' (as I call them) discovered in the neighbourhood of this place, this by far surpasses all, even indeed it is questioned whether any 'fossil' remains were ever discovered equal to that of this wonderful specimen of the tribe. The specimen is almost entire, without I believe, more than a small number of joints wanting, and very cleverly excavated (if I may say so myself) from the strata in which it was found. Perhaps there has been no animal created of a more extraordinary form than this. In the length of the neck it exceeds the longest necked birds. (If I can be sure where the neck ends and spine begins - which I intend to be). The trunk of the body equals the length of the tail and matches the head and neck combined. The head is enormous, with huge eye sockets. Its beak furnished with rows of vicious teeth. From the whole physiology of the animal, that it was aquatic is evidence from the form of its paddles; that it was Marine is equally so, from other remains with which it can be associated; that it may have occasionally visited the shore, the resemblance of its extremities to those of the turtle, may lead us to conjecture. Its motion, however, must have been very awkward on land. It may I believe be concluded that it swam up on or near the surface, darting down powerfully at any fish which happened to swim within its grasp.

Of honey laden bees....

Carey's late-flowering interest in the science of alum manufacture, had led him to a close inspection of each trade, visiting the cooperage and smithy, observing the specialists in lining, hoop-rolling and tempering.

There had been unusual activity in the cooperage and the tun house. Soon enough a new cask – identical to others in planking and end-plates, in hooping and caulking - appeared in the tun house.

It was never baptised in liquor, nor crystallised out its body shape. Never packed its truncated torso with alum flour. Its contents were installed furtively, and it held an awkward cargo. Certain items were not only awkward and heavy, but brittle too. Wrapped in cloth, padded with wood shavings, and set carefully in a sand base. Each part was marked with a chalk number, before wrapping. Each cloth parcel tied with twine. Each parcel carefully separated from its neighbours, and yet in such a way that, filled between with gently tamped down ballast of sand, each helped to stabilise the others.

They said that if the manager noticed, he thought little of this. More likely he had not noticed. After all, they said, he had other preoccupations.

It was marked how often he seemed to be just rounding a bend in the lane, or coming back from beside the barns, or strolling back from the overgrown wyke, with a vermilion flag at his shoulder.

Men joked that out at sea ships would spy the manager, with the red banner, and assume it was time to approach with contraband. Or simply misread the light and be smashed on the scars. Some saw the flag fluttering on the cliff, others at the quarries. Sometimes between the works and the cottages. In an upstairs window of the manager's house. Others claimed that, for its frequency of flying, its variety of location, foreign armies, pirates, would assume a legion of trained bands, or military garrisons, or beacons linking defences, and would fear to invade.

Men surmised that if, on a particular day, the red banner was flying, then the management of the works was reliant on the diligence and skill of those working in the various sheds and houses. And this reliance seemed to be shouldered most responsibly. Because in certain buildings and places work-rate and productivity seemed to rise when the flag was abroad. Sparks flew in the forge, hammers rang. Carpenters sawed and planed.

On the whole these men were few, and circumspect. Cash, unusually, rather than poor commodities, had bought not only their labours but also their confidentiality. In addition, fear of the purpose had to be financially overcome.

Women noticed, and said nothing. Other women, smirking, nudged each other. Word spread, among the kelp leachers, local spinners and dyers. A grain of it stained the cloudy view that Liz beheld. Smoke drifted from that prospect. At last she saw sense of certain behaviour among the women. At last, saw red.

As a matter of course, the tallyman strayed infrequently into the lower world, preferring the rarefied air of the quarries, or the introspection of his hermitage, the hut. He had not inspected the monster for some time, since Carey had ordered the covering with tarpaulins of the enclosure. Edged with planks propped on end, with driven wedges. Strapped and roped, overlaid with more planks, and all weighed down against the flapping wind that tried to tear it off. This formidably lashed, loaded and tightly secured edifice deterred even the tallyman.

The fall in the yield, the rationing of the barrow loads, and the frequent trips to the old quarries kept the tallyman occupied. Monitoring the excavations, inspecting the spoil or tussling with exactly how to represent all this in his ledgers kept Fox busy.

Liz had a coy look in her eye. She tested him with her desire.

Robbie had scarcely entered the house. He sat in the chair and she pulled his boots off.

"I was thinking of you just now, handling the egg."

Her mood was in stark contrast to his, of barely concealed anxiety. He smiled weakly. In their recent lovemaking she had complained that he seemed distant. He looked vaguely in the direction of the table.

"I'm a bit peckish."

"Not as much as I am."

Lifting her skirts.

She tugged apart his breeches and pulled out his cock, sucked it a couple of times and planted herself on him. Fidgeting to encourage the reluctant distension. Fucking awkwardly and slow until he stiffened, and then hard and fast till they came.

'You took your time today.'
Almost gloating.
'Weren't you in the mood?'

"Where does this line of enquiry appear to take you?"
Alcuin had listened in silence for some time as Carey had fleshed out the outline of his account of the monster.
Carey leafed through his papers.
"Father, this is what the great Leonardo wrote."
He turned to a passage and read, in his own translation.

In the mountains of Parma and Piacenza multitudes of rotten shells and corals are to be seen, still attached to the rocks. And if you were to say that such shells were created, and continued to be created in similar places by the nature of the site and of the heavens, which had some influence there – such an opinion is impossible for the brain capable of thinking, because the years of their growth can be counted on the shells, and both smaller and larger shells may be seen, which could not have grown without food, and could not have fed without motion, but there they could not move.

And if you say that it was the Deluge which carried these shells hundreds of miles from the sea, that cannot have happened, since the Deluge was caused by rain, and rain naturally urges rivers on towards the sea, together with everything carried by them, and does not bear dead objects from sea shores toward the mountains. And if you would say that the waters of the Deluge afterwards rose above the mountains, the movement of the sea against the course of the rivers must have been so slow that it could not have floated up anything heavier than itself.

Alcuin sensed the drift of this, but he repeated his question.

'Still. This takes us.... where, exactly?'

"Forward, Father."

Adding gleefully.

"Farther forward, Father, forward!"

Alcuin shook his head ruefully. Carey spoke fervently.

"And faster. That's where we're headed. I'm headed, we're all headed. You only have to look around you. Well, perhaps not here, but the wider world of science, of machinery and organisation. Exploration, discovery. Understanding."

"Perhaps."

"Not here I admit. In this primitive business they seem to muddle on in the old ways decade after decade. Nevertheless, in organisational terms its effective. Just look at the topography!"

"Yes, the whole place wrecked, stripped bare."

"I've heard Father, of your complaint about the spoliation. But we must move on. Frankly, it's impressive. More than impressive. For fifty miles the whole edge of the country reshaped, modified, excavated, removed. By hand! By a few hundred impoverished souls. The whole coastline levered off and tipped into the sea!"

Alcuin frowned.

"My venerable predecessor at the Society. You will have heard of him. Robert Hooke. His legacy, and those of others that followed, is a single-mindedness of purpose."

"Yes. Your assistant showed me his snakestones. Impressive."

"The least of it. The stones impressed Hooke, and he was criticised for what he made of them. As we will be criticised still. At my school - he was there too, you know? - they would hold him up as inspiration for us schoolboys. He could have become a minister, did you know?"

"Really?"

"Oh yes, like his father and brothers. His father would have wanted it. But then he hanged himself."

"My God! Hooke?"

"No. The father. So they say. But Hooke took himself in another direction. The scholars were determined to extricate a fuller understanding of God's world, and the ministers were to teach it. Which is where you come in perhaps?"

"Perhaps."

"Oh, Hooke's ambitions were varied. He branched out into every field. Provoking much jealously, not only at the Society."

"From his fellows?"

Carey laughed. He swilled the grounds round in his drained cup.

"Oh yes! But that is not at all unusual at the Society. A gathering of the mistrustful, envious and cantankerous! Of course he was an irascible man, but a brave one. He wouldn't let torturing a few dogs stand in the way of progress. Quite right too. We will be harvesting the benefits of Hooke's boldness for many a year while we try and knock this century into shape."

Sharks' teeth, thought Alcuin, and the title of Steno's book, mentioned to him by Carey.

'Forerunner to a Dissertation on a solid naturally enclosed in a solid.'

A stone within a stone.

It made him think of the church within the church. A cave within a cave.

As Carey had told Alcuin, Steno had given up science, taken a vow of poverty and, starving himself in the process, despite being made a bishop, attained the next world prematurely.

"Of honey-laden bees I was first born, but in the forest grew my outer coat, my tough back comes shoes, the leather thongs, an iron point in artful windings cuts a fair design, and leaves long twisted furrows like a plough."

Carey's assistant handed Alcuin's book back to him.

"An easy riddle, for a book, but perhaps not for this one."

Alcuin flipped over the pages.

"No, but perhaps they had grand intentions for this book. The bindings would have been last. This book is incomplete. Hardly started."

"Yes, it seems the intent was there."

The assistant gestured to take the book back. Alcuin continued.

"My father's friend told me the inscription would have been copied, many times, from older manuscripts. Other riddles would describe the preparation of the vellum, or the making of reed pens and quills."

The assistant turned to the brief written text, its solitary paragraph with one illuminated capital. The sketched outline of a second capital heading up intended further lines that were never inscribed. The assistant attempted to read a few words.

"Ród wæs ic aræred; ahof ic ricne Cyning."

"Sadly, I don't know how to say it either. Nor how to read it. I was, however, told what it says."

He recited.

"As a cross I was erected; I raised up the mighty king."

The assistant leafed through the mainly blank pages. Here and there were strips of paper tucked in bearing, presumably, Alcuin's hand.

"These are your writings?"

Alcuin flushed.

"I have not the confidence to add them to the book yet."

"But you have a few drawings."

"These faint lines I have dared."

The assistant studied the sketch of the hand stone. Alcuin blushed, from some memory, and knowing the assistant's draughtsmanship.

"Can I read?"

Alcuin nodded.

"How frightful it will be when all the wealth of this world will stand waste even as now variously throughout this world walls are standing swept by the wind, covered with hoarfrost, the buildings ruined...."

"Good stuff!"

The assistant adopted a mock solemn expression.

".... if a little gloomy."

"This I translated from the Latin, but I believe its origin is English, it would have been in the old script."

The assistant was scrutinising the pigmentation of the partially-infilled decorative capital.

"The colours are still bright."

"It may not be old."

"Though it wishes to be."

Alcuin smiled.

"They used alum, according to Father Kenelm, but only to size the pages, not to fix the paints."

"No, these they would have made with egg white, or perhaps with fish glue. The colours from plants, like madder. They ferment the root. They would have used the local flowers or roots. Rhubarb even, for red. They did sometimes use alum, boiling it up with lye – leaching it from the wood ash. Or piss – as used in everything! These they could mix with egg white."

"Wild madder we have, they call it bedstraw, and use it for that purpose. It's yellow."

"That is surely something else. But they would have found their own colours – just as our ancestors used the indigo woad.

They would have used metals too. Hanging copper in vinegar. Or lead. They hung it over their piss and buried it in a dung heap."

"Really?"

"Of course. They scraped off the crust and ground it down."

Alcuin fell silent. Feeling inadequate. Not sure what to add. He covered his uncertainty by taking up the book again and peering at the pigmentation in the decorative capital. Finally he ventured a remark.

"The colours overlap."

"Yes, they would have made the colour in layers. More layers for more intensity."

"Then they would have stitched the pages together."

The assistant, puzzled by a page of dark cross-hatchings, crossings-out and incised charcoal slashes, frowned. He flipped through the remaining pages, all of them blank. He suddenly brightened.

"Father Alcuin. I think you should draw. And write. Blank pages have no tales to tell."

Alcuin smiled, stowing the book.

After parting from the assistant Alcuin walked in the deepening dusk along the cliff edge path. There was no moon but the stars started to spark up in a darkening blue sky. Alcuin stopped and squatted, resting his back against a stone wall. He looked out beyond the indistinct cliff edge, listening to the rising and falling cadence of the sea's murmur.

Gazing at the multiplying stars he though of Caedmon, hymning how he *"wrought first for the race of men Heaven as a rooftree."*

Alcuin watched the interlacing branches of the tree, fruiting with stars. The fragment in his book told of how another tree was attacked, felled and brutalised. Lopped, uprooted, it was bound to the man, the man strapped to it. Carrying the king. Carpenters' nails clenched in their teeth, odd job men, hammering in the nails.

A pagan tale, thought Alcuin. The king strapped to the log.

Like the midsummer rituals. Keeping the oak burning. Drawing the figure of a man on the oak. The green king of the groves. As men cut the oak, lopping the limbs to the trunk. Willow thongs bind the wrists and ankles of the naked young man to the log. In some versions the log is whipped. In some the man is sacrificed, beaten, flayed, blinded, castrated and dismembered on the oak log altar. The blood sprinkled for renewal and fertility. So they said. Long ago. No longer sacrificed, no longer tied, whipped and killed. The dream song in his book recounts, he sees, his own king, crucified. His king and the pagan king, tied to each other, oak to oak.

Barrowman and general labourer, Peter Hogg lifted the pail with its few meagre coals from the ground and, rising, twisted to shift it onto his shoulders. Sudden pain knifed through his spine. He checked awkwardly and staggered, dropping the pail. Coals rattled out onto the gravel.

"Argh!"

A bolt of shock and fear surged up from his hips to shoulders, wrapped in the pain, but in a split-second outdoing it, twisting up through his backbone.

"No. Fuck. Fuck!"

Sweat broke out, wind-chilled instantly. He couldn't stand straight. Pain coursed through like a rill in spate. He twisted and in an agonising effort made himself upright, tried to step forward but the spasms intensified.

"Fuck!"

No, he thought, no, no. I have to work. Not now.

A slight breeze rolled the pail gently on the gravel, taunting its lightness.

Gingerly he explored the vertebrae with his fingertips. Nothing seemed displaced but he felt sure something had slipped out of kilter. Still and slightly stooped, it subsided a little, but try and move and it stabbed back.

A sudden image wriggled into Hogg's mind with the illumination of a lightning bolt. The obscene black twister of thick snaking ossified rope that suggested itself as the monster's backbone.

The curse.

Hogg's fear redoubled. There was no one in sight. Tentatively, gasping and swearing as palliative, he tried edging forward. He had a strong conviction that if he fell down he could not rise. At the same time he could not imagine how he could achieve a crouching position, let alone lie down if he wanted to.

There was no alternative and, sweating and chilling, his jaw clamped, he shuffled forward. Pathetically, with minimal shuffling kicks he slowly rounded up the stray coals and tapped them into the fallen pail. Finally, after a few attempts when the coals slid out again he managed to flip the bucket back on to its base. Then he looked around for a stick and seeing none, limped over to a hazel. After much agonized riving, he returned with a ripped-off branch that near the base held a twig-snapped stub. With this makeshift stave he shouldered the pail by its handle.

After an age he approached the cottages and saw his perennially pregnant wife.

"Sara...!"

Constantly amazed at her ability to conceive, Hogg noted her heavy gait as she came over, frowning. She would fall with child if a cloud simply strayed across the face of the moon.

"Peter?"

He saw his anxiety mirrored in her face.

"It just went".

She took the pail.

"How bad?"

He shrugged, but that triggered a flinch.

"I'll know tomorrow, I suppose".

She noticed the strained, bloodshot, watery look in his eyes that spoke of pain.

He moved forward again, in small steps, using just the toe of the right foot, on the side where the pain was deepest, just above the right buttock.

A hint of something in her look made him question her sharply.

"What?"

She resisted his demand, muttered vaguely.

"Something had to give."

She thought of all the shale shovelled, barrows filled, trundled, as Hogg worked to capture the thin spoils of extra piecework.

She was surprised by the vehemence of his response.

"It's that fucking monster!"

The cask

"Mr. Fox, you know time is running out."

In the hut, Fox and Carey talked quietly, intently. Fox smoked. Carey nurtured, as ever, his poisonous coffee.

"There is rumour everywhere of unease about our specimen. The imbeciles blame it for every bad fortune – from inclement weather to gumboils, their employer's avarice to their wife's lack of interest."

"They will not do anything."

"The manager keeps the lid on it for now. But it will blow."

Carey scratched his cheek, drilled a finger into his ear and rummaged around.

"There is someone..."

He paused.

"Someone who will happily acquire our friend Reynard. This is unusual. Many interested parties care not to associate themselves with this.... this underground world."

"Others will?"

"Yes, to some the esoteric nature of these specimens, their ripeness for controversy, adds value."

Fox nodded.

"What about you Mr Fox? Do you see creatures from the Flood? Extinct reptiles? Conundrums from Him, waiting to be solved?"

He glanced skywards, and back to the tallyman.

"I don't think about that. That's for others."

"Money?"

"Interest, sir. They fascinate me, and they have their own... beauty."

Outside, shouts of workmen, noises of spade and pick.

Inside, conspiratorial gloom.

"We have to spirit him away. The owner must not know. He is not a man to let anything of his walk. Mr. Wynter however, with your persuasion, can come to a price."

"What price?"

Carey removed his glasses, looking slightly lost without them as he wiped them absently with his handkerchief. Back on, his gaze snapped back instantly. He tapped the side of his nose.

Propped up on pillows, in Fox's bedroom, in the tallyman's cottage which had been allocated to him and the assistant. Fox temporarily elsewhere. Carey unfolded the paper that he carried with him. To bolster his resolve, just before he gutted the light, he read the familiar words, transcribed from the Society's annals, in his own hand.

The other experiment (which I shall hardly, I confess make again, because it was cruel) was with a dog, which by means of a pair of bellows, wherewith I filled his lungs, and suffered them to empty again, I was able to preserve alive as long as I could desire, after I wholly opened the thorax, and cut off all the ribs, and opened the belly. Nay, I kept him alive above an hour after I had cut off the pericardium and the mediastinum, and had handled and turned his lungs and heart and all the other parts of its body, as I pleased. My design was to make some enquiries into the nature of respiration. But though I made some considerable discovery of the necessity of fresh air, and the motion of the lungs for the continuance of the animal life, yet I could not make the least discovery in this of what I longed for, which was to see, if I could by any means discover a passage of the air of the lungs into either the vessels, or the heart; and I shall hardly be induced to make any further trials of this kind, because of the torture of this creature: but certainly the enquiry would be very noble, if we could any way find a way so to stupefy the creature, as that it might not be sensible.

There came a daybreak which failed to reveal the world. Mordant fog has seeped into the rimmed pan of the vale, spilled over the brow's thorn-edged rim into the dust craters of the quarries. Flowed over the headlands and down into the wykes, like fumes over the lip of a laboratory flask. Filled and thickened into the spaces between glimpsed grey gables of silent sheds. Stuck between the branches of ash-stricken trees, which line an ash-strewn track. On which, dampened slow and heavy sounds of hooves and wooden wheels, suggested a source, a thickened, darker smudge amongst the white enveloping fleece of roak. A smudge of movement, smothered. A smudge that diminished, and paled, whitened into itself as a contaminant, diluted to invisibility. Muffled sounds faded with it.

"Gone?"
"Yes sir."
"When!"
The tallyman was astonished.
"It was early Mr Fox. They said before light."
"This morning?"
"No. They said it was yesterday. Yesterday morning. A cart, sir, with galloways."

He blinked. Yesterday was a blank. He struggled to remember. Fret. Yes, it had squatted all day, and he had not left his hut.

"And a driver?"
"Yes, of course. With a driver. Mr Carey and the other. On the cart behind the driver."
"Extraordinary."

Fox was moving papers around as he spoke. Cloaking his confusion in acts of ritual. Tidying the ledgers. Stacking them. Fussing with the quill. He bustled about in his hut as much as space would allow. The barrowman moving occasionally, trying to keep out of the way.

"On the cart was something like a tun, sir. A cask."
"A cask?"
"Yes."
"An alum tun?"
"Something like..."
"Why?"

The man lifted his shoulders, and dropped them. He went on.

"On its side, they said. Wedged, presumably, to stop it rolling. Wedged and roped, and covered with a tar. Then more ropes over the tar."

"They saw all this?"

He was still battling to get this information to register.

"In the dark?"

The barrowman paused.

"Well.. they said..."

He hesitated.

"That's what they told me. Well, told him that told me."

Fox bustled past the barrowman and suddenly into the harsh bright sunlit day outside. The mist had evaporated overnight, leaving awful clarity.

"Come!"

He rushed over to the contraption of tarpaulins, planks and stones, pushing aside the ropes and guarding.

"Give me a hand here! Get that cover, lift these stones."

It took a little time to remove the top layer of weights and planks. Fox threw aside the tarpaulin and kicked away the props and framing.

He stared into the empty pit.

Fox realised bitterly. So, the monster was smuggled out in a barrel. The way, it was said, that Chaloner had smuggled the German workers in, to start the work that had provoked the curse. It had conjured up the monster. Now spirited away.

The manager leaned back on the inside of the hut door, closing it, and stayed put, waiting for the tallyman to explain. Fox lifted his face from the ledger, dropping the pen and casting Wynter a concerned and anxious look.

Fox and Wynter had agreed a price with Carey. Half now, and half later. This 'later' was to be consequential on Carey making his sale. Nothing had been mentioned about timescale. Carey had paid the half. It was not a big sum, but useful to men with little.

However, seeing that Carey had gone almost immediately, they now thought over the deal with more care. What if it is years before he sells? What if he never sells? What if he barters? These unanswered, unasked questions preyed on their minds. They know they have no idea what Carey might get. It was irrelevant to the deal. Even so, they would not want to be thought idiots. Now they realised, that could be the last they would hear of Carey.

Wynter was grim. Fox fuming. While not exactly warm, Carey and he had at least established an acquaintance built on mutual interest. Or that's how it had seemed. The assistant had been even more amenable. However, he had vanished too.

They were also left with a problem. It was not theirs to sell.

Fox was incredulous.

"Smuggled him out in an alum tun. The same way Chaloner brought the foreign workers in, with the alum mystery, to begin this whole sorry business, all those years ago."

"How appropriate."

Fox bridled. Wynter tried to appease the tallyman.

"Foxy, at least that solves one problem. Back to the newer quarries. Start digging, find its mate."

They both knew that they had been told to cut back on new quarrying.

Fox knew that a monster of that pedigree was a once in a lifetime find.

As the late afternoon blues into twilight, a languid flap of wings. The floating moon of the white owl's face drifts across the purpling valley.

Wynter pulled the front door of his cottage shut behind him. He sat down on the upper of the two sandstone steps, and leant back against the panelled wooden door.

It was a soft evening and, in the pinkish blue light, except for a few songbirds, unusually quiet. A long doughy loaf of fog lay over the headland, and the ember-red disc of the sun had cooled and set. A swirl of greyish contaminant surrounded the bright gleam of the higher clouds and in front of this a few worn-out dishrags of grey drifted over.

A sharp clipped-off fingernail of moon.

With a decent meal inside him, the slight breeze failing to chill the last of the day's warmth, his mind was free of focus, with a kind of relief.

He was absorbing the landscape rather than observing it. As the gloaming deepened a couple of small bats dipped and dived. Visible against the remains of light in the sky, hidden when they dropped below the horizon.

Straight ahead the stone path led directly the short distance to his gate. If he went in a straight line down the path, through the gate, and kept walking and walking, and never came back.

Fog and straw

Dusk. Lights along the scores of wharves and jetties illuminated the shadowy figures of workmen. A constant activity among the crates and barrels on the shore, on both sides of the river, as he steered downstream of the Pool of London. Lanterns in the purple twilight. Soft pin-points of indrawn pipe glow. He saw the last daylight drain through a gauze of rigging. The jagged outlines of pegs and stumps that were the roofs and gables of the riverside buildings, the ragged skyline. Shouts and banging, muffled and sharp, drifted to him over the slapping water. Growing fainter as he moved into the wider waters of the estuary, relishing the fresh wind that scoured the sharper edge of the piss smell. The much-scrubbed decks that, saturated as they were from years of the trade, refused to give up their stink. The boat would be invisible from the banks he thought, but anyone downwind would be certain what kind of cargo was passing.

Dark cloud massed above. Remnant light only, low down port-side. Heading out into the sea, there was no one else on deck. Not many hands needed to run a chamber lye ship to Scarshead. Felt his customary melancholy creep – a wistful peace, languor and loneliness.

He thought of Ana. He missed her, though her presence was often disconcerting. Where had this mysterious child of theirs come from? Physically so like her mother, but with another temperament entirely. Ana would be dull, dark for long periods, then smoulder a bit, glow intermittently, then flame. She would gather rumbling storm clouds around her for hours, days and then rip them apart with the bright piercing ray of her own smile.

Ana at Turner's works, a useful temporary arrangement? Something nagged at the captain. He peered into the gloom ahead of the boat, as into an uncertain future.

She was naked at the window, looking out. Robbie was standing behind her. The rough wool and leather of his clothing on her back and thighs. His bare forearm came round across her small breasts and squeezed them back tight. His lips and teeth pressed down on the hard neck muscle and his hand plunged into the sudden wetness between her legs. Quickly and forcefully he oiled and rotated her swollen cam till she gasped and with startling suddenness trembled up from the toes and subsided. In a few moments, with both hands widespread flat to the wall, leaning forward to the wall she pushed back. He fucked her extravagantly with slower and slower movements until speeding up he withdrew at the last moment and splashed up on her taut back, where it trickled down the muscled trough of her spine and into the buttock cleft.

"No more than six Boiling Pans."

Wynter slapped his palm down hard on the desk. In the corner Ana jumped.

"Six! But that is what... a few tons a month? If we only...."

Turner interrupted sharply.

"Not even all six over twenty four hours."

Wynter raised the same palm level with his temple, fingers outstretched, and dropped it with a slap against his thigh.

"It's not even our share of the region."

"There will be a compensation."

The manager waited.

"A financial arrangement."

Wynter could imagine in which direction that would flow.

Turner seemed to sense his doubts, lowering his voice.

"Mr Wynter, this is between us."

His eyes strayed to the far corner of the room. Ana was polishing glassware quietly, making herself invisible.

"No entiendo."

Robbie had mumbled under his breath, but Turner caught it and shouted suddenly.

"What's that? Don't mock me Mr Wynter! This is a serious matter. Not a single breath do you hear?"

He drew near and whispered fiercely.

"Or she goes!"

Nevertheless, with panniermen plying all the routes between the works, shifting lime, bringing fish, carrying news, the works were rife with rumour. Speculation that spread like scarlet fever up and down the coastal trods. Whisper of stockpiles, of overproduction. Of cutbacks, layoffs.

At the same time, after the brief blaze of hot summer, it was as quickly shrouded and for days on end the coastal fogs would not be dispersed. The world shrunk to a steam-filled boiling house, but that steam was chilled and clammy. From the manager's yard there was no sight of the quarries, although the caustic smoke of the clamps was locked into the fog and choked the atmosphere even within his dreary dwelling. Often even the nearby cottages were invisible.

Wynter made his way down to the works by habit, the grass was monochrome, and soaking. Figures shuffled by. People were never where they should be. Pilfering increased, useful tools were mislaid. He navigated by smell, past the rotting kelp, veered wide of the stale urine vats, coughed at the whiffs of coal dust.

Once, he came across a solitary pack donkey, approaching it out of curiosity, through the dense precipitation. An intense retch-inducing stench. Strapped to it were two panniers of rotting fish heads. From somewhere in the whiteness beyond he could hear the sound of urination. Deciding against admonishing this waste he hurried on to the little corner of patched-up outbuildings and crossed to his lab.

Where was Ana?

He couldn't settle to his research. The fog pressed flat against the windows, as though they had been lime-washed. It was eerily quiet. The fog seemed to have soaked up any sound. No sea, no gulls, no wind. Not even the usual faint ring of distant hammering from the tun house.

He put his jerkin back on and went out again – touring the sheds at random. Hardly anyone was about – a few idlers concocting makeshift activities. Gloom penetrated each of the houses, a few candles were lit, although it was close to midday.

Finally he found Ana, squatting by a cistern stirring the liquor absently with a branch. Again he held back from scolding. The contamination.

"There you are."

She shrugged.

"You weren't there."

His irritation came back.

She didn't look up from the tank, stirring it slowly, lethargically.

He remembered then that in this weather she withdrew. Some cistern of melancholy. Steeped, her spirit leached out. The fog was not the only cause. Drizzle in autumn, or the lowering overcast skies of February, or the cold winter sleet. But the summer fret, that drowned the sun, was the worst. Ana looked shrunk, pale, like someone wearing alum paste. Her eyes were blank. She coughed dryly.

She generated no warmth. Usually, in the sun, she not only flowered, she gambolled and glowed – she radiated light like her own sun.

Now Ana wilted. She ailed like a sick lamb.

His irritation left him. He wanted to embrace her, but felt constrained. There were others in the next shed. They could troop through soundlessly at any moment.

"Come to the lab. I'll light the fire."

She rose obediently, but listlessly. Dropped the stick to the floor.

The blade was criminally sharp, barbaric. The point popped the taut, moisture-glistened skin and the edge swam beneath its surface, sliding through the interior flesh snug to the backbone. Oily pinkish slivers slid free of the long bloodied slit, onto the wooden board. The point rasped back along the knuckled backbone and filmy translucency seeped out, was scoured out.

Liz worked the knife to the backbone, wasting nothing, freed the soft boned spine from the surreptitious flesh, the ill-gotten gained herring, filleted for the pan.

She flushed to remember the hot embarrassment of the transaction. Malice and lust swam together in the narrow single eye of the walnut-roasted face of the pannierman, to which her own face rose, drawn and repulsed, and a rough handful of the morning's catch slid from the pannier into the pouch under her woollen skirts. And that same hand wiped its herring slime up her tense thighs that nevertheless eased apart. Fearful of the seclusion, and at the same time of being discovered on the cliff path, she quickly spat on her hand and guided the pannierman towards a quick conclusion of the trade. The patched eye remained aloof but the mouth squeezed tight a tooth-clenched grin, a tight-jawed grimace that finally released a curt grunt.

His swimming fingers released her too soon, but it was a relief. The pannierman went on his way. Liz, sat down at a vantage point where the path was clear in each direction and, knees wide to the cliff edge, in the cool air wide to the sky and her lover the sea, completed the trade with the pannierman, alone.

Things were desperate, she rationalised, but a strong whiff of guilt hung over the herrings as she sifted the weevily flour over the fillets and salted them. She put the heads, tails and bones with the pink flesh clinging to them in the heavy pot with half an onion and set it to simmer. She wondered how to make the meagre provisions available to her into something like a special meal, for Robbie. She wondered how plausible her story would be. How she saw a quantity fall from the panniers and how on an instinct, although she could have gathered them up, she had shouted to the man with the eye-patch. She was not sure about this detail. How she had shouted that some had fallen and that in his gratefulness he had given her a few.

Robbie came in late, and a little drunk. He'd passed the Flask, he said, and had a couple. He was vague, and oddly aggressive, about why he had gone that way.

"Why not!"

Her triumph with the herrings was spoilt. He wolfed them down, without comment. Her sense of guilt evaporated, but the tension wouldn't dissipate, and she felt tearful.

Robbie had been angry about the fish.

"A biblical sense of honesty! You could have had a dozen."

"They weren't mine."

She allowed the held-back tears to gather.

"Half a loaf and two fishes."

"You ate them fast enough!"

She felt he had hardly tasted them. Unnoticed, the stock his crusts had soaked in.

Behind Robbie's pent-up resentment was a desperate sense of loathing of this atmosphere. Domestic routine he had always enjoyed, now claustrophobic, combined with hating to hurt Liz. Yet, even with his words, doing so. Seeing her crestfallen. He wanted to soothe, but he wanted to break everything in the place.

What Liz did with a handful of strewn-together leftovers was a miracle. He had marvelled at this for years. But he felt thickheaded and resentful. Dulled by the beer, unsettled by the underlying strain. Trapped.

They were stuck in a bog which dragged them down. But if either of them moved they sank in deeper.

Liz took a bowl with the pots outside to wash and there she cried. Back towards him, through the open door Robbie noticed her shaking shoulders. He was desperate to hold her but knew it could trigger violence. Something locked tight in his throat that he could hardly swallow. A panicky feeling fluttered across his chest.

Instead Robbie went to the front door and sat on the step. He watched the last dregs of the twilight drain away over the headland. He sat there a long time, till he felt cold. Going back inside he saw Liz at the table, peering intently at some sewing repair work, to stave off tears. Cautiously he put his arms around her, standing behind her chair. She stopped and he tentatively tightened his squeeze. Salt water brimmed at the rims. She blinked her eyes closed on it, breathing out with a deep sigh. He bent forward and rested his mouth against the top of her head, breathing her hair. He felt her tension ebb.

"Liz. I'm sorry."

She was quiet.

"It was delicious."

She shrugged.

"Really. As always. I shouldn't take it for granted."

She was silent.

But she snuggled back to him over her shoulder and he kissed her cheek. She swivelled round and embraced him and her face swam up towards his, mouth opening, and kissed him fervently.

Robbie fought back a sudden unwelcome surge of revulsion and kissed grimly back, making up for reluctance with additional movement and pressure. Liz sighed heavily. He squeezed his eyes tight and chomped through the kiss like a guest gamely gulping down unwelcome fare.

'Robbie why do you still make me feel like that?'

He had broken off as soon as he felt he could and was looking hopefully around the kitchen for something to drink.

'I love you.'

He squirmed inwardly under the intensity of her look, and fearing to repeat her words without conviction, he re-embraced her, so tight she yelped with pain.

In bed he couldn't sleep. He was hungry. The fish had fuelled it. Rather the dullest fare that simply fulfils the need. He felt dry and his head ached with a dull persistence.

But I do love you too.

Liz was, thankfully, sleeping an exhausted sleep.

Robert's neck was still stiff with tension. He felt cruelly, grainily awake, dreading a long night of sweating wakefulness.

But I do.

Robert could not imagine anyone with whom he could feel more whole, more like a man, than with Liz.

Ana was exasperating, selfish, elusive, immature. He wanted to slap her. But he wanted to draw her to him, the desire to simply hold her tight against himself. It was he that was drawn, like the moth.

He watched Liz in the fields, in the kitchen, he watched her talk to others, he watched her buoyant walk over the crest of the meadow. He was full of ... admiration.

Usually, in bed he simply hugged her sleeping body and his every sense relaxed and subsided, like lying in the sun. She radiated comfort.

Every waking day, with Ana in his mind, he pounded the baked roots of the works paths with energy flaring off him like a furnace. It surged through his boot soles from the primal source within the ground, driving up the shoots, and surged up through him to his mouth, head thrown back, full throated, roared at the sky. At night his body wouldn't settle, his mind churned.

He lay, not touching Liz. The room would soon be flecked with light. He craved sleep.

It was August, but again there was a heavy sea fret. Liz told Robert curtly that she was going for a walk, and abruptly went out.

She marched up the path in intense thought. Robbie had dissuaded her from confronting the girl. He had taken the fish knife from her. He insisted there was nothing to get worked up about. But his moods lurched from sullen to euphoric, and this was nothing to do with the situation at the mines, whatever he said.

The fog was low cloud. It scattered droplets on the grasses and meadow flowers that hugged the track up to the old tower. Beyond the first few yards nothing was visible.

The choking smell from the works infested the fog until, thankfully, she came to where fresh air from the sea channelled up the wyke.

A little further she reached the wooded beck where the smell of wild garlic always lingered. By habit she cut across soon after, taking the path that would come to the head of the cliffs.

I could lure her up here, she thought.

Through the roak, navigating by sea hiss and salt spray. She picked her way crossways down the face below the headland. It would be high tide, but she had heard there would be no ships in today.

Two-thirds of the way down she suddenly came below the cloud and saw the molten lead of the sea. The overlapping plates of its surface slid heavily to the base of the cliff.

Glancing north she could see the cascade of water from where the wyke's divot clove the top edge to half its height. Its liquor spilt over into the larger vat of the sea. Just beyond, the vertical hoist track and the steep rake of the packhorse causeway wound down to the staithe. There was no activity there.

Near to her, on the strand of fallen rocks that was now appearing, where the tide had started to recede, was someone gathering sea-wrack. She didn't recognise the person, and in any case wanted to remain unnoticed. She turned in the other direction and scrambled down the last part of the slippery way onto the small cove immediately below the headland. She stared at what she thought might be a couple of dogs on the beach – strange dogs were to be feared. Then for a split second puzzled over why two sheep might be on the shore. In the same instance she saw they were two fat seals that quickly slithered down to the edge and rolled in. She sat on a rock. The sea had a rolling heave to it but few waves.

The two dogs' heads of the seals in profile. They lifted their heads clear of the water and turned their faces to her, observing her with keen interest. She saw there were others beside these two and soon counted over a dozen. As she sat quietly they all came up into the water close to her. A couple dragged themselves onto a flat rock and lolled there yawning. In the water several faces – with open expectant gaze – looked at her. She smiled at them. A great knot of tension had loosened in her and slid free. Their meek faces. Liz thought of the faces in church, towards the pulpit, but behind the eyes adrift from whatever the minister might be intoning. Lost little ones, she thought, directing this silently to them. The congregation received in bewildered blessedness.

On her way back she noticed the mess and waste in the compound where the rogation revels had taken place. Liz had not been down to that field since. No one had bothered, she realised, to tidy up. Overturned trestles and jugs. Gobbets of meat gristle and bones. Snapped-off pipe stems. The churn of mud that the dancing had wreaked. The boggier areas settling to release a beery stink.

Liz walked about, collecting anything unbroken, gathering any discarded kerchiefs or trampled caps. The heavy sky loomed over, and wind roamed among the tussocks, disturbing shards and fragments. The place appeared deliberately wrecked. A couple of large gulls scavenged. Liz waved them away from a bundle of straw lying at the edge of the field. Some effigy figures she realised which, perhaps in her inebriation, she had not noticed at the revels. Probably someone forgot to throw them on the bonfire.

A bit of ribbon trampled in the mud caught her eye. That she had worn on the day, and stooping to pick it up she frowned at the straw. The smaller of two figures was a crude semblance of a doll, arms and legs wide. Mixed in with the straw a quantity of mud and black dung. Stuffed between the legs a bolt of red cloth. But it was not that which had drawn her eyes to the straw – it was the noose around the second figure, at least that was how it struck her as it trailed out into the mud – Robbie's neck scarf.

Shards

The shortening evenings of summer. Light still lingers. The blue purples, and a few stars hang low and bright. The day cools, the breeze freshens. Ana shivers. When does she not shiver? Only these long hot summer days, the brief season of her flowering. Opening up to the sun, heliotropic. So soon, as soon as the sun passes behind the long golden-baked loaf of the headland, she shivers. Mood melancholy in an instant.

But with Robbie the long summer evenings expand.

On the cliff edge, just below the crown, sheltered by bushes. Watching the tracery of fishing cobles etch across the calm bay. Sheltering her with his body, arms wrapped round, cradling vermilion.

Ana's skin glows in the last rays. The deep brown she has acquired in these summer days glows. Her eyes glow. She is the kernel in a seed. The hull to burst or wither. He knots his bony fingers, sinewy forearms around her. He teases her out of her melancholy that falls with the dusk.

Resting his chin on her shoulder, he points out whinchats and white-arses. Summer visitors, he calls them. They winter in the sun. If I could, she thinks. Buries his face in her black hair sniffing up its scent. Tickles her ear with his tongue. They avoid words. A few inconsequential things. Words can only lead into difficulty. Why things can not be. When things would not be. Which things could not be. The urgency of what should be, could be. Cannot be.

The evening balm keeps these things at bay. The light that will not yet fail completely this night. These last few summer nights. Will not fail them.

But soon it is time their absence from elsewhere will be noted. They part.

Ana takes the direct route. Stumbling in the dampening grass. Bats flit by. The sky deep violet light, the ground a deep violet shadow leaching into black. She stumbles and swears.

Wynter takes time, walking into all the yards and passages between the alum houses, the smithy, the sheds. Everything in an unnatural glimmer, empty gravel or dew-damp flags. Each surface of indeterminate distance. He walks carefully so as not to trip. He refrains from lighting the lantern. Idling, he spins out time. Fidgeting, feeling strangely self-conscious. He makes himself do another round, walking over his own footsteps on the gravel, on the flags.

Suddenly she is there. She has wandered off her track and then on impulse sought him out. Half-angry he whispers fiercely.

"Ana, it's dangerous."

Her eyes widen like moons. He means to push her away, to turn her around. Send her packing. But he finds himself pulling her urgently towards him. Their faces collide in a gasping lip-smash of wet mouths, sucking life into each other. His hands roam all over her, feeding on every texture and surface of her clothing and hot skin among the layers. Their heads and faces slide and bump over each others. His hand has found the hot secret place, it swims in her. His other has brought himself out she grabs it with her surprisingly cool fingers. Urgent movement in the desperate agitation of their bodies. Only a few moments and she feels her fingers moisten with the milky glisten. Simultaneously gasps exultant and fearful, he fills with sudden remorse. Holding her back with one hand and draining his cock with the other, stuffing it back.

"Go!"

The whisper is almost a shout. She is gone in an instant.

Wynter heads off into the shadows between two gable ends. He tramps the perimeter. Mind whirling to invent a reason to be late, as he is yet later and later.

He stays out an age. Finally he lifts the latch gently, hoping Liz will be asleep. He moves into the interior gloom.

Startled by her silhouette against the last cinders. She speaks to the dying coals.

"Where were you?"

"Sorry. I went further than I planned."

She waits.

"To the village. I ended up going the whole way. Not sure why. It was a lovely evening. But I went too far and came back in the dark."

She doesn't speak for some time. He makes movements as if to get ready for bed. After a while she speaks again.

"You could have taken me with you."

He feels sick, almost tearful. Thankfully it is nearly pitch black in the house.

"Sorry."

She drains the jar and hurls it. He hates picking up smashed glass. Imagines the tiny fragments working their way into soles of feet. Into food, picked up at fingertips.

Wynter's wife is furious. She cries.

She drinks more.

He hates it when she drinks to fuel her anger, to boil up fury.

The glass shatters, the wine loops in an arc and flicks across the ceiling. Like the time he unhinged the top of his thumb in the workshop, with the plane. Threw his arm backwards over his shoulder, an arc of red over the workbench, and the wood shavings.

For years after he will make love on his back – looking at that stain on the ceiling.

"Why should I pretend it's all right? Fuck you."

She tries to bite him.

"I'm not going to pretend. I'm entitled to..."

Grabs at his groin. Fends her off. Wild, she assails him, with all limbs.

It's like a tarpaulin lashing out in a gale. He tries to protect himself, tries to hold down every corner, as gently as possible. He doesn't have enough arms. She doesn't want to blow over. The loose ropes lash out at him. The wet cloth is heavy. The flail slaps him off balance. It's hot, wrestling the tar. Stings and rope burns. In the close thunderous dark of their room, where the coals blaze.

"So say something."

What?

Nothing he can say will not stoke it. His silence, likewise, enrages her.

"Your...fucking.... whore!"

It started with a noise in the attic. Dripping. He was aware of what might be sleet hurled at the windows. Watery noises outside the bedroom. In the dark he paddled to the window. Outside seemed to be snow blown blank against every pane. Then it was liquid – it seemed a wall of water. The thick whitish liquor lapped against the window, streamed down like milk. Noise welled up alarmingly, a storm. In the roaring dark he crawled over to the door, liquor seeped through the keyhole. It seeped under the door. He rammed the bolts across. The key dropped out of the keyhole pushed by a thick sludge of white liquor. It coiled out like thick spunk and crawled down the back of the door. Dripped on the flags. The liquid sweated across the ceiling, the walls ran, the floor streamed with it. Robbie paddled. He heard the fire sizzle, the hearth gushed liquor like a spring, like a burst cistern. It poured down the chimney. The ceilings sagged, they dripped, the water surged, he waded. Water swirled around the walls, like a sea cave. He breasted the surf, breakers engulfed his mouth and face. The whole cottage churned wildly in a tidal violence of white foam and glue. The water sucked back. Robbie's feet were tugged by the water. It ebbed under the door. The mud floor sucked, his feet sank and as the water retreated from every surface and object, crystals grew. They encrusted the walls. The ceiling dripped icicles of them, stalactites of them. The floor thrust up geometry and facets. The room shrank – sharp octahedrons of crystals pointed in at Robbie like a phalanx of spears, like an ambush. The crystal darts, the alum spears closed in on him, glinting and shining and glittering like quartz daggers. His wife shook him. Robbie. His strangulated cries trying to emerge. He was half sitting up in his sweating bed roll. Robbie. It's alright.

Valerian

Liz moved among the meadow flowers. Looking for the sweetly-scented pink or white petals. Hunting in the rough grassy areas for the sprays of small five-lobed clusters. A balmy summer day. Hot on her bare forearms. She caressed her hand through the stems and tubes below the blades and surface leaves. It was cool and moist near the ground.

Along the cliff edges the grasses were alive with swaying colours: buttercups, saxifrage, mouse-ear and vetches. Over the edge she could see purples amid the sorrel and sowthistle. Plenty of yarrow, she picked some. Scabious, from a distance she thought might be the valerian.

Robbie's night sweats were waking her. He would turn restlessly, muttering. Wake and mumble. Sleep again. Leaving her awake, to bitter imaginings.

Her tentative remedy: valerian. She asked around the women too. Murmured agreement. Although one argued against it. Said it would cause night terrors, not appease them.

"Attractive to rats."

Marion had said that. The rest cackled, exchanging knowing looks. But Marion remained stern, bitter since Launde's disappearance.

It was a beautiful day. She curled her bare toes in the cool tubers, watching out for thistles. The sea was an immense blue. Small boats, cobles, tacked to and fro.

The breeze was pleasant, waving fescue and coltsfoot, oatgrass. She stopped by a tiny beck, little more than a trickle. Aromatic, water mint and meadowsweet. Then she saw, smelt, the parsley smell of dropwort, remembering the other advice of the women.

"Look for the purple-blotched stems. Tall and musty-smelling. That would make a fine tea. For the rat, or the cat!"

Here the dropwort, its hollow stemmed cousin. Equally poisonous. Hemlock.

Finally she found the valerian. A small patch of sprays among the swaying grasses, mixed in with the vetches and outshone by solar outbursts of fleabane.

She gathered the valerian. Sleeping draught. Cure for restlessness and anxiety. Robbie's and her own. Perfume for some. The leaves nibbled and tracked by tiny brown-edged holes. Where the butterflies hatch out.

She hummed softly to herself as she continued. Picking from the other flowers too, a colourful spray for the hearth jug.

Valerian – bait the traps, catch the rats.

Valerian – agitation, headaches and night-frights. Smells of piss. Not the flower, the sour oil of the root.

Valerian, the stems and florets, in the jug. Wilting slightly, although watered, after time in the hearth jug.

The roots, dried. Liz had squeezed out a few pungent drops of the oily liquid. Like catnip to the cat, redolent of animal piss. Liz took the strong liquor of the root oil, and boiled water with it to make the brew.

Passing the valerian tea to Robbie. He winced, sniffing it.

"Here, my dear, drink this."

Affectionately, she pecked him on the forehead, ruffling his thinning hair.

He sipped the tea obediently.

"Can't be doing with wringing the sheet out everyday."

He looked into the cup, sniffing at the urinous steam. Sheepish.

"For my sake, too!"

Still cheerily, she smiled at him.

"All your anxiety and fear, me dear. Too much seaweed, not enough. Too little quarried, too much waste. Too much quarried, not enough used. Too scarce, too flush. The thousand and one contradictory judgements of the trade. The owner bearing down, the men glaring up."

"All this solved by a mouthful of piss."

Her expression a rebuke.

"Be thankful it's from the weeds!"

Some small but significant bulwark of tension in him released, relaxed. He exhaled it slowly, a slow sigh. Bitter medicine of valerian. He sipped it steadily, savouring only its warmth. In his thaw he beckoned her with a sideways nod. She came over and perched on the stool, drawing it up next to his chair.

"Robbie...."

She squeezed his forearm, raised to hold the cup with his fingertips. He switched it to his left, gripping it more easily now it had cooled a little. His right he stretched round her shoulders, drawing her in close.

No moon and only a little starlight. The light played over the bare earth, rock and dust of the quarries. No one was about. The clamps smouldered. Identified as always by the irritant smoke. Visible only as vague darker shapes against a dark background. Closer, little chinks of smoulder winked occasionally as the breeze fanned. The forlorn sweep of the black scoop of the quarry face, overhung with straggling bushes. Devoid of men the processes activated worked themselves. Exchanges of materials and heat, flame and gases, stones and accretions and efflorescence.

The clamps plastered over with new mud, to dampen down the swiftness of conflagration. So the flicker of glow through the cracks was intermittent. In the interior furnace of the self-immolating rocks any body, man or monster, would be baked to coal.

The wan starlight played on the mercury sheen of the steeping pits. The dark water barely shivered into a ripple. The still ponds inscrutable. Below their blank surface, nevertheless, things changed unseen. Old slow time, primitive, unrefined by the grasshopper escapements, the coiled strings and bi-metallic adjustments of the latest portable chronometers, worked its irrepressible transformation upon mute stone. Leachings and seepings. Thickenings.

To one side the black silhouette of the tallyman's hut.

Then shadows of men appear.

They carried the mellow mood with them, holding its spell, early into bed. Neither made any attempt at lovemaking. The embers glowed dim, reflected on the low ceiling. He nestled close in to her under the covers. Sweet savour of the stable. His head resting in the hollow between her shoulder and collar bone.

Arms wrapped around, inhaling her body scent, his thoughts drifted to Ana, and back. He felt he wouldn't sleep. A tension threatened to return. He squeezed round Liz tighter. She was asleep already. He felt the deepening rhythm of her breathing, slowing.

It is very late when Fox, down at the works, completes his tally of milled alum flour, gathers his papers and closes the door of the warehouse behind him. A bitter gust slaps round the corner of the building. Instinctively he tugs up his already turned collar. Across the yard he opens the field gate and in turning to close it his eye catches a spark in the distance. Some kind of bonfire up at the quarries which, striding up the track, he peers ahead at. With the clamps manned at all hours it is not unusual for someone to be up there in the dark. Nevertheless, something about the bonfire strikes him as odd.

Realising, with a sudden inner liquefying fear, he breaks into a run.

"No!"

The tallyman runs to the end of the track, where it meets the footpath, crunches across stones, and vaults the dilapidated fence. He runs heavily up the meadow, registering bogginess, trying to anticipate the unevenness of the dark ground. He stares down. Meanwhile, his peripheral vision carries the glittering starlight of the distant fire, which gets bigger. Swearing and gasping, heaving the cold air into deepening lungs, where it burns at each gulp, heart pounding. His every out breath is an obscenity. He slows perceptibly, but driving on. Gorse makes a grab at his thighs and elbows, but he breaks free from it, forcing himself uphill over heavy sodden ground as the fire grows. He is aware of its corona, like solar flares off an eclipse, in the surrounding darkness. There seem to be dark figures, satanic stickmen around the flames.

Before the top of the field he has to stop, bent double with the screaming pain of his lungs. Frothing and spitting curses. He forces himself to resume and clambers heavily over a second decayed boundary. On the flat upper path, shale slag crushed into mud, he regains energy and speed.

As he approaches the fire, wind roars through its white-hot centre.

Workmen prevent him, though he swings madly like a furious child, from reaching the blazing hut. Men threaten him with their picks but he flies at them. He is thrown to the ground where he falls awkwardly, on his back, seeing the pitiless stars wheel over.

Lifting his head, in the firelight he registers the ledgers, piled up tidily, clear of the flames. A blaze of sparks streams from the collapsed and settling planks of the hut. They fall to a convenient pyramid through which the updraft spirals, crackling and roaring.

"No!"

He struggles violently against greasy wool and leather.

"You stupid fucking superstitious idiots. You're going to blame the stones?"

He receives a vicious blow to the head for this, and his arms are pinioned. Several men attend to his violent wriggling. Hard fists strike his face and ribs. A heavy stave or pick handle cracks against his legs. He is forced back to the ground.

Eyes straining, chest heaving he is forced to witness the smashing of the stones. Placed on other rocks they fly off dangerously or chip and split. Sometimes they powder, sometimes they are hard, and with thoroughness the men retrieve the stones that skim off and bring them back, and pulverise them.

The work goes on a long time until the hut blaze dims, and the tallyman's collection is obliterated.

5

The parting keel

The alum cartel

"....Alum of all kinds stops mortification and haemorrhage"

Next morning Fox arose stiffly. He tested each limb painfully for damage.

Upright, head splitting, body aching, a sickening wash of loss seeped through him.

He felt drained. After the men left him he had lain in the dirt and wept. Then slept. He had awoken among cinders to the smell of wet ash. Half frozen and in a daze. Stumbled back in the pitch darkness to his cottage where, cut and badly bruised, in a spiralling frenzy of self-blame, he had drunk a quantity of spirits, and finally slept again. Or passed out.

It was not long past first light, he realised, despite his fitful night, and in the cold early mist he dragged himself back to the deserted quarry.

A wisp of smoke came from the manager's chimney. Vapour drifted from the cooling clamps. It was eerily quiet, overcast, grey. Landscape drained of colour and light – an empty hearth, bare of life, cold ashes.

There was little to see. Only the barren dusty waste of the excoriated ground. He was listless, like someone too shocked or exhausted to mourn. There was nothing but rubble left from the systematic destruction of the hammermen. With his boots he kicked apart the blackened spars of the hut remnants. It was cold, not a single ember. Squatting down, he brushed aside the ash gingerly with his sore fingers. Wrong. Beneath the damp surface a residue of warmth. He picked charcoal from the baked earth and blew. A splinter-end bloomed into a tiny glow-spark. Dropping it he picked up a scorched fragment of something else, a knurled quadrant of ridged spiral. He spat on the fragment and rubbed it tenderly, and then he pocketed it.

Robbie awoke in a tumbled confusion. It was light. Something was in the bed, fighting for space between his clammy legs. Some kind of wriggling monster. Some manifestation of his suffocating dream world. He wrestled to free himself.

Fully roused, realising, he laughed.

"Hey!"

Liz had crept under the bottom of the blanket, and her hair tickled his thighs.

"Agh...."

He wrestled the head-shape under the blanket, she was already licking his balls. His erection, and an acute pressure on his bladder. He threw aside the blanket. Her bright intense eyes brimming with mischief.

"Wait..."

He jumped out of bed and dashed for the back door. Easing it ajar only enough to piss through the crack as he rapidly detumesced in the chilly, morning air. A hint of woodsmoke and ash.

Finished, he pushed the door open a little and, over the dew-soaked grass, the wall's pale lichens, misty foliage, a low-gliding owl skimmed the space between door and jamb, some two fields away. It was still early he realised.

He scampered back to the bed, where Liz lay on her back under the covers. Her hands working. Ardour sharpening, he slipped under the foot of the blanket where she had earlier entered and slid up between her legs. Amphibian, he slithered. One long movement of propulsion, of rummaging fingers and he sucked greedily.

Disregard for the works could be observed at every stage in the production. At the quarries, vegetation was being allowed to build up on the rock face. There was not enough bare rock made available to fuel the clamps. Terraces were unshored and collapsing in places. The quarry floor was a quagmire. Spoil was encircling it when it should have been carried down the slopes. In the quarries and at the works, men tripped over rubbish, snagged on neglected equipment or stumbled into potholes. Liquor leaked from the troughs.

The failure to keep the goods in order was damaging the quality of alum produced. It also undermined the morale of the workers. In addition to lack of incentives, deficit of payment, and resultant hunger and ill-health, foul and drossy alum was being made.

Wynter felt he teetered on a cliff-edge, like the works, between Turner and the deep blue sea. When the men came to him for pay he had to authorise produce of inferior quality, old mutton or corn, rather than wages. At other times, bushels of rye or peas. Turner's measures of these were never fair.

The manager cast his mind back to the previous winter. It had come early, and hard. In late November a bone-clamping cold had materialised. Wind scouring over the waste. At sea the bay filled with white. Stinging lead-shot hail flung at the doors of the houses. It had been amusing when it came down the chimneys and bounced into the rooms. Less entertaining outside, where it whipped the cheeks and ears like a cat of nine tails.

Under the blanketing snow, water frozen in the rut puddles to malicious intent. Torn knees and smashed elbows in the quarries.

Reservoirs frozen. The brittle machinery of the pumps, frozen.

In the cottages, heat from the dung fires reaching no further than the grate. Icy draughts creeping over the earth floors. Rags under the doors and over the windows inadequate.

Some men had bargained with Turner for bushels of oats. Taken their sacks to Turner's house and left them for filling. There was heavy snow for a fortnight, and when they returned the oats had been deemed neglected and sold on. For this Turner had reduced their wages by the missing amount.

In the laboratory the glassware was as if fashioned from ice. You feared sticking to it on handling. The urine froze in the jars, which was some relief, as the smell locked in. Frost crazing on the panes set hard.

All before Ana had arrived. Wynter could not imagine how Ana would cope if the coming season was as bad. But where would she be next winter? Where was she now?

In the lab, Wynter feels hemmed in. Dispirited by the neglect and Turner's unwillingness to sanction its remedy. A figure of resentment to the men, forced to implement the owner's policies. Tension in the assay house with Ana, and brooding anger at home.

At the clamps, he squeezes his temples to massage a headache, as he absorbs their abject condition. Clamps that if properly built on two hundred foot square bases, with tapering layers of shale and brushwood, rose to pyramids a hundred feet tall.

Now they were more like tips of shale and wood, strewn over the plateau.

He tries to insist on everything being done correctly. To keep the works afloat as tidily as any well-run ship. But Turner undermines his diligence as 'excess' - *a fine artistry we can't afford*. Wynter would have plastered the pyramids with damp earth, but the labour was lacklustre and so the rough clamp heaps fired up rapidly and combusted too quickly.

He stitched and patched where he could. A couple of weeks before Launde's departure the manager had sent him up on the raw liquor cistern roof. To patch the holes that let the diluting dust-polluted rain in.

It depressed Wynter to enter the house of boiling and settling. The crumbling brick furnaces, the distorted, fractured, worn supports. The battered lead pans. Only half the full tally of pans suitable for use. The crumbling edges of the settlers. Their debris polluted the tanks.

But no money was forthcoming to make any of this good.

'If you're so concerned with the aesthetics of it Mr Wynter, then it can be embroidered with a deduction from your wages.'

The general heedlessness was compounded, the manager knew, by wilful damage. Anonymous revenge took the sting off anger at Turner and himself. Momentarily. It could only rebound on the workers. There was also a gradual increase in pilfering.

Wynter felt himself brought down, notch by notch, as he noticed the smirking disdain, insubordinate anger and occasional violence among the men. The whole listless, downhill trudge of it.

That last winter a barrowman had broken his thigh, slipping on ice with a load of mine tipped over him. Laid up in a draughty cottage a winter chill had taken him before Christmas.

Wynter shivered. Sky overcast, puddle glitter. The wind picking up. The leaves had already turned. How soon till next winter? Even if everything staggered on.

Turner and Mulgrove were sipping brandy after despatching a brace of pheasants, some smaller fowl, cheeses and bread.

Mulgrove was a landowner. At least two alum leases had been granted on his inherited estates. They monopolised long stretches of the coast, including several small harbours.

Turner was an upstart adventurer to him. Stormy Hall was little more than a castellated farmhouse. Mulgrove Hall was a substantial country seat, with family roots delving back to the time of Richard the Lionheart.

Mulgrove recognised the increasing stature of the merchants, whose ability to lend money, for mining and other labour-intensive enterprises, was underpinned by the flood of gold receipts circulating. Underneath this overextended system the power lay in London, with the goldsmiths and the recently founded Bank. The finance stretched back to the landowners, for their ability to administer rights for exploration. With strings attached.

Turner recognised the same power trail. Risk and responsibility moved in the opposite direction, to people like himself, who hoped to exploit the rights agreements and to pass on the numerous risks. They avoided overextending investment in buildings and equipment, before passing on the rights to the next opportunist. Turner envied Mulgrove's depth of reserve, which was sunk deep into the land beneath the richly fixed colours of the rug, the immaculately flagged stone of the hall floor, beneath their feet.

Landowners had nevertheless been known to overreach themselves. Pouring quantities of borrowed money into ambitious mining and manufacturing, taking an over-optimistic view of the advantages of granting quarrying rights on their own lands. The headlands over Mulgrove's own cliffs had been drastically altered over the last fifty years. A hundred tons of shale to produce one ton of alum. Great amphitheatres of dust had been gouged out and the bare stumps of headlands were bereft of vegetation, and devoid of seabirds.

If alum was extracted at too high a cost, or failed to find its price in the market, that cost could quickly undermine the cliff of finance standing behind it. Mulgrove was not exposed in this way, but was aware that other landowners had eroded the edifice of their inheritances, causing the comfortable accumulations of generations to subside.

The landowners feared the collapse in the markets, threatening any percentages promised the Crown. The rights' owners feared the call on debts to the London merchants. The merchants, to their wealthy patrons, or the Bank.

For some of these reasons Mulgrove and Turner, unequal rivals in industry, retiring now to a pair of stout upholstered armchairs, discussed the price of alum.

"Loft House, Saltwick agree. Others are not persuaded."

"Scarshead?"

Turner demurred.

"Lythe are in. Wath definitely not, they say they can't afford to cut back whilst the price is so low."

"The whole problem in a nutshell Mr Turner."

"They feel a disadvantage, being further from the sea."

Mulgrove frowned.

"They have local coal, and I have heard their shale is plentiful and richly bearing."

"They say we have the entire coastline to level onto the beach."

"Well there is some substance to their argument for they are a local trader whereas we have to wage a global war. Perhaps we can afford to leave them be. On the other hand if we cut back production and they flood the market our... arrangement... will be worth little."

Mulgrove paused.

"What does your Mr Wynter say?"

Turner felt a brush of anxiety at the mention of his coveted manager's name. Robert Wynter was a manager whose understanding of the balancing act of alum manufacture had a reputation in this region. Recently he had been reassured by a rumour – the captain's girl would keep him here. But with a precipitous fall in alum prices things could change. Hunger would oust lust.

"The workers have no wind of it. A full barrow earns a barrowful's pay. The whole tendency of the process is to improve efficiency – to make more."

"Mr Wynter, being a magician, an alchemist, an 'alum-chemist' they say, makes even more appear."

Turner winced. What was Mulgrove getting at?

"He's a practical man, sir. If we must cut back he will see the logic of it."

"For that we need unity Mr Turner. Or else managers and other useful souls might see other opportunities."

Ah.

Turner changed the subject.

"What will our London merchants feel about it?"

"If they get to hear."

"Is it not in their interest?"

"Some would say so, others not."

"It's the imported alum we must stop, and prevent the smuggling. They could lobby for progress in those fields. Using their influence."

"Indeed, Mr Turner, but that is a long game. Here we have a stalemate. You must go back to the dissenting mines and persuade again."

Turner saw he would do the dirty work. Mulgrove would draw into the background – the gentleman and the farmer, touring his tenants' smallholdings on his mare.

"Sup up, Mr Turner. I feel a late afternoon torpor. Let's talk again when there is better news."

Yield

Turner was confused and more than a little angry to hear that Mr. Carey and his assistant had vanished. And the monster apparently gone with them.

"And did he pay you well?"

Fox said nothing.

"Well?"

He saw Fox was irked.

"Then you are a fool."

Wynter spoke up.

"I wouldn't sanction it."

"Oh?"

"I mean.... I wanted it removed. The curse."

"Nonsense man! You planned to steal from me and then you were double crossed!"

"It was just mine spoil."

Fox kept silent.

"It seemed precious to Mr. Fox?"

He swivelled to the tallyman who, colouring slightly, met his gaze.

"Of interest only, sir"

"Who says they only have curiosity value? We burn from other unpromising rocks, from shale and coal, much richness."

Wynter and Fox were quiet.

"I should sack you both."

They kept quiet.

"For planning to steal from me and for failing to prevent me being robbed!"

"It's best gone, sir."

The owner turned on Wynter.

"The curse?"

He mocked.

"Is that why you failed to prevent the destruction of Mr. Fox's premises?"

Fox's eyes swivelled to the manager.

Wynter kept his eyes fixed on Turner's.

"Mr. Fox, get back to work. I have more to say to Mr. Wynter."

Fox left. His steps were heard receding.

"I didn't order anything."

"You failed to protect it Mr. Wynter. What's the difference?"

For a second Wynter's face blazed.

"Mr. Wynter. When I have had a chance to consider this matter further we will speak again."

Turner sat down, waving his hand dismissively.

"You may go."

Under Turner's instructions Wynter had cut back the wage earners to a minimum. Therefore daytime pieceworkers supplemented the rump sporadically. According to mood Wynter either mixed these together to create competitive anxiety, or kept them separate to avoid animosity. Some part-timers were baring rock. Others battled to keep the terraced gangways clear. A group was digging out mine and breaking it into pieces small enough for calcining.

Scurrying barrowmen in perpetual motion. Close to, however, the near-terminal weariness of the barrowmen. Wynter knew the pace was a fine balance of hoarded strength and striving for maximum barrow-loads. Misjudged one way would lead to injury or collapse. The other to insufficient pay to feed back the strength dissipated. That judgement was a matter of indifference to Turner. One shattered worker could be replaced with another unbroken.

Nevertheless, the whole motion at the quarries made a convincing simulacrum of a machine. Like a loom, clattering under the shifting of the shuttle and the beater, and vibrating with activity.

Cummings, the manager's new foreman at the clamps, was scowling at the furnace uproar as a stiff sea-breeze fanned the brushwood into flame. Men staggered back from the fire, their hands scorched. These men, with difficultly, were attempting to line the outside of the heap with heavy lumps of mud and clay. The constant settling of the clamps made this awkward enough without the gusting heat and flames, and the men resorted to lobbing on lumps of wet soil, hissing and popping, and poking it with sticks, faces averted.

Wynter made a note to discuss with Cummings how this haphazard performance could be made more effective. He thought about wrapping the clay around strips of sacking, bandaging the mud onto the sides of the clamps. Cummings was shouting into the choking fumes, for the benefit of anyone near, as the manager drew alongside him.

"The whole fucking journey an educated guess, fucked up by whatever weather comes along."

Wynter and Launde had tried many times to measure and analyse the variables that created the best soup. They cooled the clamps quickly or slowly, they roasted the ingredients fast and slow. The men allowed the calcined heaps to cool slowly, mellowing the shale. If the clamps cooled too fast no end of tinkering with the later processes would address the problem sufficiently. The liquormen would cluck around the steeping pits like broody hens, estimating the thickness of the soup, waiting to lay their eggs on the surface.

But with Launde gone it all had to be learnt anew by Cummings. Years of straining to interpret the subtle colour changes of the gases off the clamps. However detailed Winter's notes, they would be inadequate to convey that sense of experience Launde had picked up here since being an apprentice.

Fox and Wynter were grim. The yield was down. Unmistakably, their own records showed the yield was down. The worst news to present to the owner. Output, as a proportion of all the other costs, down. Even, he had remarked bitterly to the tallyman, with the fucking monster gone. He knew it was largely a product of neglect. Manager and tallyman considered all the stages in the process at which alum could be lost. But was it, he feared, a misjudgement in the introduction of kelp? Wynter was sure he had been making progress with kelp. But this showed otherwise? He would have to go back through all his records again. Painstakingly. Searching for clues.

Wynter sucks in cold air, trying to clear his thoughts. His feet pound the track, trundling the ground beneath like a treadmill. Deformed trees crowd in. Light sieves through.

He goes over it all again in his head.

Struggling to optimise the yield, while cutting back on production. To perfect the balance of piss and kelp.

No way to square the circle anyway. The quicker he reaches capacity the faster cutbacks will become necessary.

He stops at a fork, momentarily undecided.

By the tree he notices the gnarled bark shrunk away from a dry oval. Resinous, smooth-centred, ringed by dry crinkled lips. He thinks of her puckered arsehole, her peeled open sap-glistened cunt.

Fish to Fry

Fog, thought Ana. I arrived in this fog. In the nithering fog. I will leave in it.

Born into mist, lived in fret.

Mis sueños son llenados de niebla.

One day I will enter the fog, as into my fog-filled dreams and walk through. Pass through and finally emerge, into hot sun.

"We've been careless."

"It's alright."

"It's not alright! Neither of us can afford for that to happen."

"I mean it's fine, *sin problema*. I took alum."

"What! How? I mean, why?"

"It stops it."

"Who said?"

"The rockman. He came for work."

"And did he get it?"

"I think so."

"So, he simply came to ask for work and you had a conversation about what alum might do?"

She shrugged.

"Well?"

"Robbie......"

"So he's here two minutes and you are discussing how to fuck without consequences."

"Robbie, don't be angry. Just talking."

"Some talk!"

Struggling to control his jealousy, he made an outward effort to calm down. She cast him a loaded look. He demanded a reply.

"Who was it?"

Shrugged.

"Who?"

"Robbie, you must not interfere."

"Who?"

"Alleley."

Alleley! A placement of Turner's that they didn't need. He grabs her wrist and demands.

"So how did you take it?"

She shakes free.

"I didn't. *Solo hablando*!"

"What?"

"*Que.*"

"Que. Que....What!"

"It was talk, talk!"

He was shouting now.

"I don't understand you!"

Then she spoke softly, gently.

"Robbie, it was only talking"

"What I meant was, how?"

She raised a mischievous eyebrow.

"You don't know?"

She teased.

His anger rose again.

"No - why should I?"

"You must use something...."
"Ana, you know what we..."
"With your wife!"

No need, thought Robbie. He shook his head. Exasperated.

"She is too old."

This she didn't believe, or ignored. He was insistent.

"So?"

"You want me to show you."

Extravagantly, coquettishly.

In an instant she wheeled round and stuck out her arse.

He was shocked. Baffled.

A second later she had hysterics. She flung herself to the ground and rolled over and over, laughing helplessly.

Robert blushed and floundered.

"Sopa, sopa!"

She laughed and laughed.

"It's a soup Robbie, it's a soup."

"What is?"

"He said it was a soup."

"Alleley?"

"Yes, Roger said."

"Roger!"

Roger. The preposterous appropriateness of the name. His anger suddenly seemed absurdly stern. The name cracked it into a laughter he couldn't prevent or, with watering eyes, keep under control. Ana was hugely amused, if bewildered. Watching him shaking his head, giggling helplessly.

Alleley was a sly one. A languid eel, never quite where he should be. His work was slipshod. Reluctant, Wynter had been forced to employ him. Some second cousin or other of the owner. His attitude was a kind of smirk against authority and this facile rebellion seemed to appeal to Ana. Wynter hated the apparent empathy between them. Not that he was a known philanderer, more drawn to innuendo and gossip than activity. Ana's rebellious streak was drawn to it perhaps. Whatever, his dirty insinuations provoked the guttural bark that was her conspiratorial laugh. The tail-side of her infectious nose-wrinkling giggle.

Ana and Alleley would slide round the gable of the tun house for a smoke, and Ana would return with wide-eyed insolence. It infuriated Wynter, not that there was anything specific to be jealous of, but that she could just as happily spend time with Alleley as with himself. They emanated a careless attitude to work and indeed Ana never really cared for her contribution to his own work. Only occasionally enjoying praise for some individual task. She would listen or at least watch as he demonstrated a refinement, but later she would remember nothing of the explanation. I just like to listen to your voice, she told him.

Increasingly she smelt of drink and smoke. Where she accessed these tipples was a mystery she didn't care to divulge. One of the men. Just a mouthful. Said with a shrug. Small beer was ever present around the works, but stronger stuff was discouraged. She seemed tired and lacklustre, was absentminded. It almost seemed that any excuse to linger in the sheds, around the tanks and tuns was preferable to being in the laboratory.

Yet being in the lab was also a constant source of tension. It lacked privacy, with people coming and going with materials and samples. With the door wedged open in the summer. With Liz unaccustomed to knocking.

The other lab assistant, the apprentice boy, was usually present, and could not be trusted. Ana had befriended him like a kitten but Wynter sensed his adolescent gawkiness attracted her too. She was nearer the boy's age than his own. And his daily hangovers and pocheen tales entertained her, but those children's drinking bouts would be rife with disgusting speculation about Ana and the manager.

Nevertheless, she tolerated his attention when an opportunity arose. He would slide his hand under her shirt and up the clammy flesh of her back and her strong body odour overlaid with alcohol and smoke would stir his chemistry. They would kiss for a few seconds, breaking off quickly for fear of discovery. Leaving only dissatisfaction.

Ana, darkened by the sun, her skin the colour of unpolished jet, that spirit of hers, that would flare up in an instant, that would never shine with a veneer of burnished respect.

What was she thinking?

His constant nagging question to himself.

Liz could articulate every nuance of her hurt with the merest tensing of her mouth line. Or stooping of the shoulders. He could detect it in a change of gesture and movement, over simple tasks. Or she could tell him exactly what he thought.

I knew she had witched you, she had said. Before you even noticed.

But what was *she* thinking? This he wondered incessantly. What was in Ana's mind? Where did she go, inside herself? She would almost never articulate her thoughts, although sometimes her overt feelings seemed clear enough. He would have to press her reluctance, and even then it would be fruitless. Don't know. Can't say. Shrugs. Headshakes. Bemused smiles. You must be thinking something. Robbie, don't get angry. I'm fine. I know you're fine – it's me that's not. Sorry. It doesn't matter. And so on. Ultimately she found this boring, or exasperating. Losing her temper.

"Robbie, don't explain everything!"

He loves her lower lip, its fullness, and he draws it into his mouth over his own. His tongue travels its interior, just as it does his own, unconsciously, concentrating on a task. In the field he chews fresh grass and leaning over her face drops the spittle onto her closed mouth. Her lips part to receive it, and she licks, and open opens her mouth to receive more.

"Robbie....."
She smiles sadly.
"....I wasn't expecting....to feel."

Ana, on the grass. Lying face down to the cool earth, by the roots. Hot, her upward ear tip and cheek. Cool, her down cheek feeling the pressed mat of tangled grasses imprint itself there. Close by, the moist white roots. Through the palisade of slanting stalks, in the far distance, she sees Robbie, waist up, like another small creature among the beetles and ladybirds, moving down the slanting horizon. Sinking to his shoulders, then head only. Then gone. Her own head is crawling with emotions and feelings that fail to clarify into a single thought.

Garboard strakes. Lapped elm wrapped. Wrapped around the blunted stern, the snubbed nose. Either side of the bow. The high arch bow. Iron roves, scarf and luting. Trenails and trunnels. Grown and compass timbers, elm again. The keel plank, the bilge keels – draft or sand strakes. The cobles, boats little changed from those of the Vikings. Rigged for oars and a lug sail. Built in the lapstrake or clinker manner. Luting, of animal hair, from cattle. Experts in the boatyard, making the last adjustments and personalisation. Final perfections, to the joggling, to oak and pine planking, to the cuddy. For the fishermen, for the alum smugglers.

The captain. In the boatyard, negotiating repairs to his boat. He notes with interest the making of the local small craft, the cobles. He waits, unhappy with delays, unhappy with the price. Feeling vaguely that Turner is somewhere behind it all. Anxious to sail. Clean timbers for his stinking piss-washed planks. He tries to consider Turner's motives. Arranging trade with him, urine for alum. Then surely behind all these excuses and absences and delays?

He admires the gansey of the carpenter. The particular twists and patterns of the woollen sweater. Although the carpenter ignores him, having already indicated that the boss is away. The captain has turned down offers to have one knitted for himself. Although he knows that each design is specific to the village it was made, he also knows the gansey's usefulness, in identifying the home village of the fisherman, on whose body the gansey still clings, dragged overboard and drowned.

The captain remembered the ravaged landscape of the dusty hills around Mazarron. One hundred and fifty years of the alum trade. Transported by the Genoese until the papal decree designed to limit its production, which was prolific enough to cause a collapse of the price. Limited again by the war with England. The Velez nobility had profited from the King's allocation, and had been given the White Castle to which they gave their name – Velez Blanco. Its sheer walls – cliff faces – erected on a rock summit.

He thought of Cartagena – a walled town. The Romans had mined silver. Santa Maria Cathedral built of Roman stones, they liked to say, on the base of the old burnt down theatre.

The captain was never going to be a pig farmer. He had decided that as a boy, from his lookout in the tree, peering out to sea. But he had been shocked at Cartagena. The vast acres of activity, the mines, the desolate miles of baked earth, mine spoil and dust. The hovels where the workers lived, ovens. The Moors' castle glowering aloof. It had driven him on further, to foreign cities. To Genoa, where the emperors Nero and Vespasian had once imposed a tax on urine. Money doesn't smell. That comment had earned Vespasian the right to be celebrated by name in all the Genoese latrines, the Vespasiani.

To London, and the loss of his wife, and at last to this shrouded coastline, to more ash and dust and waste.

But its bitter wind to be put behind him, to speed him on.

In the flag-floored, bare, tough little inns by the harbour the captain picks up scraps of news, of opinion, speculation.

"Even in Whitby the cutbacks will be felt."

"Shipbuilding in this town was founded on the alum trade. Its status in the region rests on that."

"Then it will have to look elsewhere."

"The first ships from London are looking for the leviathan."

The captain thinks of a phrase he has heard. Perhaps there are bigger fish to fry.

Wynter always awoke with his collar soaked from fitful sleep. Immediately he would be aware of a tension in his throat. He would stare up at the stained ceiling, seeing beyond it into the day ahead.

He was hardly working these days.

How would she seem?

Would she be friendly? Or just tired and distracted, skulking off with Alleley or the others. He projected the day's routine. Could they be alone at any point? If not, the tension would squat there all day. His mind would drift off continually from his tasks, imagining conversations that would never be held, situations that would never arise. She would be indifferent to him, but if challenged say sorry, just tired. He would be constantly agitated, but turning it inwards, and he would be short with everyone else. The more mundane tasks were a trial of utter tedium that made him convulse involuntarily, the more challenging ones suffered from lack of real concentration.

He lay next to his wife, drained of energy to get up, drained of desire for her. Rigid, unmoving. Yet if she rolled over to him and put her arms around him he would melt into her warmth as into a tub of hot water, all his tense body relaxing into it with exhausted relief, except his throat which gripped its tension and would not release.

"Robbie, you're soaking again"

She felt his brow. No apparent fever. Was it helping? The valerian. She dragged herself from the bed.

With Liz, every conversation was tinged with tension of a different kind. Each action contained the seed of argument. Each activity a kernel of distrust.

"This place cannot carry anyone who hasn't work to do."

"Where can they go? Besides, if they work harder it runs out quicker."

"Don't be evasive Robert. You know who I'm talking about."

He did know what she was driving at. He screwed up his eyes, shaking his head, scratching it.

"It's not up to me. It's some kind of deal."

"The lopsidedness of which would be more apparent if you didn't shield her."

"How should I know? The arrangement with her father - it may benefit the works."

Her voice was full of scorn.

"It may benefit the owner."

He was sharp with her.

"Well we can't know."

She flew to her feet and started sweeping noisily and clumsily. Behind her back he rolled his eyes. She muttered.

"It may benefit the manager."

Robbie snapped back.

"Oh for goodness' sake!"

She glared at him.

"Fuck you. Well, do something to make me think different! Feel different. Do something to demonstrate. Talk to me. Notice I exist."

Robbie sighed hard, angry. Suddenly so tired. It was hopeless. He got to his feet and grabbed his coat.

"Well?"

He opened the door.

"I'm going out."

He saw she would cry.

Quickly he left, slamming it.

He was shocked by the ferocity of Ana's anger. He had ticked her off, mildly it had seemed to him, about her concentration. There had been several workers nearby.

She had stormed off, leaving Wynter in embarrassment, his authority undermined. As soon as it was possible to take a natural break in the proceedings he went to find her, pursued by smirks or sneers.

He found her on the cliff top, near the old alum-grinding stone.

"How can you insult me in front of them?"

She was wild-eyed and, he suspected, had been drinking something.

"It was barely anything."

"When I am leaving soon."

Information or threat?

"It was just a small comment."

"You're happy to be careless when it suits you."

"Ana...."

"But not when I do some small thing."

"That's not true."

"You want them to see how you treat me."

"Ana, calm down..."

"Fuck you!"

"Ana come on, come back to the works. I'm sorry. I apologise. It's just that I can't have double standards."

"One for you, one for me."

"How can you say that? I give you a lot of leeway, I just don't want them to see it."

"For you to give, when it suits."

"When you want Ana, when we both want."

She was silent, but her body trembled with fury.

"Ana, please, just go back."

"Everything nicely managed."

He rolled his eyes, struggling to rein in his impatience.

"You treat me like a child."

"Ana, I don't, it's just that things have to be proper. I have to be the manager. You have to respect that in front of them, or they will become mischievous children."

"Like me!"

"God!"

He was exasperated.

'Ana, for this thing to work..."
"Work for you."
"For both of us!"
She seethed.
"You go."
"What?"
"You go back."
"And?"
"I come later."
"Ana!"
It was hopeless. He went back to the works.

The parting keel

One day, Ana's father arrives unannounced. Everyone is busy. She dismisses herself for the afternoon and they walk south along the cliff edge. They pass the headland below the old tower where, remembering where Robbie says he found it, she fingers the jet at her throat.

Winds whip their words away, between silences, fragments.

The captain tries to interpret her appearance – the cut hair, boyish clothes, the red woollen. She responds, off-hand.

"I'm foreign anyway."

After a pause he broaches it with her.

"Ana, I can't wait."

He says nothing of what he has been hearing about her.... situation.

"This man Turner promises, but I have learned he is not to be trusted. He will make me wait for ever."

Ana tries to digest what this would mean.

"But to break the arrangement? It's surely dangerous."

His gaze strays out to sea, to the horizon.

"I will be far away."

They have both stopped walking.

"And me?"

On their return she shows him the assay house. He is reassured by the presence of the boy. Everything looks in order here, he thinks.

Outside, some distance away, the manager seems to be oblivious. The captain instructs Ana to apologise to Wynter for his lack of time and, as he leaves, salutes from his horse.

Solitary. Ana's father sat on the jetty. A fine mist, part spray, part drizzle, part cloud, obscured the sloops that plied in and out of the harbour mouth as the tide reached its height and started to fall back.

He didn't need to see the boats. The sour reek of coal dust told him the origin of one ship. The wheeling gulls and their cries another, the clean smell of fresh caught fish. The richer, saltier, pungency that the pots and nets carried. The undertow stink of a scant-scrubbed urine ship, restocked for the return journey with clean sacks of alum flour, raised in timber boxes, and covered with the tar. Slap of oars. Shouts of sailors. Harsh screeches of the gulls. The sting of the waves. The rhythm of trade – incoming, outgoing.

He sniffed a deep draught of the mingled aromas. Searching for the urine ship. His ship. He had traded his post for passage. Not without a tugging regret.

Sure, no more the butt of ale-room ridicule. The piss-captain, the admiral stinker.

Who has made discreet enquiries. Whose new berth would be packed head-to-tail, like sprats, with the black sovereigns. Currency of souls, who would work their passage in revenue, on arrival in the Americas. No value in the weak ones, naturally they would fall away in the unavoidable test of the voyage. Savage justice.

Regrets for his home? None. He had not been rich there, although respected.

No, there was no going back to his home. His daughter, however? Ugly rumour in the taverns. More than he had bargained for with the owner. Little enough trade from the works. Hardly worth swapping the lye for. Her passage, worked her passage. He would kill any one of them. He wouldn't. This collection of English savages. Any excuse to teach him a lesson. War over or not. But that had finished him here. What had he traded here? Her? Pointless to think on it. That rebellious streak of hers was also his own.

The drizzle intensified, it was muscling up into rain. Soon it would be a heavy net of water. Curse this English fucking cold. He craved Africa, craved the Americas. But that route, through the eye of the hot sun, driven through the doldrum furnace, might not be safe for her. For them.

Out loud, into the squall he spoke the overheard phrase.

"Bigger fish to fry, Spitzbergen way."

"Ana...you do know.... don't you.... how I feel? About.... you."

For a moment Ana looked profoundly sad.
"Robbie...."
She paused.
"Yes."
"Nothing."
She shifted uncertainly.
"Ana...."
He saw her eyes. The slight liquefaction.

"And that.... I. Well.... I.... I'm in...."

Saw the solitary tear tremble on the lip and roll over the edge.

"Love.... with you."

Ana looked down. Time passed.

"Damn you Ana!"

She looked up timidly.

"Say something".

From the other eye. The second tear.

"Robbie...."

She started again.

"Robert. I don't know how to use that word."

"Ana, use any words. Just say what you feel."

"Robbie, please. I didn't think that we would have to say.... that word. I am afraid."

Robert closed his eyes. In the great stretch of the region, of England, of the empire, of the world.... spreading out, the vast surfeit of everything....now dissolved, reduced, diminished....to this. Everything dependent on this – on how, what, she....

"How can I know what to think, Ana?"

"About what?"

"About everything."

She resolves not to cry.

"Everything?"

"Yes. Us. We. You. Me.... everything."

"I don't know."

"Don't know what?"

"To say."

The tears roll down.

"Just say what you feel."

They roll down, stream down.

"I am confused. I....Liz....this place. Robbie. What can I say. I can't."

"Oh God!"

He clasps her to him. He hugs her fiercely.
It escapes as a sigh.
"Oh God. Ana...."

Salt tang in sea fret. Hiss and roar of the unseen tide. Massed outcrops looming in whiteness, over whiteness, in supersaturation. Below, rich pickings amongst the cliff-fall rubble? Above, a blurred stain, blood seeping into lint, moving in white, with the semblance of a girl's figure.

There was a little turquoise left in the twilight. She pitched suddenly into the deeper gloom along the alleyway at the far side of the roaching shed.

There was a scraping and scuttling along by her feet. Rats? She stamped, shuddering. The crisp crunch told her something else – insects? Beetles, grasshoppers?

The left hand, dragging her fingertips along the rough sandstone of the blank wall, for guidance. The wind continued to whip and drift the dry autumn leaves along the track. She kept closer to the wall – knowing brambles and nettles filled out the hawthorns that formed the other boundary.

She reached the corner and peered round. A whiff of peat smoke, laced with caustic air from the sheds. No one. Straying out of the shadows she nipped across the open space in short, quick steps. She moved into the similar shadow of the cooling house. Listened for any giveaway sounds. Boots stirring on the loose stones, breathing. The cold deepened a degree, hint of frost.

There is a fence post, some wire.
On the post a twist of fleece snags.

Ana bowls down the arid ditch between two spiky armies of marram, like rags flung by the wind.

The hard crunch of the keel parting pebbles.
High up on the beach, past the sand, the hard keel clearing the knuckled shell-stones, the rounded berm of storm-heaped boulders. The rudder lifted, as it moved over the foreshore scars, the weed-sleeved spurs clear only a couple of feet down as the flat-bottomed coble floated over wrack and anemones.

The iron-wrapped forward keel, a battering ram to the shore. The two iron-wrapped rear keels, snug to the sea like cart wheels in rutways, landed on the slippery rock fingers through which the incoming tide trickled.

The cobles, oared softly in moonlight, slipping over the millpond bay like leaves in a millrace. Rolling with the swell. The sweet lapping of timbers up to the high sharp bow.

At the last second the rudder lifted clear of the bony rock outcrops. The coble expertly turned, sliding round like a flat pebble on ice, to land stern first. Men leaping out on all sides into the slippery shallows carrying ropes, sacks, lanterns, sticks, knives.

The harsh light-fall of the moon, washing the gaunt faces of the cliffs. Washing the shadowy gaunt faces of the rogue panniermen. Washing the patient galloways, swell of sacks, dusted with alum flour. Moon shadows, long over the rocks, shadowing in the potholes and postholes, the rock pools, the flooded rutways, tide coming up twin channels, parallel rails of hard reflective water. Unwelcome moonlight, on a cloudy night, suddenly breaking onto the stage, a curtain accidentally drawn back. The cobles, jammed into the foreshore or hanging back, bobbing on the surface glitter. Half-shadowed anxious faces of the ruddermen. Grim haste. The sacks awkwardly borne on the slick of black seaweed over the pitted, barnacled rocks. A hard fall, sprawled in the shadows, a trickle of blood. Black in the moonlit water. The spilled sack, ruined in shallow water, scooped back anyway tipped into the waiting cobles. The dry and dampened sacks heaped together. Hastily balancing the load. Heaving men, hard straining to push the beached cobles off the foreshore rocks.

The panniermen, bells silenced, lead the galloways along the foreshore, quickly to avoid being cut off by the tide, but eschewing the causeway. Too risky.

A light on the cliff?

Urgent activity.

The panniermen splashing the baskets, scour the carts. The spilt alum on the foreshore, will be cleared by the tide.

Under his greatcoat, swaddled. Scrambling over the stern as he steadies the buoyant craft and follows beside her. Squeezed in beside the crammed cargo. Redraped in his layers, sipping the proffered flask that has emerged from them, eyes closed to shut out everything but the cold and this bitter-sweet draught.

The boats hard-heaved off the scars, helped by the lift of the incoming tide. The cobles slide round, like leaves in a whirlpool, oars move in unison. Swiftly, deftly, following the line of water between the raking outcrops of the scars. Listing slightly, from the sacks.

The cliff light a briefly revealed star?

The moon's face as quickly withdrawn. Heavy cloud-curtains re-draped. Somewhere, out beyond the vanished ghosts of the silent cobles a sloop?

The restless tide rolls forward, over itself, and attains the foot of the cliff. Renews, its ritual attrition.

6

Meniscus

The jet bible

Alone in the tumultuous dark, in riving winds, Alcuin worked his way along the narrow cliff-edge path. Underneath the uproar of the squalling, of the gusts, and the slap of wet cloth, was the persistent nagging hiss and deeper moan of the sea, far below.

Pushed through bushes, thorns caught sides of pants and sleeves.

Darkness, not quite complete. The vague blacker smear of the intermittent track was picked out sporadically with a dismal gleam on standing water. Gusts flung sleet at him. Handfuls of gravel-hail. Stung, head aching from the persistent numbing chill on his cheek and brow.

North towards Scarshead once again to minister and teach, where a message he has received tells him Kenelm will be. The cliff path he now knows well, and the huge plummeting drop beyond it. He had not meant to finish in the dark. The day had started mild, and he had dawdled, but autumn had struck back with malice.

Alcuin hardly dared look up from the semblance of the path – the ache of concentration. Nevertheless, he kept sensing that far off to the east was a glimmer. Something like an unseen moon, behind storm clouds, but too low where, in this weather, he doubted there could be a ship.

Not so much to keep his spirits up as to regulate the heavy momentum of his soggy boots he mumbled a part of Caedmon's hymn. Just a couple of lines to a repetitive dirge of his own making. To counteract the drudgery that was undermining his sense of attention to the danger, invisible and close, of the cliff edge. Not quite consciously – it was more or less a part of his rhythm, of his sodden-footed trudging. It had been like this for hours, like a primitive incantation, the raw material of prayer.

A rubble wall started to pick itself up out of the blackened grass to his left, and soon it had assembled into a rough barrier. He leant to it and felt its lichened surface. It meant he was passing the old tower.

Alcuin knew from the map he had himself illuminated that behind this wall was a boggy field, kept short by sheep, that ranged down from the tower's ruined stone to this boundary wall which from sea resembled a battlement. A useful illusion he mused, for the security of the works. Following the wall was easy. It was taller than him and he looked ahead, as another drab hint of sail flapped once out of the inky sea-sky.

Illicit?

Following the assistant's encouragement to make a mark in his book Alcuin had embarked on a kind of map of the locations of his journeys.

Rounding the wall the land opened out, he remembered, picturing the distant curves of the quarry brow and the wide sweep of the bay.

On his map the leaf greens and earths and aquatints – shot through with sunlight – refracted the warmth of spring. None of this was visible tonight but with this image held, he pitched forward more recklessly down the long slope in what he felt to be the right direction. Strode over sandy tussocks of soaking marram with new determination.

Overnight the trees had been swept bare. The ragged flags of russet and amber dragged from their rigging. They were herded into heaps in the corner of the yards. They rustled over the cobbles.

They wasted by the trackside, dumped into ditches like so much slam.

A few days of bluster had emboldened overnight into a gale. Under its howl the big tides crashed. The cottages were buffeted like sloops straining their anchor ropes in the harbour. Draughts explored every cranny, the timbers creaked. The pantiles lifted.

Alcuin's initial shock at first seeing the despoliation of the coast had finally resigned itself to a deeply pessimistic acceptance. Seemingly all the land along the sea slopes and sea cliffs was being churned to waste. Monumental labour was levelling peaks and filling up the wykes and hollows with their grey dust. It was not just Scarshead, and the Ness. All the time more places added to the list: Stoupe, Mulgrave, Sands, Murkside, Fell, Boulby, Burnside, Loft Houses. More added year on year.

Chaloner's Pope would not be cursing now, but laughing mirthlessly about the poisoned chalice of the alum secret. Alcuin's thoughts turned often to this parchment, not a *mappa mundi* or *marinari*, but of the country. A *mappa Angliae* – made of skin, in thin bloodless layers. A fraying corner, lifted and peeled would soon peel back the whole green swathe of the land, uprooting the grass. Trees would topple in its rolling tide as more and more of the grey cadaverous flesh was revealed. Honeyed sandstone cottages shaken to bits as the relentless stripping back of the map, curling and crumpling, levelled the hills and hamlets. The flesh a suppurating grey, nearing death.

Alcuin murmured the chant:

In flagellis potum fellis
Bibisti amarissimum...

While being whipped you drank the bitterest draft.

Kenelm's eyes light up. Leafing through Alcuin's book, long ago his gift, he looks at the work in progress of the map. He looks at the sketch of the hand stone.

The moors, he explains, are a territory staked out by God. The moors are God's maps – laid out over the earth, stretching from the western vale eastwards, over the riggs, to the sea.

A holy map, criss-crossed by trails, held down by stones, that stop it flapping up like a cloth laid out in a breeze. The standing stones, the moorland crosses, the marker stones – they all hold down the map.

Alcuin listens, impressed.

After the dissolution, Kenelm explains, that map is largely vanished, torn, disintegrated, blown away. Still, a few fragments are pegged down by the stone crosses.

He tells Alcuin: your travels combine to re-draw the paths that stitch that map back to the landscape. Your ways re-create the old ways, joining the sheep tracks and pannierways to the monks' trods. Only your threads tie in the coastal works, and string them back to your source.

Back to the church under the church, thinks Alcuin.

Then he thinks, no. As Kenelm, inspired by his own words, lapses back into a silent reverie. He thinks no. No, I am like a lost sheep. Vainly crossing and recrossing the same paths, wearing in the evidence of my directionless searchings, incising the pattern of my waywardness.

Ken picks up the sketch again. It reminds him, naturally, he tells Alcuin, of the stigmata. The palm held out to be examined, by the doubter.

Use of the alum block, thinks Alcuin. Styptic, to staunch the flow.

"Thumbs up?"

Ken is startled by this sudden question.

"What?"

"Thumbs up, thumbs down?"

Kenelm is puzzled.

"Thumbs up?"

"Yes, here, on this one. But on the other stones, down. And they are carved out. Not in relief. So one cannot say if the hands, one facing left and one right incidentally, are seen from the front or back. If the back of the hand then this would most naturally be from the front. Like this."

Alcuin raised both arms, facing Kenelm, hands out, thumbs down.

"But then again, seeing the palms, would be from the back."

He turned. His back facing Kenelm, thumbs down.

"Why does it matter?"

"Well, palm out, thumbs up. It could be approbation, or assent. In any case it's the natural shape going in to a handshake."

"Yes. That would be a firm handshake, if only it could move to grasp!"

"Also the position of our Lord's hands, on the cross."

Kenelm nodded seriously.

"But the thumbs down?"

"Dissent? Goodbye? I don't know, it doesn't seem so friendly."

"At least not the concealed thumb. Peeking through."

This made Alcuin laugh. It was rare for Kenelm to refer to an obscene gesture so casually.

"Indeed, indeed!"

Kenelm closed the book, handing it back to Alcuin. He grew solemn.

"Stick to the path, Alcuin."

Peered at him over knitted brows.

"Oh I will."

He smiled.

"When I find it."

Alcuin tested Kenelm with ideas he had picked up from the dissenters.

"They don't fear the pit. Too abstract. In any case some have little choice between good and evil. If men can't eat they must steal."

Kenelm shook his head. Alcuin tried another tack.

"Some have lost faith in the church. They look to help mankind – in more practical ways"

"Alcuin, this is mere carpentry. What of the holy spirit?"

"Ken, the Gnostics believed that man's spirit could be released from its substance, the body."

"Alcuin!"

As usual Alcuin created a ferment of fluster and discomfort within Kenelm.

"Yes. I know. It offends you. Shocks you. But these are just the words, Ken. Why not consider these words? To speak of promiscuity is neither to preach nor practice it."

"I don't want to hear any of these words!"

"The spirit is released when we die. I know. But is that to say that the effectuality of a Christian life is not an objective? In a better world who is to say that the spirit cannot be released while we yet live?"

"It's hearsay, alchemy..."

"Down there..."

Alcuin indicated the alum works.

"...they hone the art of transformation. They improve and purify, taking the rough stones and bringing out the white alum flour. It's experience, judgement, like all the honest passed-down trades of the past."

Kenelm, agitated, held his tongue.

"And yes...it's luck, guesswork, it's what you could call faith."

Ken waited.

"But those men. Those women. Their children. They are largely indifferent to our message. They are treated wretchedly, they subsist, if lucky, little better than wild things."

"This is old ground between us."

Sadly, thought Alcuin. It widens.

"Knowledge increases its layers, of the world, of science, of things..."

"Things of the world, as you say. Not gnosis."

"Secret things Kenelm, hidden things, things dug up, broken down, revealed, discovered...."

Kenelm raised his voice.

"Alcuin, you fear the alum trade! How many times have you referred to it? That devilish business with the egg."

"But now I understand it. I have watched everything. Its aim is sincere. It brightens our world. It's stuff done with the raw materials of the world. That is not the evil part - the wickedness is in the people. The way they are treated."

There was a pause. Both men breathed steadily to calm.

"This will be my world from now on."

Kenelm shook his head sadly, smiling. Alcuin breathed in slowly, and exhaled.

"Everything led me to this Ken, even you. My father, my book, the many paths over the moors, the monster, the egg..."

Alcuin trailed off, like a trod disappearing over the rigg, into the mist.

Kenelm is exasperated. Shouting.
"In the old days?"
He spat.
Alcuin looked down.

In the old days it was no different from now.'

"Quieter, Kenelm."

'Pah! In the old days it was no different from now. Look at their faces. Your liquormen, your pitmen. Moving this earth to get to the next."

"There was more hope."

"Rubbish. We provide the hope. They're still suffering, still starving. At least we're not being put to the sword. Why were the brothers' houses burnt down? What about the Pilgrimage of Grace? A spiritual pilgrimage yet the abbots hanged! The old days."

Alcuin sniffed.

"Oh, you have your old book. Your old book from before the dissolution. Yes, the one, for my sins, that I gave you! Why don't the colours fade? Yes, of course you know. Well? Fixed in alum. The same starvelings fixed it then. Why? So your predecessors could float their leaf, and fix His Majesty."

"Perhaps."

Kenelm was insistent.

"Of course they did."

Alcuin shrugged dismissively.

"Of course they did. The Romans used it. The great books of the dark ages - created laboriously in the freezing cells of these isolated houses, fixed by the lay brothers. These forgotten monasteries, tucked away in the wooded dales, reached by a barren trod. These were the only lamps of learning in those good old days. When the raiders from the east trampled over the Holy Roman Empire and laid waste across Christendom"

Alcuin was stirred, flushed. He blustered, spluttered.

"It's now they need hope! Here, in this world. Hope to remain on it. Hope that the ceaseless labour will give them something to eat. That won't be stolen away by their masters...."

"Oh there you go, *ranting* again."

"Don't preach to me about that pack of lies and falsehoods."

"Alcuin!"

Kenselm sighed. He turned to the fire and played with it for a spell. He fussed with his pipe. Twilight had retreated from the windows and a deeper gloom was growing in the room corners.

Kenelm resumed more gently.

"Alcuin, my friend."

"Alcuin, I have seen you writing and drawing in that book of yours. It has pages as yet unfixed. That book came to you from the fires of the dissolution. That was your gift. You don't need to complete that book. That space is yours for now. You're a lodger. A travelling player."

"Yes, Ken. And what I write in it is that if He chooses not to be more merciful in this world then He knows His purpose in creating dissent."

"That's enough!"

Kenelm frowned hard, he burnt with indignation. Genuinely shocked he inspected minutely some scuff marks on the flagged floor.

Alcuin was shocked too. He got to his feet and slapped some life into his thighs and buttocks. His face was hot from the fire but his feet were chilled, and legs cold. He shuffled around a while, avoiding Kenelm's face. He flung a handful of branches on the fire and jabbed it with a stick.

Kenelm absorbed the meanings of these movements. Noted the jabs. They seal the points, the way ink settles under the skin from the pin.

Alcuin's physical presence, slapped back to life, a challenge to him to knock him down. At the same time he saw Alcuin's bulk was wrapped bones. He saw the fire-red cheeks, and the careless shaving. Alcuin's wrist projecting from his sleeve, delicate, wiry, artistic. Poking the fire like someone impaling a leaf with a rapier – accurately, but with the force in check. Holding the rapier, holding the brush, the charcoal, the pen. He loves Alcuin, and he despairs of this deep well of stubbornness, that he also admires. He sees himself as an enclosing cave – providing shelter if no comfort – that Alcuin throws his words into, to see how altered they are when they echo back.

"Alcuin, Alcuin."

He started gently, kindly again.

"In Whitby the other day I saw the bible that someone has carved out of coal."

Alcuin glanced up at him. He knew this.

"The cover, I mean, is carved with great..."

What? He thought. He would not say devotion.

"... with great dedication. A prodigious feat of strength with delicacy. Someone hacked this lump of coal out of the earth. One of your miners from the good old days perhaps. Someone from that century, or this, or the next. That you recognise in the faces down there by the clamps, by the tanks. Some brute with a pick, a taste for ale, a beaten wife."

Kenelm looked at Alcuin. He smoulders or sulks? He went on.

"Some other face. That you recognise by the settlers, or walking down the lane on Sunday, in this generation, or the last. That man takes the coal and with homemade tools, but with a surgeon's skill, carves his message of the bible into this stone and weighs it down by its cover, as black as any ancient leather, clean and black, and...as beautiful."

"Yes. I've seen it. It's jet.'

Kenelm nodded in acknowledgement, waited. It was smouldering. He let the breeze die off it for a few seconds.

"That's our work too, Alcuin. We take the book. We work with it. With the same patience as they did in the 'old days'. As you do in your book, in your work. We work it, and it takes a lifetime of infinite care and judgement and that lesson we tell shines out with its depth, its gleam, its figure, and relief."

"And that bible lives on the dusty bookshelves of some so called gentlemen..."

"Alcuin. That is not our business. That bible lives undiscovered for some ages, like your book. Fixed in alum, carved in coal, one day, unearthed, it catches the light and shines into the dark corners."

Alcuin remained silent. In all his simmering he had suddenly conjured the dark eyes of the Spanish girl, their wide intensity, as they burned a clearing though the dense steam of the boiling pans.

"Alcuin, my brother, you are a free spirit."

"Don't call me a heretic!"

Ken opened his palms and widened his arms, in a gesture of exasperated resignation but he went on.

"You used to be able to take a goad, Alcuin. But perhaps this one gets close to the bone."

Alcuin was quiet. But if I were of the Free Spirit, I would go to that girl.

The fire was very low now. It was quiet in the room. A slight hiss came from the hearth.

"The soul in union with God cannot sin."

It was a provocation. Kenelm suddenly lost the will to argue. He felt tired. But Alcuin stoked up.

"Well I too was in Whitby the other day too and I saw a man who might have carved a cover for a jet bible. He was carrying an armful of bad corn, which stood for a month's wages. The traders talked it down in price till they might have just as well have kicked it down to the quayside and floated the dust of it out on the falling tide. When you see a family man with tears welling in his eyes like that with some gloating crowd mimicking his desperation for sneers, you want to kick over the tables in the temple."

He paused.

"And I do not just mean that metaphorically – from Turner to His Majesty."

Ken just looked at him.

Alcuin stood up and, after a second or two, left the room.

In Alcuin's mind there is a journey he will never take. Climbing out of Rosedale. The comfort of the valley soon dropping away as the track opens out onto the wide expanse of the moortop.

They come to the stone marker. He is her guide.

"Crosses were frequently erected where four roads met, at the entrance or centre of a village and where, during the perambulation of boundaries, the processioners rested and regaled themselves."

Alcuin and the girl wade through the heather. Birds explode from cover, flap out on either side and skew off.

In his mind it's high, high summer. There is no care or fear.

The road is an old one, he tells her, that the monks took. It led to the church that is now underneath the church.

And she tells him – like the monks took to *La Cartuja*.

Yes, he says.

The walk through bracken, through heather, the soft droppings of the sheep and the adders. The heather honey. The monks' mead. The woven grasses, like her hair braided. The stepping stones. The rowans. These things link back, to his childhood, and forward, to the life he might choose.

Yes, she says.

The cork oaks, the olive trees, the black vultures glide. Some water left in the stream in May. Afterwards no. Food is not their problem. Thirst. The cruelty, she has been told, of the sun.

This track is not deserted. People pass, with their packs. They unwrap food, and sit at the base of the stone cross, eating.

In summer this path is made of light. Their souls open like the pages of an illuminated manuscript.

The fire started in the kitchens, it spread quickly to the refectory. Perhaps the enforcers started it, perhaps the fleeing monks; perhaps it was a cinder spat from the fire. Roof timbers collapsed.

It was clear frosty night. Sparks shot into the air, they swirled towards the white smudge of the milky way, their hot brass splinters glittered and moved in challenge to the old, cold aloof whiteness of the stars.

The fire spread to the ambulatory, the cloister and the nave; or was carried there. The fire raged behind the stained glass of the rose window until it finally poured upwards out of the shattered panes – its sinewy twister an obscene gesture to heaven.

He had stoked the fire up before bed. Engulfed in his heavy, clammy bedclothes. In the hot, damp dark Alcuin drifted out of dreams of Dissolution flames to dreams of the girl. Hard with diffused desire, against his usual practice, he simply succumbed. Gripping himself, as the Log King grips the log. Movements brought little waves of prickling euphoria, that circulated in him when he paused, eyes closed luxuriating in the ebb, resuming energised by the surge. Slowing toward the completion. Warmth flooded through, relaxation, eyes closed, he dozed.

Waking again, he rose in disgust. The uncomfortable, chilling, sticky damp. The clammy cold of his sweaty clothes. He stripped, and shivering, taking the cold water from the bowl splashed first his face and then with the rag squeezed the cold water over the glued hair of his belly and thighs. Freezing, awake, he dressed and looked to relight the fire.

Avoid studying the Roman gods Kenelm had said. Their domain is not only the fire in the grape, the sap thrusting in a young tree, the blood pounding in the veins of a young animal. Nature's mysterious and unruly tides rise and fall.

El Azabache

Something fell away inside him, as the shale cliff, repeatedly probed, at its foot, by the receding and returning tide, suddenly shears off and falls into the sea. In a few muddy washes the cloudiness disappears. The cliff looks the same. Blue sky, the seagulls wheel, and the world has turned.

"Where?"
The owner turned to Wynter, a hint of malicious smile twitched at the corner of his mouth.
"Spanish colonies....? The Americas...?"
The fluttering, panicky feeling rose in Wynter's chest.
"When?"
Turner shrugged.
"Irrelevant now.. irrelevant, when they went."
Wynter knew he looked foolish. He forced himself to ask no further questions. He kicked at the ground. He looked around desperately. Itching to move, he was rooted.
"Wise course."
Wynter stared at the ground.
"Lye trade all pissed out."
The manager remained quiet.
"Africa first perhaps."
Quiet.
"Or duty-free fishing?"
Wynter looked up. Confused.
"Not the Americas?"
"Depends how you measure them."

"I don't follow you."

Wynter was unable to make sense of this. Was Turner simply goading him?

"Fishing the big 'un. Maybe."

The manager stared at him. Desperately trying to read the owner's taunting half-sneer.

"Greenland?"

Turner was losing interest. Wandering off along the quay. Some yards away he half-turned.

"Makes no difference either way."

Wynter's imaginings were toxic with slam.

The blunt facts sharp sediment in Wynter's clouded thoughts. He tried to sift each out, and examine. He tried to think of nothing, trying to allow the muddy mixture to settle itself out. Just resting, letting it settle. Letting the finely divided shale, the iron suspension, added finings, slowly settle. Hoping by this method to finally separate out the mind's slam, and get rid of it.

"Why?"
He flinches.
"Why did you..."
Liz is struggling for words.
"...nurture me. Raise me up, reassure me. Why trick me, let me go on pretending all was fine. Why ridicule me. Leave me out of the party whispers. Let all the world know. Except me. Victim of glances and concealed gestures and turned-away faces. Why!"
"That's not...."
What can he say?
"....how. It was...."
"Oh! And how was it?"

"It just..."

"Oh yes! It just happened. Just happened. The word fucking no.... never fucking...."

"Liz...."

She glared at him. She looked ugly and raw. Blotched and streaked.

"Liz...she's gone. It's over. It's...."

"Over for you maybe. Oh poor you. I'll mourn for you. I hope she's dead anyway."

She was crying.

He stood helpless.

She was furious with herself. Most of all because she did feel sorry for him. Infuriatingly, she felt for him instinctively, as for a wounded animal, but she would not comfort him. She saw he was bereft and it pained her and she wanted to hit him and throw everything in the house at him.

Robbie resented her pain, that seemed more raw than his.

There was a wild invisible mad child in the room who would only rage soundlessly, refusing to scream.

High up on the track. Silhouetted, wobbled by heat haze, a tiny figure. Eyes squeezed, Robbie peers into the glare. A pounding in his chest has started up, thinking the impossible: that she might be back. Nothing. A boy, some urchin ragged waif, idly kicking stones, decapitating the hogweed.

Robbie felt listless. On a day like this he just couldn't get started. The fire wouldn't light. Nothing bored him more than the view from his window. The outline of the headland. Inert stone. The drab grasses, quivering in the tiresome nagging wind. Passive obstinate stone. The blank face of the stone walling. The stubborn gloom of the cloud. This day, like so many identical previous days. He felt tired in his bones. His head wouldn't clear, all dullness. The wind whined in the chimney. There was a damp chill in the air in the house.

He thought of his father, whose hard-won fragile status as a head liquorman, was always at risk from the whim of the resentful lackey who had been the manager at that time. Irrepressibly cheerful, he had seemed, when Robbie was a child. But at fourteen or so, Robbie was apprenticed in the assay house, where his early prowess at literacy and numeracy led him away from the easy camaraderie of the trades, and into the long solitary silences of the lab. At fourteen he became aware of his father's first difficulties, saw that his encouraging grin was stretched over deep strain and tiredness. Having to drag himself up the slopes to the quarries. The daily strain of appeasing the manager in those days, or the owner, wary of their moods. Aware of the hovering presence of the younger cheaper liquormen ready to usurp him. Getting clumsy, with the collection of sprains, tiredness, rheumatism. Never well-enough fed. Nearly forty years old and Robbie had seen the thin fabric of his good humour, his threadbare youth, worn through with the years.

Now it was Robbie.

Stepping outside the front door, the wind wrestled him. Sometimes the wind was an unwanted playmate, jostling him out of boredom, like a bullying child. He shook it off, unintimidated, and hunching into his coat, brusquely crunched the gravel.

The solitary trudge down to the works. Every blade of grass in its usual place. Robbie felt the weary acquiescence of his father's steps in his own walk.

He felt more alone than ever. Gulls jeered him. Crows croaked their scorn. Unsmiling men nodded briefly, or doffed ambiguously. Groups of workers seemed to have some derisive joke between them, as he passed.

He faced the familiar worn door of the lab – felt the lock's stiffness as he half-turned the key, released it and then turned it fully. Lifting the door slightly to clear the scrape over the stone step he allowed the door to swing clear. The wooden stool, by the empty hearth, simply there. Where Ana used to sit. The room was bright and bare and empty like a Quaker chapel. It promised nothing. The hearth neat and bare, the fire irons, a thin coating of dust. The empty stool.

The paperwork, the samples, the instruments, the assay dishes, the dull mahogany gleam off his desk. Dead objects without interest. There was an inward draining of him, the listless emptiness sinking down into a sudden inward physical sob.

Robbie laid his face on the cold surface of his desk. So tired he could close his eyes and sleep. He found himself repeating her name quietly, and he tried it aloud, matter-of-factly, like a statement.

"Ana"

He slapped his hand down hard on the desk, so that it stung. He shivered at the chill in the lab, and this finally roused him. There was dry kindling, and some papers, and coals. Methodically he set about lighting the fire. When it was going well he put a couple of dry logs on, and some coal, and wafted it to a roar with a plate. Then he put the kettle on to boil.

Other days Robbie has long mundane spells. Things happen instinctively. Following the usual rules. Flowers that open and later close. Birds issuing their familiar cries. Things seem routine. Then he remembers. The shock is a heaving breaker, catching him unawares, rocking him back off balance. Knocking him over, forcing him under.

When he remembers she has gone.

He finds the jet.

Dry-eyed, his body sobs.

He wants to think she has left it as some kind of gesture of reconciliation. Something he should assume is finally for him to give to Liz? Something perhaps just to keep for himself, which will bring back in a flash the smack of vermilion? Something she overlooked, tucked away in the back of the drawer, when she left so abruptly? He knows. Knows it is probably something she might just have forgotten to take. Something she probably forgot she had.

Robbie remembered how he had felt, the time the little jet charm was all Ana had worn.

Amazed.

Robbie was amazed. Simply amazed.

It had happened.

Ana and Robbie in the room.

It was quiet. Completely peaceful. Robbie felt completely at peace, completely calm.

Ana smiled. She made a little shrug. She seemed.... not happy, simply.... at ease.

Robbie smiled. He exhaled softly, closing his eyes gently. Reopening them.

Some small noises, birds, outside. It had happened. They had made love.

It was the most natural thing. They had made love and now this was after they had made love.

Every tension, fear and desire, had simply gone. Lifted. Vanished.

After a while he moved closer to her. He hugged her gently. Her skin had cooled a little.

They stayed like that for some time.

Finally, she spoke.

"Robert."

He smiled.

"Robert, I have to go."

He sighed.

"Yes, I know."

"No. I have to leave. I am leaving here. Leaving this place."

After a second or two he understood.

"Going away?"

She nodded.

"You're telling me now?"

"I..."

She looked at him. A look he couldn't interpret. She continued.

"Robert. I... have to. I have to go. Something arranged. I should have said before. I ..."

"No."

He shook his head sadly.

"Not now."

El azabache.

On her breastbone, the jet brooch a third eye between Ana's dark swollen buds.

What might have been said before. What might come later. What would inevitably come later. The end, as always, unravelled with the beginning. Their lovemaking, even the second time, some small time between, already more knowing. More known. There was a moment when they both opened their eyes and saw each other. In the certain knowledge of the unravelling, the cord tightened.

He has been left with everything. Still he struggles to understand why it feels like nothing.

Liz took the oatcakes off the hot tray. Blowing her fingers. She prized them off, and into the bowl. She put the hot tray on the hearth flags. She took the honey jar, and the jug of small beer.
There was a mingling of aromas. The hot oatcakes on top. The vinegar tang of the ale. The sweet undertow of the honey.
Sometimes, when Liz smiled, each benign warm part of creation assembled to shine through it.
In a tempest, he thought, tie yourself to the wheel.

She senses that he wants to wallow in self-pity. Wants to be maudlin. It's a way, she sees, of continuing the severed relationship. It gives credibility to it, although it's over. She knows it's not fleeting, not in moments, not occasional reflection. It fills up all his thoughts, everything else is pushed out, or forces in by dint of sheer necessity.
A long period of recuperation, following illness.

She loses her patience, seeing him mope.
"Robbie, you know full well. Dabberlocks or sugar kelp, curls in a bucket of sea-water. For however long it lies there. Weeks, months. Just keep topping it up. Taken out it quickly dries. Brittle, it snaps."

In fact there is a weight lifted. He hates to acknowledge it. He can enjoy the abstract pleasure of his meticulous measurements of kelp and piss. He even feels he is making progress with the efficacy of the crystallisation, of the purity. Though it is extremely hard to tell. He no longer begrudges this work as something in the way, of time with her, of little importance. A different anxiety, but one he is familiar with, used to, has returned. A whole community to feed, to support.

Liz had gathered an armful from the hedgerows and, the wind having dropped in the late afternoon of a honeyed autumn, returned to the house. She put a jar on the window board and arranged loosely a long russet-leaved stem, two drooping clumps of dry puckered elderberry, a thistle with small purple heads, a sinewy bent twig of hawthorn, with its wine-dark berries, and some copper-tinged rowan. She rotated the jar half a turn on its base and the twigs silhouetted against the sky, against the grid of panes. The last of the sun glowed translucent through the autumn of the rowan leaves. She sat in the chair and looked at it, and then softly began to cry.

At Hilda's well

A shepherd, rounding up a few strays in the fields below the old tower, heard a noise. Puzzled he looked up. There was something. He frowned. Something different. He couldn't place it. Some alteration in the line and the edge, between the land and the sea. Hawthorns on the edge? Or were there? A haze hovered beyond. A slight haze – like faint smoke, or perhaps dust. He started walking towards it, with a vague anxiety and, moving faster, vaulted the gate, breaking into a run.

It had rained for days. Briefly it had eased, but the heavy grey clouds promised no more than momentary respite. Alcuin's cloak was wrapped tightly, his hat pulled down, as he sat on a tree bole, hoarding a handful of cob nuts, which he munched absently.

There was some sort of commotion, and he saw two men struggling up the hill towards him. He separated himself from the urgency of their shouts, maintaining his meditative attitude, until they were hard to ignore.

He must come.

It was an irritation.

Finally he understood the garbled urgency of their mission.

The Ness had gone.

He rose immediately and followed them.

The sky bruised, and blackened.
The sky bruised to black.

Unrelenting, water bucketed from the leaden skies. It sluiced down the slippery gullies. It spattered onto the heaps of shattered slate, pressing fragments down into the mud-shale.

The Ness had gone.

The cliff above it had gone over. The kelp-burners' cottages below, beneath the cliff that had buried them.

Surface water poured over the new edge of the collapsed cliff face, dragging down the sodden grasses. The raw rubble-face was streaming with water and the rough surface was still alive with creeping movement, sifting pebbles, and now and then bigger stones rolled down. They clattered onto the ruined heap on the Ness promontory.

Ragged distraught women harried Alcuin, like crows mobbing a merlin. Their keening was swept into a thin vortex of sound, and his mechanical crossing was no protection against it.

Down below, men were crawling over the rock pile like ants over a carcass. Pieces were carried away down the lines, lightly, like leaf fragments. Rain streamed over Alcuin's face. His soaked garments fought against him as he slithered down the loose chute that formed a short cut across the looping sludge of the pannier track. Which ran like a beck.

He could see the stove-in roofs of the hovels simply filled up with stones. Like so many chessmen heaped back in their box. In a couple of places the gable walls yet stood, their chimney stacks and pots above the rubble, still smoking serenely.

Closer, he could see how the rain hampered the rescue work. The ants became slither-footed men, the leaf fragments heavy unyielding rocks that could barely be passed down the line. The work was a cruel parody of their normal work. The men had been scrabbling for several hours. Alcuin saw a boy of about twelve, repeatedly dropping the rock at his turn, tears and rain washing dirt into his eyes. Alcuin shook off his restrictive outer garments and took his place in line, to protests from some, but his fresh strength lifted them. The boy was sent to help children manhandling a timber pole, as lever, to wedge apart the edge-boulders. They floundered and wept as frantic women shouted at them to dig, dig for their own fathers or brothers.

Soon Alcuin's thin frame was exhausted. He was dragged from the line, and replaced by another. He was taken to inspect some blood-sodden rags that the pitiless rain flattened. Leaching the blood into the grey grasses. Odd bits of bone and hair stuck to them. Eyes closed he intoned, a murmur, almost inaudibly, beneath the heavier drone of the rain. Bewildered and sobbing onlookers took it for whatever kind of benediction it might be.

The day went on into the murky twilight. The more practical women found food somewhere, begged from neighbouring farms, and forced the rescue workers to eat. They dragged the inconsolable away. Two children had been working with the men, and they had not yet been found. A woman was said to be under the rubble somewhere, or, others said, fled. The manager was sent for, and a message conveyed to the owner. Carts came for the bodies and crawled back up the dreary track, as with the usual loads, wet sacks of kelp or coal.

A man called Hogg limped over to him, raving about the monster. He ignored him. Alcuin felt redundant. Worse, people looked at him as if he was in some way to blame, some connection with responsibility. He could explain nothing. In his place he knew Kenelm would find a tone of sympathetic judgement. Allowing them to find fault among themselves. Those who had strayed from the track. Drawing an admonitory lesson from it even as the ragged sleeves and crushed heads were uncovered.

Alcuin found himself staring at a piece of dressed stone, a broken lintel that had been dragged aside, the chisel-marks in diagonals either side of the centre line, like the quill-shaft and vane of a feather, petrified. Or of a frond, petrified. A result of regularising the stone, not intended as an evocation. Like a pattern in the shale, hidden for eons. Or another, its relief shaded with a little coal-dust, and buffed up, like a stone on the tallyman's shelves. Or a charcoal rubbing among the papers of Carey's assistant. These kind of thoughts. Among the mayhem, what use are these?

Alcuin resolved to leave, but he couldn't think where to go. He stood, shivering.

Hands, cut and bruised. Dried mud and blood. Broken fingernails deeply incised with black dirt. From the fallen rocks, from prising at the hard-interlocked slates and boulders. Dressed stone, fallen stone, smashed-in stone. Muscles aching from heaving out tight-wedged stones. Rolling them away from limbs, from caved-in, sticky, black, hair-matted heads.

Gestures. Hand-shakes, hand-wringing. Moving the hands in the air, up, down, across, back. Forming the shape of the trefoil, clover. The shape of a looped rope, a simplified knot for rigging a hopeful flagstaff, the air-shape of a cross. He'd worn out the gesture.
Stone still, the hand stone. Thumb up, thumb down.
Felt there was no more he could say. Words of encouragement, of sympathy. Words of anger, sorrow. Spontaneous words, inspired words, wooden words, incantation, spells, charm-less words, empty words, worn-out words.

Alcuin felt there was no more he could do.
The rickety contraption of his worn-out body rotated into levered movement against the heavy ground. Automatically, to walk. He walked away, around the curled outer shell of the bay.
He cut inland, keeping clear of the impoverished fishing hovels clustered like sores in the mouth of the wyke. He regained the cliff, keeping back from the torn edge. Expansive pool-strewn rocks were exposed below and, beyond, the sea was impassive.

Above Mulgrave's makeshift port with its pebble-scattered sand and jutting staithe he cuts inland, heading for the well.
Trudging up the sodden track, the sea receding behind. Into the overgrown churchyard, past the pitted, closed-up wall of the building. Legs trembling as he moves down into the cleft of grassy banks, hearing the water before he sees it.

Exhausted, Alcuin stops by the clear spring that flows out over a simple boulder placed beneath. He rinses his hands methodically and thoroughly until they began to ache with the cold of the water. He wipes them on his dirty clothes. He cups them and scoops up the water to drink.

Its holiness springs from this. Named for Hilda. Like others he knows from his wanderings. Hackness, Aislaby. Other wells named for her. Houses where the wells spring. Chapels, shrines. Those around the church beneath the church, for the early abbots – for Cedd and Chad and Ovin.

Cloak wrapped around, shivering. Meagre shelter from the slope of the land behind the old, neglected church. No one around. He has seen no one since Ness.

Images from the landslip, the ruined alum houses.

His thoughts bitter. In the village he has bypassed there had been a sickness. Claimed to be washed ashore from a stranded ship. Many deaths. A foreign plague over a century before. Now He had visited the rock fall at Ness. Where would He spring His next mystery?

Sharpened by the slice of slaked ice coursed through. As tired, more awake. Thoughts flitting, dipping, a bird hopping from pebble to pebble, in the shallows, under the tree-shadow, by a stream.

He rouses himself to move, through the churchyard, to the yew. Under its canopy, back to the trunk affording shelter from the wind.

How many years will a yew last?

The disaster of survival. The horror of escape. Lost ones, missing ones. The grief of the remaining. Crying of nighttime foxes. Daylight screams of the gulls.

Bodies entombed in rock, hammered flat, like the monster in the shale.

The fragile tearing of a frail body. Temporary lodgings. Lesser deaths. The departure of a friend. The end of a friendship.

Abandoned lovers. Vanished sons, daughters. Dotage, the body nearly intact, mind worn threadbare. Not, quite, here.

The girl. An abyss, of longing.

A life unpredictable, like a day's weather.

Sun, sliding off the rock. The cold shadows. Shivers across the grasses. Lights, trail off into a blackness. Moon, fails to rise.

A flash of red.

Sun, blazing in the sky, heat pouring onto the earth. Tomorrow.

Or just this, cold damp grey wash?

He tries to concentrate on small things. The muscled coil of the water. Light straining through it. Blackness of the pool. A leaf, caught at the edge, neither stuck fast, nor floating free, lifting and trembling with the flexing flow of the water.

Tired, but afraid of sleep.

Cold, but afraid of movement.

Words he has spoken to Ken. He remembers his book. Damp, within his garments that have dried a little, pressed hard and flat, it has protected itself. Trembling, he finds charcoal. Shaking, he writes words he has spoken.

This will be my world from now on.

Where yellowish grasses shuddered under successive scourings of the low, scattering wind a little group of aspens stood. He has wandered from the yew, and from the well. Alcuin shivers. The leaves, which in a dead calm would tremble, sensitive to the slightest stir that a man might not detect, are a frenzied blur. It is like an agitated crowd of doomsayers, and the frantic rustling of the twigs seems to voice discontent, and warning. In this wind the whispering voice of the spirits seems roused to alarm. Not just trembling in shame for the wood of the Cross, but exorcising it through a fit of shaking.

None of this gives any comfort to Alcuin. He trudges across the desolate tract, skirts the wailing aspen copse, and tucks in for meagre shelter beside a long low mound.

At Lingra Howe Alcuin rests on the ancient hummock. The rain has stopped. The grass is damp and soft. He lies face down. He imagines himself sinking down like the paved trod into the pannier way, gradually, over many years, sinking in the bog.

He imagines himself inhumed in an oak canoe, his bronze pin on hazel branches. In his oak grave, laid over with stone and turf. Encased in an oak tree, in the howe. As in his stone boat the crypt.

He remembers Kenelm's offer. Its generosity. Its subtlety of seduction. Its desperation. To be the minister of the church above and the church below. Kenelm to stand aside. It's the final move, the last. He had watched Kenelm's face. The hope, faint, then resignation.

When Alcuin was a child he understood the bible stories – they were clear and didactic, like fairy tales, but without the dark ambiguity. But the abstractions of the holy spirit, of god out there, or in here, were more elusive.

Gradually, without knowing how it started, presumably when he was very young, the moon, particularly the face of the full moon, came to represent the nocturnal presence of a benign god. Unlike the sun, which represented a force he could not look directly on, but flinched away from. He could gaze at the moon. It could be reduced to a child's drawing like the image on the face stone. It was simple. It represented peace.

The moon made less fearful the night travels, modelling with shadows the uneven paths, sudden potholes. Flashing off lurking bogs, or by a linked seam of sky-bright puddles laying out the course of the path ahead. Ploughed fields shown by their rutted shadows. Dense, spiky nests of bramble clumps and hawthorn twigs with their snares of tugging thorns, hatched in criss-cross lines by the moon shadows. The moon made manifest that the night was God's landscape too.

Alcuin had fallen asleep and awakening, saw the hare. He was lying on his side, his head on his rolled cloak for a pillow. Where he had lain down, gazing up into a starless twilight, there now hung a huge pale disc. The hare was etched on it like a shallow pitted relief on an old millstone.

It was unsettling. He didn't move. He imagined his inner self sitting up and looking at the familiar face. The inscrutable upright beneficent face. He held the two images in one. He remained on his side, watching the hare. The disc of the moon lifted, and shrunk perceptibly. Its stone disc lightened, brightened a shade.

Behind the face of the moon, as it always had, thought Alcuin, sat the hare. More wily, cunning, alert, more still, wiser, stranger, and far, far older.

Sea fret

"Robbie never knew my father, you see."

Elizabeth and Alcuin walked along the track. Evening. Pinpricks bloomed in the heavy violet drape of the sky, tiny moth holes leaking starlight.

"He was killed in an accident. Just a few weeks before they were to meet. He'd moved away, back to his home village, being no longer fit enough for a heavy trade. Hoping to find lighter work."

Shapes of a few late swifts flitted. Or early bats. A mild breeze carried night scents.

'What happened?"

"It was a very unlucky, very unlikely accident. A bolt out of the blue, as people said."

"Oh."

"One morning, on a lane such as this, a steep one, at a bend below trees. A runaway axle, heavy wheeled, broken away from an oxcart, somewhere uphill, out of sight, struck him."

Alcuin shook his head slowly.

"They say he may have never known anything about it."

"The sound perhaps?"

She shrugged.

"Perhaps, watching something in the field, or the hedge, he was dimly aware of it. Becoming aware of a sound. Perhaps like a cart approaching. But not quite registered enough to become curious. Curious enough to turn."

"What rare misfortune, unnatural ill-luck."

She shook her head now.

"That depends. An accident like that would have a cause. Immediately, for example, a bump in the road. A stone. A pothole. Prior to that perhaps, metal fatigue – the wear and tear. The split pins, ill maintained, missing. Uninspected. Careless loading of the team perhaps? The cart unattended – inadequately chocked?"

"Meaning?"

"In a sense no accident. A fact of carelessness or cost-cutting or neglect. Or a combination of things. In other words a fact, a certainty, simply waiting to be unrolled."

"There are many accidents...."

Alcuin thinks of the landslide at Ness.

"Yes, father. Many facts."

Alcuin listened to their footsteps on the loose stones of the rubble track.

"Here in the alum house, Father, there are many accidents too. Scalding in the boiling house, the evaporating room. Acid burns at the clamps, scorchings at the clamps. Poisoning perhaps. Broken limbs, torn muscles at the quarries. Men falling, men under rocks, falling objects, collapsing scaffolding."

Alcuin had to be careful. The manager of course, her husband.

"Are you saying...."

Liz was animated, anger overlaid by conviction, tautly reined.

"Neglect of course. Lack of care. Equipment well past its best."

"And the men?"

"And the men. Underfed, working off the last vestiges of energy and strength. Asking, no, being asked, being told to slip. Told to fall. Made to aim the pick wildly, made to spill the scald. Men worn out like blunt files, like loose axe heads, like frayed ropes, like rusty blocks, cams, pins, cables."

Liz paused. They walked on a little in silence.

"It must have been a shock to you, Elizabeth. Your father..."

"Yes. Ah. That's what I was talking about. Yes, yes. It was. We were very close, and as I was saying, Robbie and he never met. I wonder..."

She trailed off, picked up again.

"My father was a radical you see. He always did heavy work. But he could read and write. It was in the family, and they prided themselves on their links, all the way back to the early separatists. Baptists, Barebones, Newgate..."

Alcuin listened hard, but he waited for explanation.

"He named me, you see, after Elizabeth Lilburne. He came from north of here, and the Lilburnes' memory still burned. Still burns I hope. Of course he, John Lilburne - John was my father's name - Lilburne was exiled for complaining about the stealing of land in the north-east, a practice which still goes on."

"You read well too Liz, I know."

"Yes, that Elizabeth's example was to stand by her man – and to fight for her family. Though I have only Robbie, that's my role. But I'll not hold my tongue with the owner if Robbie won't stand like my father and like that other John."

"You might turn to the Church?"

She shrugged.

"Elizabeth and John became Quakers. But I come to my own decision. *We are born without convictions, we acquire them.* As Mr Locke wrote."

Alcuin raised an eyebrow with a tilt of the head.

"I'm impressed."

"Father Alcuin, you educate the children here. That they will learn, as well as labour. For labour creates no wealth here. No property, no security, no well-being."

She paused.

He nodded, frowning.

"And Mr Wynter?"

"He is not the pamphleteer revolutionary. He wants to muddle along."

"That's not how I see him at all."

"No. At work, no. His texts are tables of additions and subtractions. More of this, less of that. Methodical pursuit of perfecting the process. The process made imperfect by ignorance, disdain and greed."

Liz sighed.

"Ah if Robbie could hear me.."

The path had reached close to the cliff, where it would follow the edge north. By tacit agreement they paused here and, the shadows clustering thickly now under the hawthorns, and a chilly edge having entered the breeze, they turned to set off back. But Alcuin stopped again. Embarrassed he addressed the darkening void above the cliff edge.

"Elizabeth, I have undergone a hard transformation. Useless now, asleep, dead almost. Only I hope, like the oak, felled carelessly, or half-upended by landslide, or almost died away some hard winter, to sprout new growth."

Behind her sympathetic look, a shadow of pain. Alcuin faltered.

"Everything dying has a hope. Mine is still in this world."

She waited till he looked at her again.

"Father, there are things you'll need to know if you plan to spend more time in our world."

After Ness a taking stock of course.

Business as usual, but not quite. No dwellings now allowed on Ness. Kelp-burning cut back. Labour lost or damaged through injury at Ness not replaced. The fall an accident of course, no question of compensation. An act of God, as the owner himself pointedly remarked to Alcuin.

Hardly a week passed without trouble with the workers.

Even after the destruction of the tallyman's hut, after the disappearance of the monster. These provocations had been replaced with keener ones of fear and hunger. There was a fraught atmosphere of potential unrest.

The manager dressed down too. Turner throws in every item – negligent of monitoring, ill-judged over the monster, allowing deliberate sabotage, apparently distracted, according to rumour. Wynter listens, stone silent. After the accusations, the blame, Turner enlightens the manager about the message to be conveyed to the men.

Liz preaches to Alcuin.
"Is this what we fought for?"
He watches.
"Wycliffe, Lilburne, Clarkson, Winstanley..."
Her look an inquisition.
"Learning to read by the scriptures, practising on the pamphlets. Fighting with fierce pride. And now he won't stand up to it. Not Robbie. None of them will."

A pause. Liz fights back anger and tears.
"I thought it would give him something to bounce back with. To reject what he's told he must do. I mean, now she has gone. To throw himself into an act of bravado. But in her absence he moons around the place like a spare part. Like an old farmer who can no longer remember how to hold the hoe. No fight left in him."

Alcuin speaks thoughtfully.
"I think...he will have considered things...in his way. Decided there is no point?"
"No point!"
He raises a hand gently.
"Elizabeth. Listen. I will do what I can."
She scoffs.
"Pah! Platitudes. Scrape your knees on the dirt, see what miracle that performs."

"Not that way."
"How then?"
"We call everyone together. As into a church. But any shed will do. For one of your sermons. Breathe a little fire into them."
"What about him?"
Alcuin frowns.
"Turner?"
"The manager!"
He looks at her straight. She looks back. She is, he sees for the first time, magnificent. He speaks.
"He will come in his own time."
Her turn to fall silent.
"Liz. I'll talk to him."

The twilight twigs of the birch tops finger the soft creams and pinks and pale blues – like the gnarled hands of crones fingering petticoats.

"I am like this machinery here. If I'm not in use, I rust."
Wynter gestured towards the pump, the implements and tools.
Alcuin was silent. He turned and looked at the flask on the lab bench. The clear liquid within. The double line of the surface, seen through glass, that Robbie called the meniscus. The crescent moon.
Wynter waved aside the priest's protestations.
"Don't lecture me Alcuin. I have called a meeting. It's already in hand. You would do well to take up Kenelm's offer. Go back to your calling. Look to promote a better future than this".
Alcuin shook his head.

"Robert. This is what I've heard say. Many a day I'm apt to believe it. There is no afterworld, in a sense no this world. Just a flow of time through us, through men."

In his book Alcuin writes:

It's like we are at the meniscus of an infinite vessel. Below, infinite depths. Call it the past. Above, infinite air. Call it the future. Waiting to be fulfilled.

In the tension of the present we are suspended, like grains of dust on the surface. Being pulled upwards. Being pulled down. The circumference of the meniscus, even of an infinitely wide vessel, holds us trapped in a thin band, which can easily snap. For any individual that band is infinitely brief – although to each it has, however short, duration.

The meniscus. The surface skin of our modern world, infinitely thin, on which we float like the water boatman until a drop, a disturbance, ever so slight, drowns us.

We don't make our own shape in this world. We're poured into a container like the liquor into the trough. If we are strong together we will rise up, like the mercury in a weather glass, plumped up like the ocean rising to the moon. When we're weak we sag, like water in a jar, our meniscus hollow, our centre depressed. We take the shape of the vessel that holds us, it circumscribes our world, until, it breaks.

Wynter surveyed the matted, snagged, straggling and unravelled flock before him.

Rockmen, pitmen, liquormen, coopers, workmen, carpenters, carters, smiths, pickmen, urinemen, stablehands, mothers-men, boilers, coolers and roachers, plumbers, coalmen, their wives, and children: a multitude of poor snakes, tattered and naked, ready to starve for want of food and clothes.

"Men, I'll come straight to it. From Friday week we must lay idle the works."

A hubbub bubbled up and they fell to arguing amongst themselves.

"There's good alum to be made here."

"We can never make a penny on it."

"It's cheaper to buy abroad, haul it up the cliffs and resell it than make the stuff here."

"No. It's that the owners take more than can ever be made. They'll gamble a month of our wages on two wood lice racing across a saucer."

Murmurs of agreement.

"Well, it's our pay that paid for those pipes and pans. They're ours."

When Wynter caught wind of this last, with its implied threat, he spoke again.

"Men, we don't know how long we are to lay idle. Hopefully a short time. Whichever, there is nothing to be gained from any mischief in the works. We will all need to revive the business as briskly as we can, given the word."

He felt a need to emphasise this.

"All this property is the owners'. They will back up this fact by recourse to the law, or at least their own trained bands."

The men were angry, or grim. The women bitter or in tears. The children bewildered.

"You shall be allowed to stay in your houses. The works shall be off limits. You shall seek work, in the meantime, elsewhere."

Wynter thought about the effects of this closure down the line. The urine traders, seaweed gatherers, kelp fetchers, coal merchants, shop owners, carters, innkeepers, sackmakers, tanners and dyers, cochineal importers, the pay-escorters, agents of sale, leadmakers, toolmakers.

He dismissed the flock, which dispersed bleating.

Wynter walked back up to his gate. He felt a chill as he walked up the path to the door, and entered the house. In the parlour he stood at the window gazing out across the bay, to the headland.

Out at sea two boats that were first sharp, in a few moments dissolved.

On the long back of the headland the horizon softened. The cloud flocculated and steadily lowered its obscuring gauze on the cliff. The near distance grew indistinct. The sea no longer visible.

Wynter felt the fret rise, its first drifts crossed the wall and the fence, its white fleece drew across the scene outside the window like a dragged curtain. The wall dissolved, the gate vanished, and white vapour streamed up from the earth to the sky, filling the whole world with dense white opaque sourceless light.

* * *

Postspect

Alum of every kind has warming, astringent powers, purifies the pupil from darkening, melts the superfluous flesh on the eyelids as other overgrowths of flesh... Alum of all kinds stops mortification and haemorrhage and, if mixed with vinegar and honey, comforts flaccid gums and tightens loose teeth. With honey it relieves thrush and eczema, with polygonon discharge from the ears. It is a good remedy against lepra when cooked with cabbage juice or honey. With water it is a fomentation for itch, psoriasis, unguium, ingrown nails and chilblains. With the faex of vinegar (tartar) which has been heated with an equal quantity of gallnut it is used against eroding ulcers; with tar-water it makes a lotion against dandruff. It is applied with water against nits and lice, and as a salve against bad odour. It prevents conception and applied locally is an abortifacient. Finally it helps against gumboils and swellings of the uvula and the tonsils, and is used with honey as an ear salve.

"Gentlemen, those are the words of Pedanios Dioscorides, a Greek army surgeon under the Emperor Nero, who graced this world only a few years after our Lord's ascendance."

There is a spontaneous outbreak of cheering and applause at this entertaining opening. He holds his hand up graciously to acknowledge it and allow it to fall silent, and turns to the cloth-covered array on the theatre podium's table, brought in especially for this evening's event.

Sharp intake of breath, followed by murmuring from the assembly.

The assistant rolls back the cloth to reveal.

At first blackened lumps, blackened stumps.

Then a shape seems to form....

The eminent members gasp. Leaning down from the steep tiers of the horseshoe-shaped lecture theatre, straining to make sense of the pieces and the spaces, which seem to be, might be, an alarming, black, monstrously deformed....

A cough signals commencement, as the figure at the lectern moves on to this, the main theme of this evening's lecture.

****

Acknowledgements:

Thanks to: Tammy Storey, for typing my scrawl; James Bowman, for proofreading; Adrian James, Martin Bunce, Ted Farrant and Wendy de Silva, for reading early drafts; Andrea Arnold, Frank Watson, Helen and Bob Matthews, for comments on extracts; Jon McGregor, Sara Maitland, Becky Swift, for early advice; San Cassimally, for the alum joke (heard by him as a boy in Mauritius) told by Fox to Launde; Hardieillustrator.com, cover design and illustration; Cleveland Industrial and Archaeological Society, Tees Archaeology, Tees Valley RIGS Group, Whitby Museum, Scarborough Archeological and Historical Society, for their enthusiastic investigations into such arcana as rutways, slam, post-holes and floating eggs.

Note:

Ana Cross – the original One Howe or Ainhowe Cross - lies in Lastingham crypt.